Lunch with
Mussolini

At the age of sixty-five, with near accentless English and a stable of friends whose knowledge of Italy was almost solely acquired from cookbooks, Colombina had every reason to feel she had escaped her past. Indeed, she never even thought to distance herself any more. There was no need.

But Australia hadn't become haven and home just to the victims of the war, but to some of its villains as well — those clever enough to escape retribution and convince authorities of the validity of their newly assumed identities. To her horror, Colombina was soon to discover that not all the shadows of her past had been laid to rest. And for the first time in as long as she could remember, the Italian passion that she'd kept dormant deep within her flared and took shape and form.

What she felt was pure hatred.

Derek Hansen was born in England, raised in New Zealand and now lives in Sydney, Australia. *Lunch with Mussolini* is his second novel a ~~~~~~~~~~~~~ ~hich began with *Lunch with the* ~~~~~~~~~~~~~~~~ ~ory that writers are a ~~~~~~~~~~~~~~~~ ~cts about which they ~~~~~~~~~~~~~~~~ ~irty years in advertisi ~~~~~~~~~~~~~~ ~tor, Derek believes he

*Also by Derek Hansen
and available in Mandarin*

Lunch with the Generals

Lunch with Mussolini

DEREK HANSEN

ARROW

Reprinted in Arrow Books, 2003

3 5 7 9 0 8 6 4 2

This edition first published in 1995 by
Mandarin Paperbacks

Arrow Books
The Random House Group Limited
20 Vauxhall Bridge Road, London, SW1V 2SA

Random House Australia (Pty) Limited
20 Alfred Street, Milsons Point, Sydney,
New South Wales 2061, Australia

Random House New Zealand Limited
18 Poland Road, Glenfield
Auckland 10, New Zealand

Random House (Pty) Limited
Endulini, 5a Jubilee Road, Parktown 2193, South Africa

The Random House Group Limited Reg. No. 954009

www.randomhouse.co.uk

A CIP catalogue record for this book
is available from the British Library

Printed and bound in Great Britain by
Bookmarque Ltd, Croydon, Surrey

ISBN 0 7493 1995 X

For Carole

Acknowledgements

How easy writing a novel would be if there were no need for research, no verification of facts and no acknowledgement of history. This story would never have been written but for the generous assistance of others. My wife and researcher, to whom this book is dedicated, bore the main burden and I thank her for all the trips to the libraries and the back-breaking loads of books she staggered home with. I am also indebted to Tommy Tomasi, one-time soldier with the Alpini and partisans, for sharing his knowledge and experiences; Wolfgang Bose, Alex Popov, Ian Hart and Ira Kowalski for the specialist knowledge they provided; Rob Kelly for his art direction; and Phil Bellamy. I would also like to thank three people who expect no thanks — Don, Jo and Willsy. Thanks, guys, for the 'literary grant'.

WRITERS' BLOC

THE READER IS ALWAYS RIGHT

Contents

FIRST THURSDAY

Gancio watched for the four men as he began seating the early arrivals, mostly junior executives and secretaries whose time was limited. Anyone who knew him would have found him unusually subdued. He was a big man who dominated the restaurant with his size, his booming voice and his extravagant mannerisms. But not today. Nobody could find him remotely entertaining — in fact, they'd probably dismiss him as morose.

Gancio was worried and made no attempt to hide his concern. He wasn't sure the four men would come. He cursed Ramon, the blind Argentinian. No one had rung to cancel but, then again, who among them would have taken it upon himself to ring? He glanced across at the empty table. Ramon would come, he was certain of that. But if he was left to sit alone it would be unbearable. It would be an indictment, a condemnation of both Ramon's character and his storytelling ability. It would mean he had lost the game, his friends and their respect forever.

For four years they'd met without fail to share their passion for storytelling. But it was more than that. It was a contest of wit and intelligence, of put-downs, insults and clever deceit. As in all games where no quarter is given, tempers sometimes became inflamed. But their ability to incite was more than matched by a will and determination always to part as friends, and the tension served only to heighten their enjoyment. But Ramon had changed all that.

'Bloody fool,' Gancio muttered to himself as twelve thirty came and went and still their table remained unoccupied. He liked Ramon enormously both as friend and business partner, but he was under no illusion as to who was at fault. Ramon's vanity and arrogance had led him to gamble with his companions' friendship. Now it appeared the gamble had failed and he had no one to blame but himself. He should never have told that story. There was no need. He was in a new country and he'd made a new start. Why rake over the ashes of his past? But, of course, Gancio knew why. His friend had to gamble, he had to take risks and chance everything he cherished simply for the thrill it gave him. Having retired and with little left to challenge his brain, he used his friends shamelessly to provide him with the sort of adrenalin hit he used to get from playing his corporate games. Gancio glanced once more at his watch. Twelve thirty-one. Ramon would arrive soon. What would he say to him?

'*Come sta, compagno?*'

Gancio spun around, a smile broadening across his face. 'Lucio! Thank God! I wasn't sure you were coming. You're the first. Where are the others? You're late.'

'Neil's right behind me.' Short, fat, balding Lucio was the joker among them, a man whose libido seemingly never knew a moment's peace.

'So you're all coming?'

'Yes, Gancio, despite the slops you serve us, we're all coming.'

'Thank God! After last week I wasn't sure. How could Ramon have been so stupid? Sit! Sit. Let me bring you some wine.'

'Not yet. I'll wait for the others. But Gancio, you make a mistake if you think Ramon is stupid. Ramon is never stupid.' Lucio's voice became decidedly less friendly. 'We're his playthings, his toys. Oh I know if any one of us asked him for help he'd go out of his way to give it, no questions asked. In that sense he is a true friend. But it is time someone taught him a little respect. What do you think?'

'What are you two wogs up to?' Neil had arrived and seemed to have sprung the two Italians in deep conversation.

'We were discussing you, Neil. We were just saying what a warm, sensitive human being you are and how rare it is to find those qualities in a property developer.'

'Bullshit,' said Neil affably. 'What are we drinking? Just atmosphere?'

'I have a new wine chilling for you to try. Italian, of course, a Pinot Grigio. Santa Margherita.'

'Great, but I'm one of those blokes who prefers the taste to the label. So, Gancio old son, if you don't mind . . .'

'*Va fanculo*, Neil.' Gancio turned to fetch the wine. He could not keep the smile off his face. It was a smile of relief and of victory — his friend's victory. Ramon had won! The bastard had done it! He felt like singing, so he did. His regulars turned to one another and smiled indulgently.

'What's this *va fanculo* bit, Lucio? Your mate often says that to me.'

'It's Italian for "right away".'

'Yeah? Well, what do you reckon? Have you changed your mind since last week?'

'No. I think the understanding we reached last week is still valid. The bastard played games with us. Unquestionably parts of his story were true but the story itself wasn't. He took bits of stories from here and there and blended them with fiction to string us along. When you think about it, it was brilliant. But I wasn't so amused at the time.'

'Yeah, I think you're right. He's a bastard.'

'Tell him yourself, Neil. He's just arrived. And he's got Milos with him.'

If Ramon was at all nervous about confronting his friends once more, he didn't show it. He strode confidently through the restaurant with his usual measured step, following the carpet runner unerringly as it made its one ninety-degree turn on its path to their table.

'One of these days I'm going to get Gancio to shift the tables around.' Neil was the only one insensitive enough to make fun of Ramon's blindness.

Ramon laughed. 'Don't bother. Just get someone to stick out a leg. That works much better.'

'Afternoon, Ramon, nice to see you're in good form.'

'*Buon giorno*, Lucio. Milos has just told me that you are telling the next story.'

Milos shrugged his shoulders helplessly. 'I had a story ready but Lucio asked me if he could go out of turn. What am I supposed to do? Refuse him?' Milos was the eldest among them, a classic rags-to-modest-riches story, and their self-appointed chairman. He took it upon himself to keep the peace and mediate in disputes. 'We're all supposed to be friends, no?'

'It was very kind of you, Milos.' Ramon smiled to himself. Everyone was so eager to re-establish their bona fides and kinship. Obviously, he'd really rattled them. 'I must confess to some disappointment. I was looking forward to your story and more of your central European wit.' Ramon smiled thinly. 'If that's not an oxymoron.'

'A what?'

'A contradiction in terms, Neil. How many Hungarians do you know who have made a living out of their sense of humour? But never mind. Lucio never disappoints and besides, I imagine we could all do with some light relief.'

'After the story you told, you ain't kidding!'

'Now, Neil,' cut in Milos. 'We agreed not to reopen old wounds, no? We stayed on until nearly midnight last week, Ramon, discussing your story. In the end we decided to give you the benefit of the doubt, and in hindsight that seems a wise decision. We don't believe that what we heard was your confession nor do we believe that you are evil like the villain in your story. But we also agreed for the sake of our friendship and our lunches to leave your story in the past. And I trust you will never again be so cavalier with our friendship.'

'You're still an arsehole, Ramon.'

'Yes, Neil, but a contrite one.'

Watching from the kitchen, Gancio saw Neil laugh and took that as a cue to bring the wine and *antipasto*. 'Eggplant, artichoke, capsicum, *prosciutto*, salami, *alici* and olives,' he announced grandly. 'I tell you this Ramon, so you know if Neil steals anything from your plate. Who's telling the story today?'

'Lucio.'

'Oh Mother of God, more lies!' Gancio always affected embarrassment at Lucio's stories because they both came from the same region of northern Italy — Gancio from Bellagio, Lucio from Varese. 'How will you shame us today? More sneaky seductions?'

'No.' Today Lucio had a surprise for them. 'The rules have changed,' he said. 'Ramon has changed them forever.' He motioned with his fork. 'Please begin. That is another rule that has changed. I will give you my reasons and introduce my story while we eat.

'We once had a rule — no, not a rule, a convention — that we would not bring ourselves into our stories. For four years we've told stories without revealing anything about ourselves until Ramon chose to break that convention. We agree his story was only true in parts, yet those parts were revealing. Indirectly we learned much about his early life in Argentina and his new beginning in Australia. Sure, he gave those experiences to someone else — his characters — but there is no doubt that the experiences he drew upon were his own. So no longer do we all meet here as friends and strangers. If you think back, we each of us revealed as much about ourselves as Ramon did in the way we reacted to his story. At various times we were vindictive, pompous and self-righteous. Ramon's story breached our defences, our carefully constructed façades, so we can't just sit here and pretend nothing has happened. Perhaps the time really has come to lift the veil a little on our true personalities and our lives. You are not eating. Why?'

'Lucio, you surprise us.' Milos gestured to his other companions. 'We were all expecting froth and bubbles. Instead you sound like me.'

'You are not taking me seriously.'

'It's not easy when the clown decides to play Hamlet.'

'Neil, that's unfair!' Milos reached across the table and put his hand on Lucio's arm. 'My friend, you are giving voice to my thoughts. You are right. Things have changed. Ramon has changed everything. But tread carefully. For four years we were quite happy to know little about each other. If we are to know each other better, let us learn gradually and be selective in what we reveal. Ramon's story was a crack in the dam. Be careful not to burst the dam and turn it into a flood. Now, perhaps we should eat first, no?'

'No. I am Italian. I can talk and eat at the same time. Gancio, you're wanted in the kitchen.'

'Okay, okay. But before I go, this story that lifts the veil, what is it about?'

'In a way it is both our stories. I am going to take my friends back to Lake Como, to Ravello in the hills above Menaggio. My story begins before Il Duce went mad and dragged Italy into the war on the wrong side.'

'I would like to hear this story. Maybe I'll join you later. Okay?' Gancio returned to his kitchen and to the other diners whose patience was beginning to wear thin. Lucio watched him go and turned back to his companions.

'I will not put myself in my story other than in the small part I still have to play. When I finish my story, I will be grateful for your advice. But I will not attempt to do what Ramon did. I do not have his skills. No, the story I am about to tell is different to any I have told before. This story is true. There is no invention and no distortions. There is nothing I can or need add to it. You expect me to give you beautiful women and there are beautiful women. But some of these women are more than just beautiful, they are extraordinarily courageous. So are the men. That is the thing about war. It clarifies things. War has no tolerance for the bystander. It sweeps up everyone in its path. It forces people to take sides, willingly or unwillingly. It makes the courageous show their courage and the cowards their cowardice. That is why there are so many books about war, why there are so many stories to tell. But my story is not just a war story. It is above all a romance. It has passion, triumph, treachery, tension, and tragedy. It has everything a good story needs and it is all true. On the Holy Bible I swear it is all true.'

Lucio's voice had begun to shake. The others looked on bewildered. This was not the friend they knew. This was not the light relief they were expecting. Lucio had opened the door to something infinitely better and more exciting.

'*Bravo*,' said Milos quietly. He looked at Lucio's largely untouched plate. 'Now eat.'

And as they ate the audience considered what their story-teller had said and what they were prepared to believe. After all, every storyteller wants the audience to believe that the story is true and Lucio, as his friends now realised, had seized upon the uncertainties caused by Ramon's breaches of convention and turned them to his advantage. He had been handed the perfect set-up. The rules certainly had changed, but had Lucio? Was he clever enough to exploit them? His audience eyed him with new respect.

Chapter One

April had come and brought the breath of spring and the promise of an end to the war. That should have brought joy and relief to the women in Ravello's one and only square. The church of San Pietro occupied almost all of the southern boundary, bar a laneway on its eastern side and Ravello's main street on the other. The street and its neat row of houses formed the western boundary. To the north was the village noticeboard — a featureless two-storey brick wall, part of the building which housed the Parente family and their car repair workshop. Hasty brush-strokes defiantly proclaimed anti-fascist sentiments in a variety of coloured paints, and extolled the virtues of the PCI, the Italian Communist Party, the GL Actionists and Christian Democrats. Also plastered on the wall was a defaced poster which warned against supporting or taking part in partisan activities. The eastern side of the square was the social centre of Ravello where people met to exchange information, ideas and gossip.

But on this day nobody was in the mood for idle chatter. There were few people about other than those women who felt most need for the comfort the church offers. The *panificio* was closed, and the café unattended. By the garage wall, old Mentore Parente gathered up the stones and pieces of old bricks into a pile, all the while crossing himself and muttering. Occasionally he would shake his head and stare in disbelief at the shame-faced women as they climbed or descended the few steps into the church.

Gradually Mentore Parente became aware of the sound of a truck grinding up the hill from Menaggio but he took no notice of it. Neither for that matter did anyone else, though later some would claim that on hearing the labouring engine they felt a chilly premonition which had nothing to do with the fact that one of Lake Como's resident winds, the *breva*, had just sprung up. Why would anybody be concerned? Certainly Ravello harboured its share of partisans, every village did. But the Ravello partisans were careful to do nothing which would draw German attention to their homes. Ravello had never been targeted for reprisal shootings as villages closer to Como had. Now with the Germans pulling back out of Italy, there was even less reason for fear.

The old man looked up out of curiosity when the local German commandant's Lancia Aprilia drove into the square followed by a truck full of soldiers. A few older women paused on the church steps, also curious. A young woman, Giuseppina Cerasuolo, waved shyly. Only one, Maddalena Ortelli, a plain, sad-faced woman who wore each of her forty years as an intolerable burden, guessed what was about to happen. She turned to Giuseppina.

'Run! Run, you stupid girl!' she hissed.

Giuseppina hesitated, uncomprehending. It was a fatal mistake. The tailgate of the truck crashed down and soldiers poured into the square. They grabbed the women standing on the church steps. They grabbed the screaming Giuseppina and they grabbed Maddalena Ortelli. Maddalena spat in the face of the young soldier who took hold of her shoulders. He didn't retaliate. The Oberstleutnant climbed out of the Lancia and began to issue instructions. He was a man everyone in the village knew and grudgingly respected even though he was their enemy.

'Against the wall!' he commanded, and the soldiers lined their eight captives against the garage wall.

'Out of the way, old man! Unless you wish to be shot as well.'

Old Mentore looked at Oberstleutnant Eigenwill in disbelief, but shuffled along the wall away from the women. When he judged he was safe he stopped and watched. What else could go wrong on this most terrible day?

The Oberstleutnant spoke good Italian, so the women were left in no doubt as to what was going to happen. Immediately some began to wail. Many prayed for forgiveness, seeking absolution in their final moments on earth. Giuseppina pleaded with the soldiers in her halting German, begged them for her life. Only Maddalena stood silently, defiantly.

Mentore Parente watched as the soldiers formed up in two ranks. The front rank down on one knee, the rear standing.

'Prepare to fire!' ordered the Unteroffizier.

The women, fearful and breathless, looked up to face their executioners. Only one spoke.

'Men!' said Maddalena disgustedly, and spat towards them. 'You should all be drowned at birth!'

'You . . .' hissed the Oberstleutnant. 'You can say this? After what you have done?'

Old Mentore closed his eyes as if struck by sudden, blinding pain. Now he understood. He wanted to cry out, to speak to the Oberstleutnant. At least he could save Maddalena. But how long does it take to have these thoughts? How long does it take an old man to react? Mentore never heard the Unteroffizier shout the order. He just heard the sudden explosion of gunfire that cut the eight women down and left a bloody pock-marked memorial on his wall.

Chapter Two

Colombina Galli was sixty-five years old and a widow of two years. She lived in a small house in Clareville overlooking Pittwater on Sydney's northern peninsula. The house had originally been built as a weekend beach house but had been added to over the years until it had achieved some kind of respectability as a permanent residence. It faced north-west. Colombina could look through the forest of yachts moored beneath her home and across the estuary almost to Lion Island.

Her late husband, Mario, had provided well for her. He had been a kind man, eleven years her senior, and she had married him for his kindness. Colombina had learned not to expect too much from men and Mario had seemed the exception. She always maintained — and said so in front of her husband while he was still alive — that marrying Mario was the one smart thing she had done in her life. Mario had loved her for that.

Mario was a prisoner of war who had chosen not to return home. He had been captured in North Africa by an Australian patrol. He had been out on patrol himself during the night and had become separated from his squad. He was relieving himself with his trousers down around his ankles when the Australians stumbled upon him. They burst out laughing and Mario joined in. What else could he do? The situation was absurd. The Diggers were laughing so hard, they nearly killed him when one of their Lee Enfield rifles accidentally discharged. The bullet missed, but Mario had felt the wind of it as it passed overhead. His captors were apologetic and gave him a cigarette to calm him. They escorted him back to their base and wished him well before handing him over for interrogation. Mario shook their hands, glad to be out of the war — like most Italians, he had no quarrel with Britain or her colonies and no desire to fight them. He was put on a troop ship with almost a thousand others like him, and sent to wait out the war twelve thousand kilometres away in a country none of them knew anything about.

He was sent to a prison camp in Cowra in south-west New South Wales before being released into the care of a local farmer, Charlie Dwyer, and his family. Mario loved this new country, so far from the politics and turmoil of Europe, and he loved the Australian people. As his English improved he embarrassed the Dwyers with his enthusiasm for the land, the people, the weather and everything Australian he came across. Rather than being a prisoner, he became part of Charlie Dwyer's family and worked hard and willingly on their behalf.

When the war ended, Mario chose to stay on in his new home. That is not to say that he didn't miss Italy. He yearned for Italy, for his home in Lecco, for his job in the factory making tyres, and for his friends. But he knew there was no job waiting for him back in Italy and decided he was better off trying to make a life for himself in Australia. There was one other thing Mario yearned for — an Italian bride.

He wrote to his family to see if they knew of any girl who would like to come to Australia and marry him. They found girls who might consider marrying him, but none who were prepared to go half-way around the world on the off-chance, when there were American soldiers with similar offers right on their doorsteps. So he wrote to the newspapers in Lecco and asked if they would run an advertisement in the personal columns. He asked if they would withhold his name so that he didn't embarrass his family.

Only one woman replied and they corresponded for six months before she consented to exchange photographs. Mario could not believe his luck. The black-and-white photo was very poor quality because of the post-war shortage of silver, and was already beginning to fade. But it helped flesh out the meagre description she'd already sent him; that she was nineteen years old, that her hair was light brown, her eyes also light brown, and that she was 177 centimetres tall. Mario could see clearly that the woman in the photo was a beauty — far more beautiful than his wildest dreams. But a thought crossed his mind which brought an abrupt halt to his elation. She would now be looking at his picture. He was much older than her — eleven years older — and no prize. Not ugly, but not handsome in the way that she was beautiful. What would she see in him? How could she possibly accept his proposal? He sat down immediately and wrote to her, explaining that he had seen how beautiful she was and releasing her from any obligations she might feel towards him. He told her she did not need to write to him, and apologised in the event that he had misled her. He offered to return her photo if she wished.

Fortunately for Mario, Australia had opened its doors to immigration and boats sailed regularly to and from Europe. He received her reply two months later and could not contain his joy. She had accepted. All he had to do now was get official blessing and send her money for her fare. He couldn't know that his bride-to-be was as elated as he was, not so much at the prospect of marriage, but of leaving Italy and a past that held nothing but sorrow.

When Mario met her at the boat in Sydney nine months later, her skin was pale from four weeks of sea-sickness, and she stood apprehensively in her new, white suit. He put his arms around her protectively and immediately christened her Colombina, little white dove. That is what she reminded him of.

* * *

From that first moment, Colombina knew that she'd been right to follow her instincts. She hadn't been sure until she'd received the letter absolving her of any obligations. That was the insight into the man she'd been looking for. She was desperate, but not so desperate that she would allow herself to be trapped like her mother had been. Nor so desperate that she would allow herself to be used once more. In that one kind gesture when Mario reacted instinctively and took her into his protective arms, she felt an overpowering sense of relief. It made her light-headed and her knees bent beneath her. She would have fallen but for the strong arms that held her. Only then did she realise how tense she'd been.

'Colombina . . . ?' Mario asked gently. 'Colombina, are you all right? Would you like to sit down?'

Colombina didn't answer immediately. She was distracted by the sound of her new name. Colombina. Yes! She would happily become Colombina, little white dove, symbol of peace. The irony was not lost on her. Her real name belonged in the past. She would leave it behind along with Italy and her memories. She would walk away with this man, with a new name and a new life and she would never look back.

'*No, grazie. Va bene, va bene. Grazie a lei.*' For the first time she looked up into the face of her husband-to-be and was astonished to read the concern in it. She smiled and the face before her lit up in response.

'*Bene! Molto bene!* Come. I have a friend with a truck to carry your things. Where are your things?'

'This is all I have.' Colombina pointed to the battered, brown suitcase on the floor beside her. He reached over and picked it up.

'Dear God, there is hardly anything in it.'

'There is everything I need for the moment.'

Mario put his free arm around her and hugged her to him.

'Colombina, I promise you. God as my witness I promise you. One day you will have everything you want. Just say it and it will be yours.' Mario's voice shook. Where has she come from? he wondered. What has she been through, this poor girl?

Mario walked her out of the Customs Hall and into a world as foreign as anything she'd imagined. She laughed out loud when she saw the truck Mario had borrowed to carry her and her suitcase. The old Ford belonged to the builder Mario worked for and had been emptied of tools for the occasion. Mario had even given it a wash, but no amount of washing could disguise the purpose for which the truck was used, and it bore all the scars of the trade. 'M. L. McKeown, Lic. Builder' was barely legible on the driver's door. A young man with curly red hair looked out of the window at them.

'Colombina, this is my friend Harry.'

Harry climbed down from the cab and offered his hand.

'G'day,' said Harry. He looked hard at her. 'Jesus, Mario! She got any sisters?'

Colombina couldn't understand a word, but she understood the sentiment. She put her head back and laughed. She felt good, really good. Was this what her new life would be like? She climbed into the cab and perched on the edge of the seat between the two laughing men. Could she really be that lucky?

* * *

In the nine months that Mario had waited impatiently for Colombina to arrive, he wrote to her twice and often three times a week. He told her all about his new country, his new job and his new friends. Her letters in return spoke of how much she was looking forward to joining him and how quickly — or how slowly — her papers were being processed. Other than that they told him nothing. So Mario had no information upon which to flesh out the beautiful young woman in the photograph before him. He did what anyone else in his position would do — he created a personality for her, one which naturally had no defects. He couldn't help comparing other women with this woman of his imaginings and, of course, Colombina always came out on top. His new friends warned him, pointing out that his expectations were unfair to his bride-to-be and to himself. When he finally met her, how could he not be disappointed? No woman could be that perfect.

But Mario was not disappointed. The instant he saw her he fell in love. Probably he was already in love, that fact needing only the confirmation of her presence. He needed to love, and the pale, vulnerable and beautiful young woman needed to be loved by someone kind and gentle. So the foundations were in place. Yet the truth was that Colombina lived up to the image of perfection that Mario had created. His friends all remarked on it.

Colombina adapted instantly to her new country. She had banished Italy from her mind so made none of the sort of comparisons that can leave immigrants feeling disgruntled or homesick. She accepted every aspect of her new life. When people grew impatient with her lack of English, she calmly accepted that she had to get better at her new language. When people called her a 'wog', she calmly accepted that if Italians were 'wogs' in Australia then, as an Italian, she was also a 'wog'. She bore no resentment. When Mario put her into lodgings with a family from Naples until their wedding day, she calmly accepted the propriety and necessity for it. That was the thing about her that everyone remarked upon. She was always so calm, so serene, so ... well ... un-Italian.

Mario would have liked Colombina to have been a virgin on her wedding night but, given the war and her flat refusal to discuss her past, he had virtually conceded that he was expecting too much. Colombina was not a virgin but Mario was not disappointed. She admitted him to the pleasures of her body and the delights of her love making as she had all the others before him: the Count, the Oberstleutnant, the partisan and, in her desperation, the faceless men in Lecco who'd given her money so that she could survive.

*   *   *

Throughout her marriage, Colombina put Italy behind her and refused to discuss any aspect of her past with Mario. She even refused to discuss his past in Italy. When she judged her English good enough, she insisted they spoke English in their home. This was too much for Mario and caused their first serious argument. Significantly they argued in Italian, and when Mario woke up to the fact, used it to end the debate.

'See?' he demanded. 'Italian is a language of passion. We are Italians, we are passionate. How could we possibly express what we are trying to say in English, with all the right meaning? And even if it were possible, even if one of us could do this, the other would not understand. Where is the point? Besides, there are other things. I refuse to make love in English.'

Colombina had to laugh and a compromise was negotiated. Everyday matters and unimportant things were thereafter discussed in English. Serious matters or matters of passion were always discussed in Italian. When their daughter Alessandra was born, Colombina only ever spoke to her in English.

Another problem confronting Colombina was the fact that they lived among the Italian community in Leichhardt and most of their friends were Italian. From the day they were married and moved into their rented flat, Colombina began a campaign to move on to another suburb. She also made a special effort to strengthen their friendships with non-Italians — Mario's workmates and people they met at church socials. The breakthrough came when Mario's boss sent him over to the lower North Shore to help a friend who was building a patio and terracing his garden. Mario discovered three things. First, that he had a talent for landscape gardening — an occupation he never knew existed — which he immediately demonstrated by making suggestions that his boss's friend seized upon. Secondly, he discovered he loved the job. He loved being outdoors, surrounded by flowers and bushes and the ubiquitous gum trees. He loved the visiting lorikeets, galahs and cockatoos. If he'd come across a black snake, he probably would have loved that too. He saw landscaping as a wonderful act of creation in which he could play a part. But more than anything, he realised, he had discovered the opportunity to do what every immigrant dreams of doing — to set up his own business.

Colombina was quick to see how Mario's plans could advance hers. She encouraged him and promised to find work to help support them while the business was starting up. 'But how,' she asked him continually, 'could he succeed in Leichhardt, an old suburb with no need for landscaping? Surely they would be better off in a new area where there were hills and where properties sloped? Like the lower North Shore?'

Mario loved Leichhardt and his friends there, but he had to accept the sense of what Colombina was saying. The most important thing in his life right then was to start his new business and make sure it was a success.

'Okay,' he said finally. 'We look.'

*　*　*

Bit by bit, Colombina shook off the shackles of her past. But there were always new obstacles to overcome. When Alessandra turned four, Mario decided they should all visit Italy so he could show off his family to his relatives. How could Colombina refuse to go? Yet she did, though she had to play a card she never wanted to play.

'You remember when I first arrived in Australia and you saw the few possessions I had in this world, you made me a promise. Before God.' She looked beseechingly at her husband. 'You promised me I could have anything I wanted, anything at all. Mario, I have not asked you for anything till now. But I want to stay here when you go back to Italy. I never want to go back there. Take Alessandra. I am sorry, Mario, but I beg you, please, let me stay here.'

Mario reluctantly had to agree to her request, but what sort of triumphant return would it be without his beautiful, loving wife? Not for the first time nor the last he wondered what could possibly have happened during the war that made her this way.

'Besides,' she said, 'one of us should stay and look after the business. I can run the supplies yard, and send the boys on small jobs they can't muck up. I can manage the business while you're gone.'

Once again he had to acknowledge the wisdom of what she said.

'Go quickly.' Colombina smiled at her unhappy husband and put her arms around him. 'Then you will come home sooner.'

* * *

Colombina's calm and control also served her well in business — she projected confidence and that is a most precious asset. When Mario returned from Italy she stayed on as manager, leaving him free to do the landscaping, which was what he loved and was good at.

They moved house again as their business prospered. They bought a three-year-old brick home in Roseville with an acre of land, mostly bush, which sloped steeply toward the river below. Mario could hardly wait to landscape it. When they

put Alessandra into the local primary school they were surprised to discover she was the only Italian child in the class.
To Colombina, the move was another step away from her
heritage, a little more distance between her and Italy.

But Colombina failed to give Mario the large Italian family
and the son he desperately wanted. To be fair, she was hardly
to blame — she had suffered an ectopic pregnancy. Colombina
ignored the pains in her stomach until her tubes burst and
her abdominal cavity erupted with peritonitis. She lost the
child she was carrying and the ability to conceive another. It
was something of a miracle that she didn't also lose her life.

No family is spared grief and some would say that Mario
and Colombina were fortunate that no other tragedy or disaster came their way. When Mario sold the business and
decided to retire, they bought the little cottage in Clareville
on the shores of Pittwater. They could easily afford a larger
house but had no need for one. Their daughter Alessandra
was now a married woman with children of her own. Besides,
the cottage needed work and had a garden that needed
landscaping. It would keep Mario happy until the day he
died, building a seawall from sandstone blocks.

* * *

At the age of sixty-five, with near accentless English and a
stable of friends whose knowledge of Italy was almost solely
acquired from cookbooks, Colombina had every reason to
feel she had escaped her past. Indeed, she never even thought
to distance herself any more. There was no need.

But Australia hadn't become haven and home just to the
victims of the war, but to some of its villains as well — those
clever enough to escape retribution and convince authorities
of the validity of their newly assumed identities. To her horror,
Colombina was soon to discover that not all the shadows of
her past had been laid to rest. And for the first time in as long
as she could remember, the Italian passion that she'd kept
dormant deep within her flared and took shape and form.

What she felt was pure hatred.

Chapter Three

Colombina was born Cecilia Ortelli, third child and eldest daughter in a family of seven children. Her father, Primo, worked a small plot of land one kilometre uphill from Ravello. He maintained that the house and land had been given to one of his forefathers in return for services rendered during the Napoleonic wars. Primo was never exactly clear which side his illustrious ancestor had actually fought on, nor what the services were that justified the reward. But if the land was a gift, Primo had every reason to question the motives of the giver. The rough-hewn stone and timber house that occupied the land had been there for as long as anyone could remember and, even new, would have been considered poor payment. As for the land itself, it would always struggle to support them.

Primo did his best and the whole family contributed any way they could. Yet every day, every week and every month of every year was a battle. They kept sheep and sold the lambs and the wool. They kept goats and made cheese. They kept cows and sold the milk and made more cheese. In spring they sold calves. They kept chickens and sold their eggs. And every year they harvested almost enough fodder to feed their livestock through winter.

But their problem was one shared by peasant farmers throughout Europe. Their land was simply not sufficient to support a family. So, in addition to running the household, supervising the cheese-making and raising seven children, Cecilia's mother was forced to find paid work.

In the long hours while her mother was away washing other people's linen and cleaning other people's houses, Cecilia became mother to her two sisters and four brothers. By the time she was nine years old, she washed and cleaned and prepared the evening meal as a matter of course, ever grateful for any assistance her mother could give her.

In the beginning, her two elder brothers, Alfredo and Elio, exercised their right as males to order her to wash their clothes and clean their shoes, but they soon learned that things got done a little sooner and a little better if they just kept out of the way, and left her to it. Gradually Cecilia assumed responsibility for running the household, without anyone except her mother being aware of it. Cecilia accepted her lot calmly and worked methodically. She never seemed tired, she never got angry, and she was never too busy to help anyone who asked. Accordingly, she was taken for granted, as most mothers are and always have been. But Cecilia was still barely nine years old.

The only time her workload was lightened was during school hours and on completion of the evening dishes. Then her mother insisted that she study or read books. It didn't matter what she read as long as she read.

'Promise me you will not waste your life as I have,' Maddalena would urge her eldest daughter when they were alone together. 'You are special. But if you don't have an education the world will never come to realise this and you will never escape. You must read books, Cecilia. Imagine you are in a castle, in a prison, and you are digging a tunnel under the wall so you can escape. Every book you read is another bucket of earth, Cecilia. Every book you read takes you further away from these walls.'

Sometimes Cecilia read school books, sometimes bedtime stories to her younger brothers and sisters. On the only occasions she read for pleasure, she read aloud. She even had to share her one pleasure with her family. But, the fact was, she didn't mind. On the contrary, she read stories out loud to her family whenever there was an opportunity. Cecilia knew she could work her fingers to the bone and that would change nothing. The reading was something else. It gave her power, respect and an identity. She became not just her mother's favourite but the whole family's favourite because she read to them. She became their entertainment, their radio, their movies, their theatre and their magazines.

Cecilia had a good voice and her mother encouraged her to cultivate it. She adopted the enunciation and cadence of her Milanese school teacher, and his sense of drama and timing. Over time, she began to sound less and less like a peasant girl and more and more like an educated city girl. The change was so gradual that her family assumed it was the way she had always spoken.

When she sat down to read, she had a cushion to sit on and a pillow to rest against, rare luxuries brought by a family eager to hear the latest instalment of whatever story she was reading. Her brothers turned up the wick of the single oil lamp she read by. They all crowded in around her except Maddalena, who took the opportunity to iron or fold washing while she listened. Cecilia took them away from the crowded stone cottage and the monotony of their days. She transported them to other lands, and filled their heads with adventures and romance. Sometimes she'd leave her audience weeping, other times with eyes bright from excitement and begging for more. This was the gift Cecilia gave her family and why they loved her. She was the glue that helped keep the family close, and helped them forget those nights when Primo came home drunk.

This was the family shame though, in fairness, they were not the only family in Ravello or any other village for that matter to be shamed this way. Cecilia could not remember a time when it had never happened. Probably the shouting and the crying had wakened her as a baby. Probably, until she had learned to turn a deaf ear, she had cried along with her mother. It was a fact of life she'd learned to live with, however unhappily.

Primo was Cecilia's father and so she loved him. She hated what he did to her mother when he was drunk, but he was her father. Love is not always a matter of choice. Even battered children protest when the authorities come to take them away from their parents. Besides, her father was always so distraught and ashamed in the morning. He was the one who needed love and consolation, comfort and forgiveness, and Cecilia gave him all those things. His victim was left to lick her wounds, and bear the indignity of her bruises and swellings before her neighbours.

Primo was not a bad man. In the main he was a good father and loving husband who worked hard to support his family. His short, nuggetty body showed that he did. His skin was tanned by too many hours in the sun and the veins in his arms stood out like knotted rope. He worked hard and none could doubt it. But when he went drinking, he would return and stand before the crude cottage and know that, no matter how hard he worked or how hard he tried, life would give him no more than the little he already had. His disappointment would give way to anger, and his anger to rage.

On these nights, Maddalena would resign herself to the inevitable, and try to lose herself in Cecilia's story so that she would stay calm. On the one occasion she'd ever cursed him and fought back, he'd beaten her senseless. She learned not to resist or show fear and tried hard not to cry out in pain, because that only served to enrage him more. She also learned to blot out the pain and whisper soothing endearments when he forced himself upon her afterwards. Maddalena always prayed nothing would come of these couplings. Whatever would become of a child conceived this way?

Cecilia may have loved her father, but she was devoted to her mother. She flattered herself to believe she was also her mother's closest friend. Her mother spoke to her and shared confidences in a way she never did with any of her other children. But her mother would never discuss the beatings or allow her to be critical of her father, even when Cecilia was bathing her bruises or rubbing away soreness.

'You see what will happen to you, Cecilia?' was all she would say. 'You see why you must read books? Don't throw your life away. You are too good for this sort of life. Look at me. I am nothing. I am old and tired before my time. Promise me you won't throw your life away.'

Cecilia promised. She never cried for her mother. Either she'd inherited her mother's stoicism or she'd learned it. She seemed to accept the beatings in the same way she accepted her endless household chores. But was it an inner strength she showed, or the symptom of a child who had put away her deepest feelings, tucked them away where they couldn't intrude upon the reality of her life?

On those nights when her father failed to come home before dinner, she would stay up with her mother long after the storytelling had ended, cleaning and tidying so there'd be fewer things for her father to find fault with. She'd put his nightshirt by the fire and make sure there was warm water for him to wash in. Then she'd flee to the bedroom she shared with her brothers and sisters as soon as she heard her father's heavy footsteps on the path outside. Sometimes all the preparations worked and her father's anger would dissipate for want of fuel, but most times the effort would be wasted. Then Cecilia would lay awake wondering what she'd overlooked that had unleashed her father's anger; or what else she could do to soothe it away. That — and the reading — was how Cecilia tried to help her mother.

Primo did not come home drunk every night or even every week, or at any specific interval. No one knew what it was that made Primo decide to go down to the café in Ravello and exchange however much money was in his pocket for cheap, fiery grappa. But on average, once a month he'd wander down the hill and join in whatever debates were taking place. Sometimes the men would discuss football, other times women, but always they ended up arguing over politics. Primo loved the political debates, anxious to discover a party or leader who could provide him with a better life. For a while he supported the Socialist Party of Proletarian Unity. He liked their Utopian vision, but gradually realised that a vision was all they offered. They would not change his life. He shifted his allegiances to the Italian Communist Party. The idea of everyone having an equal share in the common wealth appealed to him. The idea of the strong helping the weak and the fortunate helping the less fortunate seemed only fair and just. As one of the less fortunate he would undoubtedly benefit. If anyone could improve his life, it would be the PCI.

But the PCI had its power base in the cities and in the trade unions, and Primo had the peasant's deep distrust of city people. He heard how the PCI organised strikes and disrupted industry the length and breadth of Italy and failed to see how that could possibly help him. Indeed, every time there was a strike, the papers talked of massive losses suffered by the industries involved. It seemed to Primo that the communists were destroying the very wealth they'd promised to share. How could that possibly help him? Then one night, Primo heard Mussolini on the café radio, and it seemed that the leader was speaking directly to him. That night, he went home preoccupied and forgot to beat up Maddalena.

It could be argued that Mussolini was responsible for the break-up of the Ortelli family, the catalyst that caused the glue to become unstuck. Primo adopted the cause of fascism, and the more ardent he became the more often he took himself off down the hill to argue, debate and get drunk. The beatings began to happen once if not twice a week and the children could no longer turn a deaf ear.

Cecilia blamed herself for the change in her father and for her mother's suffering. Her father loved listening to the stories she read as much as anyone, and whenever a good story had him in its grip, there was no way he'd risk missing an instalment by going to the café. Then Cecilia would milk the story. She'd do whatever she could to make the story last longer and keep her father from going down to Ravello. She'd read more slowly and more dramatically, and finish reading as soon as they came to a suitably suspenseful part. What made these moments even more delicious was the knowledge that her mother knew what she was up to, and they'd exchange little glances of complicity.

Her talent did not go unnoticed. At the age of eleven she was already the best in the school at reading aloud. In scripture lessons she was invariably chosen to read the selected passages and she made the ancient words come alive in a way that none of the teachers or Father Michele were able to. Even the dullest and most reluctant of students could not resist her spell and listened as raptly as any. That, according to Father Michele, was a miracle worthy of Cecilia's elevation to sainthood. Of course her teacher did everything he could to encourage her precocious talent, and begged and borrowed books for her.

So when her teacher gave her a book on Mussolini to read and she discovered her father's interest, naturally she used all her skills to sustain it. When she spoke of the march on Rome, she made Mussolini sound like the saviour of their nation, a hero come to rescue Italy from the grasp of a corrupt, incompetent government. When she told how he'd disbanded and outlawed the communist trade unions, Mussolini became the one man who could save the country from industrial anarchy and put it on the road to prosperity. Then there was the other matter of his North African conquests. Just why Italians felt they needed to own large chunks of inhospitable country was never made clear, nevertheless the bright lights of triumph reflected upon all Italians. It wasn't difficult for Cecilia to impart such a rosy image of Mussolini because the book was blatant propaganda, a product of Mussolini's own ministries which had been distributed to schools. Nevertheless, Cecilia brought the words to life and gave the lies the ring of truth.

Primo could see that Mussolini was the man who could change his life, who could make Italy a rich, powerful and proud nation in which all would share the spoils. The book confirmed his beliefs, and the more his friends in the café argued against Mussolini the more committed and angry he became. No one suffered more from his commitment than Maddalena.

Primo lost interest in Cecilia's stories. All he wanted to hear about was Mussolini. He told her to bring more books home from school, but if there were more books on the Duce, they hadn't yet found their way to the small school in Ravello. So Cecilia and her brothers and sisters scoured the village for discarded newspapers and fascist pamphlets, anything at all that had stories about Mussolini. Cecilia read everything first, and quickly discarded any story which voiced criticism or contrary political views.

Primo, who resented spending any of their precious money on school clothes, now insisted that all his sons had new cadet uniforms so that when the *Balilla*, the Italian Fascist Youth, paraded, his sons would stand out and bring him credit when they marched and saluted the flag every Friday. Maddalena obliged, even though it took every last *lira* she'd hidden away for emergencies.

If the family hoped their efforts would keep Primo from the café, they were soon disappointed. News simply didn't happen fast enough for him, and the stories Cecilia would read from one newspaper were often repeated in others. He got bored. The family did their best but all they succeeded in doing was arming Primo with more facts with which to regale the anti-fascists in the café. He'd argue his belief that Mussolini would make Italy rich and powerful, and that everybody in the café would share in the wealth. Il Duce was the one man who could change their lives. He filled the café with his vision and his conviction, gathering converts to the cause. One night he caught the eye of a Fascist Party organiser. If God himself had reached out his hand to Primo, he could not have been more overwhelmed.

But his passion brought little joy to his family. The beatings increased until there were days when Maddalena could no longer get up and go to work. This incensed Primo even more for it meant there'd be less money for him to spend in the café. Cecilia called her two older brothers together and told them it was time they did something to protect their mother. They refused. They didn't enjoy lying in the dark listening to Primo beat her, but he was their father and they wouldn't go against his will. Besides, their father's position in the Party and their new uniforms had won them both promotions in the *Balilla*. They enjoyed the little power it gave them and were proud of their father.

Fortunately for Maddalena the weather turned, and the morning wind from the north, the *tivano*, announced the arrival of autumn 1938. Primo was now the local fascist organiser, but the blood of generations of farmers also ran in his veins. The time had come to harvest and store the winter feed, and repair the holes in the sagging roof. For a while he became the Primo of old, and the family did everything to convince him that he should stay that way. Alfredo rallied to the cause and became his right-hand man while Elio and his younger brothers gathered, cut and stacked firewood. They fussed around him in the evenings and Cecilia would read the sort of stories he once loved. For a while, Primo succumbed to all the attention, and seemed to enjoy the role of dutiful father and husband. Then the man who had approached Primo in the café sent for him, and the cycle of beatings began all over again.

On her twelfth birthday, Cecilia decided she would no longer stand by while her mother was slowly and agonisingly beaten into her grave. When Primo went down to Ravello, she stayed up with her. She watched her mother as she folded the washing and sat down to mend the clothes that had torn or needed patching. But her tired fingers couldn't pick up the needle, and when Cecilia handed it to her, she couldn't see the eyelet to thread it. Frustration compounded her exhaustion, and her aching, battered body finally gave in. Her shoulders sagged and her head fell forward onto her arms. She began to sob, great heaving sobs which robbed her of what little strength she had left.

Cecilia took the needle and thread from her mother and began to sew. She sewed as she always sewed, calmly and methodically. She sewed until her mother's sobs died away and she composed herself.

'I'm sorry, Cecilia . . .'

'It's okay, Mama . . . okay. You rest.'

'No. It's no good. I can't take any more.' She looked up at her daughter, her voice barely above a whisper. 'What will happen? What will happen when your Papa comes home?'

'I will talk to him. He won't hit me. I will make him some food and read to him until he falls asleep.'

'No! No, no, no, Cecilia.'

'Yes, Mama.'

'No, Cecilia.' But Maddalena was too weak to argue.

'Yes, Mama. Now let me help you to bed. Rest and get some sleep. I will take care of Papa.'

Maddalena didn't protest, couldn't even if she wanted to. She let Cecilia help her up and lead her into the bedroom. Once her mother was comfortable, Cecilia began her preparations. She put away the sewing and the folded washing. She put a plate on the table where her father sat at mealtimes, with a chunk of bread, cheese and some olive oil. She picked up the newspapers her brothers and sisters had gathered that day, clipped out every story and photo of Mussolini and spread them around the table. Then she picked up the straw broom and swept the floor. There was little to sweep up because the floor was swept three or four times a day, and more often if needed. But that wasn't the point. Cecilia swept what little dust there was up to the front door then, broom in hand, sat down to wait for her father. As soon as she heard his heavy footfall, she opened the front door and finished sweeping.

'What are you doing?'

'Sweeping, Papa.'

Primo paused, uncertain whether to let her finish or just push past.

'Come in, Papa. Mama has put out some cheese for you. Come sit down. I will fetch you a glass of wine.'

Cecilia never gave orders and she was never the voice of authority. Her family, even her father, generally did what she suggested because it always seemed to be the most sensible thing. Her voice was always sweet and reasonable. Primo was nearly taken in, but then he remembered what it was he really wanted.

'Where's Mama?'

'She was feeling unwell, Papa. She asked me to stay up and read to you when you came home. See? I have all these stories about Il Duce for you.'

'Fetch your Mama.' Primo's voice had grown thick and was beginning to take on the sound Cecilia knew only too well.

'Mama is not well, Papa. Here, drink your wine while I read —'

Her father smashed the glass from her hand. He stood up, kicking his chair backwards so that it toppled over.

'Fetch your Mama!'

Cecilia stayed calm. She ignored the broken glass and the fallen chair. She smiled and stood her ground.

'Papa, this paper has a picture of Mussolini and Hitler. Don't you think Mussolini looks —' She never finished the sentence. The back of her father's hand caught her across the cheek and knocked her sprawling. Then her father was over her, dragging her to her feet, shaking her like a rag doll.

'Stupid girl. I don't want your newspapers! Did I say I wanted newspapers? I want your Mama. Your Mama! Not some pissy newspapers! Not some pissy wine. Why would I want more wine? I don't want wine. I'll show you what I want!' He picked her up and carried her into his bedroom.

Maddalena heard what was happening but was powerless

to help. Her muscles failed to respond when she ordered them to get her to her feet. She'd left an oil light on for Primo so that he wouldn't blunder into anything in the dark. Now she saw her husband burst through the doorway with Cecilia under his arm.

'No, Primo! No!'

'Don't you worry, old woman!' he yelled. 'I'm not going to touch you. Who would want to touch you? Look at you!' He threw Cecilia down onto the bed alongside his wife.

'Who would want to touch you?'

*　*　*

When Cecilia awoke the next morning she discovered she had become an outcast. No one would look at her or speak to her, not even her mother. Her brothers and sisters didn't even look up when she finally came out of her bedroom. Of course they knew what had happened. In such a small house there were no secrets. Alfredo and Elio would have heard the whole thing. But why were they blaming her? What had she done wrong? All she'd done was protect her mother. She poured herself a glass of milk and sat down at the table. Her father slowly pushed back his chair and struggled to his feet. He grabbed his hat and old woollen pullover and, without a word, left the house. Alfredo reached across the table and slapped her face. He and Elio also got up and left.

'Today you're not going to school. You're coming with me.'

Cecilia looked up at her mother, her bottom lip quivering as she fought for control. But her mother was not more forthcoming.

'Give your books to Paola. She can take them back to school.'

Cecilia turned to her sister but Paola wouldn't meet her eyes. She couldn't understand why the world had changed and turned against her. Sure, she knew what her father had done was wrong. But why couldn't they all forget it and pretend that nothing had happened, like they always did? What was the difference? She'd seen her father naked plenty of times before. She'd even helped him bathe in the tiny tub when he came in from the fields dripping wet and covered in mud. As for erections ... ha! Alfredo had turned fifteen. She could hardly remember when he didn't wake up with an erection. Anyway, he seemed to take some sort of peculiar delight in making sure she saw it. But they all knew what had happened the night before and why. They all knew it was not her fault. Why couldn't they just forget it? Her father hadn't hurt her ... well, not much, not like he hurt her mother. He'd only hit her once. She knew what she had to do when her father threw her onto the bed. She knew what she had to do so he didn't get mad. She'd done nothing wrong. She squeezed her eyes shut but was powerless to prevent the tears from rolling down her cheeks and mixing with the milk in her glass.

* * *

Lucio finished speaking and looked up towards the kitchen, looking for Gancio. It was their custom to take a coffee break in the middle of each day's storytelling. Normally this was a cue for discussion, for the listeners to comment on what they'd heard. But today the audience was reticent, nobody keen to speak first. Naturally, it was Neil who finally broke the silence.

'You wogs go in for a lot of that sort of thing?'

'Well, Neil,' replied Lucio evenly. 'No more than you bloody Aussies. No more than any other country in the world. What did you think?'

'Neil doesn't think, do you, Neil?' Ramon turned to Lucio and reached for his arm. 'Lucio, please don't make the mistake of assuming Neil is human. He doesn't think, therefore he isn't.'

'Give me a break.'

'Five coffees, five grappas. Let me put down the tray and get a chair.'

'Gancio to the rescue. Jesus guys, it was just a joke. Maybe you have to be born here to get it. You weren't offended were you, Lucio?'

'I've been here long enough, Neil. When Italians take offence nobody is left in any doubt.'

Neil and Milos made room for Gancio.

'Okay . . . tell me the story so far. What have I missed?'

Neil laughed. 'What have you missed? Holy shit! Over to you Milos. You tell him.'

'Nothing that you want to hear, Gancio. Your compatriot has kept us spellbound with his story — well told too, no?' Milos looked around at the others for confirmation and got it. 'Not his usual style. More the pity perhaps. His story has depressed me when I had hoped for a good laugh. Again, I have the painful suspicion that his story may also be true. If it is, Ramon, it is your fault and your legacy. Anyway, I'll quickly bring you up to date. If I miss anything important, somebody jump in.'

Gancio listened while the others drank their coffee and Lucio gathered his thoughts for the next part of his story. Milos was a good listener and had a keen ear for storyline and nuances. His précis was excellent.

'Mother of God, this story better be true, Lucio. If you made up this story you should be ashamed. There are plenty of things you can make up that don't involve things like that. That is terrible. But Milos has missed one thing out. The girl . . . when she is grown up she is called Colombina. When she is young she is called Cecilia. Cecilia who? Italy is full of Cecilias. What is her full name?' Gancio finished off his grappa, and rolled it around his mouth.

'Cecilia Silvana Ortelli.'

Gancio choked as he was swallowing. He grabbed a paper napkin and coughed into it.

'Ugh! Who gave you this grappa? Who gave you this shit?'

The four friends stared at him, not least of them Lucio. They were all obsessed with lies and half-truths. Gancio hadn't fooled any of them. He hadn't choked on the grappa. Besides, the grappa was very good. Gancio's grappa was always very good.

Chapter Four

Colombina didn't gasp and drop the photograph, nor did she cry out. She was always too much in control to do that. But she felt a chill throughout her body as if her blood had suddenly lost its warmth. She studied his face, so smiling and kindly — looking like everybody's grandfather and not at all like a murderer.

'Colombina? Are you all right?'

'I'm sorry, Helen. Who is this man?'

Colombina was one of the many volunteers who put themselves and their cars at the disposal of Warriewood Meals-on-Wheels, which provides low cost hot meals for those unable to prepare their own.

'Heinrich Bose. He's an absolute dear. Do you know him?' Helen organised the rosters and had been standing in for absentees for so long, she'd got to know all of the recipients in the Warringah–Pittwater area. She knew all there was to know: who delivered to whom; who was diabetic; who was vegetarian and who was low-salt. All anyone needed to join her circle of acquaintances was a medical certificate or a referral from Homecare.

'I'm not sure.' In truth, Colombina wasn't sure. Now that she'd had time to look at his photo, she began to perceive differences. It had been nearly fifty years. Of course he would have changed, and so would her memory of him. But there was something about this foolish old man in the Christmas party hat that had touched a nerve. Perhaps it was the impression she gained from looking at the whole of his face or the way he sat that was familiar. But there was nothing she could pinpoint, no one feature that said to her, 'Yes! This is him!' The more she studied the photo the more uncertain she became. She only knew she would have to find out, one way or the other.

Colombina put the photo down on the table among the others. Most of the pensioners had been picked up by a bus on Christmas Day and taken to the community hall, where they could sit down to turkey and ham and roast potatoes as one big, happy family. But there were always some whose circumstances prevented them from going. Heinrich Bose was one. He had the misfortune to fall and twist his right knee two days before Christmas. There was no permanent damage, but old bones take a while to heal and the journey from bathroom to bedroom was all he could manage. So the kind men and women who volunteered to deliver meals that Christmas Day had taken party hats and bonbons with them, and stayed with their customers for an extra few minutes to help make their meal more of a celebration, and less like another lonely lunch. One of them also took a camera.

'Who does his route?' asked Colombina.

'Let me see.' Helen mentally consulted her list. 'Bose ... Bose ... yes! John and Edna ... the dynamic duo.'

'Thanks, I'll have a word with them.' Colombina turned to see how far her partner had got in loading up her car. 'Oops! We're ready to go. See you later.'

Colombina climbed into the driver's seat and smiled apologetically to her partner. But she didn't engage in the usual small talk and gossip that made delivering meals less a chore and more a social occasion. She was too preoccupied. John and Edna were a legend in Meals-on-Wheels. Easily as old as many of the people they looked after, they'd hardly missed a day in fifteen years. Edna would deliver to one house, John the next and so on. Then, the following day they'd swap places so that both of them maintained a relationship with every one of their recipients. They were indestructible. If Colombina listed herself as a reserve for their route, it could be years before she'd have a chance to meet the man in the photo who called himself Heinrich Bose.

'What do you know about John and Edna?' she asked suddenly.

'Welcome back.'

'I'm sorry Ann . . .'

'Don't apologise. As a matter of fact, it's good to see you less than your normal, ever-cheerful self. Does me the world of good. There's nothing more annoying than having a friend whose life is perfect.'

Colombina laughed despite herself.

'When people are perfectly happy — as you always seem to be — they become unutterably boring. They have nothing worthwhile to talk about. So suffer, babe. Join the rest of the world. Now, what was the question?'

'John and Edna.'

'More perfect people. Mind you, I suspect they're into kinky sex and wife-swapping. They don't smoke, don't drink and don't even swear at old men who wear hats and drive old Volvos. Nobody could possibly be as squeaky clean and civic-minded as those two seem to be. When they're not doing meals I've seen them helping boy scouts across busy streets. They even take Sunday school at Saint Luke's. Maybe when they get home from church they dress up in each other's underwear.'

Colombina laughed. Ann was outrageous. But in among her ludicrous assertions and speculation, Colombina sought to glimpse a ray of hope.

'Are they very religious?'

'No more than Jesus was. I hear they even say grace for their customers.'

'You're kidding.'

'Yeah, but I wouldn't put it past them. When those two croak, God will roll out the red carpet and organise a choir of angels to receive them.'

'Then let's hope they're wearing their own knickers.'

'Colombina!'

* * *

Colombina appeared calm but inside she was in turmoil. She thought she'd escaped the war and Italy forever. But what if Heinrich Bose was the Oberstleutnant? What would she do then? She thought of her mother standing back to the wall facing her executioners, and used the injustice and the bitterness she harboured to steady herself. She decided to question the old couple about Heinrich Bose. Undoubtedly they'd know all about him. She'd quickly learned that old, lonely people love nothing more than to tell their life story. In her heart she hoped she was wrong about the old man. After all, the chances of her mother's murderer turning up nearly fifty years later just a couple of streets away from where she lived were, well . . . if not impossible then so remote as to make no difference. Besides, she'd found the peace and contentment she'd hungered for all her life and was loath to see that destroyed. She clung to the hope that she was mistaken. Perhaps a few innocent questions would settle everything. But the problem was, if the impossible had happened and if Heinrich Bose really was the Oberstleutnant, then she had no choice. She would have to make him pay for his crime. God as her witness, she would make him pay! But she also accepted the need for caution, for the control that had served her so well. John and Edna might inadvertently put him on his guard. She couldn't let that happen.

The following Tuesday, Colombina was first to arrive at the Warriewood centre. She knew John and Edna always came early. That would be the best time to talk to them, before the food was ready for loading. She watched as John turned his car around and backed it up as close to the entrance as possible. No matter who arrived first, that space was always left for them.

'Hi. How are you?'

'Hello, Colombina. You're early.'

Colombina took a close look at the old couple smiling up at her. Their eyes radiated health and energy, and they had a spriteliness most sixty year olds would envy. Yet she knew both were closing fast on eighty.

'Have to be early to beat you two. You deserve a medal.'

'Nonsense.' John and Edna laughed away the suggestion, but were nonetheless pleased to have their efforts recognised. 'We've nothing better to do.'

'Yes, but five days a week . . . Don't you ever need a break?'

'No, we look forward to it. Gives us something to do. Something worthwhile.' John put his arm around his wife's shoulders and squeezed gently.

Colombina groaned inwardly, but persisted.

'But surely there must be times when it's inconvenient, when your duties here clash with doctors' or dental appointments?'

'We try and work around those,' cut in Edna. 'Though there have been one or two times when we've had to get Helen to stand in for one or other of us.'

'Why Helen?' Colombina knew exactly why they always asked Helen to cover for them. They'd adopted a proprietary interest in their recipients — 'their people' — and didn't want just anybody going around to them. Yet she sensed an opportunity.

'They know Helen,' said John. 'That's important.'

'Couldn't agree more,' said Colombina. 'Anyway, if you ever need help on any days other than Tuesdays and Thursdays, remember me. I can't think of anybody I'd like to help out more. Helen knows how to contact me.'

'That's very, very kind of you,' said Edna.

'Very kind,' agreed John.

'Oh well, dinner's ready. Off to work.' Colombina congratulated herself on her manner. She'd been kind, thoughtful and charming and not shown any of the tension she'd felt. And she'd planted the seed. She'd keep buttering them up and maybe one day she'd get the call. What else could she do?

* * *

Offering to cover for the dynamic duo was not the smartest thing Colombina ever did. Helen immediately interpreted that as an offer to go on stand-by should anyone else fail to turn up on their rostered days. Every week she got called up to cover for somebody but it was never the call she wanted. Occasionally, she was forced to interrupt her bowls day at the Newport Bowling Club, and sometimes her canasta afternoons. But no matter what else she had on, she always obliged Helen and responded to her call.

By the time two months had passed, Colombina was beginning to question her motives. The extra days on duty had become a drag on her social life. She never knew from one day to the next whether she'd be called upon and she'd grown tired of apologising to her friends. Besides, her memory of the man in the photograph had begun to fade. She no longer had a clear image or impression of him, and couldn't recall quite what it was about his picture that had caused her to react. Besides, she'd known the Oberstleutnant for less than a year. Could she really hope to recognise him from a photo after forty-eight years? She decided to see Helen and get herself taken off the stand-by list.

Helen understood. That was the way it went with relief volunteers. But Colombina had been more reliable than most and Helen didn't want to let her go entirely.

'What if I put you on my emergency list?' she asked.

'What's that?'

'It's a list of people I call when I run out of stand-by volunteers.'

'Okay,' said Colombina reluctantly. It seemed churlish to say otherwise.

Five weeks passed before Colombina was asked to put in an extra day. It was a Wednesday, the busiest day, when the volunteers also distributed frozen meals for the weekend when the centre was closed and there was no Meals-on-Wheels service. Those recipients with microwaves and no relatives or friendly neighbours to look after them gladly paid the eight dollars for the two extra meals.

Colombina groaned. It was her bowling day and they were due to play competition against a visiting team.

'Isn't there anyone else?'

'Well, yes there is,' replied Helen. 'But John and Edna have asked for you specially. They've got to go to Melbourne for a funeral and for once I can't help them out. Apparently you offered to help them if they ever got stuck.'

'Yes. That's right. I did.' Now that the opportunity to meet Heinrich Bose had finally come, Colombina was no longer certain that she wanted to. She'd put him right out of her mind.

'Then you've only got yourself to blame,' said Helen. She laughed and hung up.

* * *

When she drove up to the centre, Colombina was as bright and cheerful as always. She met her partner for the day, a retired bank manager called Ted, who insisted that everybody appreciate the sacrifice he was making by giving up his Wednesday. He was the type who made the people on his route feel guilty for being helpless.

'You drive. I'll take the food in,' he told Colombina.

'I'll drive and we'll both take the food in,' replied Colombina brightly. 'I like to meet my customers.'

'Suit yourself.' It was going to be one of those days, Ted could tell. Next time he got called up he'd go down to the club instead and have his usual roast beef and potatoes, and hope some of his mates turned up.

'Right,' said Colombina. 'Who's first?'

She served lunch and spread her cheer through eight homes before she reached number fifty-seven Blaxland Street, the stone and fibro cottage where Heinrich Bose lived. Ted took the hot meal out of the insulated box on the back seat and led the way down the path.

'The odds are a million to one,' Colombina told herself.

* * *

'Good afternoon, I am Heinrich Bose. Thank you for giving up your time.'

The front door had been left ajar and Ted had marched right in, barely bothering to knock. Colombina heard Heinrich Bose greet Ted and certainly heard the welcome in his voice. Yet there was something about it which chilled her. It was both familiar and unfamiliar. The accent was strange — then again, she'd never heard the Oberstleutnant speak in English — but the tone of his voice and the intelligence it conveyed touched a nerve.

'Good afternoon, I am Heinrich Bose.'

'I'm Colombina. This is Ted. Please don't get up.'

The old man wouldn't be deterred. He rose to his feet without hesitation, his right hand firmly planted on the arm of his chair to protect his right knee. Once upright, he stood to attention as Colombina knew he would, and formally bowed his head before extending his hand to her. She took his hand and knew immediately.

'I am pleased to meet you . . . Colombina?' Heinrich arched his eyebrows as if querying the name. 'People say we Swiss are neutral but we are never neutral where beautiful women are concerned.'

Colombina laughed, but her mind raced.

'Colombina Galli. I'm pleased to meet you.' She calmly placed the two frozen meals she was carrying on the table beside her and shook the murderer's hand. 'You seem surprised by my name.'

'No, delighted. Little dove. I cannot think of a more suitable name.'

'Do you want the soup now?' Ted cut across their conversation, miffed that Colombina was the centre of attention, not him.

'No thank you, Ted. Put it in the fridge if you don't mind. I'll keep it for dinner.' Heinrich answered Ted but never took his eyes off Colombina. They'd lost little of their intensity and she felt as naked before their scrutiny as she had as a seventeen year old.

'How did you get the name Colombina?' He turned from her finally, placed his hand back on the arm of the chair, and slowly eased himself into it.

Colombina very nearly told him. His inspection had unsettled her. In fact if he hadn't looked away she would have told him, and that would have begged the question as to her real name. Absurd as it seems, she hadn't considered the possibility that he might recognise her or question her. It was such a long shot. Besides, surely she was no more than one young girl among many who had shared his bed. She cursed her foolishness. She knew the calibre of the mind she was up against. Whatever happened next she knew she would have to be careful and always on her guard. She watched him for any small sign of recognition, but he was now more interested in his lunch.

'I was a very small baby . . . tiny . . . not more than two kilograms. My father said I looked like a little featherless bird.'

'A little like my lunch perhaps.'

'Roast chicken,' said Ted proudly, as if he were personally responsible for cooking it. 'And roast potatoes and broccoli. Delicious.'

'Nutritious, yes. Delicious, no. Tell me, Colombina, would you describe this meal as delicious?'

'Nutritious will do nicely.'

'Indeed. Please do not think I am not grateful. I appreciate the system that provides it and the two of you for bringing it. For giving up your afternoon for the likes of me. I imagine you both have many better things to do.'

'Any time,' Ted responded. 'It's a small sacrifice in the overall scheme of things. My friends will just have to do without me for a while.'

Colombina was tempted to laugh and she suddenly realised that Heinrich was playing up to her, implicating her, making her side with him as he'd done with Cecilia so many years earlier. Ted was oblivious to such subtleties. She carried the two frozen weekend meals through to the small kitchen and stacked them in his freezer. She looked back at the Oberst-leutnant, taking the opportunity to look at him more closely. His straight back had bent with age, and the broad shoulders had grown gaunt. His face was more angular and his slightly beaked nose more pronounced. And his lips had retreated to become thin red lines. But his attitude, his bearing, had not given in to the years. She fumbled for the right word . . . what was it? . . . patrician! Yes, he was patrician. Intelligent, aloof, aristocratic. And there were other things age had not and could not change. The burns on his hairless hands and the scar that tracked from above his left ear to the back of his skull.

'Will I see you again, Colombina?'

Columbina started. Had he caught her staring? Colombina was flushed with guilt. But how could he have? He hadn't looked up. His attention hadn't wavered from the meal in front of him.

'If you behave yourself.'

Heinrich laughed. And if Colombina had any vestiges of doubt left, his laugh dispelled them. It was more of a throaty chuckle really. Warm and genuine and unforgettable. More the laugh of a lover than a murderer.

*   *   *

Colombina was glad to leave the house and review everything that had happened second by second. 'Heinrich Bose' was no more his name than 'Colombina' was hers. He was no more Swiss than Attila the Hun. She knew exactly who he was, but did he know who she was? She shuddered when she recalled the way his eyes had seemed to bore right into her; to seek out her thoughts and hold them up for inspection. He'd seen through Ted quickly enough, but what had he learned about her? Probably not much. Would a murderer knowingly make jokes and play games with the daughter of one of his victims? She didn't think so. If he had recognised her it would have shown. She felt sure of that. Then another thought occurred to her, stunning in its implications. What if he *had* recognised her? What if he was now sitting there in his armchair, tray on his knees, eating his lunch and wondering if she had recognised him! What if he was playing her game? That was exactly the sort of thing he'd do.

If Ted noticed any change in Colombina, he didn't mention it. When Colombina suggested she stayed in the car while he delivered the rest of the lunches, he had only one thing to say.

'About time you came to your senses.'

The following day, Colombina did her normal Thursday deliveries with Ann. Once again, her partner accused her of being insufferably content.

'Come on, Colombina,' she pleaded. 'Tell me all about your secret lover. You must have one. Your smile gives you away. There's only one thing that makes a woman smile like that, and that's a good, healthy bonking.'

'Don't you wish.'

'Who is he? You can tell me. I won't tell anyone outside of the centre, the bowling club, or our card games. In fact I won't tell anyone outside of the peninsula.'

Colombina began to laugh. 'Thank you. You're not usually so discreet.'

'Good, then that's settled. Tell me everything. I want to know everything. Even the naughty bits. Especially the naughty bits.'

'There's nothing to tell.'

But of course there was. Colombina was desperate for someone to talk to. She couldn't get the Oberstleutnant out of her mind. He had been her lover and the first man to reach her heart. Some of the things she'd loved about him, she'd glimpsed in him still: his gentleness and his charm; the keen brain behind the kind eyes; his quiet confidence; his sense of humour, often ironic or mocking, and often self-deprecating; and, the thing that worried her most, his immense self-control.

Colombina now realised that if he had recognised her, he would have given no indication. She had no doubt at all about who had controlled their encounter. He'd taken charge the moment they'd walked into his home. He'd worked Ted out and realised he had an accomplice in her for his brand of humour. He'd achieved this in just a couple of sentences. But was it pure intuition? Or had he recognised her and tested her for confirmation? This is what worried Colombina. The exchange had been brief, but oh so familiar! So practised! So instinctive. It was as if the intervening years counted for nothing. If he'd set out to trap her, he'd succeeded. She was no match for him. She never had been.

'Are you going to tell me?'

'Sorry, Ann.'

'We're getting worried about you. You keep doing that, drifting away while we're talking to you. Are we boring you? Am I?'

Ann was joking of course, but Colombina had to concede the substance behind her comment. She'd have to be more careful. She didn't want her friends noticing a change in her, not now. She laughed once more, as she was expected to, as she always did.

'No, Ann. Without any doubt you are the most exciting person I ever get to talk to. As a matter of fact, because you are my best friend, and because I know I can count on your discretion, I will tell you. There is a new man.'

'Really? Tell me, tell me!'

'Well, he's very intelligent.'

'And . . .?'

'Very charming.'

'And . . .?'

'And at least twenty years younger than me with ears that stick out and a thing that doesn't.'

'Colombina!'

'Maybe I'll be luckier next time and get it the other way around. Now on your feet, we've got customers waiting. You take this one in and I'll do the next.'

Colombina sat in the car and wondered what she should do. If she had to rely on John and Edna being called away to funerals, she'd get nowhere. She had to see the Oberstleutnant again and the sooner the better. But what reason could there be to call in? She needed a reason and a good one. She couldn't just turn up on his doorstep. If he hadn't already recognised her, then that would make him suspicious. And if he had, that would be the ball game. If she was going to avenge her mother, she'd have to find a way to get close to him. Then she'd deal with him. Exactly how, she'd no idea. But one thing was for sure, she had no intention of martyring herself in the process.

*   *   *

Two weeks passed before Colombina's son-in-law inadvertently handed her both the means to make contact with the Oberstleutnant and to exact retribution. Her daughter Alessandra brought her family up to Clareville for their monthly Sunday visit. They dragged Mario's little runabout down the slipway, and motored out to the last of the moorings and tied up. Her grandchildren loved fishing but they particularly loved it when they dragged lures behind the boat to jag squid. They loved the way they squirted black ink everywhere and tried to crawl up their arms. But Colombina wouldn't let them catch squid when she went out with them. They made her flesh crawl. In her mind, the only good squid was a stuffed squid.

So they sat on the mooring and dangled lines over the side and caught illegally small bream and tailor and talked. Her son-in-law loved his food, and he particularly liked the small fish they caught cooked whole. He begged Colombina to cook them for dinner, so outrageous in his flattery and praise of her culinary abilities that he gave her no choice.

'Everybody deserves to eat well,' he said. 'Good food is like good sex. Without either, life is not worth living.'

'I don't know about that.'

'It's true, Colombina. Think of the people you deliver your food to. Do they wake up every morning — or even any morning — and say, "Aha! Today I will have a meal I will remember for the rest of my life"? Do they? No! They are just waiting to die, knowing they will never again have good sex, and never again have a good meal. Life no longer holds any pleasure for them. What you do is a necessity, Colombina, not a kindness. Imagine their faces if you were to cook a meal for them. Eh? With rosemary and basil, with bay leaves, garlic and ground black pepper. Imagine if you took these little fish and made them *misoltitt*. Or made them your *risotto Gorgonzola*. That is something to live for!'

'Probably kill the lot of them stone dead.' Colombina laughed — but she now knew how to get close to the Oberstleutnant. It was true. The way to a man's heart was through his stomach. Perhaps it might also lead the way to his grave.

* * *

Colombina knew Heinrich wasn't on a special diet, otherwise his lunch would have been specially marked. So on the following Saturday she made a pot of *Blumenkohlsuppe* — cream of cauliflower soup — a *Rouladen* — braised beef rolls stuffed with bacon, mustard and pickled cucumber — from a German cookbook she'd bought the day before, and baked an *apfel strudel*. To a man faced with the prospect of reheated tomato soup, reheated roast lamb and a garishly coloured strawberry mousse, this meal would seem nothing less than miraculous. This would give the Oberstleutnant something to live for.

On Sunday morning, Colombina went to Mass. She did not take the Sacrament, nor did she consider going to confession. If she had, what would she say? That she had every intention of becoming a murderess? No, all she wanted was a little of the comfort her mother had found in her religion. And she wanted to feel close to her and say a prayer for her. She didn't say a prayer for herself or ask forgiveness for what she was contemplating, because even thinking about it probably put her beyond redemption, and Colombina wasn't a hypocrite. She didn't deny the existence of God — indeed she'd never had a moment's doubt that He existed — but she had little use for the church or its servants. They dealt in platitudes and wishful thinking, she in practicalities and reality. How would the church deal with the Oberstleutnant? They'd preach forgiveness and suggest she leave judgement to God and the proper authorities, whoever they might be. Either way, the Oberstleutnant was certain to escape retribution in this life and that, to Colombina, was unacceptable.

She hurried home and packed lunch. Three servings of soup because Heinrich Bose would probably want to keep some for his dinner. Three servings of strudel because he'd probably want a second helping. And the *Rouladen*. She parboiled some potatoes and sliced some cabbage and onion into a steamer. She taped the pot lids down and wrapped the plate holding the strudel in a tea towel. She packed her best china, enough for both of them, and her best silverware. At the last moment, she remembered the silver salt and pepper cruets. There was no time to waste. Heinrich Bose would be accustomed to eating at twelve forty, which was the time his meals normally arrived. But there was no guarantee he wouldn't take his Sunday lunch earlier. She decided she had to be there before twelve fifteen.

As she loaded up her car for the five-minute trip to fifty-seven Blaxland Street, she concentrated on the good deed she was doing, and the pleasure she'd bring to the charming old man. Her motive had to appear unambiguous. An act of kindness, that's all. She would have to take on the role as surely as any actress. But, then again, Colombina was hardly inexperienced. She rang his doorbell and took a deep breath. She prepared her smile. She could see movement through the frosted glass beside the door.

'Yes?'

The Oberstleutnant showed no sign of recognition. He swayed a little as he squinted at her. Colombina was perplexed. She didn't quite know what to do. Then she noticed the little indentations on the bridge of his nose. She flashed her mind back to the last meeting. Was he wearing glasses? No! Yes! He put on glasses when he began to eat. So he could see his dinner! They were reading glasses, but did he need glasses to see normally? Yes! She was certain he did. It was clear in the way he squinted and swayed. He was trying to focus. The Oberstleutnant was short-sighted, probably quite severely. Colombina was elated. He couldn't have recognised her. Dear God, he was lucky he even saw her!

'Heinrich, it's Colombina. I've brought you some food. Real food. *Rouladen*. I thought you deserved a change.'

'Colombina. Forgive me. How could I be so impolite? Come in! Come in!'

'Thank you. I couldn't bear the thought of you sitting down alone to the same old Meals-on-Wheels food, day after day.'

'So you have made *Rouladen* for me?'

'And for me. If I'm invited to stay, of course.'

'I can't believe it. I haven't had food like this for so long I've forgotten what it tastes like. And you made it for me?'

To Colombina's surprise, the old man's voice shook and he seemed close to tears. The iron control was showing the wear of age.

'Please, please ... put it down here so I can lift the lid and smell it. To remind me. You see, there was no point in remembering. Why remember something you never expect to taste again? Growing old is bad enough. Why make it worse?'

'Sit down and I'll take the tape off. Then you can sniff all you like while I go out to the car and bring the rest in.'

'There is more?'

'What's *Rouladen* without *Blumenkohlsuppe* before, and *apfel strudel* to follow?'

'*Blumenkohlsuppe*? And *apfel strudel*? Colombina you are an angel. You are an answer to an old man's prayers. What have I done to deserve such kindness?'

'What indeed!' thought Colombina as she turned to go back out to the car. So far so good. But she knew the test was still to come when he put on his regular glasses.

Heinrich had his head over the casserole dish and his reading glasses lodged firmly on his nose when Colombina returned.

'Colombina, this is magnificent. Absolutely magnificent!'

'Wait till you taste it. You might not think so highly of it then. Now let me into the kitchen so I can start warming things up. Out of the way.'

The Oberstleutnant sat back.

'Colombina, if the Lord struck me down now, before a morsel had passed my lips, I would die a happy man.'

'Can't have that,' said Colombina.

'I beg your pardon?'

Colombina waited the right amount of time, till the silence begged a response, then turned around to face him.

'Can't have the Lord striking you dead now. I've gone to too much trouble.' She smiled then held up the *Rouladen*. 'The least you can do is live long enough to enjoy it.'

Heinrich put his head back and the laugh Colombina had once loved tumbled from his throat. She set the table with her fine china and silver while the soup heated and the potatoes resumed boiling beneath the cabbage-filled steamer. She noticed that Heinrich still wore his reading glasses.

'Do you want me to find your other glasses?'

'Later, perhaps. I'll manage with these. With these, I can see what I'm eating. With the others, I can see where I'm going but I cannot see what is right in front of me. I fell over just before Christmas because of that and injured my knee. Both glasses do their job very well but there is an area perhaps one metre to two metres away where neither work satisfactorily. But I manage.'

Colombina smiled. Inside, she was elated. That was why he had studied her so intently the first time. She was in his blind spot. He couldn't have recognised his own mother.

'Reading glasses it is then. Now, let me see if I can poison you with the soup.'

* * *

Mario had always enthused about her cooking, and her son-in-law raved. But Heinrich made Colombina feel her efforts were world class. He drank each spoonful of soup with reverence and obvious appreciation. He was like a small child opening Christmas presents, each mouthful a wonderful gift, each course a new delight. The *Rouladen* left him speechless, as he renewed his acquaintance with hot mustard and dill-pickled cucumbers. The strudel was the perfect conclusion. He watched as Colombina smothered his portion in cream.

'So much cream will kill me,' he said. 'But please, don't hold back.'

Colombina didn't. Her own portion was much smaller because she wasn't used to large meals in the middle of the day, and she finished before Heinrich was half-way through.

'I'll put the coffee on,' she said, rather than sit and watch him eating.

'Thank you, I drink tea.'

'Of course.'

'Why "of course"?'

There it was! A reflex remark and he'd seized on it. He stared at her intently, squinting, searching for focus. Forty-eight years on the run had made him wary. What could she do? That was the odd thing about the Oberstleutnant which she knew well but had forgotten. He only drank tea. Her mind raced. How could she have been so stupid?

'Because it always happens. If I offer somebody coffee, they always drink tea. If I offer them tea, they always drink coffee. Don't ask why it happens that way, it just does.'

Heinrich relaxed.

'This strudel is wonderful. I haven't enjoyed strudel so much since I left Switzerland.'

'I'm sorry I didn't make you a Swiss meal. I don't actually know what Swiss eat. Your accent sounds German so I made German.'

'The Swiss dip their food in melted cheese. It is a disgusting way to eat. It smothers the natural taste of the food and makes cheese taste revolting. But then, I am not Swiss. Switzerland was my adopted home. Both my parents were Silesian. My father was half-Jewish. They thought it prudent to move to the German-speaking part of Switzerland in the early thirties. I grew up in Sankt Gallen. My accent is typically Swiss–Silesian.'

Colombina had to smile at his cleverness. There would not be enough Swiss–Silesians for anything to be considered typical. How better to conceal Saxon origins than to claim an accent that was uncheckable?

'And your accent?'

'Australian. I was born here. Both my parents were Italian, of course, and we always spoke Italian at home. I have an Italian accent without ever having been there.' *Touché.* 'Where did you learn to speak Italian?'

'Ah ... yes. In Switzerland. The Italian Swiss are very attached to their language.'

'Rightly so.' Colombina laughed. 'Now, what would you like next Sunday?'

'You are going to do this again?'

'Every Sunday. My son-in-law says that without good sex and good food, life is not worth living. At least I can help with the food.'

Once again Heinrich put his head back and laughed. For half an hour they discussed favourite dishes while they drank their tea and Colombina cleaned up.

'I have left you soup and some strudel for your dinner tonight.'

'I cannot believe that I could possibly eat again today. But I will. And I will enjoy the soup and the strudel again as much as I enjoyed having it for lunch. Come, I will see you to the door.'

'That's not necessary.'

'It's okay, I know the way.' He leaned heavily on his cane as he made his way to the front door.

'Thank you, Colombina.' Despite the fact that Colombina was loaded up with the pots and plates, he took her arm and leaned close to her so that she came within range of his reading glasses. He peered intently at her.

'I don't know how to thank you for this wonderful surprise. You have given this old man immense pleasure.'

Colombina held herself tightly under control, her smile fixed. She sensed his words were just camouflage, a distraction while he examined her. He took his time then held her eyes.

'You remind me of someone I met a long time ago.'

'Who?' Colombina met his gaze, hardly daring to breathe.

'Mother Teresa.' Heinrich let go of her arm and laughed.

Chapter Five

After her brothers and sisters had gone to school, Cecilia wrapped up the few clothes and shoes she had in newspaper, and tied the little bundle together with string. As hard as she tried, she couldn't stop her tears. She was being thrown out of her home, separated from her family and, what hurt most of all, abandoned by her mother. She never thought she would ever lose her mother's love, her friendship and her closeness. Her tears stung her eyes and she sobbed silently. Why? Why? She'd done nothing wrong! But of course she had. She'd brought shame on her father and therefore the family. Her best intentions counted for nothing. It wasn't fair!

'Come.'

Her mother had put on her hat and shoes and was standing grim-faced by the open door. Head down, eyes averted to hide the shame of her tears, Cecilia did as she was told. To her surprise her mother took her hand and led her up the pathway to the road. She glanced up but her mother's face was as hard as it had been all morning. But at least they were holding hands. As they set off down the hill Cecilia couldn't help herself. She squeezed her mother's hand as hard as she could. Then came a sound as sudden as it was unexpected, a sound she instantly recognised — she'd heard it often enough through the thin walls. Her mother sobbed, just once, but it was a cry of pain and despair that Cecilia knew came from the depths of her heart.

Tears sprang afresh to her eyes, yet she was also gladdened beyond description. Her mother still loved her! She loved her! Cecilia didn't know where her mother was taking her or why, but she now went willingly. Her mother still loved her!

They walked through Ravello, past the square, the café and the church. Old Mentore Parente watched them pass by from the doorway of his garage. His eyes took in the mother's weariness and the apprehension in the daughter, noting her age and the discomfort in her walk. For once he didn't call out a greeting. He knew better. He'd seen it all before.

They continued down the hill towards Menaggio until they came to the white-washed walls of the Villa Carosio, home of Count Vincenzo d'Alatri. Bougainvillea and jasmine spilled recklessly over the walls, but autumn had already deprived it of its splendour. They walked past the imposing iron gates and turned down the laneway that ran along the southern wall. Two-thirds of the way down, Maddalena stopped at a small gateway and rang the bell suspended above it. Then she settled down to wait for somebody to answer it.

Cecilia's mind raced. This is where her mother worked, where she scrubbed linen and kitchen and bathroom floors. What was her mother doing? What did she have in mind? She looked up at her mother, but she turned away and gazed through the grille in the gate to the garden beyond. They waited in silence for perhaps five minutes, but to Cecilia it seemed like an eternity.

'Maddalena! It is good to see you.'

The gate creaked open and Cecilia could see an old man framed in the doorway. He was smiling and wore clothes like her father wore. She'd foolishly expected the Count to open the gate, after all, it was his house. Cecilia had never seen anybody more important than the mayor of Menaggio and the prospect of meeting a real, live Count terrified her.

'Buon giorno, Roberto. I have brought my eldest daughter. Cecilia, say hello to Signor Bertani.'

'Buon giorno, Signor Bertani.'

The old man smiled at her but Cecilia had seen the look of concern that had crossed his face when he realised her mother was not alone.

'Roberto, I would like to speak to Signora Mila.'

'Of course. Come, come!'

The old man ushered them both through the gateway and led them down the pathway towards the rear of the villa. In the cold autumn air, the garden was far below its best, yet

Cecilia was awestruck. She'd never seen anything so beautiful in her life. Beyond the busyness of the gardens she could see a sweep of immaculately manicured lawn crossed by white pathways, some of which led to an ornate gazebo. There were fountains that played into pools alive with red and golden fish. And there were more statues than she could count. But why was her mother bringing her here?

Roberto led them in through the back door into the rear of the villa. He sat them down at a heavy wooden table that had known many uses. The top was not polished but worn smooth and had acquired its own glossy patina.

'I will find someone to fetch the Signora.'

'Thank you, Roberto.'

'Mama, who is the Signora?'

'Signora Mila is the Count's housekeeper. She runs the house for the Count. She makes sure the house is always spotlessly clean. She looks after the servants and supervises the day workers. People like me.'

Cecilia looked around the room and noticed the washing tubs and copper boiler. She began to recognise it from her mother's description. She knew without looking that there was a shelf at the opposite end of the table where soap and scrubbing brushes, starch and bleach were kept. But the room was so much bigger and the ceiling so much higher than she'd imagined. If this was just the laundry, what was the rest of the house like? She began to feel frightened. The room was cold but that wasn't why she shivered. She reached across and took her mother's hand. Her mother squeezed her hand gently and smiled encouragingly. Then she turned away.

'My mother says to tell you she'll be here shortly.'

Cecilia spun around to see a girl her own age standing in the doorway. She recognised her from church — not from the church in Ravello but from the Sanctuary of the Madonna of Peace in Menaggio which they attended on saints days. Cecilia had envied her for the clothes she wore and the assurance with which she carried herself. She'd often looked at her and wished she was as pretty.

'*Grazie*, Signorina Carmela . . . *grazie*.'

Cecilia was stung by the humility and deference in her mother's voice. She recognised it. The cleaners at school used that tone of voice when they spoke to the teachers. And even to the older students. The reality of her mother's status came home to her. Now she understood why her mother made her read books. Now she understood the shape of the prison from which her mother wanted her to escape. She fought back tears and stared hard at the table top in front of her. How much of its sheen did it owe to her mother?

'Ah . . . Maddalena.'

'*Buon giorno*, Signora Mila.'

Her mother stood, so Cecilia instantly did likewise. She would have stood up anyway, not just because it was polite to do so, but because the Signora was the most formidable woman Cecilia had ever seen. Even her headmaster would cower before this woman.

'Where have you been, Maddalena?'

'I must apologise, Signora . . . I have not been well.'

Even the Signora was aware of what it was that made Maddalena unwell. She knew all the gossip. Primo's excesses were scandalous.

'I am not unsympathetic, Maddalena, indeed I think you will agree that we have been most tolerant.'

'Yes, Senora, I am most grateful . . .'

'But you make a problem for us . . . you understand? While you are unwell, there is still washing that must be washed, there are still floors that must be scrubbed. Am I making myself clear?'

'Yes, Signora.'

'Personally, I am very sorry, but I am sure you understand.'

'Yes, Signora. I understand, and I appreciate that you have been very good to me. It is for this reason that I have asked to speak to you. I am not here for myself because to be honest, I am no longer up to doing the work. I have come to see you for the sake of my daughter here, Cecilia.'

Signora Mila turned to Cecilia as if noticing her for the first time. She peered at her as if she was a stray and unwelcome animal that had followed Maddalena in from the fields.

'*Buon giorno*, Signora Mila,' Cecilia said, then bowed her head and curtsied. Nobody was more surprised than Cecilia herself, but instinctively it seemed the right thing to do. The Signora smiled.

'A fine girl, well mannered. But I don't see why you have brought her to me.'

Maddalena hesitated, wondering how to phrase her request in a manner most likely to gain acceptance. 'She is a good worker. She can wash and iron, sew and darn. She can cook. She has a good voice, a voice of the city not of a peasant. And she can read. She can read like an angel. Signora ... please ... I was hoping you could find a place for her here, in your household, perhaps as a chambermaid.'

'I am sorry, that is out of the question.'

Cecilia didn't know whether to feel relieved or disappointed. But her mother had not yet given up. 'Please, Signora. She will not require wages, just food and lodgings. And she will reward you many times over, not just with the work she does but also with her reading. Look! I have brought this book. Let her read something to you.'

'I am sorry, Maddalena. I understand your situation but you must understand mine. If I take your daughter, I will have to let someone else's go. I'm sorry, there is nothing I can do. Besides, I have no interest at all in *The Count of Monte Cristo*.' She gestured towards the book in Maddalena's hand. 'One Count at a time is enough for me to worry about. I am sorry.'

'Signora.'

The resignation in her mother's voice said it all. Cecilia picked up her little bundle of belongings and followed her mother to the door.

'Come, I will walk you to the gate. Roberto is never around when I want him. Besides the fresh air will do me good. Perhaps that's what you need too, Maddalena. Fresh air and plenty of rest. Perhaps when you are feeling better we can find some work for you. Ah, here is Roberto hiding in the bushes. Roberto can take you the rest of the way ... oh, I beg your pardon, Count, forgive me, I didn't see you there.'

'Good morning, Signora. We have been discussing the pruning of my roses. Ah! Who do we have here? Who is this delightful child?'

Cecilia looked up and into the Count's eyes. He wasn't a bit like she expected him to be. He wore tweeds with a cravat and the most comical hat she had ever seen. The clothes were fine to be sure, but nowhere near as lavish as she'd seen the mayor of Menaggio wear, or indeed the bishop. Where was the gold and scarlet, where was the silk and brocade? He wasn't even tall. His face was lined and wrinkled, his eyes watery and his skin the colour of parchment. His only distinctive feature was his thin black moustache, which he'd waxed to a shine.

'She is the daughter of this woman, Maddalena Ortelli, a laundress . . .'

'Excellency . . .' interrupted Maddalena. The Count nodded courteously.

'Unfortunately,' continued the Signora, 'she is unable to continue with us for health reasons. I am just seeing her to the gate.'

'Excellency . . .' interrupted Maddalena once more. 'I was hoping the Signora could find a place for my daughter here in your household.' Maddalena knew she'd trespassed over the line of good manners, but she was desperate. Besides, here was a once in a lifetime opportunity and she couldn't allow it to pass by. God had given her this chance. 'She is, as you said yourself, Excellency, a delightful child. She works hard and can read like an angel.'

'Like an angel? I have never heard anyone read like an angel before.' The Count smiled, reached down and took Cecilia's hand in his. 'How old are you child?'

'Twelve, sir.' Cecilia surprised herself. Her voice betrayed none of the nervousness she felt.

'Twelve! Excellent. Come, let's find somewhere to sit where it is warm, and we can listen to you read. Come along. You too Signora Mila, and you Roberto.'

He led Cecilia around to the front of the villa, to the lawns she'd glimpsed as they'd entered. But that glimpse had barely hinted at the beauty of the place. Cecilia gazed in awe across the sweep of lawns which ended in a line as clean as any drawn, where the hillside fell away towards the lake. And there, in all its splendour, was Lake Como. Cecilia could see across to Ravenna on the far side and Bellagio on the tip of the peninsula, the crotch that separated the two southern legs of the lake.

'Here we are. Sit, sit!'

The seat he indicated was concrete, curved to fit the line of the garden behind it, and far more ornamental than comfortable. The adults sat and waited for Cecilia to take the book from her mother and read to them, with the magnificent view as her backdrop.

'*The Count of Monte Cristo*,' read Cecilia, her confidence returning now that she was doing something she knew she did well.

'Old family friend,' said the Count mischievously. 'Please continue.'

And Cecilia did. She knew the story well and did what her teachers had taught her to do, what all good readers of stories do; she looked up from the book and into the eyes of her audience as she read. And more and more she singled out those eyes which held sway over her immediate destiny. For his part, the Count never took his eyes off her.

If the Signora was discomfited by Maddalena imposing upon the Count, she forgot the transgression and allowed herself to be swept up in the story. Cecilia read on and on, the cadence of her voice hypnotic, the words magical, till at chapter's end she took the initiative and closed the book.

'To be continued,' she said, and smiled her sweetest smile. Her eyes never left the Count as she waited for him to respond. His lips trembled. But for the magnifying effect of his waxed moustache, the trembling may have passed unnoticed. Then he dragged his eyes away from her and turned to Signora Mila.

'Indeed. We cannot allow so great a tale to end prematurely, can we, Signora? I for one would be distraught. Attend to it.' He turned to Cecilia, rose and once more took her hand. 'It is true, my child, you do read like an angel. Thank you. I look forward to the next instalment. Roberto!'

Maddalena stood at once. She made no attempt to hide the tears that sprang from her eyes.

'Excellency . . . I don't know how to thank you.'

'Nor I you.' The Count took one more look at Cecilia, then strode off with Roberto.

Chapter Six

Cecilia didn't cry when her mother left her and disappeared through the little gateway in the side wall. She wanted to, but her mother seemed so happy and delighted at the way things had turned out that she forced back the tears and swallowed the lump in her throat. She wouldn't spoil things for her mother. God knows, there was little enough that brought her joy. Now she was alone with nothing but the clothes she stood in, her ragged little bundle and the final words of advice her mother had given her.

'Be a good girl, Cecilia,' her mother had said. 'Be nice to the Count and Signora Mila. Always be polite and do what you are told. Work hard. I will come and see you whenever I can. And Cecilia, don't stop reading, promise me you won't stop reading. When you escape from the prison it is a sin against God to come back to it.'

Cecilia slowly made her way back around to the rear of the house, past Roberto and the Count and the question of the roses. She climbed the few steps and stood in the kitchen doorway, not knowing whether to knock or enter. She knew she was on the threshold of a new life but had no comprehension whatever as to what the new life entailed. So she hesitated, unwilling to move forward but with nowhere to turn. In any event, she didn't have long to wait.

'Are you Cecilia? Come with me.'

Cecilia did as she was told. She followed the housemaid with the scowling face and unfriendly voice through the doorway on the opposite side of the kitchen, and down a long, panelled corridor. When they reached the end the housemaid opened a door and led Cecilia up a flight of narrow wooden stairs.

'They're putting you in my room,' said the housemaid. 'And if you touch any of my things, you little squirt, I'll make you wish you'd never come here.' She opened the third door and entered a tiny room with barely enough room for two thin beds, a dressing table and wardrobe. Between the two beds was a small shuttered window which looked back up the hill towards Ravello and the house which, until this morning, had been her home.

'You can have that bed,' said the housemaid, her hostility plainly evident. 'Sit on it, sleep on it, leave your things on it. It's your bed but it's still my room. I don't want to see you or your miserable bundle of rags anywhere but there. Understand? Understand! What's the matter, are you dumb or just stupid?'

But Cecilia was unable to answer, didn't dare in case her voice betrayed her. Through the window she'd just caught a glimpse of a familiar figure struggling up the hill where the road curved into the village. As she watched, the figure stopped and turned so it could look back down the hill towards the Villa Carosio. It was too much for Cecilia.

'Mama,' she said, the word half-choking on a sob. The tears so bravely held back now ran freely down her cheeks.

'My God! What have they given me?' The housemaid tried to sound angry but lacked conviction. She was barely seventeen herself and it wasn't so very long ago that she'd been in the same position. She glanced through the window and caught a glimpse of the distant figure just as it disappeared from sight. She put her arm around the distraught girl and pulled her down beside her on the forbidden bed. Cecilia had not been in the room for one minute and was already trespassing.

'Here, dry your eyes.' The housemaid handed Cecilia a delicate white handkerchief edged with lace. Cecilia hesitated, unwilling to spoil such a beautiful thing. 'Go ahead, I've got two more. They come with the uniform.'

Cecilia dried her eyes and blew her nose. She took deep breaths until she had her sobbing under control. All the while, the housemaid hugged her tightly.

'Never mind, little one, you'll like it here. The Signora tries to act tough but really she is a softie. I'm sorry I was awful to you. This is the first time I've ever had a room to myself, my own room. Now I have to share again. You wouldn't be very happy either if that happened to you.'

'I shared a room with four brothers and two sisters. I shared my bed with my two sisters. I've never had a bed of my own. I'm sorry you have to share your room, Signorina.'

The young housemaid smiled, relieved that Cecilia had stopped crying and begun talking. She pointed across the tiny room.

'There you are, your own bed. And enough of the Signorina. Call me Anna. I suppose I'll have to give you a drawer as well. You can have the bottom drawer and I'll make some room in the wardrobe for your uniform.'

'Uniform?'

'Everyone here wears a uniform. Now, I'm under instructions to run a bath for you. While you have a bath, I'll go downstairs and get some clothes for you to wear. Signora Mila is giving you some clothes that her daughter Carmela no longer wears. Come with me.'

Five minutes later, Cecilia found herself sitting waist deep in hot soapy water, having the first proper bath of her life. It was the most wonderful, luxurious thing that she'd ever experienced. She lay back and pointed her toes so that the hot water could cover her whole body except for her face, and tried to comprehend the nature of her new life. She would step from her bath and into Carmela's beautiful clothes. It didn't matter that they weren't new — indeed, the fact that they'd been Carmela's only made them more desirable. She'd never considered for a second that she'd ever wear anything remotely like them. If this was what her new life was going to be like, she vowed never to return to the old one. No matter what it took she would never return. She would take her mother's advice, obey her instructions to the letter and do whatever she had to do. She'd escaped. There was no way she was going back. When she was dressed Anna took her downstairs and presented her to Signora Mila. Cecilia curtsied as she'd done when first introduced.

'Save that for the Count,' said the Signora, allowing the

slightest smile. 'All I require from you is your respect and obedience.' She turned to the housemaid. 'That will be all, Anna.'

'Yes, Signora.'

'Now let me look at you, Cecilia. Carmela will be surprised to see how well her old clothes look on you.'

'Thank you, Signora, I . . .'

'We can't have you wandering around here in rags. I will arrange for the seamstress to make you up two uniforms which you will wear at all times when you are here. You will wear your other clothes — the ones I have given you — to school and to church in Menaggio. Now pay attention, this is what I want you to do. You will report to cook at six o'clock each morning in your uniform, having first washed, cleaned your teeth, and brushed your hair. At eight o'clock you will change into your school clothes and walk with Roberto to the school. Roberto will meet you at the school gate after school and you will come straight home. You will behave yourself at all times and under no circumstances talk to boys, even if they are your brothers. You must understand, you now live at the Villa Carosio, you are part of the Villa Carosio, and everything you do from this day onwards reflects on the Villa Carosio. After school you will go straight up to your room and change into your uniform. You may do your homework or read for half an hour. Then you will report to me for your afternoon duties. If I am unavailable, you will report to Signora Fiorella. Once everything is cleaned up after dinner, you will be free to go to your room. Do you understand?'

'Yes, Signora. I will do exactly as you say. You can count on me. And Signora, I would like to thank you . . .'

'Thank me? Thank your mother. And if any blame attaches later, blame her as well.'

Blame? Cecilia had landed in paradise. What on earth was there to blame anybody for? But the Signora's face had taken on a hard look which Cecilia couldn't read.

* * *

She spent the rest of the day in Anna's care, learning the proper way to make up beds, the proper way to fold linen, the proper way to dust, clean and polish. It embarrassed her to learn that all her young life she'd done things the wrong way. It seemed that the Villa Carosio had a way of doing everything differently to the way she'd been taught. She concentrated hard so she'd never have to be told a second time. When they sat down to lunch she met the cook, Signora Fiorella, the remaining two housemaids, Carla and Antonella, the butler Signor Calosci, the chauffeur Andre, the valet Stefano and a big, brusque man called Piero who was in charge of maintenance. They were her new family and, like all families, had a pecking order which she set about learning.

Signora Fiorella was a large, unsmiling woman who ruled her domain with a scowl and a voice cast in a foundry. There'd be no smiles for a job well done, just scorn for work that fell short of perfection, and the back of her hand for cheek. Carla and Antonella were both in their thirties and were as close as twins. They'd shared a room for as long as anyone could remember and resisted any move to vary the arrangement. The valet Stefano was the one who brought life to the gathering. He was twenty-two years old and baby faced, and slicked his hair down with oil to try to make himself look older. He was mischievous and irreverent, traits that would always inhibit his career. He flirted openly with Anna right through lunch and, when the cook objected, turned his charm and attentions upon her. It took all of Cecilia's self-control not to laugh.

She spent that first afternoon with Anna polishing the silverware. She learned to apply the fluid to each utensil then polish it off when it turned milky. How they shone when she polished them! Cecilia had never done any job as rewarding before, never handled anything as precious. She only looked up once and was surprised to see the Count staring at her from the doorway. Their eyes met. She smiled and he nodded back as he withdrew. She glanced over to Anna to see if she had noticed anything.

'What are you smiling at?'

'Nothing. I just felt like smiling.'

'You just felt like smiling. And this morning I suppose you just felt like crying. You're going to drive us all mad.'

'No I won't Anna. I'm not going to cry any more.'

'Never?'

'Never ever.'

Anna looked at the girl six years her junior and for the first time sensed the strength and calm within her.

'You're strange,' she said, and returned to her polishing.

Anna was even more perplexed when, later that night as they cleaned up after the staff meal, the Count sent Signora Mila to fetch Cecilia.

'Count d'Alatri wishes you to read to him while he has his dinner.'

Cecilia was delighted, not simply because she preferred reading to scrubbing dishes and benches, but because she knew her reading made her special. Yet when she looked up at Signora Mila she found her anything but encouraging. Her lips curled as if they found the words distasteful.

'I suppose it was to be expected, given the circumstance of your hiring. Come!'

'Should I run upstairs and get my book?'

'Cecilia there are two things you should learn straight away. Staff never run. At the Villa Carosio no one ever runs. Running is undignified. We walk with purpose, that is sufficient.' Signora Mila paused to ensure that Cecilia had absorbed the lesson and the rest of the staff the reminder. 'Secondly, if the Count wishes you to read to him, doubtless he will also tell you what it is he wishes you to read. Do not presume to make that judgement for him. Now come along.'

Cecilia followed Signora Mila through the house to a part she had not yet seen. Her confidence gave way to apprehension as she moved further and further into the Count's realm, and chandeliers took over from the oil lamps and weak overhead bulbs of the servants' quarters. Everywhere she looked, the Count's family and ancestors seemed to be watching her progress from within their ancient frames. Even so, nothing prepared her for the awesome magnificence of the dining room. The sheer scale of it was daunting. It seemed to her that the entire population of Ravello could sit around the table and still leave room for guests. The centrepiece of the room was a massive crystal chandelier, flanked by two similar but smaller chandeliers. Her head spun. If someone had told her that all the stars in creation had been captured and put at the Count's disposal she would have shown no surprise. The Count! Her mind leapt back to her reason for being there. Where was he? Then she saw him, a solitary figure sitting at the far end of the table, alone but for Signor Calosci by the *credenza*, standing straight-backed and as motionless as one of the garden statues.

'Ah . . . there you are! Bring her up here would you please, Signora Mila. Sit her down here so we don't strain her precious voice.' The Count pointed to the chair nearest him, which was the first of the chairs arrayed along the far side of the table. He put down his knife and fork and delicately wiped his mouth with his napkin. He watched as Cecilia sat down.

The chair was enormous, like everything else in the room. She had to go up on her tip-toes to climb up onto it, and when she finally sat upon it her feet could no longer touch the floor, even though she barely perched on the edge.

'*Bene!* Signora Mila, perhaps you would care to wait while we determine which book we will read from tonight.' The Count turned to Cecilia. 'Tell me, child, apart from *The Count of Monte Cristo* which I must confess I have already read many times, what do you suggest we read?'

Cecilia had no idea what to suggest now that he'd excluded *The Count of Monte Cristo* and, most likely, every other book like it. 'Excellency, I have no preference. I am happy to read any book. Mostly my family liked me to read adventure stories, but when my father became interested in Il Duce, most nights I read stories about him from the newspapers.'

'Ah . . . you are an admirer of the great man!' The Count's eyes had lit up in genuine interest and delight. 'Signora Mila, please bring us the Milan newspapers. We can share our mutual interest.'

'Excellency.'

It probably never occurred to the Count how he had belittled Signora Mila by sending her to fetch newspapers for the child to read, but the slight was not lost on Signora Mila, or Cecilia for that matter. She looked up apologetically but the Signora had already turned away.

'Tell me,' said the Count eagerly, 'what do you know about Benito Mussolini?'

'He is the one man who can make Italy rich and powerful again,' she said, launching herself into her father's favourite theme. The Count listened rapturously, as she recounted how Mussolini had pushed through the law creating two First Marshals of the Empire, effectively placing himself on the same level as King Vittorio Emanuele. As she spoke, Signora Mila returned with the newspapers and set them down quietly on the table beside her.

'Thank you, Signora,' said Cecilia, desperate not to offend her any further. But the Signora gave her a look which could have melted steel. Too late Cecilia realised her mistake. The Signora had not brought the newspapers for her but for the Count. It was not her place to give thanks. The Signora was not her servant. Cecilia watched dismayed as the Signora bobbed her head to the Count and left the room.

'Now, Cecilia, read to me. We are very fortunate, see? The front pages are full of Il Duce's welcome to Herr Hitler in Rome. I was invited to attend, you know, by Il Duce himself. Unfortunately my health ... even a Count must sometimes obey his doctor.'

Cecilia was agog. The Count knew Mussolini? Mussolini knew the Count? If that wasn't enough to contend with, she'd also just discovered that her benefactor was unwell. She was about to inquire as to the cause of his ill-health, when she hesitated. What would be normal good manners wasn't necessarily the case in this house. Would her inquiry be interpreted as thoughtfulness or impertinence? She knew the answer as soon as the question formed in her head. She was learning.

'*Viva Il Führer!*' she began, reading the headline emblazoned across the front page of *Il Popolo d'Italia*. She couldn't help but fill with pride when she read how the Führer had arrived at the Ostiense railway station, newly refurbished for the occasion, and begun a procession to the Palazzo del Quirinale alongside the King. Their six-horse state carriage was flanked by mounted escorts in gleaming cuirasses and horsetail-plumed helmets. Mussolini had followed immediately behind in a black Lancia, first in a motorcade containing fascist dignitaries and Hitler's five-hundred-strong retinue. Red lights beaming on magnesium flares created the illusion that the Colosseum was burning in a spectacle that Rome hadn't witnessed since Nero's excesses, and all along the five-kilometre route, newly installed lights played upon the dancing waters of Bernini's fountains. The paper also reported that Goebbels had called the young officers lining the route 'a perfect spectacle'. And that Hitler had called Il Duce 'the last Roman'.

As she read this, Cecilia glanced up at the Count as she had been trained to do. He sat head back and eyes closed, an ecstatic smile on his face, just as her father would have had he been listening instead. She read on, over page after page, as various reporters recorded the same event with varying degrees of hysteria.

'Enough,' said the Count finally. 'They are beginning to diminish this historic event with their rantings. I would have been in the procession. I would have been there to share the glory. This day will live long in the memory of every patriotic Italian. I wonder now if that weakling in the Quirinale has finally got the message.' He reached over and put his hand on Cecilia's thigh and held it there, his watery eyes gazing into hers. 'Thank you, my child, with the voice of an angel. You read beautifully. You made me feel as though I were there after all. Because of you, I have missed nothing! Thank you once more.' He squeezed her thigh, patted it for a moment, then withdrew his hand. 'Run along now.'

'The Signora said we mustn't run,' said Cecilia as she climbed down from her chair. 'It is sufficient to walk with purpose.'

The Count erupted with laughter. His thin shoulders shook and his eyes watered even more. His laughter followed Cecilia to the door where she paused to curtsy before leaving. Even the statue-like Signor Calosci was smiling.

What was Mussolini's triumph compared to hers?

* * *

Lucio finished speaking and pushed his chair back to indicate that the day's storytelling had concluded. He reached for his glass of grappa but he'd drained it long ago. He glanced over to where he expected Gancio to be, behind his bar waiting for the signal to serve coffee. But of course Gancio was sitting next to him. 'We have a problem.'

'No we don't. Maria!' Gancio waved towards the kitchen.

'*Subito!*' Maria, the longest serving of Gancio's waitresses appeared and attacked the espresso machine.

'Well,' said Ramon. 'Your comments please, Gancio. Now do you appreciate why our Thursdays are so precious to us?'

'Of course. Well done, Lucio, your storytelling does you credit. I must admit I had no idea you were such a good storyteller. I have listened in over the years so the experience is not new to me. But stories like this I expect from Ramon and Milos, not from you. You tell your story well.'

'Hear, hear.'

'See? We all agree. But I don't understand why you chose this subject. Why rake over the past like this? Why resurrect it? Why can't you just entertain like you always do? Leave these sorts of stories to the others.'

'What's your problem? Because it is Italian? You happily listen in to Ramon when he talks of the bad times in Argentina, and Milos when he takes us back to wartime Hungary. Why should Italy be quarantined? They share their history, why shouldn't we share ours?'

'I think some things are best left alone.'

'What specifically?' Ramon's voice was gentle and persuasive. 'What is the part of Lucio's story that you feel should be left alone?'

Gancio was uncomfortably aware that he was the centre of keen attention. 'It is not the fact that the story is based in Italy.' He hesitated.

'Go on.'

'It's just that some things are better left alone.' He looked around the table helplessly. 'This story touches on the subject of war criminals. I can't see that any good is served by hunting them down and dragging them before courts. It all happened so long ago. It was a moment in history unlike any other and it will never be repeated. Times were very different. People were different. You can't judge what happened then by today's standards. People did things because they had no choice.'

'People always have choice, Gancio.'

'No, Ramon! That is where you are wrong. What do you or I know about the Oberstleutnant?' Gancio's voice had risen and become strident. 'What do you know of the pressures that were on him? The times that Lucio's talking about when those eight unfortunate women were shot, they were desperate times. The Wehrmacht no longer had any heart for the fighting. They knew they were beaten. They just wanted the war to end so that they could go home. But they couldn't go home. The SS were standing behind them with guns at their heads. Fight or be shot. Obey orders or be shot. Obey orders! Is a man a war criminal because he followed orders? Do you think in this situation a soldier has any choice? No one can approve of what the Oberstleutnant did. But to be fair, everybody knew about reprisals. Notices were posted everywhere. The Oberstleutnant acted in response to partisan activities. He had no choice.'

'That's very interesting,' said Neil. 'I'm not aware of Lucio telling us what the Oberstleutnant acted in response to.'

The spotlight fell on Gancio once more, exactly as it had when he'd choked on the grappa. 'It is a reasonable assumption.' Gancio looked to Lucio for support, but got no response. 'Reprisals took place because of partisan activities or assassinations. Or because people made the mistake of being Jewish. The women who were shot were not Jewish because they were coming from the church. Lucio told us that. They went there for comfort. So if they were not Jewish, the shootings were in reprisal. What else could they be?'

'What indeed?' Milos turned to Lucio. 'But that doesn't explain why he only shot women and spared the old man — what was his name? Mentore Parente? I think our friend here has plenty of surprises in store. Already he has opened up endless possibilities and I, from my point of view, am absolutely delighted that he has chosen this subject, and demonstrated a skill in the telling we never knew he had.'

'I agree with Milos.' Ramon was thoughtful for a moment. 'However, Gancio also has a point. Let me remind you of the Polyukhovich case. He was the Adelaide pensioner at the centre of the war crimes trial in Adelaide. He was charged with being involved in the deaths of eight hundred and fifty Jews — the Jews of Serniki — in 1942. Before the investigation he was a model citizen. He lived quietly, tended his garden and even kept bees. Then forty-eight years after the massacre of the Serniki Jews, he is made to face trial. He tries to commit suicide. He suffers two suspected heart attacks and severe hypertension. The strain on his family as his name and picture appear in newspapers all over Australia and abroad for three years is horrendous. And the prosecution spends millions of dollars bringing the case to court. For what? He was acquitted by the jury after one hour's deliberation because of the difficulty in securing confirmation of his crimes. Whether or not he perpetrated the atrocity is irrelevant. He could be entirely innocent, an officer acting under orders, or a monster. We will never know. But our system demands he be given the benefit of the doubt. So he must be presumed innocent. And if he is innocent, why should any innocent man be made to suffer this way? So, taking Gancio's point, what useful purpose did the investigation and trial serve? Are these matters best left alone, after all?'

'No way, José,' Neil cut in. 'There's far too much rhetoric here. The fact is, the prosecution must have been pretty sure they had their man or they wouldn't have brought the case to trial. If Polyukhovich is innocent then he's had the opportunity to clear his name. From my point of view, a war criminal is a war criminal. Time excuses nothing. I reckon they should all be hounded to their graves. The only thing I bleat about is the cost. I have a lot of sympathy for Colombina.'

'Do you want me to stop telling this story?' asked Lucio quietly.

'You can't,' Neil cut in quickly. 'We have broken many conventions but we will not break that one. Once you start a story you have to finish it. Milos, what do you think?'

'Lucio should continue. I've made my point of view quite clear. I think this is a story with fantastic potential. Ramon?'

'I agree. Of course he should finish. Gancio raised a point and since he is our newest member, I felt we should accord him the courtesy of having it discussed. Besides, this story has me intrigued. I don't think this is the last moral issue we will have to face either. Does Colombina have the right to by-pass the courts and take justice into her own hands? And what is our role? Lucio made it clear at the start that he would appreciate our comments. Should Lucio continue? Absolutely. Gancio?'

'I have two choices. Listen or stop listening. I can't stop

Lucio telling his story. That is not my place. But you may regret your decision today. Lucio says this story is true. Let me leave you in no doubt. Every word of it is true. Every word. Think about that while you sip your coffee and your grappa. I know your story, Lucio. It's not too late if you wish to change your mind.'

Maria began placing the coffees and grappas on the table before each of the men. But she could have been invisible. Ramon, Neil and Milos waited for Lucio's reaction.

'How . . . how do you know so much about my story?'

'When the time comes, I will tell you. Do you still wish to go on?'

'Yes.'

'Then God help us all, because I know who you are, Lucio. I know who you are.'

SECOND THURSDAY

The week's break had unsettled Lucio. It had given him time to think and he realised how far in over his head he was. The others made their storytelling seem so easy but now he knew the reverse to be true. He doubted his ability to manage the complexity without revealing too much too soon and giving himself away. Besides that, there was the question of timing. If it came to the crunch, he could always stretch his story a bit or, if the worst came to the worst, give it away. But if he could time everything right, if everything went his way, then he'd upstage them all and even give Ramon a mighty dose of his own medicine.

But first he had mountains to climb, higher mountains than he'd ever entertained climbing before. And he knew they'd watch his every step and subject every stumble to thorough inspection. Could he cope with that sort of scrutiny? And what about Gancio? The man was a loose cannon. As if he didn't have a tough enough audience to begin with, he had to contend with Gancio. The big man had stunned everyone with his outburst, none more so than the storyteller. He'd been tempted to take him aside and sort a few things out, but it was all too late. Damn him! Already he was on the defensive and that was no place to be after just one episode. He needed to shake up his audience and get them off balance. Then keep them off balance. But how on earth could he do that?

His thoughts were interrupted by the sound of Milos' chair sliding back. He looked up. Yes, Ramon had arrived and Milos had stood, as always, to greet him. Neil watched Milos stand, caught Lucio's eye and shook his head in wonderment, as if standing to greet a friend was the most foolish thing he'd ever seen anyone do.

'Ramon, I swear I don't know how you do it.' Milos took an exaggerated look at his watch as if synchronising it. 'Twelve thirty exactly.'

'If you'd set your watch by him last week it would be about six minutes slow this week. Big deal.' Neil shrugged. 'Anyway, you know he just sits outside in his cab and gets the cabbie to kick him out when it's twelve twenty-nine and thirty seconds. Isn't that right, Ramon? It's his little game and typically, he has to cheat.'

Ramon smiled. Punctuality to him was a matter of arriving precisely at the appointed time, being neither early nor late. It was a conceit, of course, like the gold Rolex he wore on his wrist. He claimed he had his own internal clock and he did, thanks to the hours of concentration and training in the first weeks of his blindness. It was only when he awoke from sleep that he was ever unsure of the time.

'Gancio has asked a favour,' he said, ignoring Neil. 'He asked if he could join us as soon as we have finished eating. Lucio, would you mind waiting until then?'

'Of course not.'

'Very obliging of you, Lucio,' cut in Neil. 'You two, you and Gancio, make a great little team. A nice little storytelling mafia.'

'What's this?' Milos' ears pricked up and he turned to Lucio for enlightenment. When Lucio failed to respond he turned back to Neil. 'Do you know something we don't, or are you just being as snide and cynical as usual?'

'Don't tell me you fell for that little double act last week. I expect more from you, Milos. I reckon Lucio here has done more cooking than Gancio. The whole thing's a set-up. It's a stew. He's doing a Ramon. Can you think of a better way to have us believe his story than contrive an endorsement from a second party?'

'Interesting.' Ramon leaned back into his chair thoughtfully. 'Is he doing a Ramon, as you put it? I have thought of involving Gancio in a similar way in the past, but my judgement was that you wouldn't wear it. Coming from me, it would be an obvious contrivance. But from Lucio, perhaps a stroke of genius. Interesting thought, Neil. Perhaps if I had your cynicism it might have occurred to me, too. What do you think, Milos?'

'Gancio was very convincing, no? He is a great chef, but is he also a great actor?'

'All Italians are actors,' growled Neil. 'Haven't you ever watched them play football?'

'Ah ... point taken. But if you've been watching Lucio here, you would have noticed that Gancio surprised him as much as anyone.'

'Jesus, Milos! Lucio acted as surprised as anyone. He *acted* as surprised, okay?'

'If that's the case, he was a very surprised actor,' said Milos patiently. 'I got the distinct impression that Lucio would have been delighted if Gancio had gone away and fallen on one of his kitchen knives, no?'

'Perhaps.' Lucio smiled. He could not believe his luck. He blessed the gods for giving him Neil. If the others had suspected complicity they would have kept their suspicions to themselves, silently gathering evidence for and against to use later or discard. But Neil couldn't keep a cold to himself, and had provided the ingredient he'd been looking for. Neil had introduced a wonderful new element. What more could a storyteller ask for? His confidence grew. 'Ahhh ... Gancio, what have you done?' He looked up delightedly as Gancio placed a large plate containing one of his favourite foods upon the table.

'*Misoltitt* ... a dish inspired by your story.' Gancio's pride was obvious as he gazed down at the platter of small fish. 'From Lecco. I found them in Paddy's Market. They are not perfect because they were tinned. But I have dried them and marinated them in my own special way.'

'Magnificent!'

'Thank you, Lucio. Help yourselves while I fillet some for Ramon.'

'You want to fillet some for me while you're at it?'

'Of course. Would you also like me to bring you a bib, Neil?'

'Maybe I'll skip the funny fish and double up on whatever's next. What is next?'

'Another dish inspired by Lucio's story. I don't know why I haven't made it before. It's today's special and everyone is ordering it. *Risotto Gorgonzola*.'

'Jesus help me! And you guys still don't think these two wogs are in league with each other?'

'What's that?'

'Neil thinks you and I are conspiring together.'

Gancio turned and looked at Neil pityingly. 'Sometimes I think you are too stupid to live. Here are your little fish, nicely filleted. I've hidden a bone in one of them. Choke on it.'

Neil gave in gracelessly, and picked at the little fish with his fork.

'Has Ramon spoken to you, Lucio? Will you wait until I can join you?'

'Today, Gancio my friend, you can have anything you want.'

Chapter Seven

Dresden, the capital of Saxony, was first settled in the twelfth century by Sorbs, a Slavic people whose origins lay further east. Nobody knows why they chose to cross the River Elbe and build their village there but, whatever their reasons, they chose their site well. It was both beautiful and practical. The hills on both sides of the valley were heavily timbered and followed the curve of the Elbe. The local stone was easily quarried and suitable for construction, so there was no short-age of building materials. It was also a natural crossing point of the river and sat squarely on the trade route between Meissen and the silver mines of Freiberg. Showing none of the creativity or imagination which would later mark their village as one of the world's great cultural centres, they named it Drezdany, the place of the wooded valley dwellers.

Over the centuries, the Sorbs became Germanised along with their village, which developed into a bustling medieval town straddling both sides of the river, and then into the most beautiful city in Germany. Credit for this transformation goes to Augustus the Strong, elector of Saxony in the early eighteenth century, who allowed nothing as trivial as finance or reasonable constraint to come between him and his baroque fantasies. Unfortunately, the King of Prussia saw fit to sack Dresden some thirty years after Augustus the Strong died, but enough of his baroque wonders remained to give visitors a glimpse of how remarkable the city had been. Indeed, even up until the Second World War, Dresdeners still maintained their city was the fairest in all of Germany.

Through the eighteenth and nineteenth centuries, Dresden became a focal point for the arts. It was home to many great artists including the Venetian painter Canaletto, and boasted one of the world's finest art collections. Richard Wagner composed his operas *Tannhäuser* and *Lohengrin* there, and composer and innovator Carl Maria von Weber gave conductors their treasured baton. However, Dresden in 1937 had fallen well behind Berlin as an arts and entertainment centre, and young Saxons looking for a good time would put aside their inborn distrust of Prussians and head for the German capital with its cabarets and American jazz. Yet Dresden was hardly devoid of life, music or theatre and, all things considered, was an attractive place to live, provided you weren't foolish enough to have a social conscience or be Jewish, Slavic, Russian, communist, gypsy, retarded or insane.

*　*　*

Christiane Frederika Schiller numbered among the more privileged Dresdeners. She was living proof of the old rhyme: '*Sachsen, wo die schönen Mädchen wachsen!*' — Saxony, where the pretty girls come from. Typically, she had long blonde hair which tumbled recklessly in a mass of vigorous curls and twists. Her skin glowed with health and vitality, not so much pale as fair, a subtle backdrop which accentuated the glow of her cheeks, the blaze of her lips, the cobalt in her eyes and the glimpses of dark brown root deep in the forest of her hair. Yes, she was a beauty, though by no means exceptional among the many beauties of Saxony.

She was fortunate, however, to be the daughter of a director of the Dresdner Bank, good fortune she shared with two younger sisters and a younger brother. Her family was well-off rather than wealthy, and their pride was their two homes. The first was eighteenth century and six storeys tall with an elaborate façade. It was in the very heart of Dresden on Prager Strasse, near the junction with Ring Strasse where the fashionable shops were, about half-way between the Altmarkt, the old Dresden market, and Dresden Main Station. The second was a country residence fourteen kilometres south-east of Dresden, set in grassed and timbered land two kilometres east of the River Elbe. It claimed the royal summer residence of Pillnitz, one of Augustus the Strong's legacies, as a near neighbour. Christiane adored Pillnitz. Even as a young child, she'd found its elegant symmetry, its pagoda roofs, Chinese lantern chimneys and tranquil gardens an irresistible attraction. She loved to picnic nearby and dream of being a princess at court, trying to place herself among the pomp and splendour of earlier times.

But as much as Christiane loved her country home, she preferred the grand old house on Prager Strasse. Her interests were those of any twenty year old in any Western city. She loved music both old and new. For Christiane, nothing could possibly compare with the opening night at the opera, especially if Elisabeth Schwarzkopf was performing. But by the same token she loved dancing, and there was no better music for dancing in the whole world than American big band music, even though it was not always successfully adopted by the local musicians. There was enough provocative theatre to keep the young entertained and stimulated, though the quality of it had fallen along with the involvement of the Jewish citizens who had been its life blood. They'd been the mainstay of German experimental theatre, providing the actors, directors and producers. She also loved the volunteer work she did three days a week at the Semper Picture Gallery, where she helped clean frames, catalogue and occasionally act as guide. But her preference for her home in Prager Strasse was very much the result of her age. All twenty year olds are hosts to biological imperatives and Christiane was no exception. Dancing has always provided an opportunity for flirting and, until recently, she had competed as keenly as any of her friends for the attentions of the most handsome and entertaining young men.

It is hard to think of Christiane as being anything other than a very fortunate young woman with a life as perfect as any could wish. She was beautiful, cultured, well educated and intelligent. But she was also immature and naïve. The young princess at the court of Augustus the Strong was alive within her, and she still harboured old-fashioned notions of chivalry and gallantry, of simpler times when good and evil were sharply defined. She hadn't yet grown up and, for this, her father could claim responsibility.

Few people are as steeped in establishment conservatism

as bankers, and Carl Schiller was one of those men who take their lead from their superiors. He negotiated a path through life, protecting himself and his family from its pitfalls and excesses. In a sense, he created his own little world, which was as unreal as any of Christiane's imaginings. The great depression had cast no pall over their house. The closest the family had come to the misery and hardship endured by millions of their fellow Germans was through charity works. Prior to Hitler's accession, Carl had also shielded them from the collapse of the German *mark* by transferring funds to other countries and investing there. When that became politically unwise, he invested in the burgeoning armament industry, seeing only the potential profits and nothing of what the new armaments might portend. He was slavishly obedient to authority and it would never have occurred to him to be otherwise. When Hitler and the Nazis came to power in 1933 he embraced them as his new masters and applied himself to helping build a better Germany as defined by the National Socialists. Now five years later he held few qualms. He firmly believed that what was good for Germany was good for the world as a whole. And he believed Hitler was good for Germany. Hitler had certainly been good for the Dresdner Bank.

Carl Schiller managed his family's social life with the same measured, narrow-sighted conservatism. He chose the schools and universities his children would attend. He even found Christiane's job at the Semper Picture Gallery for her. He shaped the family's taste in music and art. He created a world where loyalty, good manners, endeavour and a clear code of ethics could achieve anything they wanted. He gave them an honest and honourable set of values few could quibble with. Unfortunately, he gave them no real understanding of life.

The man Christiane fell head over heels in love with was a clear manifestation of this. Dietrich Schmidt could never be described as entertaining, at least not in the circles in which Christiane moved. He was not even a good dancer. Wooden Pinocchio moved with greater fluidity. But, by God, Dietrich Schmidt was handsome! In the uniform of an SS-Untersturmführer he was Hitler's vision of the master race personified. If it were at all possible, doubtless the Führer would have delighted to use him as a pastry cutter to punch out an army of others just like him. Christiane was completely infatuated, and when her arm was linked with his, she just knew she was the envy of all the other girls. It didn't matter that when he spoke, his *sächsisch* belied his good looks. While Goethe maintained that the Saxon dialect was the clearest in Germany, most Germans find it too flat and broad. They complain that Saxons don't open their mouths enough and that the words just spill out carelessly. Because of this, they like to lampoon Saxons and portray them as fat, lazy, incomparably stupid buffoons. The flat, working class Saxon accent they give these *dummkopfs* in their clubs and cabarets was, unfortunately for Christiane, uncomfortably close to the way Dietrich spoke.

But in the blinding optimism of young love, Christiane found it easy to overlook his accent, and just as easy to convince herself that she could teach him to speak properly. With the confidence and assurance she'd inherited from her father, she began a process of re-education as methodical as any set down by her school teachers. She took him to the opera and introduced him to Wagner, to recitals and introduced him to Beethoven, and to the theatre. In the theatre at least, Dietrich found something he could understand and identify with. By 1937 the avant-garde expressionist theatre which had once shocked, challenged and thrilled Dresdeners had long gone, replaced by more ideologically correct fare, not too far removed from the propaganda which had been Dietrich's cultural bread and butter.

Standing together in the foyer or taking their seats the moment before the lights dimmed, the handsome Dietrich and beautiful Christiane were a combination none could ignore. Christiane soaked up the admiring and envious looks like bread soaks up gravy. She could scarcely believe her good fortune. Often in the darkness her eyes would blur when she stole a sideways glance at the handsome profile alongside her. If this was love, then she was very much in love.

But love was destined to take second place to the problem of the Jews. As usual, Christiane's father chose to shelter the family from the harsher realities of life. When he received word that the Brownshirts were to take to the streets in yet another spontaneous demonstration against the Jews, he promptly whisked the family off to their country house.

Christiane was irate. It meant she would miss many engagements, foremost of which was a rare and prized Saturday night engagement with Dietrich Schmidt. He was ambitious and committed to the service of the SS. If she had ever had to ask him to choose between herself and his career, she knew she'd come second. She had to organise her life around him and his hours of duty. It wasn't often that he was free on a Saturday night and now she was obliged to cancel.

It would be nice to think that someone as kind, thoughtful and as involved in the arts as Christiane would feel sympathy or a sense of injustice at the way Jews were being treated. But she hardly gave them a thought. Hitler's racial policies had not reached her in her isolated little world. She was not unaware of the hatred some Germans felt for Jews, after all there was a limit to what her father could shield her from. But she was at a loss to know what the Jewish problem had to do with her. She'd had little contact with Jews. They had not attended her exclusive school and were forbidden from entering university. Undoubtedly she encountered Jews in the shops around Ring Strasse but the issue then was the purchase, not race or culture. She didn't care who served her, Jew or Gentile. To Christiane the Jewish issue was one of inconvenience, like on her sixteenth birthday when her parents had taken her to see *Rigoletto* at the Opera House. Halfway through the performance, security police had walked out on stage and arrested the Jewish conductor, Fritz Busch. At that moment, though only briefly, she was on the side of the Jews. Couldn't the police have waited until the performance was over?

Her father, who in every other way was a reasonable man, spoke disparagingly of the Jews on the few occasions the subject was raised. So Christiane, without evidence to the contrary, saw no reason to take issue with the prevailing sentiments which blamed the great depression, communism and all the accompanying ills of the world on Jewish greed and conspiracy. She fully subscribed to the Nazi-inspired portrait of the fat, cigar smoking Jew with the jewelled tie-pin, and pockets bulging with money made from the sweat of honest, hard-working Germans, even though she'd never ever seen one. This is what she'd been taught as a child and in the League of German Girls, where they were instructed in comradeship, domestic duties, motherhood and who to hate.

Despite Christiane's tearfilled protestations, they moved down to Little Pillnitz, as they jokingly referred to their country house, on the Friday afternoon. She moped about the house wondering what she would do to fill in the hours until the mobs had returned the streets to their inhabitants, and her father deemed it safe enough to return to Prager Strasse. Bed, it seemed, was the only alternative to boredom. Damn the Jews!

She woke up irritable on the Saturday morning and not even breakfast in bed could improve her mood. Her mother, Clara, tried to talk her around but soon gave up. Though she failed to see what Christiane saw in the young Untersturm-führer beyond the obvious, she knew what her daughter was going through.

'It's just part of the game,' she'd argued. 'The game of being in love. You're still too young to get serious with any young man. You're a beautiful girl. You can have any man you want. Why tie yourself down?' But Christiane had simply responded by pulling her bed covers over her head. Clara was a calm and patient woman but she was also smart enough to know when patience would not be rewarded. She left her daughter to sulk.

When Christiane finally came downstairs she went straight to the piano, and tried to lose herself in bitter-sweet melodies. But her sisters were making so much noise disputing the ownership of a pair of her shoes she'd given them that she couldn't concentrate. She decided to tie some flies. If there was one thing that could distract her and block out everything else on her mind, it was tying flies.

Being the first born, Christiane knew she was supposed to have been a boy, a situation exacerbated by the succession of sisters that followed. So she stood in as substitute while her father awaited the arrival of a son, and during that time shared his hobbies and pursuits. Only one of his passions endured in the young girl: she adored fishing. By the time she was eight, she could tie flies better than her father and cast almost as well. She learned how to play the trout that inhabited the nearby streams and the salmon that ran in the Elbe so skilfully that, when they were finally netted, it was all they could do to excrete one final time.

What Christiane found particularly satisfying was the deceit of fishing. It was not easy to replicate nature so precisely that fish could be deceived. Fly-tying was an exacting art which required a dedicated hand. As a child she'd spent hours watching her father tie a single fly, patiently removing the herls from a feather quill, and trimming and shaping it so exactly that she could recognise the insect upon which it was modelled long before the fly was completed. The whole process fascinated her, and it wasn't long before the apprentice was as skilled as her teacher. The precise nature of the art absorbed her to the point where she became oblivious to everything else. She was the last person in the household to hear the sound of tyres scrunching on wet gravel.

She heard her sisters rush to the door, grateful for the diversion. Christiane would have joined them but for the fact that her fly-tying was at its most delicate stage. Nevertheless, as she bound the strands of fox hair to the shaft of the tiny hook, she couldn't help but listen for the voices which would identify their visitor. She knew it wouldn't be Dietrich because he was still on duty until evening. Besides, although she had formally introduced him to her mother and father, her father had given no indication that he would be welcome at Little Pillnitz. The country house was her father's sanctuary and he was very particular about who was invited to visit there. Yet for some reason she felt a tremor of excitement which went beyond the relief from boredom. Who could it be, she wondered? Who else could be mad enough to drive down on this bleak December day, through the mud and slush and suspicion of ice?

'Uncle Gottfried!' The shouts of delight from her sisters, Lisl and Jutta, brought a smile to her face. He was her favourite uncle and she sincerely believed that she was also his favourite niece. She heard his deep, resonant voice as he greeted her sisters and her brother, then the voices faded as they moved from the hallway. She decided she'd present him with a gift of the flies she had just tied. He was also a keen angler, though he maintained that Christiane's flies were far too exquisite to waste on fish.

Though she loved her father dearly, there were times when she'd wished Uncle Gottfried was her father instead. Where caution and prudence marked every move her father made, her uncle was both fearless and passionate. She remembered how he'd plunged fully clothed into a freezing stream to grab a trout that had thrown the hook just as it was about to be netted. He'd missed the trout and broken his rod, but rather than get upset about it, he'd sat waist-deep in the icy waters and laughed his head off. Everything he did was larger than life. He rode his horse faster than anyone else and never backed off no matter how high the hedge or wide the stream. His confidence and energy, like his courage, were boundless, qualities that had helped him rise through the ranks of the Reichswehr to Generalleutnant.

She hunted around and found a small box which had once housed one of her brother's toy cars. She covered the bottom in cottonwool, making a bed which both protected the flies and showed them off in all their glory. Then she did what any beautiful twenty year old would do: she tidied her hair and clothes, and rubbed her cheeks to bring back the colour the cold and her inactivity had drained away. Now she was ready.

As she closed the door to her room, she heard the gramophone burst into song in the lounge room. Uncle Gottfried had obviously brought them some new jazz records from Berlin, and her sisters and brother had wasted no time giving them an airing. That meant her father and uncle would be in the study, for her father detested modern music. He thought it was decadent and worse, black man's music. The door to the study was slightly ajar. She was about to knock discreetly before entering when she heard a voice she didn't recognise. She hesitated. She peered through the tiny gap and saw a young officer sitting in the chair next to her uncle's. She was immediately struck by his manner. He seemed to show no deference to either her uncle or her father, nor any respect for her father's prized Scotch whisky. Uncertain whether or not to interrupt, she chose to wait and pick her moment. In the meantime, she was happy to eavesdrop.

'So you witnessed the bombing of Guernica,' she heard her father say. 'How was it really? You are the first person I have met who was there. The foreign press have been very critical of the bombing of civilians, as you are no doubt aware. What do you say? Was it a great victory for our Condor Legion or an atrocity? You may speak bluntly, Captain.'

'Don't worry, Carl, the Captain always does.' Gottfried gave Christiane's father a wry smile.

'All war is an atrocity, Herr Schiller,' the young Captain replied. 'Before you draw any conclusions, however, for I know that may sound like a strange observation for a soldier, it is my father's wisdom not mine. I know you once met my father, but are you aware he won the Iron Cross with Oak Leaves on the Western Front? In fact, he won so many medals the weight of them on his uniform made it impossible for him to stand upright. He credits this fact for his survival, as the British bullets passed over his head. Yes, the bombing of Guernica was an atrocity, as it must be whenever human flesh is torn apart by flying metal. But militarily and strategically, it was both a success and a necessity. General Franco needed to capture Guernica and its industrial capabilities. For our part, it was a valuable lesson in the use of combat aircraft. That is why we sent the Condor Legion to Spain. To learn and put our theories into practice.'

'Did you take part in the fighting?'

'No, sir. I was there merely as an observer for the Lieutenant-General.'

'Hah!' exploded Gottfried. 'Tell them how you used *Tann-häuser* to wipe out the Republican machine-gunners.'

'No. If you like the story you tell it.'

Christiane gasped. The young officer had refused his superior! And in such a manner. Now he was laughing at him. Christiane was appalled, but undeniably also fascinated.

'Let me tell you, Carl, there has been nothing to match this since ... I don't know ... since those cheeky Greeks used their hollow horse to get inside the Trojan walls.' Gottfried began to laugh. It reverberated around the room. He was in his element telling stories. 'Young Friedrich here decided to take a closer look at the Republican defences. He took a couple of riflemen with him. God knows how, but they got to within fifty metres of the enemy lines before they were spotted. A machine-gun opened fire on them. Luckily they were right by a shell crater and dropped into it. The machine-gun stopped firing. The trouble was, it had all happened so quickly, they had no idea where the machine-gunners were. On the other hand, the machine-gunners knew exactly where they were. Worse, it was getting dark, and once dark, they knew the Republicans would send out a patrol to finish them off. They didn't know which line of withdrawal would provide the best cover. One of the Schutzes took off his helmet and held a clump of grass to his forehead for camouflage. Then very slowly he rose to peek over the rim of the crater. The poor fellow took a bullet between his eyes before he even had time to blink.

'So, what could our gallant Captain do? I'll tell you. He waited until it got dark. Then he launched into the Pilgrims' Chorus from *Tannhäuser*. If Friedrich hadn't decided to become a soldier, I tell you he would have made a fine tenor. He has a beautiful voice. The Republican machine-gunners thought so too, because when he finished they applauded. Friedrich listened to the applause, worked out where it was coming from and hurled stick grenades at them. That shut them up!' Gottfried stopped talking, speechless as tears of laughter rolled down his cheeks. 'Can you imagine it, Carl, laying flat on your back singing the Pilgrims' Chorus: "*Durch Sühn . . . und Buß hab ich versöhnt . . .*" then BOOM!'

'What did you do next?' asked Carl, as soon as he managed to catch his breath.

'We ran like rabbits. Very frightened rabbits.' The young Captain rose to his feet and picked up his host's bottle of Scotch. Without begging permission, he topped up their glasses and his own. Christiane winced. Her father was a stickler for formality and he would not have enjoyed the Captain's presumption.

'Why *Tannhäuser*?' her father asked somewhat tersely. 'Why the Pilgrims' Chorus?'

'I don't think Wagner intended it, but in the Pilgrims'

Chorus he seems to capture the essence of everything that is good in the soul of man. If he doesn't capture it, then at least he touches it. Has anyone ever heard it and not been moved by it? Also, it is probably one of Wagner's best known pieces. My gamble was that the enemy could not fail to recognise and be affected by it.' The young Captain laughed gently. 'You may think it a bold gamble, Herr Schiller, but what was I risking? My life? At that moment, a wise gambler weighing the odds would not have bet on my existence continuing for very much longer. My life was all I had left to bet with, and it wasn't much of a bet.'

'Still you survived, Captain, and doubtless you learned from the experience. What else did you learn in Spain?'

'Enough to fill volumes of reports which I know the Lieutenant-General will never read. Enough to learn that the outcome of any battle is usually determined by two factors. Firstly superior armaments. Tanks will usually defeat rifles and machine-guns. But more importantly, battles and wars will more often than not be won by the side which makes the fewer mistakes.'

'What about the quality of the soldiers? Do you not take that into consideration?'

'Yes, of course, Herr Schiller. Perhaps the greatest lesson I learned in Spain was this: never, under any circumstances, put German soldiers in a position of fighting alongside the Italians. I was also a guest of the Italian motorised corps at Jarama in February when they mounted their flanking attack on Madrid. What a disaster. Fortunately I could see it coming and hijacked a despatch rider's motorbike. Further to your point, if I'd had one hundred thousand Saxons as my troops we could have cleaned up the mess in Spain in a week.'

'At that stage, the entire Reichswehr barely numbered one hundred thousand, at least officially,' cut in Gottfried drily. 'But the point young Friedrich is making is valid. In a situation where soldiers are more or less equal in ability, the side which makes the fewer mistakes will win. And that need not necessarily be the best equipped.'

'Are we going to invite the young lady to join us?'

If the Captain's question caught his companions by surprise, it was nothing compared to the shock Christiane felt.

Her cheeks flushed hot with embarrassment. She wanted to turn and run but knew that option was no longer open to her. She had been caught red-handed in the act of eavesdropping. But how could he be so rude? How could any friend of her uncle be so thoughtless and tactless? Her ears burned.

'Is that you, Christiane?'

She took a deep breath, and found courage in her sudden dislike for the impudent young officer.

'Yes, Father.' She pushed the door open and entered. 'I wasn't sure it was the opportune time to interrupt you.' She turned to greet her uncle, formal in the presence of the stranger, but her uncle wouldn't have a bar of it. He'd risen from his chair the instant she'd entered and now rushed to embrace her.

'My dear Christiane! Dear God, look at you! You grow more beautiful every day!'

'Please Uncle, you embarrass me!' She nodded towards the Captain who now stood with an infuriating smile on his face.

'Oh, take no notice of him. He is an arrogant and rude upstart of no consequence. I will introduce you in a moment. What's this?'

'A present for you, Uncle. It's nothing. Open it later.' Christiane had overlooked the flies. Fishing may be fine for a young girl, but it was hardly an appropriate pursuit for a young woman in her twenties. How many times would she be made to look a fool in front of the stranger?

'Nonsense! I know it is not a toy car. If it is, it is identical to the one I gave your brother two or three Christmases ago.' He opened the box and examined the contents. 'Oh Christiane, they are beautiful and doubtless equally lethal. Look at them! What fish could possibly resist them? I will add them to my collection. I have had your flies mounted in glass cases and hung on my study walls. Thank you once more.' He drew Christiane to him and kissed both her cheeks. She saw that he had at last noticed how flushed they were but he, at least, had the good manners not to draw attention to them.

'Now let me introduce you to my young friend and comrade in arms, Hauptmann Friedrich Eigenwill. His father is also involved with the Dresdner Bank.'

'Hauptmann Eigenwill,' she said, as frostily as good manners permitted.

'Fräulein Schiller.' He clicked his heels together and bowed stiffly. Then turning, he addressed her father. 'Herr Schiller, I formally request the hand of your beautiful daughter in marriage.'

Christiane's mouth fell open and her eyes flared wide in astonishment. Was there no limit to this appalling man's impudence?

'Really, Friedrich!' Even her uncle seemed put out. 'Sometimes you go too far. You shame me. I insist you apologise.'

'I apologise. To you, Fräulein, and to your father and your uncle. It was not my intention to be rude. But I do have good reason.'

'Really. We would be interested to know what could possibly excuse such behaviour.' Christiane did her best to look aggrieved and haughty, but the young Captain took not the slightest notice. In fact, he seemed to be enjoying himself immensely. To her further surprise, he stepped towards her and extended his hand. She hesitated, but had been reared too well to refuse it. She allowed him to take her hand.

Immediately, a change seemed to come over the Captain. He softened. Where she had only seen arrogance and insolence she now saw sincerity and charm. And what charm! Christiane was utterly confused.

'You see, Fräulein, when the war comes, we will have our one hundred thousand Saxon soldiers and probably more, all of whom will look handsome and magnificent in their uniforms. All of them will seek to marry beautiful Saxon girls and you, Fräulein, are as fine a prize as any man could wish. Do you blame me for endeavouring to establish prior claim?'

Christiane listened spellbound, and wasn't aware that the Captain still held her hand captive until he'd finished. She withdrew her hand immediately. His voice had a sincerity about it which helped calm the anger within her. But she was still a long way from forgiveness. She was unaccustomed to being humiliated. It was a new and entirely unpleasant experience.

'I accept your apology, Captain, though regret the necessity for it.'

'Don't be too harsh on him, Christiane, though God knows he deserves all he gets.' Uncle Gottfried put his arm around her and led her to a chair. 'I must confess, I like his unpredictability. I can always count on young Friedrich for truth and contrary opinion. Nowadays, that's as rare as salmon in the Rhine. We're producing automatons.'

'Captain, you said if I may quote you, "when the war comes". You believe there will be a war?'

'Yes I do, Herr Schiller. But it is an opinion the Lieutenant-General does not share.'

'And what is the basis for your belief?'

Christiane settled back into her chair to listen, relieved that she was no longer the focus of attention, and flattered that her father permitted her to remain. Such talk was the province of men and her father had always discouraged similar discussion within the family. This was a rare opportunity. Besides it gave her the opportunity to examine the tall, aristocratic young officer more closely. He was handsome enough, but not in the same class as Dietrich Schmidt. His accent suggested his family came from Leipzig though at times his *sächsisch* was barely detectable. What impressed her most was his confidence and sophistication. He was the antithesis of Dietrich. Once more the little girl inside her began to dream and wonder.

'Herr Schiller,' the young officer began, 'I believe the cause of the next war will be the same as the last — the dream of *Grosswirtschaftsraum*.' He paused to see what effect this observation had had. He wasn't seeking agreement but disagreement. He had no intention of spending the rest of the day engaged in a political debate with his host, a debate which he would not be permitted to win. When he got no reaction he continued.

'From the German point of view, the creation of a large, economically self-sufficient, unified Germany is an admirable aspiration, particularly as it would also be militarily impregnable. If you are not German, however, it is a fearsome prospect. The question is, how far will the foreign powers allow our Führer to go? Herr Hitler is making great capital out of the cause. How could any loyal German not support such a dream? Will the foreign powers allow us to bring all

German-speaking people into the Fatherland? Will they stand by and allow the Führer to bring Austria, the Sudetenland, and anywhere else that has a German-speaking population into the Reich? And how will Hitler cope with the question of East Prussia? A wise man would not count on France or England giving their blessing to any of this. So what does a wise man do, because we cannot have our *Lebensraum*, our living space, without it?

'The Führer has already shown us what he intends to do. Already, we have remilitarised the Rhineland and introduced conscription in direct contravention of the Versailles Treaty. Our armaments production has increased fivefold — maybe tenfold — in just the last few years. Our weaponry, our tanks, our artillery, our navy, our airforce are fast becoming the most advanced and most powerful in the world. Hitler has the means to realise his dream of a unified Germany, and I believe he will use it to take on France and England once more if they object.'

'It is my opinion that they will back down,' cut in her father. 'They have no will for war. Furthermore, they are not unaware of the strength of our military. Of course they will protest, but I believe we will achieve a unified Germany without a shot being fired.'

'What then?'

'What do you mean, "what then"?' Carl Schiller was obviously irritated. As far as he was concerned his argument had ended the debate. He looked to his brother for support but found none. Indeed, Gottfried seemed amused by his discomfort.

'Would the Führer be happy then, do you think? If the foreign powers cave in, don't you think that will only feed his ambitions? What of the thousand-year Reich? What of his dreams of a *Herrenvolk*, of a master race? Of a *Weltzeitalter*, a new world age dominated of course by German culture and morality? My father once told me that Germany can defeat any country in the world, but we can't defeat every country at once. Do you think the whole world will cave in, Herr Schiller? Do you think America and Russia will give in as easily? I do not, and regrettably I don't think our Führer does either. Yes, Herr Schiller, war is inevitable. The only question is, with whom will we make war?'

'That's enough, Captain. Gottfried, I don't know why you put up with him.'

'Carl, that is precisely why I put up with him.' Gottfried laughed to defuse the situation. 'You don't have to agree with Friedrich. Half the time I'm not even sure he agrees with himself. But it's good to hear an opposing voice. They're all too rare these days.'

'Perhaps,' Carl agreed reluctantly. 'But to use your words again, Captain, a wise man would be careful where he expressed his opinions. And that is a caution I extend to you, Christiane. It is not a bad thing that you heard Captain Eigenwill's somewhat free analysis, but you are not to repeat so much as a word of it.'

'Your caution is not necessary, Father.' Christiane had been thrilled at being allowed to take part in the discussion, even if only as audience, and she was in awe of Friedrich. His performance had been spellbinding, nothing less than she'd expect from a senior lecturer at university. But this brush with reality distressed her, particularly the talk of war. The Captain made war seem inevitable and with all her heart she wanted that not to be so. His words chilled her. She slipped from admiration to apprehension, and the little dreams she'd been allowing to unfold in her head now seemed ridiculously childish. Her father and uncle were still watching her so she continued. 'I too find the Captain's opinions distasteful. I do not believe the Führer wants another war. He wants only what is right. Why shouldn't the German people be one again? Why shouldn't we unite and nurture our own race?' Christiane did as she was expected and echoed her father's views. It would never have occurred to her to do otherwise. 'We would be in our home on Prager Strasse right now but for the Jews.'

'Ah, the Jews! A cunning race no doubt. A race of cheats and deceivers.' The twinkle was back in the Captain's eye and Christiane wasn't sure whether he was agreeing with her or mocking her. She allowed him to continue.

'You have heard no doubt of gefillte fish? The Jewish wife buys a fish too small to feed her family. So what does she do?

She strips the flesh off the bones and mixes it with bread and anything else she has handy. Then she puts it back on the bones to make the little fish look like a big fish. See how Jewish mothers even cheat their own families?'

Gottfried burst out laughing. Even her father was amused. But Christiane was furious. She smiled weakly. She didn't know what gefillte fish was and so didn't understand the joke. Once more the Captain was making fun of her and that was unforgivable. No one, certainly no man, had ever treated her in such a cavalier fashion before. Colour rushed back to her cheeks and in her anger she found the confidence to strike back.

'Is the Captain staying for lunch?' she inquired. 'If so, please excuse me. I'll go and tell mother to add some bread to the salmon we're having.' She left the room with as much haste as dignity would allow.

Chapter Eight

The day Untersturmführer Dietrich Schmidt was due to meet with Christiane, he awoke with a young woman's naked body pressed against his back. Her arm hung slackly over his. At first he couldn't remember which one she was, then a smile spread slowly over his face. He felt the soft flesh cushioning his back like pillows. Yes, she was the one with the big tits. What tits! Like zeppelins, and on such a fine stem! Slowly memories of the previous night came back to him. He'd been insatiable, rampant, and the steel in his member had neither flexed nor faltered. If only it was always like this! They'd fucked like rabbits and he'd even screwed those magnificent tits. He laughed softly at the memory of their drunken contortions. Last night he could have fucked anything. He'd never felt so high in his life. He wondered if the money he'd paid her extended through to morning, and even if it didn't, he decided he'd fuck her once more anyway. True, she'd already given him his money's worth, but hadn't he returned it in kind? Her orgasms certainly hadn't been faked. Ha! She should pay him!

He slowly turned to face her, gently so he didn't wake her and eased the cover down to look again at her body. For once the woman beside him had not aged as they usually did between the small hours and dawn. She was still as young and as magnificent as he remembered her. He bent forward to wake her with a kiss, but changed his mind as she exhaled and he caught the ardour-killing breath of stale wine. Instead he swung out of bed and pulled the covers back over her. What a night! And what a day!

Dietrich had been given the responsibility of leading a

93

squad in the action against the Jews. It was a huge compliment to be acknowledged by his Hauptsturmführer in this manner. And he had excelled! SS-Captain Gorgass had been quite specific in his orders. He had given Dietrich a list of Jewish businesses and families to target, with strict instructions to limit his activities to those names on the list.

'You see, Lieutenant Schmidt,' Captain Gorgass had said, 'all Jews make donations to the Party. Those Jews who are spared this time will be encouraged to believe that it was their contributions that saved them. They will then be further encouraged to increase their contributions, and we do not believe they will be of a mind to refuse. In this way we make the Jews pay for the costs of the action against them. It has a certain logic, don't you agree?'

Dietrich agreed wholeheartedly. The idea of Jews paying the cost of their own persecution delighted him, and he saw the cleverness of it as further evidence of German racial superiority. He looked through his list, noting the names and addresses until he came to one he recognised. He hesitated for the briefest of moments, but it had not gone unnoticed.

'You have a problem, Lieutenant?'

Dietrich realised then that this was a test.

'No, Herr Captain!' Dietrich was relieved to see the Captain's close scrutiny melt to a smile.

'But you do recognise a name on that list. Dr Shapiro? We have evidence that he has been sending money abroad even though the Führer has forbidden it. German money. Money he stole from the good German people. Money that might be better used in cleansing the Fatherland of his kind. Agree?'

'Yes, Captain. With all my heart!'

SS-Captain Gorgass had chosen well, for he could hardly have found a man more suited to the job. Even in the Hitler Youth Dietrich had demonstrated his political and ideological suitability by denouncing everyone who showed less than total commitment to the cause. In the early days, he had even denounced one of his closest friends who had a talent for mimickry, for doing a light-hearted impression of a Nazi Party official who'd come to address them. To Dietrich, it was all a question of loyalty, and absolute loyalty was owed to one's superiors. There was no grey area, no tempering or softening, no forgiveness. In loyalty there was honour, in disloyalty dishonour. He was duty bound to point out those suspected of bringing them dishonour.

It was inevitable that Dietrich came to the attention of the SS recruiters. He was strong, tall and handsome, the ideal model of Aryan youth, and his mind was like blotting paper the way it soaked up and absorbed Nazi teachings. Naturally, those teachings which appealed to him most were to do with racial cleansing, eliminating the elements that might threaten the propagation of other racially-pure Aryans similar to himself. He fully embraced and advocated compulsory sterilisation for the 'hereditarily ill', those with symptoms or family histories of mental illnesses, or suffering from blindness, deafness or diseases like multiple sclerosis. As a result of his enthusiasm, he was invited to play the part of a student in an educational film advocating euthanasia for the incurably insane and handicapped, called, *Life Unworthy of Life*. Every one of the propagandists' words were gospel to him. Why should the young and healthy support the sick and the weak? Why should they divert money which could provide housing for workers to the care of the incurable who made no contribution to society? That ran contrary to the laws of nature. From the beginning of time only the fittest survived. Everything was so clear and obvious to the young Dietrich. The sick and the weak had to be sifted out and eliminated for the good of the German race. It wasn't a question of hatred, but of common sense. Hatred was something reserved for the Jews and Slavs.

Dietrich wasn't born hating Jews or even raised to hate them. The doctor who had delivered him, Dr Shapiro, was Jewish and had remained the family doctor until the relationship had become politically unwise. It was only when he was inducted into the *Deutsches Jungvolk* at the age of ten, and the Hitler Youth at thirteen that he discovered the treachery and avarice of the Jewish race and, along with this discovery, his vocation. There was nothing the Jews weren't to blame for. Furthermore, he believed that they were not just bent on undermining the German economy and enslaving its people but, like the hereditarily ill, were a threat to the purity of German blood. It was a threat that Dietrich believed passionately should be eliminated.

Dietrich's was only one of a number of spontaneous demonstrations planned for Dresden that night. Along with his area, he'd been assigned a mob of Party members mainly from the ranks of the SA, some posing as outraged citizens. Dietrich had taken part in similar actions before but never as a section leader. Nevertheless, he knew what to expect and was determined to excel. The Brownshirts would also need a demonstration of his right to command along with his own troops. He decided to begin where he could best show the steel from which he was made. He began by bursting into the home of Dr Shapiro. It was Friday night, the beginning of the Jewish Sabbath.

The doctor's wife recognised him immediately. Her expression changed from outright fear to one of faint hope.

'Dietrich! Thank God it's you! Tell them it's a mistake. Tell them to go away! Tell them we're friends. Loyal Germans.'

Dietrich could sense his troops watching him, waiting to see his reaction. He looked at her coldly. He felt no compassion for her whatsoever. He enjoyed her weakness, the way she cowered back, eyes pleading. He watched as her daughter Hannah put a comforting arm around her and glared at him. As children they'd played together and even bathed together, taking sneaky looks at the parts that made them different. Hannah was the first girl he had ever kissed. However young and foolish he'd been at the time, this Jewish girl had been his first love. Dietrich now found the memory repugnant.

'Where is the doctor?' he demanded.

His wife hesitated. 'No, Dietrich. Please go! Please, I beg you, please leave us!'

Dietrich slapped her hard. She screamed in shock and fear and burst into tears.

'He is in the toilet.' Hannah met his eyes without flinching. 'Just as you —'

'Fetch him!' Dietrich ordered. 'Now!' Two soldiers ran off to obey. He looked around the room but was disappointed by what he saw. It hadn't changed much from when he was young. There was no obvious wealth, no evidence of a Jewish conspiracy, just the furniture and decoration he'd expect to see in any comfortable middle class home. It angered him that they failed to live up to the stereotype, and failed to feed the prejudices ingrained in his troops. They didn't seem much of a threat to the Fatherland. His thoughts were interrupted as the soldiers returned with the hapless doctor, his trousers still trapped around his shins. He was shaking with fear.

'You are under arrest for crimes against the State,' said Dietrich. 'You and your family.'

'Dietrich, for God's sake, what are you saying?' Dr Shapiro looked up at him, pleading. 'What crimes? What possible crimes could I have committed?'

'Is it not true that you have been sending money abroad in direct contravention of the Führer's wishes.' Dietrich watched as the doctor's face went even paler. He sensed the absoluteness of his power and decided to add to the list of crimes. 'Furthermore, under the guise of attending to honest German folk you have attempted to introduce hereditary illnesses into their blood. Your patients are willing to testify to this.' Dietrich could sense that he'd struck a chord with his men. He could almost feel their approval. Here was something they could understand. His confidence grew.

'Dietrich, that is nonsense! You know that is nonsense. For heaven's sake, I brought you into this world. I was your family's doctor for more than fifteen years! Please, I beg you! Stop this nonsense!'

Dietrich sensed the situation had reached the point where it could get away from him. The mob were getting impatient. They wanted action. They wanted blood. But Dietrich wanted more than that. He wanted to set an example for his men that they'd never forget. One that would mark him as a man to be reckoned with. One that would impress Captain Gorgass. The soldiers had followed the exchange and watched him closely. Would he go soft on the Jews because they were once friends of his family? Would he stumble at this first hurdle? Dietrich took his time and considered his options. Catching the doctor on the toilet had been a stroke of luck. Yes, he'd give his men something to remember. He'd give them something to boast about!

'Doctor, you have not finished your business!' He pointed

to his trousers still trapped around his ankles. 'Please, finish your business.'

'What do you mean?'

'Finish your piss, Herr Doktor! Here! No, not on the carpet. On your wife!'

'No!'

'Now! Now, Herr Doktor!' Dietrich dragged out the syllables, mocking him. 'Now!' He turned and pointed his pistol at Hannah. She flinched suddenly, and her fear encouraged him.

'Now!' he screamed.

'Yes, yes! Don't shoot!' Dr Shapiro could not look at his wife's face. 'I am sorry, Edit, forgive me.'

'It is all right, Walter. Just do it. Just do as he says!'

A cheer went up when the doctor managed to turn the first few pathetic drops into a brief flow that splashed onto his wife's lap. He turned on Dietrich, tears of shame burning in his eyes.

'There! Are you satisfied now?'

'Not quite, Herr Doktor. There is the matter of the rest of your business. A man does not take down his trousers just to piss.'

'No Dietrich, you've humiliated us enough!'

Dietrich turned to face Hannah. Her face was contorted with rage and hate. She'd risen to her feet, her fists clenched. Despite the pistol pointed at her, she took a step towards him. It was enough. He pulled the trigger. The sudden explosion caught everyone by surprise, even Dietrich, but he recovered first.

'That is what happens when Jews resist arrest,' he said calmly. He pointed to the disbelieving doctor and his wife who looked on open-mouthed in horror, so stunned they were not yet able to give voice to their grief. 'Take them away!'

His soldiers did as they were ordered and the mob set about ransacking the house. Dietrich felt exultant. Hannah was the first Jew he'd killed and he felt the full force of his power.

'Well done, Herr Untersturmführer!' He turned to see the grinning face of one of his soldiers, one of his comrades.

'Right in the Jew bitch's face! Unbelievable! Where next?'

Dietrich consulted his list. There were five more names remaining. He could barely restrain his excitement. They beat up two more Jews that night, one for resisting arrest and the other a passer-by who, in escaping from one mob, had the misfortune to run into Dietrich's. They wrecked a toy shop, burned a bakery, and looted a watchmaker's shop as they rampaged through the streets. Ironically, many of the watches confiscated were in for repairs, and the property of non-Jewish citizens. Dietrich had stood back as the night progressed, exhorting his troops to greater and greater excesses. He'd set his example as a good leader should, and then ensured that his troops followed it. His squad arrested a total of nineteen Jews and dispossessed them of everything except the clothes they stood in and whatever shreds of dignity they could muster.

Later that night Dietrich and his fellow junior offices celebrated their triumph. Already the story had got around about the way he had humiliated the doctor and shot his daughter. It marked him as a man to be respected, a man whose steel was beyond question. Dietrich knew the story would find its way back to Captain Gorgass and his chest swelled with pride. He'd covered himself. He'd made sure the shooting could be construed as an act of self-defence. What did it matter that the girl wasn't armed? God, he was high! And the beer he swilled did nothing to diminish the growing presence in his trousers. Some woman would be lucky tonight!

* * *

Lucio paused and glanced around the table at his companions. That they'd found his story distasteful was beyond question. He decided it was time for coffee. Besides, it would give him the opportunity to move the story on. He wasn't enjoying the telling any more than his listeners were enjoying hearing it.

'Lucio, is all this really necessary?' Milos spoke softly but there was a note of censure in his voice.

'Yes, why do you take us back over all of this?' It was

Gancio, back on his favourite theme. 'We all know what happened. We all regret what happened. Why bring it all up again? Do you think anyone enjoys hearing about these atrocities?'

'It is precisely because they were atrocities that Lucio has raised them.' They all turned to the blind man. 'Have you all been sleeping? All war is an atrocity. Remember Lucio saying that? What that young SS officer Dietrich did was an atrocity. The bombing of Guernica was an atrocity. And the execution of the women in the square at Ravello was also an atrocity. You're both listening to the examples and missing the theme.'

'Ramon's right.'

'Thank you, Neil.'

'You're welcome. Now where's our bloody coffee? What sort of a place do you run here, Gancio?'

'Excuse me. Maria!' Gancio's bellow startled some of the remaining diners, but the regulars just smiled.

'I think Lucio's wallowed sufficiently in that mire for the time being. Am I right?' Ramon turned to where Lucio sat, his back to the window.

'Yes. But we are not yet finished with Germany. Please don't think I enjoy telling this part of the story. But it *is* part of the story and so I have no discretion over whether it is or isn't told.'

'Oh come off it!' cut in Neil. 'I can accept that what you told us on the first day actually happened, particularly after Gancio's little outburst. But surely this business with that young prick Dietrich is just colour — pure invention — a rather sickening example of the sort of things that happened. How can you possibly maintain that part of the story is true? You weren't there. Of course you had discretion.'

'Of course I wasn't there, but that is exactly what happened, Neil.'

'Bullshit! Look, I accept your need to cover the extent of the atrocities. Even the blind can see that that is one of the key issues in your story.'

'Thank you, Neil.'

'Shut up, Ramon, I was speaking figuratively. But there is no way that this part of your story is true. It's just colour. We can accept that so why not just admit it?'

'Because it isn't just colour, Neil.' Lucio spoke patiently and evenly, but a note of irritation had crept into his voice. 'Everything I've told you actually happened. Don't dismiss the life of that poor, unfortunate Jewish girl as fiction, nor the humiliations that preceded it. You're right, I could have invented hundreds of examples, all equally convincing. But there was no need. That one true story is enough, I think we're all agreed on that. And it is true, Neil. As my story progresses, that will become quite plain to you.'

'Dear God,' said Gancio wearily. 'Why do you tell this story at all?'

Chapter Nine

Dietrich Schmidt had come a long way from the small boy who never knew where his next meal was coming from, or could feel with any certainty that there would be one. His father had been wounded in the war and this had handicapped him in his search for work. Fragments from an exploding shell had torn apart his right knee, and the damage had been compounded by harassed, ill-equipped field doctors. His father was grateful that they'd saved his life. He knew of others who had been less fortunate. But he'd been left with a painfully bent leg that would neither straighten nor bend further. The result was a pronounced limp that often saw him passed over for what few available jobs there were.

His strength was his persistence. When there was no work for wages, sympathetic shopkeepers would sometimes employ him for a few hours of stacking and packing and pay him in kind. He'd come home with a bag of bones and some sausages after helping the butcher, or a bag of tired vegetables after helping vegetable sellers at the markets. Mostly, whatever he brought home went straight into the large pot to make soup which the family devoured with large chunks of bread. Dietrich's father could lay claim to two pieces of good fortune. One was his relieving job in a little village-style bakery, where he kept the wood-fired oven burning two nights a week. His payment was a large, daily loaf of coarse bread made from both white wheat and dark rye flours. Dietrich had the job of collecting it hot and fresh each morning. The second piece of good fortune was his relationship with Dr Shapiro. Dietrich's father tended the doctor's garden and did simple maintenance jobs for him. In return, the doctor cared for his family and kept him supplied with the pain killers which, on some days, were the only things that kept him on his feet at all.

His mother had helped by taking in washing and ironing. His two sisters assisted and their combined labours brought in a steady, if rather paltry, flow of cash. It was enough to keep them clothed. Dietrich and his two younger brothers had chipped in whenever they could by doing deliveries for local merchants. But for all their effort, Dietrich could hardly remember a time when he wasn't hungry, when the most beautiful sight in the world was the rows of sausages in endless varieties hanging in butchers' windows. He could never pass by without flattening his nose against the window.

National Socialism had been the salvation of Dietrich's family and eased the chains of poverty. Through the mid-thirties at Hitler's direction, armaments and munitions factories mushroomed and enticed workers away to the west. Those who'd remained flocked to Siemens, Zeiss-Ikon and the Sachsenwerk plants, and the new factories that blossomed around them. For the first time in his life, Dietrich's father found regular employment, and the *plockwurst, leberwurst, blutwurst* and *bratwurst* Dietrich had lusted after now appeared on the dinner table as a matter of course. But the new age of affluence did more than ease the pains in his belly and fill out his growing body, it gave him freedom to think beyond the next day and to plan a better life for himself.

Initially, the SS had been the sole foundation for his plans. They rewarded those whose loyalty was unswerving and whose ruthlessness was absolute in the service of the Führer. They also rewarded those with street cunning and in this attribute Dietrich's credentials were among the best. A successful career in the SS was assured. But Dietrich wanted more. Yes, one day he might make Hauptsturmführer but he had his sights set on loftier ranks. After all, hadn't the Führer himself once been a humble corporal? SS-Captain was not enough for him. Oberführer or Brigadeführer better fitted his aspirations. But he needed help to get there. He needed patronage, influence and wealth. He needed Christiane.

Meeting her had been no accident. Even if she'd had a face like the working part of a pig's backside he would have asked her to dance. Or, if not her, someone equally pedigreed. Christiane had matched his criteria perfectly. Her family was not so wealthy that she would dismiss a junior Lieutenant out of hand, nor her father so senior that his plans would be obvious. She was well connected. It had taken no time at all to discover the existence of Uncle Gottfried and his exalted rank. She was also young, beautiful and childishly naïve. She was putty in his hands.

He loathed opera and cursed the day that Richard Wagner was born. But at least opera had some semblance of a plot, however ridiculous. He was at a total loss to know why people paid to sit down and listen to an orchestra. Dietrich could imagine nothing more stupefyingly boring. At first he had agreed to escort Christiane because it was necessary to foster their relationship. Yet Dietrich soon realised that an apparent knowledge and appreciation of German culture could be more important to his aspirations than proficiency with weapons. Suddenly he found himself rubbing shoulders with generals, leading politicians and captains of industry. How could they not notice him and speculate upon his contacts? After all, he and Christiane were by far the most attractive couple there, a glowing tribute to the future of the German people. If the subtleties of opera eluded him, the potential of these evenings did not. He kept a record of every notable and influential person he met. He learned how to conduct himself and, more importantly, the art of saying precisely what his peers wanted him to say.

So he expanded the foundations upon which he would build his career to include Christiane and the Schiller family. He began to pay her the little courtesies and compliments he'd learned by observing others. He went out of his way to see her whenever he was off duty. And, instead of waiting for Christiane to take the initiative, surprised her by buying tickets to hear the Staatskapelle Dresden, the Semper Opera Orchestra, and to performances by the choir of the Kreuz-schule. He could see that Christiane interpreted this latest development not only as a burgeoning appreciation of the arts, but as clear evidence of the fact that he loved her as much as she loved him. He even began to respond to her lessons in elocution. Ah! If only everything in life could be as simple!

He courted her parents as diligently, though less successfully. Her mother, Clara, seemed to like him well enough but he could see that her opinion counted for little. Herr Schiller was another matter. He was courteous as expected, but cool and distant. The only approval he'd ever won from him was when he'd announced his promotion to Obersturmführer — full Lieutenant — following the first demonstration he'd led against the Jews.

But Dietrich had inherited his father's persistence and he persevered. One day Carl Schiller would have to face the fact that his daughter was in love with him. He couldn't help but notice. She could hardly stop smiling and radiated happiness. Even the Semper Picture Gallery's most prized exhibit, Raphael's *Sistine Madonna*, paled in her presence. In the meantime, Dietrich pretended to enjoy the tiresomely formal dinners at Prager Strasse where he was clearly out of his depth. Little by little, they drifted inevitably along the path towards marriage.

Throughout it all, Dietrich made no attempt to sleep with Christiane and their embraces, though warm and genuine, had none of the fire and passion he showed with his whores. Often he could hardly wait to bid his love farewell, before dashing off to the beer cellars to join his comrades in their drinking and whoring. Ambition was one thing, but he still had to get on with the business of living.

* * *

For Christiane the warm embraces were enough though, in truth, she'd had few other experiences to compare them with. She was in love — a hopelessly naïve and impossibly idealised form of love. Dietrich was her gallant knight and she his pure, virginal lady. She forgave him his accent and the fact that his wit was either absent or obvious. It was a romance straight from the pages of a storybook and bore little relationship to reality. She forgot about the other young officer Uncle Gottfried had introduced her to, and the little fantasies she'd briefly entertained with him as the centrepiece. Christiane was evidence that true love is not only blinkered but often hopelessly blind.

But fate intervened just as their relationship was gathering momentum. Hitler found another use for Dietrich and his brethren. On 12 March 1938, the day before the plebiscite which would determine whether Austria joined the Reich or not, the Führer exercised his will over the democratic processes. His troops marched into Austria with the tallest, strongest and fairest to the fore, living proof of the superiority of the German race, the master race which would unite all German-speaking people. For Dietrich Schmidt, it was the proudest moment of his life. Perhaps it was the significance of the occasion or the enthusiasm with which he performed his duties, that caused him to overlook the obvious. Whatever his reasons, it never occurred to him to write a letter to Christiane.

Chapter Ten

Dietrich Schmidt was correct in his belief that not everyone in the Schiller family was as enamoured of him as Christiane. There were things about him that Carl Schiller found disquieting. Unquestionably, Dietrich was a product of the times, one of the automatons Gottfried had spoken of. His opinions weren't his own but reflected hard-line Party attitudes. In his heart Carl could not believe that Dietrich was the right man for his daughter. She was subtle, clever and sensitive, he the reverse. Dear God, the young fool spoke in slogans! Apart from his obvious good looks, what on earth did his daughter see in him?

Other thoughts troubled him. He was well aware of the persecution of the Jews and the role of the SS. He had no sympathy for the Jews but some of the stories he'd heard had disgusted him. Surely the Jews could just be arrested in an orderly fashion and taken to wherever it was they went? Was this other business really necessary? Carl Schiller knew that Dietrich could not have escaped involvement, indeed, he had to have been involved. In Carl's mind, a thug was a thug even if he was a German thug, and that was not the sort of person he wanted his daughter to marry. But what could he do? What reason did he have to caution her against their growing friendship? And even if he did, would that not have the reverse effect? He could order her to stop seeing Dietrich and he knew that she would obey. But he was reluctant to take that step. Better to let things run their course. His daughter was too clever. Sooner or later she would realise how unsuited they were.

But as time passed and Dietrich's position in his daughter's affections achieved a sense of permanence, his despair grew. He'd allowed the relationship to run too long and was reluctant to call a halt. When Dietrich was dispatched to Austria, he seized the opportunity to try to entice her out to the theatre and opera where he could arrange for her to meet other young officers. But she refused all his entreaties. Having farewelled her gallant knight, she patiently and loyally settled down to await his return. She felt it improper to go out and enjoy herself while the man she loved was away on duty. The only times she left the house were when she went to work. The rest of the time she floated around lovelorn and infuriatingly virtuous, until Carl could stand it no longer. At dinner time he made his announcement.

'Come,' he said. 'I have decided we will spend the weekend at Little Pillnitz. We need some fresh air, you especially Christiane. We will go fishing. Yes, Christiane, before you object, you will come fishing with us, too.'

'But Daddy . . .'

'Yes, you too, Christiane. We will pack and leave tonight. I am tired of your moping around here. So is your mother and your brother and sisters. It's time you pulled yourself together and took stock of things.'

Christiane bowed her head, martyred by authority.

'If your young man has written to you, his letter will be here waiting on our return. He knows the address. The question I'm tempted to ask is, does he know how to write?'

'Oh Daddy, that's unfair! How could you?'

Christiane rose from the table and fled in tears. Her father shook his head. He'd gone too far and he knew it. Still, what had been said was said and there was no changing that. Probably do more good than harm. He turned to his wife.

'Go to her, Clara. Help her pack. Tell her I apologise for my remark but I haven't changed my mind.'

The moment his wife left the room his son and daughters began to giggle. His son looked up at him mischievously.

'Well, Father? Do you think he knows how to write?'

Carl Schiller looked steadily at his young son. This was normally a prelude to a scolding and, Lord knows, the little upstart deserved it for his impertinence. Instead he began to smile and that was enough. His son and daughters burst out laughing. There was no way Christiane could not have heard.

* * *

Saturday dawned the sort of day that renews life in those weary of the long, cold, German winter, even though the hills of the Elbe valley protect Dresdeners from the worst of it. True, the trees looked skeletal against the soaring blue of the sky, but anyone who took the time to observe more closely could see the tinge of green where new leaves budded.

This first breath of spring even worked its magic on Christiane. She'd been quite prepared to sulk and make life miserable for all around her, but on this crisp, clear morning she couldn't work up the heart for it. Her father's remark had cut her to the quick. But the fact remained, she'd received no letters from Dietrich even though three weeks had passed. Why didn't he write? She decided to be stoic and put up a brave front, which suited her mood far better. Besides she was quite looking forward to wetting a fly, despite her earlier protestations.

Knowing how cold it would be, particularly if the wind came up, she changed into the heavy winter underwear she kept for fishing, the fine, high-necked, inner pullover and heavy twill trousers. She pulled her slippers on over the thick socks, threw her heavy-knit pullover across her shoulder, and went downstairs to join the rest of her family for breakfast.

As soon as her father saw her, his face lit up. He had been certain she'd be in one of her moods, but there she was, dressed and ready for action. He didn't question why, for the mental processes of the female of the species never ceased to leave him bewildered. He merely accepted that she'd changed and that the change was for the better. He rose from his chair to greet her and kissed both her cheeks.

'Ah, Christiane, it will be like old times! I hope you haven't given away all of our flies to Uncle Gottfried.'

'Not at all. I keep the best ones for fishing. They can't catch trout when they're in glass cases. Ah ... *Plinsen!*' Her mother handed her a plate of buckwheat pancakes flavoured with lemon rind and sour cream, and covered with a sugar beet syrup. Christiane knew she was supposed to be serene and distant but the morning, the hot pancakes and her father's excitement made a mockery of her intentions.

'We should have got up before dawn for the early rise,' said her brother.

'Ernst, there is no fish in the world worth getting up for that early or getting that cold for.' She put her head back and laughed. Her family looked at her astonished. It was a sound they hadn't heard for months.

Carl, Christiane and Ernst set off immediately after breakfast, their boots crunching on the frost wherever the pastures were still in shadow. Cows had wandered out from their overnight shelters and watched suspiciously as they passed by. Jonquils had popped up among the scattering of mushrooms that Lisl would soon gather, relishing the sun and the vindication of their early appearance. As they neared the stream they could see swifts and housemartins engaged in aerial combat as they banked and dived in pursuit of winged insects. It was a good sign. They paused just short of the bank so their shadows wouldn't fall over the water and spook the fish, if any happened to be nearby.

Carl and Ernst elected to move further upstream where the trunk of a fallen beech had partially blocked the stream and caused a pool to form. Ernst, who was the least experienced and least accurate, needed the extra room to cast. Christiane liked to fish where the stream narrowed and the water flowed fastest. Often little pools formed around underwater obstacles and sometimes trout waited in these for food to wash down to them, or hid beneath the overhanging banks.

She chose a caddis, a tiny fly the colour of a muddy puddle. Then moving upstream she cast back into the flow. As the adult caddis fly hatches on the surface of the water it swims against the current, using it to help peel off its larval shroud. Delicately she worked the fly upstream. Nothing. She cast again. Nothing. She shortened her cast where the water swirled around an underwater snag. Again nothing. It didn't matter, nothing mattered. She became totally absorbed in the pursuit of her quarry and the execution of her skills. She slowly began to work her way further upstream. Casting, retrieving, casting again. She saw the splash before she felt the trout hit. In the instant that trout take to crush insects between their tongue and the roof of their mouth, Christiane struck and the tiny hook sank home.

The fish fought hard but the force it opposed was irresistible. Christiane was patient, allowing the spring of her rod to do the work, and slowly drew the tiring trout towards her. She waited until it rolled over onto its side exhausted, before slipping her net beneath it. She was elated. The trout wasn't particularly large but neither was it so small that it was best returned to the stream. It was lunch for one but, more than that, it was proof that she hadn't lost her touch. She slipped it into her bag and prepared to catch another. She caught two more worthy of keeping before she became aware of her father and brother heading back towards her. Startled, she looked at her watch. It was almost lunchtime! Where had all the time gone?

Her father had caught five but Ernst had caught the biggest, and wanted to talk about nothing else. Christiane listened as he prattled on, describing the fight in more detail than even the most enthusiastic angler wants to hear. What a glorious day! There wasn't a cloud in the sky nor, it appeared, over the horizon. There wasn't even a hint of breeze and the sun had seized the opportunity to return some warmth to the soil.

'I think you'd better save your story,' said her father suddenly. 'You'll only have to repeat it. That looks like Gottfried's car.'

Christiane looked over to the house and sure enough a black Mercedes tourer was parked in front of it. Uncle Gottfried! The day just kept getting better. Perhaps she could take him fishing later, once her feet had had a chance to warm up. And her face. It always surprised her how cold she got when she was fishing. She never noticed it at the time.

She gave her trout to Ernst to clean on the bench by the back door, and took his rod and tackle from him. It was one of her father's mandates that fish had to be cleaned and equipment dried and put away before anything else could take place. She happily took care of the rods because, as much as she liked catching fish, she loathed cleaning them.

The sun still hadn't reached the outbuilding where they

kept their fishing gear and gardening equipment, and Christiane felt the chill seep through to her bones. She worked quickly with practised hands, eager to get to the kitchen and bathe in its warmth. She kicked her boots off at the door and removed her jacket. With her knitted hat still on her head, scarf around her neck, and slippers on her feet, she entered.

'Good morning. You are more beautiful than I remembered.'

She spun around. It was the young Hauptmann. The infernal man had a genius for embarrassing her! Her two silly sisters were standing either side of him grinning foolishly.

'Forgive me for greeting you like this, but I have volunteered to help your charming sisters make bread. Actually it is an excuse to stand in the kitchen. After driving from Berlin with your uncle, there is only one place I want to be, and that is wherever it is warmest.'

'Welcome to our humble kitchen, Captain. I'm sure my two sisters will keep you entertained. If you'll excuse me.' Christiane hurried to her room. Why was it, she wondered, that clothes for fishing can look so beautiful and elegant in magazines, yet so agricultural when worn? She pondered upon this when she should have been asking herself other questions. She should have asked herself why it mattered what clothes the Captain saw her in. And, more importantly, why she felt her embarrassment so deeply.

She changed and took time to tidy herself up. She teased up her hair where her hat had flattened it, but nothing could bring colour back to her cheeks or life to her frozen feet. There was no doubt about it. There was no way a woman could ever feel beautiful when her feet were cold. She planned to make an entrance right on mealtime to avoid getting caught in conversation with the Captain before she was ready for him. But first she had to get warm. Should she risk the kitchen or join her father and uncle in the study? Perhaps the Captain had already returned to the study. She chose the kitchen. The Captain was right. It was by far the warmest room in the house.

'Hello again.'

Damn! He was still there.

'Come in, I have moved up a chair for you in front of the stove and we have shifted our bread-making over here out of your way. You must still be frozen.' The Captain bowed slightly and gestured towards the chair with his hand. Christiane could hardly refuse. Besides, she was touched by the young officer's consideration, and in front of the stove was precisely where she wanted to be.

'Thank you, Captain . . .' She sat down and lifted her feet off the floor and held them out towards the stove. 'Ahhh . . . that feels so good!'

'When you went straight up to your room I thought you must have inherited the same blood as your uncle. He never feels the cold. Here, I have poured you some schnapps. Sometimes it is best to work on cold from both the inside and out.'

Christiane smiled and took the small glass. Again she was touched by his thoughtfulness.

'My uncle drinks a lot of schnapps. Perhaps, Captain, that is why he never feels the cold.'

'You may well be right, but I am not going to be the one to tell him.' He laughed and Christiane found it easy to join him. 'And please, stop calling me Captain. Call me Friedrich.'

'Tell me, Friedrich, have you thrown any more bombs at lovers of Wagner?'

Friedrich laughed.

'No. I've learned my lesson and I've never gone close enough again.'

'Did you really kill those Republican machine-gunners?'

'No. The story has grown in the telling. The grenades we threw fell way too short, but they confused things enough to enable us to make our escape. Personally, I think the machine-gunners were laughing too hard to shoot straight. Still, I'm glad the grenades fell short. How could anyone who likes Wagner possibly be our enemy?' He put his head back and sang the first few lines of the Pilgrims' Chorus. Her uncle hadn't exaggerated. He did have a fine tenor voice.

Slowly, in the warmth of the kitchen with her sisters looking on, the coolness Christiane felt towards the Captain melted away. At last, she managed to see the kind and sensitive man beyond the cynicism and facetiousness. She no longer disliked him, though he was a long way from winning her affections.

* * *

Uncle Gottfried and Friedrich stayed overnight and in the morning joined the party to go fishing once more. Uncle Gottfried, her father and her brother selected a place further upstream. Friedrich accompanied Christiane. That was how she discovered their common interest. When they reached the stream, she handed him her tackle box and invited him to choose a fly. It was a test. Without hesitation he picked up the fly she'd used the day before. Christiane was delighted. He obviously knew his stuff and told him so. But he had another surprise for her.

'Choosing the correct fly was easy. It is all a question of season, observing the insects, size of fish and wind conditions. Besides,' he said, 'I asked your father before we left.'

Christiane laughed, pleased by his honesty when he could so easily have used the moment to try to impress her. She watched as he tied the fly to the leader and cast expertly towards the opposite bank. He retrieved and gradually lengthened his cast. As she watched a trout struck, but he missed it.

'Too much line,' he muttered and made good his error. He made his way slowly downstream, closer to where he'd seen the trout rise, and cast again. The second time the trout struck he was prepared, and set the hook. Like Christiane, he didn't rush things but let the rod do the job of tiring the fish for him. When he brought the wearying trout to the bank, Christiane netted it for him.

'What a perfect team,' he said.

Christiane was undecided whether he was hinting at an alliance that went beyond fishing. It was inappropriate if he had, but at the same time undeniably flattering. Little by little he won her trust and Christiane lowered her guard. She found she could relax with him, and allowed him to entertain her with his stories and observations. Whenever she caught a trout, he netted it for her and removed the hook. These were things that Christiane liked to do herself for they were part of the craft of fishing, but she saw it as thoughtfulness on his part, the actions of a gentleman, and didn't object. Indeed, she found she liked the attention. For the first time ever in heavy fishing clothes, she felt feminine.

With the desperation of a drowning man, her father seized

upon her growing friendship and put aside his reservations about the young Captain. He prevailed upon his brother to return with them to Dresden and made him promise to stay on for a few days.

'Just look at them, Gottfried,' he insisted, 'have you ever seen two young people so suited to each other? See how they feed off one another? I haven't seen Christiane so talkative or relaxed since she left school.'

'You play a dangerous game when you play matchmaker with your own daughter, Carl. What if Friedrich decides your daughter is not for him? He is alert to traps. There are many young ladies in Berlin who have laid traps for him, only to have him steal the bait and move on.' Gottfried laughed. 'Will you thank me, then, if Friedrich treats your daughter the same way?'

'Perhaps yes.' Carl looked intently at his brother. 'If all Friedrich does is open Christiane's eyes to other men, then I will be grateful. If that is the price I must pay to distract her from that SS oaf, then I pay it gladly. But I don't believe Friedrich is playing games. I believe he is more honourable than you give him credit for. Besides, how could he not be attracted to my daughter?'

'Okay, okay.' Gottfried raised his hands in mock resignation. 'Hitler can conquer Europe without us. At least for the next four days. And if in the meantime Friedrich conquers your daughter and vice versa, I will be the happiest man in all of Germany.'

'Second happiest,' said Carl. 'And God knows I appreciate this.'

Christiane was delighted when she learned their guests were staying on and returning with them to Dresden. The more she got to know Friedrich the more she liked him and came to appreciate his dry wit. She enjoyed his company and seemed to revel in their banter. But if Carl had thought that that was all it took to deflect a young woman from her true love and destiny, he was due for disappointment. When Friedrich invited her out to dinner with him she declined. She was reluctant to go and be seen on the arm of another man while Dietrich was away. She would not be so disloyal. She only accepted his invitation after she'd coerced her parents and Uncle Gottfried to join them. Friedrich seemed not to mind and entertained them all over dinner, though sometimes Christiane felt his comments were a little too outspoken.

'Because of my father's postings in Milan and London, I speak passable English and Italian. Therefore I know exactly where the army will send me when the war comes. They'll send me to France where no one is willing to speak German, English or Italian and no one will understand a word I say. Or, heaven forbid, they'll send me to Russia. If we go to war against Russia we'll find ourselves in real trouble. One good German soldier is worth twenty Russian soldiers. Unfortunately, there are one hundred Russian soldiers for every good German soldier. That will be the time for all of us to start learning to speak Russian.'

Friedrich and Uncle Gottfried laughed out loud, but Christiane noticed her father frown and other diners glance their way disapprovingly. Even in jest such talk was considered unpatriotic or at the very least inappropriate. Nevertheless she enjoyed the evening tremendously. And Friedrich had shown no desire to dash off at the earliest opportunity.

* * *

A month passed between Uncle Gottfried and Friedrich's departure for Berlin and the return of Dietrich Schmidt. In that time Christiane received three letters. They were all from Friedrich. When the first letter arrived she had burned with embarrassment.

'It must be from Dietrich,' she'd announced loudly, as she rushed to pick the letter up from the hall stand. But instead of vindication of her gallant knight she'd found humiliation. Friedrich had shamed her again. Of course, her family pretended not to notice her disappointment nor did they ask who the letter was from. Friedrich's name and mailing address was clearly written on the back of the envelope. Christiane was tempted to tear it up on the spot. He had no right to write to her. She'd told him all about Dietrich and left him in no doubt as to where her affections lay. But curiosity got the better of her anger, and she opened the envelope to read the contents.

'Dear Christiane,' the letter began, 'Please excuse my presumption but I felt the need to write and thank you for your hospitality, your company and for a fine morning's fishing. I enclose a lock of my hair in gratitude.' Taped to the page was a large, crudely tied fly consisting only of a hook and a tuft of the Captain's hair. Despite herself, she burst out laughing. The letter went on to describe the amount of schnapps her uncle had consumed between Dresden and Berlin while Friedrich had almost frozen solid behind the wheel. Her uncle had even put the hood down. He described the mood in Berlin following the annexation of Austria. 'The place has gone mad for Viennese coffee and waltzes,' he said. 'Let us hope the Führer does not annexe West Prussia and Galicia because I can't stand Poles or mazurkas!' Christiane could hardly contain her laughter. Her disappointment forgotten, she read the letter out loud to her family.

As he listened, Carl Schiller came to appreciate the cleverness of the young Captain. It was no love letter to be sure, but he realised immediately that its intent was the same. Here was a man of wit and humour, of style and sophistication, and he was using those attributes to mount a flanking attack. He was putting himself up as an alternative, for Christiane to make comparisons between himself and Dietrich. Carl Schiller was delighted with this discovery. As his daughter read, they could almost feel his presence. How could the Captain not come out ahead in any comparison?

His next two letters continued in the same vein, full of witty observations and self-deprecating humour. But, reading between the lines, they left Carl in no doubt that the Captain was reinforcing his initial attack, building upon his early success. He didn't come right out and say how much he wanted to see Christiane again, or how keen he was for the two of them to go fishing once more. The intent was obvious to him, but was it also obvious to Christiane? Or had she closed her mind?

* * *

Shortly after the last letter arrived, Dietrich Schmidt reappeared on their doorstep. If anything, he'd grown more handsome. The experiences of the preceding weeks seemed to have hardened him, firmed up the soft, boyish edges. Carl had to concede he'd underestimated him. His daughter threw herself into his arms, and any thoughts she may have been entertaining about Friedrich seemed to evaporate immediately.

Dietrich talked endlessly of the march into Austria, and how proud he'd felt when the Austrians had lined the streets to welcome them, waving flowers and swastikas. He told of the gifts showered on them by a grateful populace, how he'd never had to pay for so much as a coffee or a beer. But he never told her about the whores he'd had, or the Austrian Jews they'd terrorised, arrested and sent East, whose property they'd destroyed and whose valuables they'd confiscated. But his biggest mistake was to not ask Christiane how she was, how she'd been in his absence. Women who wait while their men are away like to have their loyalty and faithfulness acknowledged. Dietrich never gave her a thought.

Nevertheless, they slipped back into their earlier routine. Whenever he could, Dietrich took Christiane to the opera or theatre and occasionally the movies, before excusing himself to join his friends. Christiane tried hard, but couldn't help but feel disappointed when Dietrich failed to deliver on her expectations. She couldn't help but compare him with Friedrich.

Still, Dietrich was her beau and he, perhaps sensing some cooling on her part, gradually became more attentive. He began to call in at Prager Strasse more often and delighted her by bringing flowers. They looked ridiculously incongruous in his hands, but that only served to make the gesture more touching. Occasionally he even gave up his late night carousing with his comrades to stay with her longer. Christiane was now aware that he was not everything she hoped he'd be, but she'd invested too many dreams and aspirations in him to let him go. Besides, she still believed she loved him as he unquestionably loved her. She felt bound to him. And people continually reminded her of how good they looked together, and how lucky she was.

Once more they drifted inevitably towards the announcement that would make their subsequent marriage a formality. But again, Christiane was spared the necessity of making a decision. The racial cleansing which would result in virtually all of Dresden's Jews being murdered or sent to concentration camps intensified, and there were other more pressing demands on Dietrich's time. This presented her father with one last chance and he was determined not to let it slip by. He blamed himself for Christiane's continuing attachment to Dietrich. He'd sheltered her too much and she lacked the experience to realise that Dietrich was wrong for her. She wasn't in love with him, he was sure of that. She only thought she was in love and was role playing, doing what was expected of her. He had to act. He couldn't sit back and watch Dietrich walk off with his daughter. He rang his brother in Berlin.

Chapter Eleven

If Dietrich thought the evening would be just another dinner party in Prager Strasse to be endured rather than enjoyed, he soon realised his error. He snapped to attention the moment he realised the rank of the other officers.

'Relax, Obersturmführer,' said Uncle Gottfried dismissively, 'you are among friends here.'

'Herr Generalleutnant!' Dietrich forced himself to relax but inside he was fuming. Why hadn't Christiane warned him of their presence? This was not how he'd hoped to meet Christiane's uncle. He was unprepared and wrong-footed. What sort of impression could he hope to make now? He was torn between his aspirations and the SS disdain for regular army officers. He knew the Reichswehr had supported Hitler only as a means to get the armaments denied them by the Treaty of Versailles, and that now many senior officers would relish the opportunity to use their new weapons against him. He instinctively went on the defensive.

'You must be Dietrich. I am Friedrich Eigenwill.'

Dietrich was once more taken aback as the other officer, the Hauptmann, casually extended his hand. This wasn't how things were done. Nevertheless he shook the offered hand.

'A pleasure to meet you, Captain.'

'Yes, I'm sure it is.'

Dietrich's eyes narrowed. He didn't understand this informality and felt lost. He wasn't certain, but he thought he might just have been insulted. He decided to stand quietly by as Carl Schiller questioned the two officers over the Führer's likely response to the clamouring of the Sudeten Germans. Why were they here, and where was Christiane? He didn't have to wait long for the answer to either question.

'Dietrich!'

He turned around to see Christiane at the doorway with a tray of drinks.

'So you've met my favourite uncle, and Captain Eigenwill. They've just arrived from Berlin. They have a habit of doing that. They never tell anyone, they just arrive.' She looked for somewhere to put her tray. Friedrich stepped forward and took it from her. She went straight to Dietrich, took his arm and turned her face up for a kiss as she usually did. Dietrich hesitated, unsure, and in the end his kiss was token, as if any show of affection on his part indicated weakness. Christiane was a touch nonplussed. Weren't they among friends?

Dinner failed to live up to her expectations. She sensed Dietrich was angry but was at a loss to know why. He'd indicated often enough that he'd like to meet her uncle who served on the General Staff. Even Friedrich was more subdued than normal. It was left to Uncle Gottfried to entertain them and he did so admirably, though sometimes she felt the laughter around the table was a little forced. As they sipped their port, Friedrich asked a question that sounded innocent enough, if a touch impertinent. Christiane had no inkling of the change it signalled, and could only look on in horror and disbelief at the events that unfolded.

'So how is life in Herr Hitler's little army?'

Dietrich nearly choked on his port. If he thought he had been insulted before, he was certain he had now.

'Excuse me, Captain, are you referring to the Schutzstaffel?'

'Yes, your lot, the SS. The army our Führer has to protect himself from the army.'

Dietrich was outraged. He had to restrain himself from rising from his chair.

'Excuse me again, Captain, but I believe you are using your rank unfairly to insult my comrades.'

'Oh, am I? Then I apologise. I was just making conversation. I know what we do, we foot-soldiers of the Reich, but what do you do? What are your duties here in Dresden?'

Dietrich swallowed. This was not a subject he wished to discuss around a dinner table, nor in front of Christiane.

'It is our duty to serve the Führer,' he said, equivocating.

'And how exactly do you do that?' Now Uncle Gottfried had joined the inquisition. Christiane turned to him astonished, but saw none of the kindness and levity she normally associated with her favourite uncle. His eyes were hard, and fixed on Dietrich.

'It is our duty to root out the *Volksschädling*, those who would seek to undermine the Reich.'

'Do you include the Jews among your *Volksschädling*, Obersturmführer?' The use of Dietrich's rank by her uncle sent a chill through Christiane. This was no longer a discussion among friends.

'The Führer has been quite specific about the treachery of the Jews. It is our duty to arrest them, and confiscate the property they have stolen from the German people.'

'I believe you have carried out your duty with distinction. Your exploits have even reached us in Berlin.'

Dietrich realised the trap that had been set. The whole evening had been contrived for this moment. He knew what would follow. There was no way anyone in Berlin would know of his activities. He must have been investigated. He looked across the table at the young Captain and immediately knew why. Yes, he had been investigated.

'Perhaps you would care to relate to us all the incident with Dr Shapiro — your family physician — and his unfortunate daughter.'

'I do not believe that is necessary, Herr Generalleutnant. You have made your point. With your permission I will withdraw.' Dietrich hadn't even begun to stand when Gottfried roared at him.

'Permission refused!' He glared across the table at Dietrich, daring him to disobey. 'If you won't tell the story, then allow me.'

Coldly and clinically, Gottfried told of the humiliation of Dr Shapiro and his wife, and the cold-blooded execution of their daughter. He was well informed and spared no detail. Christiane listened aghast, daring neither to blink nor breathe as every painful word sunk home. How could Dietrich do such a thing? The girl was his childhood friend. And the same age as herself. Christiane could not help but imagine herself in the Jewish girl's place. She was also young and beautiful and full of life, and Dietrich had calmly shot her in cold blood. A wave of revulsion washed over her and she thought she was going to be sick. She composed herself with difficulty and waited until her uncle had finished. Then, in the silence that followed, she turned to the man she'd planned to marry.

'Dietrich,' she asked hesitantly, eyes pleading for a denial she knew would not be forthcoming, 'tell me it isn't true?'

Dietrich knew he'd been out-manoeuvred and soundly beaten. Yet he was determined to give these two foot-soldiers no further satisfaction. He'd done nothing to be ashamed of. On the contrary, he had acted with distinction. If Christiane saw fit to think otherwise, then so be it. He ignored her question. Instead he met Gottfried's eyes with a steely gaze of his own.

'The Jews are the enemy of the Reich. It was my duty to set an example for my troops, regardless of personal feelings.'

'Then God help us all if that is an example of what we can expect from the Schutzstaffel!' Gottfried snapped back. 'As for personal feelings, do not claim what you obviously do not have!' He glared at Dietrich but the young SS officer didn't flinch.

'The Führer has chosen us to do this work because he knows other troops have no stomach for it.'

Gottfried rose to his feet in fury, knocking his chair backwards and scattering glasses. Dietrich also stood and drew himself up to his full height so that he towered over the Generalleutnant.

'And now, with or without your permission, I will take my leave. Herr Schiller, Frau Schiller, Christiane.'

'I will do nothing to delay your leaving,' hissed Gottfried. 'Hauptmann Eigenwill! Escort the officer to the door.'

'Sir!' Friedrich snapped to attention and followed Dietrich out of the room. As they reached the front door, Dietrich suddenly whirled around and pinned him to the wall.

'Don't think I don't know why you've done this. I, at least, don't need the services of my commanding officer to procure my women. Don't imagine for one second that I will ever forget you or that pathetic old fart!' He moved his face as close to Friedrich's as he could without touching it. 'And if I were you, Captain, I would watch my every step from now on. I would sleep with the doors barred and the light on.' He paused to let his threat sink home. 'Though I suppose you do already.' He banged Friedrich against the wall one more time, then opened the front door and disappeared into the night.

Friedrich closed the door then leaned against it while he caught his breath. What would Christiane think of him now, he wondered? One thing was certain, she wouldn't thank him for the part he'd just played. But her father's plea for help had left him with no choice. Glumly, he returned to the dining room. As he expected, Christiane and her mother were no longer there but he was surprised to find Gottfried and Carl arguing bitterly. The Generalleutnant looked up as he entered.

'He just asked if I knew what happened to the rest of the Shapiro family. Dear God! Doesn't everybody know!' He turned back to his brother. 'They were sent East, Carl! They were sent East! Don't you know what that means? Where have you been these last five years?'

Friedrich spotted the decanter of Scotch which had appeared on the table and helped himself to a triple. Both Carl and Gottfried had slumped back in their chairs sipping morosely, avoiding each other's eyes. What a disaster. He closed his eyes and drained half of his whisky in a single gulp. It stung his throat but he took savage pleasure in it. He saw no reason to do otherwise. Dietrich had lost Christiane but so had he. There'd be neither understanding nor forgiveness for what he'd done. He drained his glass and reached for the bottle.

* * *

Christiane held back her tears until she'd closed her bedroom door behind her, then threw herself onto her bed and wept into her pillow. She cried as she hadn't cried since she was a child, in great wracking sobs that seemed to begin in her toes. She cried for the shattering of her dreams; for the loss of her innocence; for her gallant knight who never was. She cried not for the death of the Jewish girl but for the glimpse it gave her of her own mortality. But mostly she cried for the humiliation she had suffered — and would continue to suffer as word got around about her break-up. And she cried, too, for the hate she felt; for the betrayal by her uncle whom she'd always loved; and for the treachery of the Captain, who she'd come to like and trust. They had done this to her and she vowed never to forgive them.

* * *

On their return to Berlin, Friedrich asked for a transfer to the Panzer school at Weimar. More and more, Gottfried was being drawn into the Army High Command and Friedrich didn't want to be stuck there when war broke out. Gottfried agreed reluctantly and conditionally. He would use his contacts to get him a posting, though not at Weimar as Friedrich had requested, but in the new Panzer school in Berlin. Gottfried valued Friedrich's company and advice far too much to let him slip away entirely. Besides, he was still unconvinced of the inevitability of war.

There was another issue that also begged resolution. Carl Schiller had written to confirm the total estrangement of his daughter from Dietrich Schmidt, but also reluctantly advised that Christiane lay the blame for her heartbreak squarely at their feet. She had expressed the wish to see neither of them ever again. Her father had pleaded with her, explained the circumstances and his own involvement, yet she steadfastly refused to change her mind. There was no reasoning with her. He suggested they ceased their visits for the time being.

Gottfried knew Friedrich too well not to recognise the change that had come over him. His normal irreverent humour now gave way to cynicism or silence. He had become moody and preoccupied and Gottfried had no doubt as to the cause. But what could he do? Time, he knew, was the great healer but that was something they may not have very much more of. If Friedrich was right and Germany found itself at war, the inevitable separation would kill all hopes of reconciliation. So he resolved to keep Friedrich on hand for as long as he could. Then at least, if opportunity arose, they could take advantage of it. Besides, Gottfried adored Christiane. It pained him immensely to think that he had caused her distress, however laudable the motive. And it hurt even more to think that she no longer had a place for him in her affections. He also knew that Friedrich was the only tonic that would alleviate the pain. The issue was, how to administer it?

If Gottfried was guilty of anything, it was in underestimating his young Captain. Friedrich had not surrendered, but merely engaged in a tactical withdrawal. What Gottfried had interpreted as resignation was in fact patience. Friedrich was not the sort of man who gave in easily when the prize was so worthwhile. Certainly he was hardly in a strong position, but was it yet hopeless? He determined to find out.

He waited two months until the first autumn flurries of snow fell, then sent Christiane a letter. He didn't expect this first shot to breach the walls of her defences, but he planned further salvoes. Each letter would chip away at her resolve. Persistence was his main weapon and, in his persistence, he hoped she would see the dedication and single-mindedness of a man in love with her. Christiane was an incurable if somewhat naïve romantic, and she had enjoyed his previous correspondence. Put the two together and he was sure that one day she would find his letters irresistible and open them.

At first he wrote every week and then, despite receiving no replies, every three days. He drew some hope from the fact that her father had not written suggesting he cease the deluge. One day she would weaken, and when she did, he would give her no opportunity to deny him. But dear God, hasten the day! His training at the Panzer school demanded his full concentration and virtually every waking hour. These times weren't conducive to patience. These were times for the strong to exercise their will and reshape the world. Of what consequence were the love-sick ambitions of one young officer?

* * *

Christiane was stunned speechless when the first letter arrived. The appalling gall of the man! She'd made it quite clear that she didn't ever want to see or hear from him again. She was outraged. But not sufficiently to shred the letter into tiny, unreadable pieces fit only to feed the fire. It fed a fire all right, but one she was not yet prepared to acknowledge. She took the letter up to her room and threw it into a drawer unopened. What she ultimately intended to do with it was unclear even to herself. Her family kept a tactful silence.

As successive letters arrived, she became less and less outraged. She complained about their frequency and unwanted intrusion to her mother, and generally affected a total disinterest in them. Yet they continued to pile up unopened in her drawer. She began to anticipate their arrival, feeling cheated and let down if there was a delay. Gradually, bit by bit, Friedrich's persistence chipped away at her defences and at last tiny cracks appeared. She began to take the letters out of her drawer and handle them, as if trying to divine their contents. She arranged them in order of arrival and bound them together with ribbon. One Sunday morning as she lay in bed, discouraged from getting up by the chill in her room and the incessant rain beating on her window, she decided to open them.

* * *

Friedrich and Christiane were married on the first Saturday of December 1938, one year to the day since they'd first met at Little Pillnitz. Following the legal ceremony at the Registrar's Office, they exchanged vows in the eighteenth century, Protestant cathedral of St Peter, the Frauenkirche. Friedrich's parents travelled up from Milan for the occasion. Gottfried, newly reinstated to the position of favourite uncle, stood as best man alongside Friedrich beneath the cathedral's massive dome. Not even the solemnity of the old stone building could suppress the joy of those who attended. When invited to kiss the bride, Friedrich did not hold back yet was still upstaged by Gottfried. The love Gottfried felt for his niece and the anguish he'd suffered at his near loss finally found release. He hugged her and held her until people began to wonder exactly who had married whom.

Was Christiane happy? Was any woman ever happier? She

was so in love just thinking about it reduced her to tears. She couldn't imagine what she'd ever seen in Dietrich Schmidt, and was horrified to think she'd considered marrying him. Light, laughter and vitality flooded back into her life. They were the perfect couple, the perfect match, indestructible and immortal. She could not conceive of anything that could spoil their perfection. On her horizons at least, there were no clouds.

After all the ceremonies, the newly-weds retreated to Little Pillnitz for Friedrich's three remaining days of leave. Perhaps Christiane would have preferred somewhere more exotic for their honeymoon, but she had no regrets. The cold north-east winds sweeping down from the Russian steppes kept them tucked up in bed for warmth or snuggled up together in front of the fire, so that the three days they had together were spent together, as close as any two people could be. They rode a wave of happiness and, if Christiane felt immortal, she was only reflecting the mood of the German people.

They, too, rode a wave, one of new-found confidence and pride. The Führer's armaments drive had meant full employment, and relief from the hopelessness of the depression, the burden of reparations, and the humiliations of the Treaty of Versailles. Hitler had also shown what strength of purpose and belief in the superiority of the German race could achieve. The annexation of Austria was proof of that. The creation of *Grosswirtschaftsraum*, the economically self-sufficient unification of all German-speaking people, was no longer a dream but a realistic objective.

Friedrich, however, was not infected by the nationalistic fervour. He did his best to shut his concerns from his mind. But in the lonely hours at night, with his new wife curled against him for warmth, he wondered what the future held. How would Britain and France react if Hitler decided to march on from the Sudetenland into Bohemia and Moravia? Would they stand passively by? And if so, what next? Would they also allow Hitler to march into Poland? There'd be another war, of that he had no doubt. What would happen to them then? What would happen to his lovely new wife?

He felt a chill course through his body which had nothing to do with the icy winds outside, or the snow piling up against the side of the house.

* * *

'What's this?' demanded Gancio. 'Another break for coffee? How come you want two coffee breaks? One has always been good enough in the past. Maria! They want more coffee!'

'No, not another coffee break,' said Lucio wearily. 'That is all for today. I'm not used to telling this sort of story. I had no idea it could be so tiring.'

'You've done well, Lucio.' Ramon reached over and patted his friend's arm. 'You've given us enough to think about.'

'Where did you get all this "Obersturmführer" and "Schutzstaffel" stuff from, Lucio? I haven't heard so many double-bunger words before in my life.'

'Italy was an occupied country, Neil. As a child, you played cowboys and Indians and cops and robbers. We played partisans and Nazis. We knew every rank of the Wehrmacht and the SS. Our bad guys were the Waffen-SS and the Allgemeine-SS, especially the Gestapo. We shot more Germans after the war than during it.'

'There! You're doing it again,' said Neil plaintively. 'What the hell's the Allgemeine-SS?'

'Thought police,' cut in Milos. 'If they thought they didn't like you they arrested you, no?'

'That's right.' Lucio laughed at the distraction. 'Allgemeine-SS were in charge of police and racial matters. They did a lot of tracking down of Jews. They were also in charge of foreign and domestic intelligence and espionage. The Gestapo was part of their most important division, the Reichssicherheitshauptampt.'

Ramon laughed. 'Try saying that, Neil, when you're full of grappa!'

'Give me a break. But where did Dietrich fit in? What division was he with?'

'He was with the Waffen-SS. They were Hitler's personal

bodyguard. They ran the concentration camps, and one corps, the Verfügungstruppe, served alongside regular troops.'

'Verfügungstruppe, eh? Lucio do me a favour. Can we have next week's instalment in English?'

The friends broke into easy banter as they waited for their coffee. But Milos looked across at Ramon wondering if he was thinking the same thing. Lucio's knowledge was more than the stuff acquired in playgrounds. It smacked of research and, if so, what did that signify? Neil's cynical observation at the start of lunch may have been closer to the truth than they'd given him credit for. Very interesting.

THIRD THURSDAY

Lucio deliberately contrived to be last to arrive. He knew his friends would expect a continuation of Cecilia and Colombina's story, and he wouldn't disappoint them. But he didn't want to be pumped for a preview. Their enthusiasm for a good story made them greedy and it was a greed he shared. It helped build a sense of expectation. Normally he'd happily titillate them with sneaky glimpses of the tales he was about to tell. But those stories were plainly contrivances, light entertainment, like bringing on the clowns between the more serious acts. The truth was, if he was going to pull this story off, he had to keep his ambition within the bounds of his ability. He'd planned exactly how far he wanted to go with the day's episode and he didn't want to be pushed into going any further. That could upset his timing and he didn't want to arouse suspicions unnecessarily by stalling later on. His story was developing its own pace as every story does. It meant he could plan ahead more accurately but, equally, any variation tended to put an alert audience on its guard. That was the last thing he needed.

He looked across to the table as soon as he entered the restaurant. As if cued, Milos began to rise to his feet. The affectation always made him smile. Milos had arrived from Hungary without two pennies to rub together and made his money by disposing of other people's rubbish. It was a hard and competitive business where street cunning was more important than nice manners. His old world courtesies were undoubtedly a recent addition to his repertoire.

'Sorry I'm late.' He greeted each of his friends in turn.

'Before you ask,' said Neil, 'Gancio is joining us later. Same rules as last week. In your absence, we questioned him extensively but he emphatically denies any collusion with you. Furthermore, he regrets that you're Italian, pisses on your grandmother's grave and admits that the only thing that stops him throwing you out of his restaurant is your friendship with us, whom he likes and respects enormously.'

'Thank you, Neil,' said Lucio evenly. 'It is good to see that he has stuck to the script.'

'I think you went too far when you said Gancio respects us enormously. It was enough that he likes us, no?' Milos turned to Lucio for confirmation.

'Correct, but not entirely. Gancio likes some of you. I happen to know that Gancio commits indecent acts upon the veal he serves Neil. I can prove this. Notice how Neil is always the first to comment on its tenderness?' Lucio gave Neil his most arch smile. 'By the way, what are we having for lunch?'

'Vegetarian *antipasto*, seafood soup, and quail. Now, where are you taking us today?'

'Back to Italy.'

'Thank God,' said Neil. 'I don't speak any Italian but it's a bloody sight better than my German.'

'And Colombina?'

'Yes, Ramon, I will tell you more about Colombina. And now I must invoke our convention. I refuse to tell you any more until we have eaten our lunch. Any objections?'

There were none, nor did Lucio expect any. The whole tone of conversation seemed contrived to put him at ease. They knew he was treading on unfamiliar ground and were making things as easy for him as they could. But it was a honeymoon that wouldn't last. As the story developed and they adopted their positions, the questions would come. There'd be no going easy then.

Chapter Twelve

True to her word, Colombina prepared another German meal for Heinrich Bose the following Sunday. She did all the preparation at home and all the cooking in his little kitchen. This time she chose something a little kinder to his stomach, something more compatible with the bland food which for years had been his diet. Heinrich had loved the *Blumenkohlsuppe* and the *Rouladen*, but he'd paid a heavy price for his pleasure. Indigestion had kept him awake all night and the unaccustomed richness had kept him running to the toilet. He hadn't complained. Quite the contrary. In explaining Colombina's unexpected generosity to a stunned John and Edna, he'd not only described every dish in great detail but also the aftermath claiming that, had he known what the effect would be, he still wouldn't have missed a single mouthful.

Colombina learned all this from John and Edna who, while praising her Christian compassion and charity, made it quite clear that they resented her intrusion upon what they regarded as their people and their territory.

'At least now the old bugger has something to look forward to each week,' Colombina had replied, shocking them with her language and her intention to continue her visits. John and Edna had marched off in a huff, their decency affronted and their faint trust in their fellow workers clearly vindicated.

But Colombina knew she was the real loser. She hadn't thought things through clearly enough. In hindsight, John and Edna's reaction was quite predictable, as predictable in fact as their future actions, should misfortune befall the old man. If there was the slightest suspicion about the manner of the Oberstleutnant's death, Colombina knew who would be first to point the finger and at whom it would be pointed. It was a complication she didn't need, but it didn't change anything. Still she'd learned something of value. Heinrich Bose might put up with indigestion and diarrhoea one Sunday, but nobody would put up with it Sunday after Sunday. Where would she be then, if he decided he didn't want her meals any more? No, she had to win his trust and put herself beyond anyone's suspicion before she acted, and that could take many Sunday lunches.

So Colombina flicked through her German cookbook until she found a dish from Hamburg which was both light and flavoursome. She bought two salmon steaks to bake in dry white wine and vermouth. The only tricky part would be blending in a *crème fraîche*, made the night before, with the juices from the baking tray. She decided to serve the salmon with julienned carrot, celery, beetroot and leeks. She'd begin with a carrot soup and conclude with simmered red berries and custard. Provided she kept the serves relatively small she felt Heinrich would have no problems digesting the meal.

When Heinrich answered the door, it was clear he'd dressed for the occasion. He wore a tie, and what hair he had left was plastered to his scalp. His excitement was obvious and he'd waited like a small boy promised a bike for his birthday. While Colombina prepared their lunch he chose the music. His collection of classical and opera records occupied three shelves that ran the width of the room. Books on opera and biographies of its better known performers occupied another two. His taste in music hadn't changed in the slightest.

While Colombina cooked and while they ate, she set about establishing the pattern for subsequent visits so that she could win his confidence and make him drop his guard. Whenever she could, she talked food — different food and different methods of preparation. She didn't want to discuss her past and asked no questions about his. They discussed opera at length, books, the weather, and the European soccer. Occasionally, Heinrich would reminisce and describe a particular dish and the places he'd enjoyed it. Colombina had to work hard to suppress a smile. It seemed there wasn't a single Saxon dish that couldn't be made to perfection in Switzerland. He even made it sound as if *Streuselkuchen* and *Bienenstich*, the sweet Saxonian yeast dough cakes, were Swiss creations. Colombina had heard these dishes described before and even helped the Oberstleutnant prepare some of them, a long time ago in another country, in another lifetime.

As the Sundays came and went she gradually succeeded in her first objective. He relaxed and seemed to trust her. The aging processes slowed and appeared to reverse. A younger man would have been accused of having fallen in love, for he exhibited all the signs. Perhaps he had fallen in love. Colombina made it easy for people to love her. Now all she had to do was figure out a safe way to kill him.

* * *

Colombina was no stranger to sudden and violent death. She had been instrumental in the deaths of many men, some no more than boys. She had witnessed its randomness, its suddenness and also its cruel, lingering slowness. But that is the price war exacts on all who engage in it, and those who survive it best learn to harden their heart and disassociate. Like doctors and undertakers.

Colombina only had to look at the old, faded photograph of her mother she kept in her locket to find the bitter, hard part within her and make herself immune to the charms of the likeable old man. She coldly considered her options. The Oberstleutnant had a gas heater and a gas cooker. It would be the easiest thing in the world to leave the gas cooker on, knowing that he always fell asleep in his chair after she left him. By the time the leaking gas found its way to the pilot light on his heater, there would be enough to blow the house apart. Gas was a definite possibility. Then there was the flex on the electric kettle. It was so worn it looked like it may also have been in service during the Second World War. It would be easy enough to contrive a short. The carpet was also worn in places, badly enough to catch a shoe and trip its occupant. Yet the Oberstleutnant seemed to have a sixth sense in negotiating these patches. She would have to trip him herself and somehow ensure the fall was fatal. Nonetheless, a definite option. Colombina realised killing the Oberstleutnant would present no real difficulty, provided she did her homework and her planning thoroughly.

But there was one major problem. The Oberstleutnant would be dead before he realised she was killing him, and consequently would have no idea why. What kind of justice was that? It is always the sentence of death and the waiting that causes the most agony, rather than the event itself which is over in an instant. The Oberstleutnant had to be made to face up to his past, to his crime, and he had to be made to face the certainty of his death just as his victims had. He had to know fear. And remorse. He had to suffer. Yes! Remorse. Horror. Terror. Guilt. Fear. Fear of death. Fear of eternal damnation. Yes! He had to suffer first. The swift sword of retribution would be too kind, a denial of justice.

Perhaps the way to a man's stomach might also be the way of his death? Colombina began to consider poisons. She'd heard that the juices from one squeeze of an oyster that had been buried for a week would kill anyone, but it might also raise awkward questions as to how the old man came to ingest them. Given that the bulk of his meals were provided by Meals-on-Wheels, there'd probably be an inquiry to protect the other recipients of the service. Colombina had no doubt where such an inquiry would lead. John and Edna would see to that. Perhaps shellfish gathered around an outfall mixed with others bought from a fish shop? Yes, this had possibilities. Rampaging salmonella and very probably rampaging hepatitis. If by some miracle he survived the first, he would never survive the second. But there was no guarantee that the shellfish would carry the bacteria and, even if they did, she would be left exposed. She would have time to inform the Oberstleutnant of his fate but, equally, he would have the opportunity to inform on his murderer. She needed something that would kill in minutes not in hours or days. He didn't need to suffer long, just long enough. Long enough to know why.

The cooking of Saxony tends to be homely and hearty with an emphasis on meat. While pork and ham tend to dominate, from ancient times Saxons have shared the German passion for hunting, and the spoils of the hunt are welcome supplements to their diet. Heinrich Bose was no exception and one Sunday he regaled Colombina with descriptions of meals he'd enjoyed. Roast saddle of venison with red wine sauce, braised hare, and pheasant with giblet stuffing. Colombina thought no more about it until, one day looking through her German cookbook for inspiration, she came across a recipe for hare. She wondered if she could make the same dish with rabbit. And as she thought about rabbits, it occurred to her that she may have stumbled upon the perfect way to kill the Oberstleutnant.

She remembered the tales her late husband had told of his first days in Australia, working on the farm. He'd always kept in touch with the Dwyer family who'd fed and sheltered him. Mario had sent them a card every Christmas with a note inside, and occasionally they'd driven south to stay with them over a weekend. When Charlie Dwyer had died at the age of eighty-one they'd attended his funeral. Even then, they'd not lost touch and had sent Christmas cards to his son. After Mario's death, she'd continued the practice and now she wondered if her relationship with the Dwyers was strong enough for her to impose upon them. Above all, she hoped the rabbit problem was still as severe as it had been, and their method of dealing with it unchanged. Yes, she had found the perfect way to exact retribution on the Oberstleutnant, if only she could acquire the means.

Domestic rabbits were first brought to Australia from Britain as a food source for the starving colonials. But it wasn't until the introduction of twelve wild rabbits at Barwon Park, near Geelong in Victoria, that the devastating spread of rabbits began in earnest. With few natural enemies to control their numbers and an abundance of fodder, they spread north and west. Within twenty years they'd spread into South Australia and New South Wales. More and more rabbits were liberated independently ahead of settlers, to provide food for them as they pushed deeper into the hinterland. Within thirty years, the threat they posed to agriculture and the land degradation they caused was recognised, but it was all far too late. In the area around Cowra where Mario Galli served out the war shearing sheep, sinking posts and baling hay, rabbit pairs were producing an average of twenty-five kittens a year, more than any other region in Australia.

Mario had often spoken of the time when drought had hit the south-west and it was commonplace to see a furry ring of rabbits four and five deep around the dams, all desperate for a drink. Even when their mortal enemies, wedge-tailed eagles, joined them at the waterholes, they didn't scatter in panic. This had surprised Mario until he noticed the birds' swollen bellies. They'd already gorged themselves on rabbits too weak to make it to the dam.

Mario helped the Dwyer family control the pests by plough-ing in and digging out burrows, but their hard work gained them little more than breathing space. Breeding female rab-bits can dig up to thirty metres of burrow in a single night. Those which escaped the assault on their homes, soon estab-lished others. It was clear the farmers needed to take more drastic measures, and to do this they set up a regular and systematic routine of poisoning. At the time, three poisons were in wide use; strychnine, arsenic and sodium cyanide. Of the three, the Dwyers chose sodium cyanide.

They mixed the crystals in with dough made from pollard, bran and molasses and spread it around the warrens. Mario hated the necessity of killing rabbits in this way because the poison was anything but selective. Over the following days they also found the carcasses of kangaroos, wallabies, goan-nas and native birds alongside the dead rabbits.

'Sodium cyanide kills everything that eats it,' he used to complain. 'One pinch will even kill a grown man in five to ten minutes. Imagine that.'

Colombina couldn't imagine anything more ideal, though obviously she needed to find out a lot more about the poison and its dosage. But first she had other duties to perform — her Thursday stint with Meals-on-Wheels. She curbed her excitement, picked up her friend Ann, and set about deliv-ering meals in her normal calm manner. Anyone privy to her inner thoughts might have found irony in this latterday Lucretia Borgia handing out meals, but it eluded Colombina. The following day she drove to the library and learned all she needed to know. Two to three hundred milligrams would kill an adult in five to fifteen minutes by interfering with the body's oxidative processes. But she would have to disguise the bitter almond smell and whatever taste it had in a suitably spicy dish. The books informed her that twenty to forty per cent of the population were genetically incapable of smelling hydrocyanic acid or its salts, but she wasn't prepared to take any chances. Every time she'd taken the old man a meal, he'd delighted in smelling it, enjoying the odours and the meal they foreshadowed. Whatever other failings he had, there didn't appear to be anything genetically wrong with his nose.

But therein lay the problem with sodium cyanide. Technicians in the Coroner's Court were tested and excluded if they were among those who were incapable of detecting the bitter almond odour. So the chances of the agent of the Oberstleutnant's death going undetected were remote. Unless ... unless she could muddy the water and obscure the real cause of death behind another which was more apparent. In his weakened state, she could drag him to the bath, undress him and drown him. If there was an autopsy, would busy technicians then look beyond the obvious, particularly when they considered the age of the deceased? Or could she contrive to make it look like a suicide?

Suddenly the task of killing the Oberstleutnant no longer seemed as simple as Colombina had imagined it would be. Perhaps she would be better off if she simply confronted him with her knowledge and provoked him so that she would be forced to defend herself. He'd know then that he was about to die and he'd know why. Of course he'd panic and he'd fall, and in falling he'd suffer a fatal injury. Again, she would see to that. But Colombina had never actually killed anyone before, not with her own hands. When the time came, she wondered, could she hate him enough?

She decided to keep her options open while she formulated her plan. For the first time she felt sickened by what she had to do. She opened the locket she wore around her neck, removed the picture of her late husband and looked at her mother's faded image beneath it. The eyes that had stared apprehensively into the lens of the camera all those years ago now seemed to stare back at her, and bore with them a reminder of all the misery and suffering the poor woman had endured. Colombina could have rescued her, brought her to Australia and given her a taste of a life that had been denied her. She thought of her mother growing old gracefully and peacefully in the little cottage on Pittwater, surrounded by water, flowers and birds more beautiful than any Maddalena had ever imagined. She thought of all the things her mother had deserved which the Oberstleutnant had denied her. That place within her that neither her late husband nor any of her friends had ever suspected existed, grew harder and more resolute.

Perhaps if she had not lost her ability to cry; or discovered the comfort of confiding in a friend and sharing her burden; if she had found and accepted any such pressure valve for her emotions, she could have put the past and all its burdens behind her. But life is not fair. It wasn't fair to her mother and it had not been fair to her. Both were victims, prisoners of events over which they'd had no control. She returned the photograph of her husband to its rightful place and snapped the locket shut.

That evening she wrote to the Dwyers expressing a need to get away from Sydney for a while, and her desire to revisit the farm where her late husband had been so happy. How could they refuse?

Chapter Thirteen

Cecilia adapted well to life at the Villa Carosio. While others might have complained at the regime she was obliged to follow, Cecilia accepted it with enthusiasm. The hours were long but no longer than they had been when she'd lived at home, and the work was nowhere near as hard. At the beginning the cook, Signora Fiorella, had ordered Cecilia to scrub all the benchtops and shelves, and wash the kitchen walls. Clearly it was just the cook's way of letting Cecilia know who was boss, for the kitchen was already spotless. Nevertheless, Cecilia had set to work with a will, knowing full well that it wasn't so much the job but the manner in which she carried it out that was important. The cook had grudgingly accepted that Cecilia wasn't just 'another good-for-nothing, lazy village girl' and allowed her to get on with the work she'd been assigned. But there was one part of her routine from which she was excused. Every evening, instead of helping to clean the kitchen, she joined the Count at the long table and read to him over dinner.

Cecilia had much to be grateful for. Her life had changed substantially for the better and she had no hesitation in expressing her gratitude to the Holy Mother when she attended church each Sunday. But along with her thanks came an urgent plea for the well-being of her mother. Cecilia had not set eyes on Maddalena since she'd glimpsed the tired, retreating figure through her bedroom window the day she'd arrived at the Villa Carosio. Nor had she heard word from her. Cecilia's problem was threefold. She no longer attended the local church in Ravello where she could expect to see her mother every Sunday. Instead, the entire staff were driven down to the Sanctuary of the Madonna of Peace in Menaggio in which the Count's family had worshipped for centuries. Furthermore, Signora Mila had forbidden her to talk to boys and the edict had included her brothers. That left her sisters, but only Paola was old enough to get any sense out of or to entrust with a message. But that course was denied her as well. Her brothers had forbidden Paola to speak to her on pain of death, or at least a savage beating.

Alfredo and Elio had accepted that their father was a hero after all, and would not allow anything to reflect badly on his — or their — newfound status. Therefore Cecilia had to bear the blame for the events that had led to her being thrown out of their home. Cecilia was their shame and their shame had been cast out. She was no longer their sister. Her name no longer had a place on their lips. She was no longer an Ortelli and would not be recognised by them.

Cecilia had been brought up to love her brothers and sisters as much as she loved her parents, and she struggled to come to terms with the fact that they'd shut her out of their lives. She'd felt as every child in a close family does; that her family wasn't simply a group of individuals but a single functioning unit of which she was an integral part, inseparable from and mutually dependent upon the rest. It hurt and bewildered her to learn otherwise. Fortunately for her, much of the pain was dissipated by the distraction of adapting to her new life, otherwise the loss would have been unendurable. Besides, she knew in her heart that her mother would never abandon her and she drew strength from that. But it also begged a question. Hadn't she abandoned her mother?

She thought of using a go-between but was no longer sure who she could trust. Children are very quick to pick up on a change in status or a fall from grace of one of their number, and her brothers had left no one in doubt that she'd been thrown out for an unspecified but indescribably shameful deed. Her school friends speculated wildly upon what that deed might have been and distanced themselves from her. In the normal course of events, things like this are soon forgotten, usurped by some other juicy scandal or gossip. But Cecilia compounded the problem by turning up at school in Carmela's cast-offs. Instantly she ceased to be one of them, the division as clear as it always has been between the haves and the have-nots, between privilege and poverty. Her friends were envious of her fine clothes and good fortune, but their envy was entwined with a sense of betrayal. Her clothes shamed them and she had put herself above them. Who would be her friend now, who could she trust?

One day she saw her opportunity and took it. As she sat alone waiting for classes to begin, she noticed a girl who had once shared her desk and been her friend, arrive through the school gates. Instead of joining the others for a last, frantic few moments of play and gossip, she slunk away to a corner of the playground where she could sit quietly by herself. There was something in the way she walked and slowly sat down that Cecilia couldn't help but recognise. As if to confirm her suspicions, the girl's chin slumped down on her chest and, even from a distance, Cecilia could see that she was crying.

Cecilia raced through her morning lessons, completing her work early so that she could write a note to her mother. She folded it and put it in her pocket. Now all she had to do was wait for her class's turn to gather in the courtyard outside for exercises. Daily exercise was another of Benito Mussolini's gifts to the school children of Italy. Perhaps he envisioned a super race of Italians in the same way Hitler dreamed of his Aryan master race, or perhaps it was just another act of kindness for which he was well known. Whatever his motive, the boys of the *Balilla* and the girls of the *Piccola Italiana* and *Giovane Italiana* welcomed the break from the mysteries of mathematics and the opportunity to stretch their limbs. Frequently the teachers were somewhat less enthusiastic and, in the time between the first blow of the whistle and the marshalling of their charges, there was often a period of anarchy. This was the moment Cecilia waited for. She held back as the whistle blew and the first wave of students charged towards the doorway and temporary freedom. She sidled unobtrusively up to her target.

'Giuseppina,' she said softly.

The girl looked up at her, her face swollen and puffy, desperation in her eyes.

'Giuseppina,' she said again, 'I can tell them that you fell over getting up from your desk and that you've hurt your knee. I'll tell them that you are unable to do the exercises. I'll tell them I bumped into you. They'll believe me because they have no reason not to.'

'Cecilia, I . . .'

'Don't say anything. I'll tell you a secret. My father used to beat me, too.' It was a lie, but sometimes lies are told out of kindness. Tears of gratitude and relief flooded Giuseppina's eyes. The last thing the battered child needed was to leap around an exercise yard.

'Oh . . . there's one thing you can do for me. There's no hurry. When you feel up to it, would you give this note to my sister Paola and tell her to read it to my mother when they are alone. Don't let anyone see you. Okay?'

Giuseppina took the note and nodded, grateful for the chance to return a favour.

'When you feel up to it. There's no hurry. You rest now.' She left Giuseppina and went to find her teachers, convinced that Giuseppina would pass on her note at the very first opportunity, and that at last she'd found a conduit to her mother.

*   *   *

That afternoon there was a change in Cecilia's routine. She didn't realise it at the time but it set a pattern that was to govern her next few years at the Villa Carosio. She'd barely changed from her school clothes into her uniform when Signora Mila sent for her. When she saw the Signora's face she wondered immediately what she'd done wrong.

'Cecilia, the Count is unwell. He would like you to read to him. Here are some papers from Milan and Rome, and some books he asked for.' The Signora paused and took a deep breath. 'I have asked Stefano to set up a chair by the Count's bed. When you read to him you will sit in the chair. Stefano has also set up a table and a lamp beside the chair so you have light to read by. Are you listening to me, Cecilia?'

'Yes, Signora. Stefano has placed a chair by the Count's bed and I am to sit in it while I read to him.' The instruction was so simple Cecilia had no idea why the Signora wished her to repeat it. Or why her tone of voice was so brusque.

'Very good, Cecilia. Begin by reading the newspapers. Perhaps you can find some reason to discuss our beloved Duce.' There was something in the way the Signora said the word 'beloved' which suggested the Duce was not necessarily beloved by her. Cecilia was confused. 'Oh, one more thing, it would be a good idea to impress upon the Count that you have lots of homework to do tonight.'

'No, Signora, I have no homework.'

'Cecilia, I asked you before, are you listening to me?'

'Yes, Signora. I must impress upon the Count that I have a lot of homework to complete tonight.'

The Signora stared steadily at Cecilia. If anything, her attitude had grown harder and Cecilia was at a loss to know why. Perhaps she was jealous that the Count was showing a preference for her over her daughter, Carmela. Perhaps she wanted her daughter to read to the Count. But Carmela struggled with her reading and read in a flat monotone. Who would want to listen to that?

'Go now, Cecilia, and remember what I told you. Oh ... and report to me afterwards.'

'Yes, Signora.' Cecilia gathered up the newspapers and books and headed for the Count's bedroom. She knew it intimately. She'd helped Anna change the bed linen many times and scrubbed the huge enamelled bath more often than she cared to think about. This was the first time she'd been allowed to enter the Count's chambers while he occupied them, but what difference did that make? Why all the fuss? She knocked gently on the Count's door and waited, uncertain whether to enter or not. To her surprise the door opened and it was Signor Calosci not the Count who opened it. He beckoned her in.

'Good afternoon, Signor Calosci,' she said politely, fully expecting him to smile in reply. But there was no smile. He wouldn't meet her look. He as good as ignored her.

'Ah ... my little angel is here! Come in Cecilia and sit down.'

But for the fact that his eyes were more watery and his breathing more laboured, Cecilia thought that the Count looked much the same as usual. She curtsied as was her custom.

'Good afternoon, Count d'Alatri, I'm sorry to hear you are unwell.'

'Oh, it's nothing child, just the burden of age. Come sit down. Stefano has made a little throne for you to sit upon.'

Cecilia looked at the enormous maroon and gilt chair beside the bed. She recognised it as belonging to one of the reception rooms below. It was a mystery to Cecilia why Signora Mila had seen fit to have this chair carted up the stairs when there were other perfectly suitable chairs in the Count's room. Nevertheless she sat upon it as instructed and nearly disappeared in its depths.

'Thank you, Signor Calosci, that will be all.' The Count dismissed his servant and waited until he'd left the room and closed the door behind him. 'Now Cecilia, where are you? I can't see you!'

If Signora Mila's intention was to put as much distance between Cecilia and the Count then her good intentions were about to backfire.

'Cecilia, that chair is ridiculous! I like to see people when I'm talking to them. I want to see you when you're reading to me. Otherwise I may just as well be listening to the radio. Come child! Sit here.'

Cecilia didn't argue, not that she had any choice in the matter. But it was plainly foolish to remain in the big antique chair where neither she nor the Count could see each other. So she slid off the chair and climbed up onto the edge of his bed.

'Not there. Here. Closer so I don't have to strain to hear you. That's it, good girl.' He patted her thigh. 'Now what have you brought me?'

'The newspapers and some books.' Cecilia remembered what the Signora had said to her. 'If you like, I will read the newspapers to you. We'll find out what our beloved Duce is doing.'

'No. I am tired of the news. I know exactly what Il Duce is doing. The radio is full of it. Read one of the books to me instead. Let me see . . . yes . . . read to me from this book.' He skimmed through the pages. 'Here. Begin reading here.'

Cecilia took the book from the Count and began to read. She could hardly believe the passage the Count had given her. It described things the boys at school wouldn't dare whisper about, even at their most wicked. She hesitated.

'Go on.' The Count stared at her intently. Cecilia was aware of a tension in his voice and eyes that wasn't there before. She felt sickened. She hadn't been raised to read filth like this. This wasn't why her mother had encouraged her to read.

'Go on! Read! Do as I say!' His temper flared and his moustache quivered.

She began to read once more. She was startled and frightened, yet still desperate to please. Her hands trembled and made it difficult for her eyes to follow the lines. She faltered and stumbled over words but the Count didn't seem to mind. She knew she was reading poorly and for that there was no excuse. In a situation she didn't understand, she fell back on her training, and exercised the control that came from deep within her. She concentrated on her breathing and keeping her voice steady. The subject no longer mattered as she concentrated less on the words and more on the manner of their delivery. But she didn't look up from the page as she'd trained herself to do to maintain contact with her audience. She couldn't bear to. She couldn't bear to look into that strained and sweat-beaded face. She could hear his breathing becoming more shallow and rapid. She could feel his eyes upon her and knew he hung on to her every word. She read them as they were intended to be read, doing full justice to both meaning and context. But it was the actor in her who was reading, not her. She retreated into her craft, closed her mind off and took in nothing of what she read. She concentrated so hard she wasn't aware when the Count first began to stroke her back and shoulders, slowly and rhythmically, as a father might to a sick child. But he was not her father nor were his interests paternal. And Cecilia now understood why the Count had overruled Signora Mila and allowed her to join his household.

* * *

As soon as she left the Count, Cecilia ran to her room. She wanted to throw herself on her bed and cry her eyes out. But it was not to be. As soon as she opened the door to her room she saw Anna. She closed the door quickly. She wasn't ready yet to share her shame with anyone. She turned away down the corridor, but where could she go? Then she remembered Signora Mila's instructions. Had she known what would happen? Of course, that was why she'd had the big chair moved in for her to sit on. Tears of relief began to well in her eyes. She wasn't alone. She wanted her mother but Signora Mila loomed as a welcome substitute. She set off in search of her and found her in the kitchen reprimanding Stefano, battering and humiliating him with a seemingly endless stream of insults. Cecilia hesitated, wondering what he had done this time to incur the Signora's wrath. Everyone other than the cook had found work to do as far away from the Signora as possible. They knew when it was prudent to duck for cover. Stefano looked up and saw Cecilia standing in the doorway. He'd heard the rumours and knew an escape route when he saw one.

'Signora . . .'

The Signora paused and caught his glance. She turned around and saw Cecilia. One glance was enough to change her priorities.

'Ah, Cecilia. Stefano, I will finish with you later. Cecilia come with me to my office.' Cecilia followed the Signora down the hallway to the little room she called her office. The Signora closed the door behind them.

'*Merda! Cretino!* That cretin Stefano will be the death of me!'

Cecilia was shocked. She'd never heard the Signora swear before nor ever expected to. And certainly not over Stefano. The Signora put her elbows on the little table she used as her desk, and cupped her head in her hands. Cecilia thought of her mother. She'd often seen her worn out and world weary like this.

'Cecilia let me tell you some things, though by now I'm sure you will have guessed. The Count, as you are aware, has a wife, though they have not lived together for more than twenty years. They have no children. There have been all sorts of rumours as to why they split up, but they are all gossip and best dismissed. But it is a fact that the Count has certain preferences. It has been rumoured that his preferences have even extended to young boys, but I have no evidence for this and I have lived in this house most of my life. Cecilia, now you know the truth about the Count's interest in you and why I didn't want you to come here. Now, tell me what he did to you. Are you all right?'

'Yes, I am all right.'

'Tell me what he did to you.'

'He made me promise not to tell anyone.'

'Of course he would.'

'He said he'd throw me out onto the streets if I told anyone.'

The Signora grimaced. 'Look at me, Cecilia. You must understand the way things are. He is rich and powerful and we are nothing. If not for the Count everyone of us here would be out on the streets. That disgusting old man upstairs knows this. Cecilia, this is a lovely house and we have beautiful clothes to wear and nice food to eat. But life here can be unbearable if you don't have someone to share your troubles with. You can share your troubles with me. I will tell nobody, God as my witness. But I can't help you unless you tell me everything. You can pretend I am your mother. Don't you think your mother would like me to look after you while you are here?'

'Yes, Signora.'

'So, Cecilia, tell me. Did he touch you?'

Cecilia bowed her head under the weight of the shameful admission.

'Did he make you take off your clothes?'

'Yes.' Her reply was barely audible.

'Did he touch you between your legs?'

Cecilia nodded. She screwed up her eyes, determined not to cry.

'Did he put his thing there?'

'No.'

'Did he make you touch his thing?'

'Yes.'

'Just with your hand?'

'Yes.'

'Did anything happen?'

'No.'

'So at least we have his age to be grateful for. Did he do anything else?'

'He said things to me.'

'What sort of things?'

'Awful things, disgusting things. Like the book he asked me to read.'

'Dear Cecilia . . .' The Signora's voice softened and she put her arms around the distressed child. 'You poor child. What are we going to do?'

'I hate him!'

'Yes, apart from Signor Calosci and Andre he doesn't have many friends here. But that doesn't answer the question. What are we going to do? You can either remain or leave. If you decide to remain here you now know what to expect. There's not much I can do to help you. But I want you to know you can always turn to me as one woman to another. Do you understand me, Cecilia? As one woman to another?'

'Yes, Signora. Thank you.'

'Oh, don't thank me, Cecilia.' The Signora let go of her and turned away, clearly distressed. 'I should send you away from here now! But where can I send you? Where can you go? Your father won't take you back. And if I dismiss you, what will happen to me? And Carmela? This is the only life I know. My parents passed this job onto my husband Guido and I when my father became sick and they went back to Varese. My family have looked after the Villa Carosio for more than sixty years. God knows I wish my husband Guido was here. He wouldn't stand for this. I curse the Villa Carosio!' She bit her lips as if regretting her outburst, and used her sleeve to wipe away her bitter tears. Cecilia decided to do nothing. A servant does not presume to show sympathy for her superiors and she wasn't convinced that the 'one woman to another' protocol was yet in place.

'Lord knows it has been hard enough keeping that dirty old man's hands off Carmela. Now there are two of you. I suppose I should be glad you are here for her sake, but I'm not. I think my husband would kill the Count if he interfered with her, and I think the Count knows that. But what use is he to us in the army? The Count insisted he join. Ordered him to join as an example to the village. Mussolini had just invaded Ethiopia and in a fit of patriotic fervour that *stronzo*, that shit upstairs, sent my husband to join them. "Don't worry," he says, "I will give him the highest recommendation." We thought Guido would become a chauffeur for a General, but the Count's fine recommendation got him a seat in a tank instead as a machine-gunner. What does my Guido know about machine-guns? What will happen to us if he is killed? Our lives are being run by madmen! What will happen to any of us? I don't know what to do!' The Signora began to weep silently and bitterly once more.

Cecilia sat staring at the floor while she waited for the Signora to compose herself. How could she leave when she had nowhere to go? Besides, her mother would be devastated if she ever learned what had happened. She thought of her mother and how proud she was when the Count had hired her. How could she leave? She thought of all the good things about the Villa Carosio and weighed them up. She didn't want to leave. She liked the nice clothes and being surrounded by nice things. She loved her little bed and the big bath tub when it was filled with hot soapy water. She didn't want to go back to the drudgery and poverty of her earlier life, and end up like her mother. She'd escaped the prison once and couldn't be sure she'd get a second chance. She thought about the Count and what he'd done to her. Was it all that bad? She felt ashamed and guilty and somehow unclean. But the old man hadn't hurt her. He'd frightened her, humiliated her, disgusted her and yes, he'd betrayed her because she'd trusted him. But he hadn't hurt her. If that was the price she had to pay to remain in the Villa Carosio then she'd pay it. She'd put aside her feelings. For her mother's sake, there was no turning back.

'Signora, the Count did not harm me. Mostly he just strokes my back and shoulders and my arms. When he touched my private place all I had to do was stop reading and look at him. He always took his hand away. He is an old man, but he is like a small boy.'

'Is that the truth, Cecilia?'

'Yes, Signora. The truth is he didn't harm me.'

The Signora looked uncertainly at Cecilia but her face revealed nothing.

'That small boy upstairs cannot harm me. That is the truth. It doesn't matter what I read to him. I concentrate on my reading and the words mean nothing to me. They're easy to ignore. He can't harm me, Signora. He can touch me but he can't make me feel anything I don't want to feel.' She hesitated, remembering something one of the boys at school had said about their teacher. She looked at the Signora in the way an actor assesses an audience and decided to be bold. 'Besides, his thing couldn't stand up even if Mussolini himself walked into the room.'

The Signora was stunned. Then she burst out laughing and reached for Cecilia once more. She threw her arms around her and held her to her breast. She wondered about this strange child who now reciprocated and returned her embrace. Most girls her age would be in tears. Most would want to run home to their mother whatever the consequences. But this child — if she was telling the truth — was mature way beyond her years. How did she become so wise? Where did she gather her strength? How did it come about that a twelve-year-old girl she'd thought would need comforting was now comforting her?

'I promise you, Cecilia, one day we will get even with that old goat.'

'Do you mean that, Signora?' Cecilia was intrigued. The possibility that someone in their lowly position could somehow exact revenge on somebody as important as the Count had never occurred to her. 'How?'

'I don't know yet, Cecilia, but we will find a way, I promise you.' The Signora was so fierce in her conviction that Cecilia was convinced. 'If he dies first, God will punish him anyway. I will plead with the Holy Mother to make sure he is sent straight to hell to burn forever. In the meantime I want you to promise me one thing. Never lie to me. If I am to help you, you must never lie to me. Do you understand?'

'Yes, Signora. I promise I will never lie to you.' The Signora had given Cecilia strength to endure the humiliations and the hope that one day they would get their revenge, so she made her promise sincerely and without hesitation. Indeed both parties to the promise had only the best intentions. But promises have a way of turning on their makers and the day

would come when they would both regret that this promise
had ever been made.

* * *

Benito Mussolini was executed by partisans on April 28, 1945,
by the front gates of the Villa Belmonte while trying to escape
to Switzerland. Arguably, it was the final act in a process
of suicide begun some nine years earlier with the formation
of the Berlin–Rome Axis. On June 10, 1940, Mussolini stepped
beyond salvation. He declared war on Britain and France.
For most Italians, this was a bewildering turn of events.
School children and parents alike recalled an old rhyme:
'With any country war, but never England.' Italians were
already wearied by the war in Ethiopia and the battering
their troops had received in Spain. All but the most ardent
fascists were convinced that Mussolini had committed them
to war on the wrong side. Even Hitler must have wondered
at the wisdom of having Mussolini on his side, as the Italian
soldiers' will to fight was often sorely lacking. But what could
be expected of men whose traditional sympathies lay with
their enemy?

* * *

'Lucio, Lucio ... what are you doing to us?' Milos shook his
head, the tone of his voice still patronising. 'What kind of
story is this? So far we've had incest, that distasteful episode
with Dietrich and the Jewish family, and now we have Cecilia
delivered into the hands of a pervert. I'm not sure I want to
hear any more.'

'I'm not sure it would matter whether you did or not
because it is becoming clear to me that you're not listening
any more.'

'Ramon, how can you say that?' Milos glared at him indig-
nantly.

'Ahhh ... a touch of outrage. At least you've stopped being
so sickeningly condescending towards Lucio. Think for a minute. We have Colombina who is in every respect an honest,
decent, charming woman. Yet she is about to commit the
most cold-blooded murder upon an old man. Why? Because

she woke up one day out of sorts? Of course not. If we are to understand her at all, isn't it important to know what happened to her in Italy? What makes her capable of murder? What shaped her? What made her like she is? We are all prisoners of our past. Lucio is defining Cecilia's prison. We are denied the privilege of choosing our parents or the circumstances of our birth. Sure, Lucio could hold back and vet his story so as not to offend your tender sensibilities, but how would that aid your comprehension? It seems to me that sooner or later we will each have to take sides. We will either have to condone or condemn what she intends doing. I for one would like to be fully informed before I make my decision.' Ramon paused to give Milos the opportunity to object if he thought he'd been treated unfairly, but his silence held unbroken. He continued.

'Let me ask you another question. What does a storyteller want more than anything else? I'll remind you. He wants a careless audience, one that doesn't listen as carefully as it should. We all of us — perhaps with the exception of Gancio here — work hard to make our listeners careless. We lull them into a false sense of security. We give them false glimpses of where the story is headed so that their egos run ahead of their brains. Then we bring them up short with an unexpected twist or turn of events. It takes a lot of skill to do this. But you make it easy for Lucio. You are sharpening his weapons for him because you still won't take Lucio seriously. You have underestimated him. Perhaps he has even underestimated his abilities himself. But when he turns on you, as he surely will, you will be defenceless. He will make you ashamed. You too, Neil, I include you in this. Your comments since Lucio began his story have not done you great credit either. Gancio is listening, perhaps more closely than any of us. Maybe he has his own reasons for this and one day he may even share them with us. There is a moral issue in this story and it has the capacity to make each of us examine our souls. We may even learn something about ourselves we don't particularly like. I have no doubt that Lucio intends to put us all on the spot and we owe it to ourselves to listen carefully. This story has barely begun yet it suggests great complexity. You must listen carefully with an ear for the main issue or you will be too easily sidetracked and regret it later.'

'Yes, Ramon is right. This story is complex and don't any of you doubt that there is a moral issue to confront.' Gancio sighed wearily. 'I have heard this story before, parts of it anyway, but not from this perspective. If I had my way, Lucio wouldn't tell this story at all. I don't know why he feels he has to. Milos and Neil couldn't care less whether you told it or not.'

'Steady on!'

'It's true, Neil. Only one person here really knows where this story is headed.' He turned to Lucio. 'Whatever happens you must remain true to the story no matter what. Don't let these two distract you. You owe it to me, you owe me the truth, the whole truth as you know it.'

'Don't cut us out of the story just yet. Perhaps Ramon is right, perhaps we have been a touch arrogant and haven't listened as carefully as we should have. But we were only trying to make it easier for Lucio.'

'Very noble, Milos, but unnecessary.' Ramon turned to Lucio. 'You have done well, Lucio. You have surprised us all with your ability. But it is time we removed the kid gloves.'

'Perhaps.' Lucio paused. 'I can't argue with anything you've said except the last point. Yes, there will be a moral dilemma and yes, you should all listen carefully. But there is another risk you should consider which has to do with my inexperience. You could outstrip your storyteller. Of necessity, I need to lay my foundations block by block. Because you've all done this before, you can see what I'm doing and anticipate the next step. Already you're further into the story than I ever expected you'd be or want you to be. I need your indulgence for a while longer. I'm still feeling my way and I'm struggling a little with the time frames. You can ask questions about what I've told you, but not about what I've yet to tell you. I feel like an inexperienced coachman with a team of horses all wanting to pull in different directions. It takes all my ability to hold them in check and keep them on the road in front of me. I can't do that and also respond to speculation.' Lucio paused and looked once more around the table. 'Well . . . will you indulge me for a little while longer?'

'That seems a reasonable request, no?' Milos looked across at Neil.

'Got me.'

'Ramon?'

The blind man began to chuckle. 'Lucio, you amaze me. I don't think your request is reasonable at all. You pull a stunt like that and they still can't take you seriously! Ha! I agree to your request out of admiration.'

'Jesus, you're boring Ramon. You've always got to make out that you know something the rest of us don't. But I have a question and I'm sure it falls within the guidelines.' Neil turned from Ramon to direct his full attention on Gancio. 'What the fuck are you going on about? I'm also getting bored with your dire little endorsements of Lucio's story. I think it's time you put up or shut up.'

'I'll get the coffee.'

'You bloody stay where you are!'

'*Va fanculo!*'

Gancio pushed back his chair, glared at Neil and retreated to the kitchen.

'He said it again, Lucio. What did you say it meant?'

'Nothing much, Neil. He just told you to fuck off.' Lucio began to laugh and the others joined him.

'*Va fanculo*, eh?' Neil tried out the word, savouring it, shifting inflections. '*Va-fan-cu-lo*. Yep. Sounds like fuck off to me. The question is, what the hell is going on here?'

'Search me,' said Lucio.

Chapter Fourteen

By Christmas 1939, Hauptmann Friedrich Eigenwill was prepared to believe that Hitler was a magician. The indecision and spinelessness of the French and English astounded him. The fact that they'd conspired with Hitler to take the Sudetenland from Czechoslovakia and give it to him was bad enough. Yet Hitler had exposed the whole of the western flank to the French during the blitzkrieg on Poland, and still the French hadn't reacted. Had they chosen to reoccupy the Rhineland or even push further into the heart of Germany, they would have been virtually unopposed. Where would Hitler have stood then? If he'd diverted his forces west, Stalin would have seized the opportunity to take all of Poland and Germany would have been committed on both flanks. The war would have been over and Hitler deposed. But the Führer had the Allies mesmerised. He remained and Germany was triumphant. Even his critics among the German High Command had to concede that Hitler's tactics and intuition smacked of genius.

Nevertheless, the Hauptmann still didn't share in the euphoria that swept through the country and manifested itself in everyone from his fellow officers to the most lowly working man. Undoubtedly the German military machine was the finest in the world and he was proud to be part of it, but he couldn't forget his father's advice: 'Germany can defeat any country in the world. But it cannot defeat every country at once.' Friedrich knew the Russian–German Pact was no more than an expediency, and the time was fast approaching when the traditional foes would meet on the battlefield. Then the German nightmare, the dread of war on two fronts, would begin. And that was a war Germany could never win.

The war in Poland had been over for two months and still the French sat mute and immobile behind the Maginot Line, their military and their mentality entirely on the defensive. Why didn't they attack? Hitler had just shown them how to go about it in Poland. Once they brought the fight to German soil the war would end, Friedrich was sure of it. But no, their tactics and will to fight had bogged down in the mud of Verdun and Flanders twenty years earlier and were beyond salvation.

Still, he had one thing to be grateful for as he shivered in the cold and thin light of the railway carriage taking him home on leave. Because of the inactivity of the French, the war had entered the phase nick-named the sitzkrieg — the sit down war — without which there would have been no Christmas leave for anyone. He glanced around the carriage crowded with officers. Apart from himself there wasn't a sober man to be found. Schnapps and captured Polish vodka which had been opened as fortification against the cold, now flowed without excuse or hesitation, relieving tension and lubricating voices. Friedrich smiled for the first time. Whatever his reservations, however dire the portents, he saw no reason to take them home with him and spoil Christmas for everyone. Besides, he had a good voice and liked a sing-along as much as the next man.

'Leutnant!' he bellowed. 'What are you drinking?'

'Zybrowka, Herr Hauptmann!'

'Zybrowka?'

'Zybrowka vodka. Bisen vodka. Very best Polish vodka. See? It has the blade of grass in the bottle.'

The men around him roared with laughter as Friedrich snatched the bottle from the young Leutnant and took a mighty swallow. They were delighted that the moody Hauptmann had decided to join them in their revelry. Celebrations love company, not opposition, so they welcomed him to their ranks. When Friedrich began to sing, the power of his tenor voice silenced them and they listened in awe. When he finished, they cheered and applauded.

'What's the matter?' he demanded. 'Haven't you heard a world class tenor before? I will now sing you selections from

Der Rosenkavalier. If any man utters a word while I am singing, I will put him on a charge.' Instead, he launched into a
ribald ditty soldiers dare only sing in their barracks or when
they're falling down drunk. That set the tone for the rest of
the journey into Dresden, so that when Christiane finally met
him at the station she needed her father's help to carry him
to their car.

The following day, as they prepared for the traditional
German Christmas festivities, Friedrich had to battle both a
hangover and a return of his misgivings. The previous evening, after he'd bathed and marshalled what few wits were
left, Christiane had made it perfectly clear to him that she
required his assistance while he was on leave to begin a
family. He had feigned delight as seemed only proper. She'd
couched the request in terms that were impossible to deny.
She'd said it was the only Christmas present she wanted, the
best Christmas present she could possibly have, and proved
her sincerity by hugging and kissing him till he was breathless.

But what sort of a future could he offer a child in a country
committed to a war they probably would not win? What sort
of a burden would this place on Christiane if he was killed
and Germany overrun? On the other hand, what right had
he to deny Christiane the child she desperately wanted? He
hid these thoughts behind a smile and the *bonhomie* of the
season. In his heart he knew he'd acquiesce. To do otherwise
would destroy the family celebrations and his precious leave.
Besides, he reasoned, a child would help take her mind off
worrying about him. And in the days ahead, he felt sure
there'd be plenty of cause for worry.

He joined Carl in the study while Christiane and Clara
busied themselves preparing for the Christmas Eve sharing of
gifts. Carl was buoyant. The ease of the victory in Poland had
convinced him of the invincibility of the German military. The
U-boats were creating havoc in the North Atlantic and the
only blight on the festivities was the scuttling of the pocket
battleship *Graf Spee* in the mouth of the River Plate. However,
the newspapers had even contrived to turn this setback into
a triumph of German courage and heroism.

'So, Friedrich, tell me all about Poland. You must have felt
ten feet tall.'

The last thing Friedrich wanted to do was discuss the war, but the war was all every civilian wanted to discuss, particularly with people who had been involved in it.

'Yes, we all felt ten feet tall.' Friedrich had learned that the only way to curtail these discussions was to confirm everything the other party knew or believed. 'The Polish army had no idea of modern tactics. Wherever we engaged them we were surprised to discover that, for the most part, they had neither tanks nor anti-tank weapons. They fought us with rifles and raw courage. And don't doubt that they were courageous. But in no area could they match us. We had total superiority on the ground and in the air.'

'Is it true that they attacked our Panzers on horses?' Carl could hardly hide his glee.

'Yes, I believe it happened. It was a gesture, a magnificent act of defiance from troops who knew they couldn't win but were determined to go down fighting.'

'How could you possibly call that a magnificent gesture? It was stupidity, sheer stupidity. If a German officer ordered his men to attack tanks on horseback, he would be shot.'

Friedrich didn't argue because he knew there was no point. 'The real question is, Carl, why did they persist with cavalry at all? Did they learn nothing from the Great War? Has the Polish army been asleep since then? Have the French and British armies also been asleep? You know our Panzer tactics were developed by Heinz Guderian, but who did he learn from? I'll tell you. From the Britishers Liddell Hart, Fuller and Martel. They developed the three principles of tank fighting. The fast surprise attack to force a breakthrough, close co-operation with infantry, and the use of air support. These are the tactics of our enemy but so far they have ignored them. Why? Our western flank is wide open to precisely this initiative but so far they have done nothing. Why?'

Carl began to chuckle. 'Sometimes you soldiers can't see beyond the walls of your trench. Isn't it obvious? The French and English are frightened. They are frightened of the Führer and they are frightened of our army, now that they've seen what we can do. They're ignoring us in the hope that we'll go away. They are frightened, too frightened to think, too frightened to act. Do you know that during the attack on

Poland, we defended our western border with loudspeakers? It's true. All we did was broadcast one message: "We won't shoot if you don't." You know I think they were grateful. Anyway they didn't shoot.' He laughed uproariously. 'Do you think they will be enjoying their Christmas, eh? I think not!' Carl crossed his arms in front of him and leaned back in his armchair, his shoulders shaking as he chuckled. Friedrich could imagine similar scenes right throughout Germany, as self-satisfied, smug and invincible citizens began their celebrations. It wasn't Christmas that worried Friedrich, it was the New Year and what that would bring.

'Time for your bath!' He looked up to see Christiane smiling in the doorway. 'You next, Friedrich, then father. We've all bathed already while you've been talking. I don't know what you men find to talk about.'

Friedrich raised his hands and surrendered, glad to be rescued from the conversation.

'And hurry,' Christiane continued. 'Our Christ Child is anxious to ring the bell.'

'Tell Ernst that patience is a virtue and that waiting heightens the expectation. I have brought him a gift worthy of the wait.' Friedrich rose and nodded to Carl.

'And me, have you brought your father-in-law a gift?'

'What? I give you Poland and you still want more?' Carl's booming laugh followed Friedrich as he made his way to the bathroom.

* * *

Ernst, being the youngest, duly rang the bell that summoned the others to the Christmas tree. Had the Führer himself been joining them, they would not have dressed more formally nor more elegantly. The dining table was covered in presents separated into groups, most of which were unwrapped. A plate filled with nuts and biscuits, chocolate and sweets accompanied each pile of presents. You'd never have known there was a war on.

'Ah, the moment Ernst has been waiting for!' Carl turned to his son and daughters. 'Let the blitzkrieg begin!'

Each person moved to their pile of presents as if guided by

radar even though there were no name tags to indicate just whose was whose. Friedrich was less interested in the gifts he'd received than in the effect of his gifts. He'd gone to a lot of trouble and risked censure from his superiors. Even so he had to smile. The bottle of whisky among his presents indicated that Carl and he had given each other identical gifts.

'Whisky!' boomed Carl who had come to the same realisation at precisely the same time. 'And where did you come by this rare treat?'

'I probably bought it from the same rascal you bought mine from. Merry Christmas!' Out of the corner of his eye, Friedrich saw Ernst scrabbling through his presents until he found the one that was wrapped. His hands shook as he tore the paper away. He stopped awestruck, and reverently picked up the watch the paper had contained.

'It's a tank commander's watch. The hands and the dial glow in the dark. You'll see later. Take good care of it, but tell nobody where you got it.'

'Herr Hauptmann, I don't know how to thank you.'

'Just take care of your sister for me. In fact, take care of all your beautiful sisters. And especially your beautiful mother.'

'It seems we have all benefited from your thoughtfulness, Friedrich.' Clara held up the length of material she'd just unwrapped and her two youngest daughters did likewise.

'It is nothing.' Friedrich was embarrassed. Their thanks embarrassed him as did any display of affection from anyone other than Christiane. 'I beat the bureaucrats into Poland. I purchased your presents before they had time to impose restrictions. We all did. You never saw soldiers more eager to part with their money.'

'Nevertheless, that good fortune won't save you from our thanks. Come here.' Clara reached over to him and kissed both his cheeks. Her daughters however, seized the chance to be considerably less formal and kissed him squarely on the lips. Friedrich flamed bright red as they knew he would.

'And you, Christiane, what has he brought you?' Clara turned to her other daughter expectantly.

'Friedrich is giving me his present later.' She glanced mischievously towards her husband.

'Not quite.' Friedrich began unbuttoning the top pocket of his jacket. 'I slipped something for you in my pocket at the last moment. It's something I thought you might like.' With the skill of a conjurer, he concealed her gift as he withdrew it. 'Close your eyes.'

Christiane closed her eyes while her family looked on. A gasp from her mother and sisters caused her to open them as she reached to investigate the new weight around her neck. 'Friedrich, this is beautiful! Where . . . how . . .?' She suddenly found herself lost for words as she tried to comprehend the exquisite jewels and intricate setting that now hung around her neck.

'There is not much in Poland now that cannot be purchased with a bag of coffee beans.' Friedrich shrugged deprecatingly to dismiss the subject. It was no time to invite speculation on who the previous owner might have been or the circumstance of its surrender. That would only diminish the gift. But he hadn't counted on Carl's reaction to seeing his first spoils of the war in Poland.

'You didn't buy that with a bag of coffee beans,' bellowed Carl, 'any more than Hitler conquered Poland with water bombs! What did you do? Steal it?'

Friedrich winced. 'No, of course I didn't steal it, nor did I buy it with a bag of coffee. But in truth I paid nowhere near its real value though, as you'd expect, I did pay a lot. The Polish have little need of finery now and a great need of food and favours. I have no knowledge of what transactions took place. I purchased it through a middleman.' Friedrich paused, looking for a joke that would ease the situation. 'We're not supposed to do such things, and I solemnly promise my Führer never to do it again. Unless my wife needs matching earrings!'

Carl laughed gleefully. 'And a brooch perhaps!'

'I think right now a kiss would be sufficient.'

Friedrich turned to his wife. There were tears in Christiane's eyes. Her hands still cupped the necklace and she hadn't moved. He took her hands gently in his own and kissed them.

'Was ever a man more lucky to have a wife like you and a

family that welcomes him into their home as one of their own? I don't think so. This day is precious to me. I will carry it with me in the battles ahead.' He gazed steadily into her eyes and she returned his look. Suddenly she felt the full weight of the words he'd just uttered and was confused. What did he mean? She was sure the war would soon be over. All the Führer wanted was to take back what was rightfully theirs. Once that happened, the war would end. Her father was certain of that. She saw love in her husband's eyes and looked beyond it for reassurance, but found only sadness.

'Don't be so dramatic, Friedrich. The British and French don't want war. Neither does our Führer. Ask Daddy.'

'We've had that conversation. Friedrich, it's time to forget about the war. It will all be forgotten by next Christmas anyway. Now we must spill some wine to prepare us for the carp. I don't know why it is traditional to eat carp on Christmas eve, I'm sure we'd all prefer salmon.'

Friedrich gently released his hold on Christiane and surrendered to the occasion. Afterwards he'd have plenty of time to think about the war. 'A drink, yes, a drink. That's what we all need.' He grimaced and held his hands to his head. 'I already have a squadron of Stukas dive-bombing inside my head. But it's a poor celebration that doesn't also bring suffering!'

That night Friedrich set about giving Christiane the second part of her Christmas present. With an effort of will, he put his misgivings aside and they made love passionately and tenderly. Once in Christiane's arms he found it easy to forget everything but the pleasures at hand. But later, sleep was elusive. Christiane lay cradled in his arms and he clung to her like a ship-wrecked sailor to a spar. His mind filled with 'what ifs' and 'if onlys' but the only certainty was what was. Hitler had enjoyed a freakish run of victories and successes, but could he maintain the pace? Could the master magician weave a big enough spell to bring about the final miracle? Victory for Germany. God in heaven, victory for Germany! Right then every sane German would have happily settled for peace.

Sleep came at last but in it he saw the burned and charred hulls of the Polish light armour, and the crews blackened and cooked like meat in a can. An icy gust crept under the covers and sent its chill down his spine. Christiane snuggled in closer to share her warmth.

Chapter Fifteen

The months passed in uneasy peace until April 1940 when the battle for Norway began. The German navy needed a pacified Norway to provide ports for its ships and access to the North Atlantic, but mainly to safeguard supplies of Swedish steel which were carried down the Norwegian coast while the Baltic Sea was frozen over. But, as important as that action was, the battle for Norway was no more than a sideshow to the battles ahead, as Hitler massed his armies for an offensive on their western flank.

Friedrich was assigned to the Seventh Panzer Division, part of Army Group A under von Rundstedt. His commanding officer was Major General Erwin Rommel, a young officer who was highly regarded throughout the Panzer corps and a darling of the press. Friedrich didn't realise it at the time, but Rommel was to become his friend and mentor and, very probably, his saviour.

On May 10, 1940, Hitler launched his offensive against the west. Instead of engaging the French along their heavily fortified Maginot Line, he ordered his troops into the neutral low countries and out-flanked them. It was an obvious manoeuvre foreseeable by all except the terminally stupid and the French. With no forces held in reserve to counter such a manoeuvre, the French folded as Poland had done.

The Germans captured not just the pride of the French army but most of their armour intact as well. But for an error of judgement on the Führer's behalf they would also have captured a quarter of a million men of the British Expeditionary Force. It would be wrong, however, to think that the German forces met no resistance. The Seventh Panzer Division and Friedrich in particular felt the steel of one such set-back.

The Panzer III tank was the cutting edge of the German forces in their advance westward and can claim a lot of the credit for the successes that followed. But although it was greatly feared by the Allies, it met its match on the advance to Arras when it came face to face with the Mk II Matilda, one of the most awkward looking tanks ever made.

The Vulcan Foundry in Warrington, Lancashire, normally made locomotives. In the late thirties it lent its expertise to the production of tanks. The Vulcan Foundry had seen fit to protect the Matildas' crews behind armour plate that was not only well sloped but up to 78 millimetres thick in places, and equipped them with a two-pound gun. Though it would never win a beauty contest, the Mk II was one of the most effective tanks of its time.

The British forces advanced southward to cut through the German lines of supply as their armoured spearheads swung north to the English Channel. It was a manoeuvre the German commanders feared because it had the potential to isolate the infantry from its supporting armour, whereupon the infantry would become easy pickings for the British tanks. And that is precisely how the battle began.

Infantry of the Seventh Panzer Division was first to make contact with the British. They set up their 37 millimetre anti-tank guns and let fly. In theory, at least, the Germans held the advantage because the great majority of the opposing tanks were Mk I Matildas, armed only with machine-guns. But the Germans had a rude awakening coming. The anti-tank gunners watched in horror as their *Panzergranate*, their armour-piercing shells, ricocheted off the British armour plate.

Friedrich arrived on the scene just in time to see the artillery overrun. He quickly identified the British tanks and instructed his wireless operator to inform the Command tank. They took up defensive positions as more anti-tank units moved up to engage the enemy. Friedrich had every reason to feel alarm. It was their policy not to engage enemy tanks because of the high rate of attrition. Tanks were valuable and had better uses. But he could see that they'd soon have no option for, accompanying them, was an unblooded SS-Totenkopf Motorised Division. Their light tanks and half-tracks would be sitting ducks for the Matildas. He was even vulnerable in his Panzer III, as the British artillery ranged in providing a protective screen for their tanks. He called down anxiously to his radio operator.

'Call Command. Tell them the armour-piercing shells are bouncing off the Matildas. Suggest they instruct their anti-tank gunners to shoot for the treads.' He heard a familiar scream and looked up. Manna from heaven. German dive-bombers had begun a series of attacks on the British tanks. Whether they'd be more successful against the advancing leviathans was yet to be seen, but at least it would buy them time.

'Hauptmann!'

He turned his attention to his radio operator.

'We are instructed to cross to the west and attack the British on their flank.'

Around them the other Panzer IIIs and the IVs they'd borrowed from the Fifth Panzer Division swung left, using the smoke and distraction of the air attack as cover. It was an impressive sight but Friedrich was under no illusions as to what lay ahead of them. The Panzer III suffered as most tanks did at the time from over-rapid development, but it also had two potentially fatal weaknesses. It was under-armoured, with just 30 millimetres of armour plating to protect its occupants. To compound the problem, the designers hadn't considered the need to shape the armour plate in such a way that it could deflect anti-tank missiles. Instead the Panzer III offered invitingly flat vertical surfaces which would greedily accept whatever shells came their way.

They cut directly across the battlefield in a bold manoeuvre which exposed their flanks to the enemy tanks and artillery. They grabbed what cover they could, as they headed for the intersecting highway. Once more Friedrich blessed the French military for insisting that highways be lined on each side with poplars to conceal troop movements. It was never intended that the movements they concealed would be their enemy's, but Friedrich blessed them nonetheless. The highway was slightly raised and the Panzers took up position with both the embankment and the poplars providing cover.

They opened fire with armour-piercing shells and watched

for impacts so that they could adjust range and direction. Friedrich had no option but to stand on his turret seat so that he could see his shells land through his field glasses, all the while shouting instructions to his gunner. He needn't have bothered. His gun was the same calibre as the anti-tank guns and no more successful at penetrating the British armour. It was every tank commander's nightmare. Again and again the advancing tanks were hit with no appreciable result. He instructed his wireless operator to pass his observations on to the Command tank, just as the Panzer IV alongside took a direct hit. Friedrich felt the concussion and recoiled instinctively. He watched in horror as the tank commander emerged from the turret hatch, his uniform ablaze, only to slump back into the inferno. He looked up ahead to where the Matildas advanced relentlessly, and reported the hit. He watched helplessly as the British tanks targeted in on the SS Motorised Division where their machine-guns and two-pounders could wreak havoc. All he could do was sit tight, calling in the range, waiting for an artillery shell to find him, wondering if he'd be next to fry.

The German policy of not pitting tank against tank was clearly vindicated as the battlefield became littered with burning Panzers. Friedrich couldn't help but be reminded of Poland, of the charred hulls and blackened, unrecognisable corpses of their crews. He realised with a shock that, somewhat illogically, he'd never expected to see German tanks destroyed in numbers the same way. Yet it was happening before his very eyes. Where was Major General Rommel? The situation was desperate.

In fact Rommel had already realised the danger they were in and taken personal control of the artillery. He brought his anti-aircraft guns into the action. This wasn't the first time anti-aircraft guns had been pitted against tanks, and it was a tactic that was soon to gain wide acceptance. Friedrich breathed a mighty sigh of relief when he heard the familiar thundering crash of the 88 millimetre guns. But he had little opportunity to rejoice. His tank took a direct hit and he was blasted unconscious from the turret.

* * *

Friedrich came to on the back of a half-track troop carrier. He felt no pain and no panic, just an overwhelming sense of peace. There were sounds, but they seemed so far away they didn't matter. He gazed at the evening sky, blue and perfect, and so very far away. He'd never before noticed how high the sky was and how very far away, and felt himself drawn to it. Instinctively, he knew he was dying but that didn't matter either. The sky swung and bounced from left to right and right to left and sometimes he felt as though he were among the clouds, strange columns of clouds that appeared and disappeared as the sky swung.

But the more he thought about dying the more puzzled he became. Why didn't he feel any pain? He knew the fate of Panzer crews as well as anyone. His mind flashed to the commander of the Panzer IV, his clothes ablaze, collapsing back into the inferno of his tank. He saw his face contorted in agony, agony that he must surely now share. But he didn't, and he didn't understand why he didn't. It began to worry him that he didn't feel any pain and that everything was so far away. Maybe that's what happened when you were dying. Maybe his body had died and his head was still dying. That seemed to make some kind of sense. It was good that he didn't feel pain from his burns because he knew that burn pain was the worst of all. He began to slip away. The sky disappeared beneath his closing lids. He was dying and dying was very peaceful and pleasant. Then the world around him exploded again.

The Matildas scored another hit as they continued their devastation. Friedrich felt himself lifted up into the air, borne on a cushion of noise, then he was falling. He opened his eyes but they could make no sense of what they saw. Then he felt pain, sudden and blinding. He felt his head strike metal and all the air was forced from his lungs. He fought for breath and fought the pain and fought for understanding. Someone was shaking him and it made the pain worse. He opened his eyes and someone was screaming at him. He could tell he was shouting by the way his face moved and the effort that he put into making his lips move. He tried to concentrate and focus on the face above him, the face of the man who was shaking him and hurting him.

'Can you walk?'

What? Friedrich listened but the voice came from so far away it was hard to hear.

'Can you walk? Wake up! Wake up!'

The shaking was becoming anoying. Couldn't the soldier see that he was burned and dying?

'God in heaven!'

Friedrich felt himself being lifted up. He grabbed hold of the arms that lifted him and forced his legs to work.

'Good! Good! Now walk . . . walk!'

Friedrich walked, the arms holding him, steadying him.

'Jump!'

Friedrich nearly laughed. Walking was manageable, jumping was out of the question. Besides the ground was so far away, so very far away.

'Jump! Do you want to burn here?'

Friedrich launched himself into space and the ground rushed up to meet him. He shut his eyes. But once more the arms closed around him. How could they be both above and below him?

'Try and stay on your feet, Herr Hauptmann. We will help you.'

We? There was more than one? Friedrich became aware that the sounds around him had come much closer. The medic wasn't shouting any more. He could hear engines and screams and shouting and explosions and slowly it dawned on him that he wasn't dying, that he was only wounded.

'Thank you,' he murmured.

'Ah . . . good! Just keep walking, sir. We'll hitch a ride when we can. More Panzers are coming and we are expecting further air support.'

'Where are you taking me?'

'Field station. You are very fortunate. Most of the other wounded on the half-track were killed.'

What other wounded? Why were they killed? Nothing made sense. His head began to thump and the pain made him screw up his eyes. He vomited and his legs gave away, but the steadying arms held firm.

'Am I burned?'

'Head wound.'

Head wound. Yes. That's what it felt like. Head wound.
Like ... like ... yes! Like Zybrowka vodka and Christmas!

* * *

Friedrich missed taking part in Rommel's breakthrough to
Rouen which helped clear the way to cross the Seine into the
heart of France. Instead, he sat in a French hospital which
had been taken over and let himself be nursed back to health.
Shrapnel had gouged bone from his skull as it ripped a furrow
through the flesh above his left ear all the way to the back of
his head. But no metal had penetrated through to his brain,
nor had his hearing suffered permanent damage. Indeed, the
doctors' main concern seemed to centre around the after-
effects of concussion. He'd been severely concussed, and his
headaches and bouts of vomiting were a constant reminder
of the fact. Still, he felt a fraud, sitting in hospital surrounded
by others far more seriously wounded than himself. He fetched
them drinks and wrote letters on behalf of those whose injuries prevented them from writing themselves. He was staggered to learn the intimate detail some soldiers included in
their letters and wondered how the censors would react. But
he paid particular attention to the tank crews who came in
with burns. The worst cases were moved on to special centres,
but the ones he saw horrified him enough. The poor men
never had a waking moment when they were free of pain,
and cried out for medication. But like everything else in
Germany, that too was rationed, and the men had to wait for
nightfall when their allocation of morphine would allow them
to drift off into troubled sleep. He could so easily have been
one of them.

Friedrich was temporarily out of the war, but he was not
out of mind. Rommel had taken note of the young Hauptmann who had calmly called in the enemy strengths and
made suggestions until his tank, like those around him, had
taken a direct hit from the British artillery. He'd decided the
young officer was worth hanging on to. Friedrich was unaware of it at the time, but it was a decision that saved him
from the Eastern Front and confrontations with the mighty

Russian T-34 tank. It did not save him, however, from further confrontations with his nemesis, the lumbering Matildas.

* * *

Helmuth Carl Eigenwill was born into a loving family and a Germany flushed with success in the last week of September 1940. He was pink and plump and radiated good health. Although rationing had limited the amount of protein, fresh milk and vegetables available, Christiane had not wanted for anything. Her family and friends had spared nothing in scavenging on her behalf. And what they hadn't been able to find on the black market or via their *Quellen*, their sources of supply, they obtained by visiting Little Pillnitz. The bureaucrat had not yet been born who could outwit farmers, besides which, the farmers of Saxony had successfully understated their productivity and deceived a succession of rulers for centuries, and were well versed in the art. The farms around Little Pillnitz kept the Schiller family supplied with eggs, milk, cheese and butter so Christiane and her unborn baby had never gone without.

In the months leading up to the birth, Christiane had adapted to her new responsibilities and become a zealous *Ehefrau*. Throughout summer she'd followed the German custom of bottling and pickling whenever particular vegetables or fruit were plentiful. The transition astonished her family, but no more so than the quantities she set aside. It had made them wonder whether she was expecting one child or an entire army. She'd dried trout fresh from the streams and salted down what extra rations of pork she could get her hands on. Christiane had already experienced one winter of rationing and knew that the second would be worse. She was determined that there'd be plenty of food in her stores in case Friedrich came home for Christmas. He'd missed the birth of Helmuth and the christening, and had yet to see his son in the flesh. She was sure that somehow he'd make it back to Dresden for Christmas. Then they could discuss setting up a home of their own. Her father was dead against it and had offered them a floor to themselves which they could turn into an apartment. It made sense. Christiane would have her own home but also have her family around her whenever she wished. But she wanted more. She was impatient to leave the nest and establish her own. She felt sure Friedrich could make her father see reason.

But it was not to be. Friedrich remained on duty throughout Christmas and then in January, instead of tucking into Christiane's hoard of food to help ward off the hard European winter, he was sent with Rommel to North Africa to rescue the Italian army. Christiane had to face the awful reality that her husband might not be lucky twice, and that he might die without ever seeing his son, or holding him in his arms. But surely, now that France had fallen, Britain would sue for peace. She comforted herself with that thought. Hitler had consistently out-manoeuvred the British and he would do so again. In the meantime, they'd get by as best they could.

Chapter Sixteen

The war came to the Villa Carosio in February 1941 when Signor Mila was sent home to convalesce. He had been fortunate enough to be in the vanguard of the Italian withdrawal from Benghazi following the capture of Tobruk, and even more fortunate to escape with his life. The Italian forces hadn't expected any opposition, but General Wavell had got wind of the withdrawal and ordered the Fourth Armoured Brigade to intercept the retreat. They cut across 270 kilometres of desert south of the Benghazi promontory in just thirty-three hours to take up position ahead of the Italian column. Guido Mila had barely made it past Beda Fomm when the British opened fire. The raggle-taggle formations of the retreating Italian forces had made easy targets for the British tanks hidden in the rough terrain well back from the road. The Italians panicked. Tank commanders fired at every puff of dust up ahead of them. Unfortunately, one of those puffs of dust was being thrown up by Guido Mila's tank. It took a direct hit from a 47-millimetre shell fired by an M13/40 tank belonging to his own unit.

Guido had been sitting on top of the tank with some infantrymen, taking his turn to cool down when the British tanks opened fire. He still hadn't figured out what was happening when his tank had been hit. He was thrown clear by the blast, but not before flying shrapnel and motor parts had torn through his legs.

In a battle where three thousand British soldiers and twenty-nine tanks captured more than twenty thousand prisoners, a hundred tanks and two hundred field guns, Guido Mila was lucky to escape at all. He was picked up by a *carro veloce*, a small machine-gun carrier, which was fast enough or ineffectual enough to escape the attention of the British gunners. He was taken to Agheila where the army surgeons were too busy organising their own withdrawal to Tripoli to attend him. Instead they loaded him onto their plane and took him with them. In hospital at Tripoli, surgeons with more time and better facilities mended his shattered bones and stitched his torn flesh together again. He had that to be grateful for.

Guido was wounded on February 6, but it was March before Signora Mila received the news. Even then, it wasn't an official advice but a scrawled, heavily censored letter from her husband which gave no clear indication of his injuries, other than that they were severe. A pall descended over the Villa Carosio immediately. Already in Ravello and Menaggio, women had been widowed. Others whose husbands and fathers were still listed as missing in action waited desperately for news of their capture. With more than one hundred and fifteen thousand Italian soldiers captured in a few short weeks by General Wavell, there was no shortage of families waiting for word. Guido arrived home unannounced in early April in an ambulance from Milan. His arrival coincided with the first warm weather of spring. Everyone took that as an omen that the worst had passed and that things would now only get better.

* * *

Life at the Villa Carosio had changed enormously for Cecilia. She no longer polished silver, made beds other than her own, or washed dishes. She was the Count's companion. She'd put aside her loathing and accepted her fate as the price she had to pay for the privileges she enjoyed. She ate her meals with him, cared for him when his illness left him helpless, and took away his loneliness. And behind closed doors, she allowed him his weakness.

But both were fast reaching a time in their lives when change is accelerated. At fourteen, Cecilia was no longer a young girl and there was no hiding the fact. For a while, the Count had been fascinated to observe the changes taking place in her body, but the truth was, the more she became a woman, the more his interest waned. One day he ceased stroking her altogether and, from then on, the only times he touched her were acts of genuine affection. However, he still liked to look at her sitting naked beside him as she read. He insisted that she wore only her dressing gown while she read and, in the course of reading to him, allow it to slip slowly from her shoulders and fall away. Perhaps it was the last futile sin of a man yielding to age, or perhaps he simply admired her beauty. Why not? His statues were ample evidence of his love of the human form. Either way, Cecilia always pretended she was one of his marble statues, just like those posing endlessly and unfeelingly in the gardens outside.

Naturally her position accorded her many privileges, but Cecilia was cautious in exercising them. She treated her elders on the staff with due deference and Signora Mila with the utmost respect. Every day after school she reported to Signora Mila even though both were aware that it was no more than a courtesy, for the Count's wishes overruled any instructions the Signora might give. Yet each of them recognised the necessity for it, because it was a way for Cecilia to confirm her acceptance of the Signora's position in the household, and to honour the promise she'd made her. Besides, there were the rare occasions when the Count left the Villa Carosio to attend to business in Milan or to stay in his apartment in Rome. At those times, Cecilia put herself entirely at the Signora's disposal, and gladly helped her friends go about their chores.

Throughout it all, Cecilia faithfully reported each twist and turn in the war to her Count, as recorded in the Milan newspapers. While Italy had taken a hiding in Greece and North Africa, the undeniable truth was that the Axis forces were winning the war, and the newspapers reported it that way. The Count had given up listening to the radio, preferring to have Cecilia read the newspapers to him, and he'd grow impatient as he waited for her to return from school. He was as addicted to her reading as he was to his medication and, of the two, there was no doubt that Cecilia was the more efficacious. But his real addiction was to Mussolini.

While most of Italy was becoming increasingly disaffected with Mussolini, the Count still revered him. There was no set-back that he could not interpret as a strengthening of the Duce's position or a further reflection of his greatness. He was their Julius Caesar, their Alexander the Great, their Hannibal. He was a man of destiny who would restore Italy to a position of power. The Count never tired of telling Cecilia how, after his factories in Milan had been occupied by workers, he had supported and secretly helped finance Mussolini; and how he laid the blame for the collapse of the old order squarely at the feet of the communists. They threatened to destroy everything his family had achieved and built up over centuries, and even his very existence. By occupying his factories, the communists had created an implacable foe. So he'd turned to Mussolini in his outrage and the two had joined forces against the common enemy. The Count had become a valued adviser, adding subtle spin to Mussolini's policies.

Cecilia learned to share in his excitement and his pride. She became his willing accomplice for, on numerous occasions, it had been her hand that had penned the Count's letters to Mussolini. It was her good fortune that she also wrote as clearly as she read and in one reply, Il Duce himself had actually complimented the Count on her writing. The Count had asked her to read that letter to him and, when she reached the part where the Duce had complimented her, the Count had leaned across, put his spaghetti-thin arms around her and hugged her.

Cecilia had felt flattered and very pleased with herself, but she'd quickly realised that that was not enough. She had to be overjoyed, speechless, and teary-eyed. Just like the Count. It wasn't so much a compliment the Duce had given her but an endorsement. There was no praise higher than Mussolini's. He was a paragon and a pillar of strength. He was everything the Count wasn't.

*   *   *

It's hard to say whether the return of the wounded Guido Mila changed things, or whether things would have changed anyway. The Count allowed Guido time to settle in, then called the staff together formally to welcome him home as a hero. They decorated the reception room with streamers and

a banner, made a cake iced with his name and set out wine
glasses for toasts. Cecilia was one of the few who had never
met Guido and was eager to see the man whose name had
dominated conversation for the past month. She felt strangely
excited, perhaps because after reading about so many heroes
in the past few years, she was now going to meet one.

In later years, the old women would claim that the damage
was done then, but they would be wrong. Cecilia felt no
hot flushes nor did she go weak at the knees when he was
wheeled into the room. She stood at the Count's side as they
sang the fascist hymn, the *Giovinezza*, and saw only a man
who looked to be the very epitome of what a good father and
husband should be. He had a strong face and a gentle manner.
His muscles had wasted and lost their tone through disuse.
Nevertheless Cecilia could see that he was solidly built. But it
was his eyes that held her. They were just like her mother's,
sad and weary beyond measure. She saw none of the pride
and certainty that heroes are supposed to have, and there
was not even a hint of immortality. She saw a strong man
made vulnerable, and her heart went out to him. She wanted
to help him and care for him. When the Count made his
speech, she was pleasantly surprised to learn that she'd be
given the opportunity. The Count magnanimously decided
to offer him her services.

'Cecilia can read to you like she reads to me,' he announced.
'And care for you like she cares for me. You have fought our
battles, for Mussolini, for Italy and for us. The least we can
do is take care of you now. Cecilia is better than any nurse I
have ever had.'

Guido had looked across at Cecilia as if noticing her for
the first time. He glanced up at the Count and then back to
her. His eyes locked onto hers. 'Thank you. You are most
kind.' He smiled at her and to her surprise she found she was
blushing.

The Signora and Carmela would probably have been happier to have had any nurse other than Cecilia, but what could
they do? The Count had decided, and probably thought his
gesture unselfish and generous. At least they could reason
with Cecilia. It wasn't that they didn't like her, because clearly
they did. It's just that they thought their hero deserved better

than to be ministered to by someone who was not only in league with the Count but . . . well, tainted. They waited until the Count had retired for the night and Cecilia had finished reading to him, then approached her.

'Cecilia,' Signora Mila began, 'please don't think us ungrateful or that we doubt your capabilities as a nurse. Indeed, you know that we have only the highest regard for you. You are like another daughter to me.' She hesitated as she picked her next words carefully, aware of the possibility of them being repeated to the Count. 'The fact is, Cecilia, you are not my daughter, Carmela is. And Guido is Carmela's father as I am his wife. It for us to give him the love and care he needs. We are his family. It is us who he must turn to, not strangers. He has had enough strangers. It is us he needs!' The Signora put her arm around Carmela and held her tightly. 'It is us he needs. Do you understand?'

Cecilia smiled. She could see both mother and daughter were embarrassed but nonetheless determined. But so was she. She felt strangely excited by the prospect of reading to Guido Mila and was not about to be denied. She didn't know why she felt so strongly about it, only that she did. She chose her words carefully, anxious not to reveal her inner feelings or offend.

'Signora Mila, you know I take my instructions from you.' It was a lie but entirely appropriate. 'I will obey your bidding. I will attend your husband only if and when you wish.'

'You are a good girl, Cecilia.'

'However, Signora, the Count does not give instructions only for them to be ignored. His wishes must seem to be obeyed. Allow me to read to your husband occasionally. There will be times during the days ahead when you will be grateful for the break and your husband for the diversion.'

The Signora hesitated. What Cecilia had said made sense, yet for some inexplicable reason she felt out-manoeuvred. She looked hard into the eyes of the girl before her as if trying to divine some secret intent. But there was nothing to read there, nothing at all to see. With a shock, the Signora realised that Cecilia's face never so much as hinted at whatever went on behind it. But what reason did she have to distrust her?

'Yes, Cecilia, you are quite right as always. The Count wants you to help so you should help. Besides, I think it's a good idea that you read to my husband occasionally. I'll let you know.'

'Thank you, Signora. Goodnight. Goodnight, Carmela.'

Neither replied but Cecilia didn't notice.

Chapter Seventeen

A week passed before Signora Mila invited Cecilia to read to her husband. She chose her day well. The low mists and drizzle, which seemed to have settled over Lake Como for the duration of the war, had suddenly lifted and been burned away by a resolute sun. Birds which had lain low in whatever cover they could find, reappeared singing the joys of spring. Blossoms appeared on the branches of trees and in the gardens, and caterpillars began an orgy of feasting which would end only when they'd metamorphosed into butterflies. On such a day, it was a sin to remain indoors. Signora Mila had ordered Stefano to wheel her husband out onto the lawn overlooking the lake, and it was there that Cecilia found him, gazing dolefully towards distant Ravenna.

'*Buon giorno*, Signor Mila, how are you today?' Cecilia waited for a reply but it was clear that he was either lost in thought or hadn't heard her. 'Signora Mila has asked me to read to you.'

'Eh?'

Cecilia laughed and her laughter so free and innocent broke through Guido's reveries and brought a smile to his face.

'I am Cecilia. We met at your reception. May I sit down?'

'Please ...'

Cecilia sat down on the same stone bench she'd sat upon the first day she'd come to the Villa Carosio, and once more her heart was pounding. Why? All Signor Mila had done was smile at her. Why did it matter whether he smiled at her? Why was it so important?

'This is where I sat when I first read to the Count. He liked my reading so much he invited me to stay and live here.'

'Yes, I have heard about your reading, Signorina.'

Cecilia froze. She wondered exactly how much the Signora had told him. He gazed at her as if inspecting an expensive purchase and she felt herself wilting before his scrutiny. She turned away to hide her shame, pretending to choose from the books and newspapers on her lap. Her hands shook.

'*Che occhi belli!*'

He'd spoken softly. Cecilia looked up surprised to see if she'd heard correctly. He repeated his words.

'What beautiful eyes!'

Cecilia felt the blood rush to her cheeks. She knew she had beautiful eyes. Her mother had told her so, as had her father and friends at school. But nobody had ever told her quite like this before.

'Forgive me. I didn't mean to embarrass you. To prove it I will not mention your beautiful brown hair. Why is it some women get all the gifts? I was merely stating what to me is plainly obvious. It must be this spring air. Today I see everything so clearly. I can even count the flower pots on the window sills of houses in Ravenna and Bellagio. I can see the trout rising on the lake.'

Cecilia began to laugh at this absurdity. But a tension and bitterness crept into his voice and he seemed unable to curb his flood of words.

'I can even see the Avanguardista parading through Menaggio. They are doing the Bersaglieri trot. Other soldiers march to victory, ours run to defeat.' He waved his arm in the vague direction of the town hidden beneath them. 'I can see that foolish man, your father, urging them on like lambs to the slaughter. Teach them to march. Teach them to look good in front of the ladies. Teach them to fire their pathetic carabinas. Then throw them up against the British tanks. God help them! Holy Mother have mercy on them! Did you know your father's boot laces are undone? Look at them. See? It is a miracle he doesn't trip. The only thing that can help us now is a miracle and we waste them on men like your father!'

Cecilia was stunned by the vehemence in his voice. Then to her astonishment, his voice began to tremble. 'Dear God! We don't even teach our men to tie their boot laces properly!'

Cecilia sat immobile, not knowing what to do. This was

not how she expected a war hero to talk. What would the Count think if he overheard them? What would Signor Calosci think? She didn't know whether to caution him or comfort him. At any event, her indecisiveness spared her from possible embarrassment. A sudden shudder which began with a shake of his head flicked through his body. He gathered himself together and looked back up at Cecilia.

'Forgive me. It's just that the war is madness. Every Italian soldier who has been in action can see the future more clearly than Il Duce can see his own pee-pee when he's taking a leak!' Once more his hands came up to his face. 'What am I saying? I forget myself. Please Signorina, forget I said such things.'

Cecilia was bewildered. What was he saying? How could he say what he had about Mussolini? She had a thousand questions to ask. Nevertheless, there were manners to observe and a patient to tend. She simply smiled and took his hand. 'Signor Mila, every day at school I hear ten times worse in the playground. There is nothing to apologise for. Tell me, you know my father?'

'Signorina, everybody in Lombardia knows your father and his fascist rantings. He was the reason I stopped going to the café in Ravello. And, of course, I know your mother. Sometimes I drove her up the hill to Ravello when she'd finished work. A fine woman. Her tragedy is that she chose to marry your father.'

'I still love my father, Signore, after all . . .'

'After all he is your father. I must apologise once more. It is my fate to spend this glorious afternoon apologising to you. It is right that you love your father but, let me tell you Cecilia, the time will come soon enough when your love will be sorely tested. Tell me, are you also a fascist?'

'No, not a fascist but a loyal Italian and I am loyal to Il Duce.'

'And you are also loyal to the Count.'

'As is the Signora and everyone else in the Villa Carosio.'

'Then I must watch my tongue otherwise you will tell the Count and we will be thrown out.'

'Signore, I would never . . .' Cecilia hesitated. She was about to add the words 'betray you'. 'Signore . . . I promise I will never repeat conversations we have to the Count. You can trust me. Ask Signora Mila.'

'Tell me, Cecilia, tell me truthfully, do you like the Count?'

'Signor Mila, I believe you already know the answer to that question.'

'So the old bastard still hasn't changed his ways. Don't worry, Cecilia, I won't embarrass you any further. I asked the Signora but she told me nothing. In truth she didn't need to. One look at her face and I could guess. I have been around this damned place too long for there to be any secrets. Tell me, is there anything I can do?'

'Signor Mila, if there was something you could do, you would have done it. I will never forgive him, neither will the Signora. One day he will pay for what he has done. The Signora has promised me. One day we will make him pay.'

Guido Mila studied the young girl, surprised by the sudden hardness in her voice. He took his time appraising her, assessing her strength. She held his gaze this time and did not falter. His eyes bored into hers, then he allowed them to wander over the rest of her. She neither looked away nor flinched. Despite her school uniform he couldn't help but notice she was no longer a girl but on the verge of womanhood. And she would be a beauty.

'Justice. Retribution. We Italians have an infinite capacity to carry hatreds. But enough! This glorious day deserves better. It is time you read to me, young lady. It is time you took my mind off less pleasant matters. That is your job from today.'

'Would you like me to read the newspaper?'

'No! Heaven forbid! How can I forget the war if you sit there and remind me?'

'But the news is good. The German General Rommel has taken charge of our troops and driven the Allies from Cyrenaica. They're in full flight back across the desert to Egypt. We've captured half the British armour. The papers say we'll reach the canal in a few weeks. The Count —'

'Cecilia, dear Cecilia, I beg you. Help me forget.' He took both of her hands in his and stared earnestly into her eyes. She could see his fears and his desperation. Once more her heart pounded. Was it because his eyes were so like her mother's? No it was something else. 'You realise once my legs have healed they'll send me back. They'll send me back, Cecilia. God help me! And if He won't, you must. The Germans will use us as cannon fodder and the British as target practice. Help me forget, Cecilia. For an hour, for a minute, for a second. Please. Help me forget.'

Cecilia nodded, transfixed. She'd help him forget. She'd do anything for him. Anything, anything. She didn't want to usurp Signora Mila's claims, or to replace Carmela. She wanted only his affection and trust and to take away his pain; to give him affection and loyalty in return. He confused her and unsettled her and set loose emotions she didn't begin to understand. He was the Signora's husband. He was Carmela's father. But did that mean he couldn't also be her friend? She could be his companion, like she was with the Count. Yes! She felt a tremor course through her body. Like she was with the Count.

*　　*　　*

Lucio sat back, finished for the day, and waited for comments. He felt good. For once he felt he'd controlled his story well. He'd shaken off his earlier doubts and finished strongly.

'Is that it?' Once more Ramon had turned in his chair to face him.

'Yes. It is enough for today.'

'No, Lucio, it is not enough. Only an optimist would think it was.'

'What do you mean?' Lucio tried to sound indignant but had a sinking feeling that he knew where Ramon was heading.

'We're waiting to hear more about Colombina. Isn't that correct?'

'Ramon's right.' Milos looked steadily at Lucio. 'You began with Colombina and you have studiously avoided her ever since. That's not how it is done, Lucio. After all, a story has to be about someone and this one is about Colombina. You can't throw a bone and then hold back the dog.'

'What Milos is saying, Lucio, is if you want to tell grown up stories you have to abide by grown up rules.' Neil motioned to Gancio who'd begun to stand. 'There'll be no coffee and no grappa until you finish your story for today. Now, tell us more about Colombina.'

Lucio sat silently, desperately trying to collect his thoughts. It was a mistake, he realised, to have begun with Colombina. What could he tell them now without advancing his story too far? He had no choice but to continue.

'I thought we had an agreement,' he said, stalling. He turned to Milos for support.

'Yes, we have an agreement.' Milos spoke gently, but Lucio could tell instantly that it was a lost cause. 'We've agreed not to anticipate your story. We haven't. We are merely asking for what we believe is our due. I think you should round the day off by telling us more about Colombina. You ignored her entirely last week and barely touched on her this week. Yet it is her story. By all means drip-feed her story, but even drips come regularly. We need more to sustain our interest and give us something to think about over the coming week. I don't think we're being unreasonable.'

'Okay ... where did we get to?' Lucio suddenly felt tired and his tiredness made him careless. 'What do you want me to tell you? There are developments, but they should wait till next week when I will tell them better. But you want more so I'll give you more. Colombina is now convinced she needs the rabbit poison to kill the Oberstleutnant.'

'Is now convinced? Present tense, Lucio?'

Lucio's mouth went dry. What had he said? What had Ramon picked up on? 'Present tense, past tense, what does it matter? I was thinking in Italian and mentally translating into English. In Italian it would be present tense.' Lucio felt sick. He'd blundered and blundered badly.

'What are you trying to do to us, Lucio?' Ramon's voice was soft and reasonable, but Lucio had no doubt that his mind was considering the implications.

'What are you going on about, Ramon?'

'Work it out, Neil. You, too, Milos.'

'You've lost me, Ramon. Please explain.'

'There is a suggestion here that the story Lucio's telling is still awaiting its conclusion. I haven't lost you, have I, Lucio?'

'Yes, Ramon you have. Let me rephrase my sentence and you'll find you have no issue with me. I'm just tired and a little careless with tenses.'

'When did you start thinking in Italian again? Your English

is as good as anyone's and your repartee as quick. There are no translation delays then.'

'When I'm tired, Ramon. Only when I'm tired. That's when I think in Italian and I'm tired now. What's more, you've asked me to tell a part of my story I haven't prepared and didn't expect to tell until next week. Now are you going to let me get on with it?'

'So long as it was a genuine mistake.'

'Mother of God, Ramon! You try my patience. All I'm trying to do is honour an obligation and tell more of my story. A story which just minutes ago you all claimed you wanted to hear. Now give me a chance!'

'Do I have your word?'

'Yes Ramon. If that's what it takes to continue with my story then I give you my word.'

'I'm very relieved to hear that, Lucio.'

'What the *va fanculo* is he going on about?'

'Neil, it's enough that I'm fucking up in Italian. Don't you start fucking up in English and Italian. Now! With your kind permission — and at your insistence — I will continue with my story. I will back-track a little. You're all so obviously fascinated by Colombina I'd hate you to miss a single thing.' Lucio prepared to continue his story but he knew that from now on Ramon would hang on his every word. He was not a man who let go of suspicions easily. He cursed his stupidity for thinking aloud, for being drawn into telling a part of his story he wasn't ready to tell, and for throwing his timing into jeopardy. And he'd had to lie to his friend. That was unforgivable. How could a day that had begun so promisingly end so badly?

Chapter Eighteen

Colombina drove down to the Dwyers' farm near Cowra with the intention of staying for a full week. It wasn't until she'd adjusted to the gentle pace of country life and its never-changing routine that she realised how tense she'd become. Duplicity no longer came as easily to her as it had when she was younger, when she was allied with both friend and enemy. She needed to relax. Heinrich was alert enough to notice any change in her and she'd already learned how quickly his caution could be aroused. Yet she knew she couldn't begin to relax until she had her hands on the sodium cyanide, if that's what they still used to kill rabbits. She decided that the sooner she told her little tale the better.

Colombina repaid the Dwyers for the hospitality by cooking dinner for them. It was something she enjoyed doing and the Dwyers lapped up the change to Italian cooking. Possibly for the first time in their lives they sat down to meals where the focus wasn't meat. Indeed, many of the dishes she served, like the beetroot *ravioli* in warm pea puree, had no meat in them at all. Still the Dwyers were happy to forgo their evening protein infusion, perhaps knowing they could always compensate for the deficiency with a breakfast of chops and eggs. But good food needs no explanation nor justification and the Dwyers were appreciative of Colombina's efforts. Very appreciative, in fact, as Colombina intended they should be. She made her move as the Dwyers pushed their chairs back from the table, replete and content. Fortunately they had a cat so they'd understand.

'Do you have any problems with feral cats out here?' Colombina asked innocently.

Country people never rush in with an answer, preferring to think the question through before answering. Stan Dwyer, like his father Charlie before him, was no exception. 'Well,' he said slowly, 'they don't come around here because of the dogs. And out there, well we've got our share of foxes. Further out they're a bit of a problem. According to the parks and wildlife people they're a real menace to native birds and the small marsupials. If we see them we're supposed to shoot them, but we never see them. They're no trouble to us.'

'Wish I could say the same.' Colombina spoke with just the right amount of resignation so that the Dwyers could see that she had a problem, but not so much that she'd appear to be soliciting their help.

'What's the matter?'

Colombina looked around the table and saw concern in all the faces. 'It's nothing really. It's just one of those things Mario was going to get around to before he died. He always said he was going to get some of the sodium cyanide he used to kill rabbits with when he was here. He just never got around to it. It's a wonder our cat hasn't joined him, poor thing.'

'Slow down,' said Stan. 'What are you talking about?'

'I'm sorry. Up on the peninsula where I live there are a number of feral cats. There's plenty of bush and parkland for them. One of them — a huge black-and-white thing — has moved into the bush behind us. Honestly, you'd think its sole purpose in life was to torment my cat Smokey. If he goes outside after dark that feral brute is on to him straight away. I spend half my life at the vet. Last time Smokey nearly had one of his ears torn off. There was blood everywhere. Great chunks of fur missing.'

'Where's your cat now?' Gwenda, Stan's wife, was clearly caught up in the tale, concerned not so much for the cat as for the effect of its misadventures on Colombina.

'I've left him at the vet. He's happy enough to stay there. It's like his second home. If I left him with my neighbour he'd be dead by the time I got home. It's hard to appreciate how vicious that black-and-white monster can be.'

'Wouldn't surprise me,' chipped in Stan. 'Parks and wildlife reckon they can pull down the smaller breeds of wallaby.'

'You're going to have to do something, Stan.'

Colombina tensed. This was it.

'Oh, could you, Stan?' She turned her eyes on him, wide and full of hope.

'What do you want me to do? Sit on your back porch with my rifle? That would wake your neighbours!'

Colombina laughed and turned to Gwenda, as if accepting that there was nothing they could do.

'You could let her have some of that poison, Stan.'

'Good grief, woman, that's not something you hand over like a cup of sugar. It's a restricted substance. If something went wrong there'd be hell to pay.'

'Honestly, Stan. All we're talking about is enough to kill a cat. Colombina will be careful. It's not as if she's going to leave it lying around.'

'I dunno. Like to help, Colombina, but that's dangerous stuff.'

'That's all right, Stan. I tried to get some in Sydney and got the same answer. Smokey will just have to learn to live with the beast. Me too, I suppose.'

'No you won't!' Gwenda was on her feet. 'Stan Dwyer, tomorrow morning you go down to the shed and get some of that poison for Colombina. I'll give you a tin to put it in. And not just one dose in case the first one doesn't work. If there's any left over Colombina can just flush it down the toilet.'

'It's okay, Stan, you don't have to.'

'Don't suppose it'll do any harm to give you some.' Stan and Gwenda were typical country people to whom words were a means of communicating, not the stuff of idle chatter. And Stan was smart enough to know that Gwenda had just communicated with him. Some country women don't speak up often, but when they do they like to be heard. Nevertheless, he saw fit to reiterate his warnings. 'Be careful with the stuff, for heaven's sake. Always wear rubber gloves and destroy them afterwards. The same goes for the spoon and bowl you use to mix it. You shouldn't put it down the toilet either but I guess that amount won't matter. Look, just kill the bloody cat and get rid of what's left. And don't tell anybody where you got it from or they'll have my —'

'Stan!'

'You know what I mean.' Stan turned to Colombina sheepishly.

'I know, and thank you.' She leaned across and kissed him on the cheek.

'I'll be honest, I don't even know for sure if I've got any sodium cyanide. It's not something we use much any more, except for white ant. Strychnine and arsenic are the go nowadays. I've probably got some somewhere. Always give you some strychnine anyway. That do you?'

'I'd prefer sodium cyanide. That's what Mario was going to use.'

'Okay ... okay ...'

* * *

Colombina drove home on Saturday so she could prepare a meal to take to Heinrich the following day. It was a vastly different Colombina who made the return trip, and even the Dwyers remarked upon it. For the remaining three days of her stay, with her prize safely stashed in her suitcase, Colombina had finally relaxed. The homestead had rung to sounds of laughter and she'd entertained them in the evenings by reading to them. It seemed she'd lost none of her old skills, and even the Dwyer children crept from their beds to crouch in the gloom of the corridor and listen spellbound to her voice. She was better than the radio and, in the Dwyer household as in many country homes, radio still held sway over television. Colombina captivated them with her charm and her energy. No one could have guessed the real reason for her visit.

She rose early on Sunday morning and began to organise lunch for herself and the old man. For once she decided to prepare a simple Italian meal. She drove down to the Avalon shopping centre where she bought some fresh artichokes to boil and serve with a hot lemon butter dip, and some fresh baby calamari to serve over spaghetti with oil, garlic, olives and small pieces of fresh tomato. Even though Heinrich's stomach was gradually becoming more and more accustomed to her cooking, she still liked to keep her sauces relatively simple. Besides, it was so much easier when she could prepare the meal all at once in Heinrich's kitchen.

Now that she had the means, she was in no hurry to kill him. She could bide her time and think the whole process through to cover herself in the event of an autopsy. She'd also need to come up with a recipe that used lots of almonds. She loaded her car and set off for number fifty-seven Blaxland Street. In a strange way, she was looking forward to seeing the old man again, to watch his face light up in anticipation of the meal. How was it possible, she wondered, to like somebody and yet hate them enough to kill them? She pulled up outside his house and banished all such thoughts from her mind. She was visiting as a friend. That was the role she had to play. She was visiting a likeable old man called Heinrich, not the Oberstleutnant. She took the food from her car and walked up the narrow path to his front door. She made a mental note to call the boy who mowed his lawns because the grass between the pavers was growing dangerously long. The ginger lilies were in bloom and she paused long enough to inhale their scent. She rang the bell and listened for his uneven footsteps advancing down the hallway. She rang again and waited. She began to grow concerned. He wouldn't have gone out, not when he knew she was coming. The arrangements had been firm. She rang again. This time a voice called out, not from inside the house but from the house next door. Colombina turned and saw an elderly, grey-haired woman leaning out from her front window.

'He's not there. He's gone. The ambulance came for him last Wednesday. Those Meals-on-Wheels people sent for it. He's gone.'

FOURTH THURSDAY

If Lucio had been concerned about a resumption of the debate over his untimely slip of the tongue, he needn't have worried. Once more Neil was his unwitting ally. He was late. Lucio kept the conversation to small talk while they awaited his arrival. And when he finally showed up, any hopes Ramon may have entertained of questioning Lucio were quickly dashed.

'Today lunch is on me.' Neil shook his companions' hands and flopped down on his seat. His face was flushed and he couldn't keep the grin off his face.

'No. We each of us always pay our own way. It avoids complications.' Ramon was not pleased and made no effort to hide the fact. 'However, we would be delighted to accept an explanation for your late arrival. We waited as long as we could. You have missed the whitebait fritters.'

'I'm sorry. Just got a bit held up. Nothing I could do.' Neil tried to look contrite but failed miserably. He turned to Milos. 'I'm sorry, okay? Just one of those things.'

'Why didn't you call us on that dreadful phone you insist on carrying around with you?'

'I was using it. I tried to ring you from the car but I must have been in a shielded area. Phone wouldn't connect. Don't tell me you were worried about me.'

'We were concerned, but not for you. For our storyteller. Look at him. It is a difficult story for him to tell and your lateness doesn't make it any easier. He clearly wants to get his story going before Ramon has a chance to cross-examine him again. I'm not sure what's going on between them, but they've been poor company. They are like disillusioned lovers, no?'

'No, Milos.' Ramon snapped at his friend. 'I came expecting to hear Lucio's story but so far that pleasure has been denied me. My frustration is only that of an audience deprived of its promised entertainment.'

'You see what I've had to put up with? For once, Neil, I'm pleased to see you. Very pleased.'

'Yeah? Well, I'm pleased to see you too, Milos. These two can get stuffed. Nothing's going to spoil my day, in fact, it couldn't be better.'

'Share your secret.'

'That deal I was trying to put together up on the north coast. It's a goer. Just got the green light from the local council. I managed to persuade them to change the zoning.'

'Congratulations!'

'Thanks, Milos.'

'Congratulations from all of us.'

'Thank you, Lucio. And thank you, Ramon.'

'Perhaps after all we should allow you to buy us lunch.' For the first time that day, Ramon allowed a small smile. 'Provided you tell us how you managed to persuade the council to change the zoning.'

'I did it the Argentinian way, Ramon. Plain brown envelopes. You'd know all about that. Now, what are we eating? When are we eating? I'm starved. Gancio, where are you, you miserable bastard? More food!'

Other diners turned to see who was shouting so rudely. They glared at Neil but he ignored them. Nothing was going to spoil his day. 'Now Lucio, have you prepared your story for us today? The full quota. No trying to cop out like you did last week.'

'Yes, Neil, I have prepared my story. All the ingredients are in place and I have been marinating them for the past seven days. All that is required now is for me to apply the flame.'

'Tell me, Lucio, does your wife know this story?'

'Jesus, Ramon, at least let him tell his story before you question him. Until the end last week you'd done all you could to give Lucio confidence. Why have you suddenly changed? You had a misunderstanding but that was cleared up. Why do you want to undermine him before he even begins? We agreed to indulge him a little longer, no?'

'It's okay Milos. It's a fair question. Yes, my wife knows this story.'

'Does she know you're telling it to us?'

'Yes, she knows.'

'Does she mind?'

'She trusts me. Do you?'

'My wife also knows this story — so far, at least.' Milos could sense another argument brewing and intervened. 'She is intrigued. She asked me to pass on her compliments.'

'Thank you, Milos.' Lucio smiled.

'Tell me, Milos, do you tell your wife the full story or a précis?'

'If it is interesting, Neil, I tell the full story with all the details and subtleties. I have a very good memory for such things. If on the other hand, it is one of your stories, I do a précis.'

Neil laughed and the others joined in.

'That's it guys, lighten up. We're here to enjoy Lucio's story. To be entertained. Nothing more. Okay?' Neil looked around the table for disagreement and found none. 'Just don't go and spoil my day, okay? Now, where's our food? Gancio, you lazy bastard, where's our bloody lunch?'

Chapter Nineteen

If the British forces had pushed on after the battle of Beda Fomm they would easily have taken Tripoli and the war in North Africa would have been over. Instead, despite intelligence which warned of the arrival of Rommel and two mechanised divisions in Tripolitania, Churchill ordered a large part of the British army and airforce in Libya to Greece. Given the speed and ease of their advance across the desert, the British High Command must have thought that the remaining forces would be sufficient to contain, if not overpower, the remaining Axis forces. It was typical of the sort of misjudgement which marked the course of the war and which many believe ultimately determined its outcome.

In Rommel, the British had an enemy of uncommon guile, courage and initiative. He was a master of the lightning thrust, the devastating penetration of the enemy's lines in strength. He realised immediately that the opposing forces were weakened and their supply lines over-extended. He called his senior officers together — among them a newly promoted Major Eigenwill — and informed them of his intention to go on the offensive. Friedrich was stunned by Rommel's audacity but couldn't fault the logic. If he was stunned, how would the British feel?

So instead of shoring up defences around Tripoli as anyone else would have done, Rommel unleashed his tanks on the unsuspecting British who were using the lull in the fighting to do much needed repairs and maintenance. Why shouldn't they? They had the enemy on the run. The last thing they expected was to be attacked.

For Friedrich, the charge across Libya was like the blitzkrieg into Poland. The British put up poor resistance and were easily defeated. The Germans recaptured Agheila and Mersa Brega. Then, with the backing of two new Italian divisions, they forced the evacuation of Benghazi and sent the British forces reeling back to Egypt. By mid-April 1941, Rommel had control of all of the Libyan province of Cyrenaica except Tobruk, and stood on the border of Egypt. If they'd pressed on, they would have seized Cairo and the Suez Canal, and the Middle East would have fallen into German hands. Again, the war in North Africa would have concluded. But over-stretched lines of supply, the bugbear of both sides in the conflict, now forced Rommel to halt, giving the British time to consolidate. It was a pattern that determined the ebb and flow of the battles that followed, as first one side then the other gained ascendancy, and they chased each other backwards and forwards across the desert.

The early successes in Libya did nothing to convince Friedrich that the war would be brought to a speedy conclusion or that Germany might ultimately win. When Rommel was forced to halt his advance on the Egyptian border, the fundamental weakness of their North African campaign became clear to him. They could not win without logistical support. Yet instead of sending them the tanks and fuel they needed, the Führer had chosen to invade Yugoslavia. How many fronts could they fight on at the same time and still win? Friedrich desperately wanted to talk to Gottfried in Berlin. But how? Young officers didn't go over their commander's head, and besides, his letter would never pass the censors. But if he could somehow get word to him, he believed Gottfried would be smart enough to read between the lines and recognise a plea for help. He decided to approach Rommel in the officers' mess. The next question was how?

Both in the military and among the civilians in Germany it was an offence to spread doom, gloom or rumours, or to question Hitler or the invincibility of the German army. It was forbidden on pain of death. This edict also had the effect of suppressing comment and observations. Even when superior officers invited their staff to speak freely, few tempted fate. So Friedrich changed his way of thinking and converted his problems into opportunities. They weren't stalled on the border of Egypt but poised on the brink of victory. They weren't perilously short of fuel but engaged in vital preparations for the final offensive. Friedrich rehearsed his lines out loud whenever he could until he'd achieved the right amount of conviction. Then he went looking for his leader.

Unfortunately, finding Rommel proved difficult and Friedrich's contrived optimism waned as the weeks passed and his frustration grew. Rommel divided his time between his headquarters in Benghazi and Tobruk, where the Ninth Australian Division remained stubbornly holed up, a constant threat to his supply lines. Twice — in May and in June — they were forced to repel British relief columns trying to fight their way through to the embattled Aussies. June was well under way before Friedrich found the opportunity he was looking for.

'Excuse me, General, may I have a word?' Friedrich had picked his time well. For once, Rommel's staff were engaged elsewhere and he was alone in his tent looking through a file of signals. The outcome of the campaign was hardly contingent on his not being interrupted.

'Ahhh . . .' Rommel paused for the briefest of moments. 'Major Eigenwill. So talkative on the battlefield yet otherwise so reticent. Come in, come in. Please, sit down.'

Friedrich was not easily ruffled, yet he felt as overwhelmed as any schoolboy on his first visit to the headmaster's office. He was staggered that the General recalled his name but more so by his informality. He had imagined himself standing rigidly to attention while barking out his request with all the enthusiasm he could muster. He'd rehearsed with this expectation in mind. Now he wasn't sure at all how he should proceed.

'Tell me, what is on your mind. You may speak openly.'

Friedrich's heart sank. The dreaded invitation. What should he do? He was damned if he did and doomed to be thought an idiot if he didn't. He decided to be himself and rely on his wit. He could be sufficiently ambiguous until he'd gauged which way the wind was blowing and its strength. Then he'd bend with it.

'General,' he began, 'there are two ways of viewing our situation. An optimist would say that we are poised on the

brink of victory, ready to seize the Suez and strike a potentially fatal blow to the British Empire. That is undeniably true.
A pessimist, however, would say that the British too, are
poised on the brink of victory with the opportunity to drive
the German army out of North Africa.'

'So tell me, Major,' interrupted Rommel, 'do you side with
the optimists or the pessimists?' There was no trace of humour
in either his voice or his face. His eyes bored into Friedrich,
unwavering. His strategy crumbled as he realised he could
no longer sit on the fence.

'That depends upon which side has fuel.'

Friedrich knew he'd gone too far, but the General's iron
gaze had unnerved him. He began to prepare himself mentally
for the consequences. He met Rommel's gaze and held it.

'Very well put.' Rommel turned away and a slow smile lit
his face. 'Perhaps if I'd spoken to you before I spoke to the
Führer we'd now have our reinforcements. Yes, very well
put. It takes a brave man to speak out these days, Major, and
you didn't disappoint me. A drink?'

'General.'

'Excellent. It is not good for Generals to be seen drinking
alone. People may get the wrong idea.' He flipped the top off
a leather-bound silver flask and poured whisky into two
tumblers. 'The spoils of war. We captured a good deal more
than tanks in the British retreat. What is it they say? Cheers?
Yes, cheers!'

'Cheers, Herr General.'

'Now, Major, what do you suggest we do? If that idiot
Mussolini hadn't got us involved in Yugoslavia we'd have
our reinforcements. Perhaps now that we are finished there,
we might get them. What do you suggest?'

'My proposal no longer seems worthy. Unlike you, I do
not speak with the Führer. I was hoping for permission to
write to Generalleutnant Gottfried Schiller in Berlin. He has
influence disproportionate to his rank. He is a good soldier
and a good friend and . . .'

'And you are married to his niece. It's in your file. No,
Major, you do not have permission to write to him.' Rommel
paused and looked steadily at the young officer. 'Instead you
will come with me on my plane this afternoon and send him

a wireless message from Benghazi. At this stage I am prepared to use every avenue open to me. It is time to find out just how disproportionate the Generalleutnant's influence is. I for one do not wish to end up on the side of the pessimists. Report back at sixteen hundred hours.'

'General!' Friedrich snapped to his feet and saluted.

'Oh, and Major, I understand you have a good voice. Perhaps we will go some place tonight where you may have the opportunity to use it.'

'General.' Friedrich marched out of Rommel's tent, his head spinning. No wonder the General was so highly thought of. The man was daunting. But if he couldn't get the necessary undertaking from Hitler, what chance did Gottfried have?

*   *   *

'The Hotel Cyrenaica was once the only reasonable hotel in Benghazi. Lately they haven't been able to attract tourists so the management offered us their establishment as a club for senior officers. Very generous of them, Friedrich, don't you think?'

'Is this the same hotel that a few months ago was the British officers' club?'

Rommel snorted in the darkness alongside him. 'I can see why you get along so well with Generalleutnant Schiller. Have you always been such a cynic?'

'Generalleutnant Schiller chose me because I was the only junior officer he could find who was prepared not only to be his driver, but drive his blasted tourer through a German winter with the hood down.'

Again Rommel laughed. 'Cynicism and irreverence ... so refreshing. I should warn you, however, there may be some SS officers present who will fail to appreciate your humour. Tell me, are you pleased with your transfer to the Panzers?'

'Why wouldn't I be? It is so much more pleasant travelling in the back of a tourer with my commander than in the driving seat with the frost and snow for companions. In fact, it is even more pleasant commanding a Panzer against those damned Matildas.'

In fact, this was less than the truth. Even though the British had been routed, the Matildas had been upgunned and had left their mark. Friedrich had witnessed several hits. He didn't mind it so much when the crews were killed instantly or if the tank was just disabled and the crew could escape. But the sight of tank crews desperately trying to claw their way out from a fiery coffin, their clothes ablaze, chilled him to the bone. His fear of being burned to death grew and his nightmares gained in intensity. As much as Friedrich had come to like his commander, he could hardly share these fears with him.

He'd overcome his initial discomfort with General Rommel, and succumbed to his charm. He found himself slipping into the old ways that had characterised his relationship with Gottfried. Rommel had helped him draft his message and questioned him on Gottfried's contacts. It was then that Rommel had told him of Admiral Raeder's and the Naval War Staff's commitment to an all-out offensive in North Africa. Perhaps the extra weight that Gottfried could muster might sway the balance their way. He began to relax for the first time in months, convinced that reinforcements would now be forthcoming.

'Ahh . . . here we are. Friedrich, you will be by far the most junior officer, but there is no need for you to jump to your feet all the time and salute. Once the introductions are over, you may relax. All the same, a wise man would keep a close watch on his tongue. We don't want any question marks over your political reliability.'

The driver held open the door and Friedrich followed Rommel into the foyer. The guards snapped to attention and saluted but Rommel ignored them. Friedrich took his cue from him and did likewise. He followed the General into the lounge room. He hadn't seen so many high-ranking officers since he was stationed in Berlin. Some looked at him curiously, but mostly they ignored him. He waited until Rommel sat down then sat opposite him. Immediately a waiter appeared with a glass of Scotch whisky.

'The same for the Major?' He looked up questioningly. Friedrich nodded. 'Ah, Friedrich, soon the vultures will swoop for the latest gossip on the progress of the war, but they will do us the courtesy of waiting until we finish our first drink.'

'Then let us hope the first drink is a large one.'

'Indeed. Now tell me, as a result of this afternoon, are you a pessimist or an optimist?'

'Definitely an optimist.'

'Good. I on the other hand am undecided.'

The smile on Friedrich's face froze.

'Why was it necessary to crush Yugoslavia so quickly? And Greece? Why are we so short of fuel and equipment when we know there is plenty available in the Fatherland? Why do they not send it to us? What do you think the Führer is planning? Why is he ignoring us?' Rommel was interrupted by the arrival of Friedrich's drink. 'It is not just me asking these questions. Everyone in this room wants to know the same thing. They won't ask me outright, but that is what they want to know. What do you think I should tell them?'

The implications had caused Friedrich's mouth to dry up. Of course, he'd done his own share of speculation, but to hear the same questions framed by his commander was another. The conclusion was unavoidable and it sickened him.

'I would suggest there is every reason to feel optimistic. We have powerful friends working on our behalf. The Führer has proved himself a brilliant tactician first in Poland, then France, and now the Balkans. We have every cause to believe that reason will prevail.'

'Except you don't believe a word of that.' Rommel laughed grimly. 'Nevertheless I will take your advice. Then, perhaps, we will seek a diversion. Soldiers must take their comforts when they can.'

Friedrich looked around the room and for the first time noticed that there were women present. Where had they come from? Why hadn't he noticed them before? He turned to inform Rommel of their presence and found the General watching him with obvious amusement.

'Perhaps you'd care to invite a couple of those young ladies over while I exchange words with my fellow officers. Our first drink is finished. The next must be earned. Then we can enjoy the evening. Off you go. I'll be interested to see how seductive your charm can be.'

'General.' Friedrich no longer had the slightest doubt who

the women were or what their purpose was. His feelings were ambivalent, to say the least. While he would undoubtedly enjoy some female company for a change, he wasn't at all keen on spending the night in bed with a stranger. He wrote regularly to Christiane and, though his letters had never embraced the lurid, detailed passion of the letters he'd written for others in hospital, they had become more passionate. He hadn't been home for more than eighteen months and he carried each day's absence like millstones on his heart. He yearned to see Christiane again, to hold her, to whisper his love in her ear, and to pick up and cuddle the young son he'd never seen. Left to himself, he'd give these ladies a wide berth. He'd be happy just to watch them and let them remind him — however sadly and painfully — of the life awaiting him back in Germany. But orders were orders, however casually given. The General wanted him to return with two women so he would. And they would be the pick of the room.

Friedrich watched them as he sipped his whisky. Some were as young as eighteen, others in their early thirties, perhaps more. He would pick two attractive women, that went without saying. But he didn't want any gigglers or scatterbrains. If they were to spend the evening together — and he hoped that was all it would be — then he wanted women who were intelligent, who had a sense of humour, and who could hold up their end of a conversation. He watched their mannerisms and gestures and was dismayed to find they were all too quick to smile. Why wouldn't they be? It was their stock in trade. The women were professional but even so he was surprised by the uniformity of their conduct. It was almost as if they had been drilled as thoroughly as the common foot-soldier, differing only in their skills. He looked for evidence of higher breeding. He dismissed those who smoked, using long cigarette holders and posturing as they smoked, as if they were in cabaret or the movies. He dismissed those who draped themselves over chairs or leaned against walls. He looked for women with good posture who had some pride in their bearing. This narrowed the field considerably. He watched the remainder as they disqualified themselves by laughing too loudly or insincerely, or by holding their wine glasses as if scared someone would snatch them away. He settled on two women, each in a different group. Now the question was how to approach them. He chose the older.

'Excuse me, Fräulein, your glass is almost empty. May I order you another?'

The woman looked at him, not at all impressed by his junior rank nor the prospect of another drink.

'The wine they give us is diluted and barely fit to drink. No, I do not think I would like another just yet.'

'Perhaps if I ordered two glasses of wine. One for me and one for you. Then we can swap. They're hardly going to dilute my wine.'

The woman smiled. Now that he was close to her she looked younger than he'd thought. She couldn't be much older than twenty-five or six.

'Then you will have to drink my wine.'

'Not at all, there is a plant behind you with the thirst of a camel. Besides, I am drinking whisky.'

'All right, Herr Major, order your two glasses of wine. My name is Grete.'

Friedrich did as he was bid. 'Now, there is something I would like you to do for me. Do you see that young woman over there in the pink dress with the pearls. I wonder if you could be so kind as to ask her to join us.'

The woman hesitated. But she was there to serve so serve she would, even the wishes of a junior officer. Friedrich watched Grete cross the room. She didn't slouch decadently or have an exaggerated roll of her hips. In fact, she glided as elegantly as any woman he'd ever seen. He watched the conversation take place, saw the woman in pink cast a quick glance in his direction, then take her leave from her companions. They returned together, unhurried.

'Herr Major, may I present Ilsa.'

For the first time since he'd arrived at the hotel, Friedrich snapped to attention. His heels clicked together and he bowed formally.

'Major Friedrich Eigenwill.' He shook Ilsa's hand not considering for a second that he hadn't extended the same courtesy to Grete. He had no idea why he'd behaved so formally other than that he'd been taken by surprise. Ilsa was extraordinarily beautiful. Once again his observations had been off the mark. Clearly he'd been deceived by the trappings of their trade. Perhaps the younger women tried to look older and the older women younger. It was a strange world he'd entered. Ilsa could not have been more than twenty-two or twenty-three. And there was an aura about her, a suggestion of hidden depths.

Friedrich looked across to his commander who was trying to disengage himself from the last of his inquisitors. 'Come,' he said with a smile, 'it is time to rescue my friend the General.'

The two women exchanged looks of surprise. The young officer was with General Rommel? Any reluctance they may have felt about accompanying Friedrich vanished. The General was a legend and, it was rumoured, not just on the battlefield.

'Friedrich! Welcome back. With such delightful company too. Sit down, sit down.'

Friedrich relaxed as Rommel took over. The man had immense charm and didn't spare any. He questioned the two women on their places of birth, their home towns and finally on their opinions as to the progress of the war. The General was clearly taking his time in making his selection. Of the two women, Grete was the more outgoing, the more attentive and slowly Rommel's preference drifted her way. Once Friedrich was certain, he began a conversation with Ilsa.

To his surprise he found himself talking about Christiane and the son he hadn't seen. He told her how he'd begun to court her alongside the trout stream at Little Pillnitz, surrounded by jonquils and tiny, shy crocuses. Ilsa seemed to hang on every word and he could barely restrain himself from revealing every single detail of his life. Possibly he would have, if his commander had not interrupted.

'I have arranged for us to stay here tonight. Your young lady will show you to your room. Why don't you both run along now?'

'Herr General. I am a married man. In view of my relationship with the Generalleutnant I hardly think this is appropriate behaviour for —'

'Friedrich, Generalleutnant Schiller is a soldier. He understands perfectly. A soldier must take his comforts when he can. And Friedrich, that is an order.'

Friedrich snapped to attention and Rommel burst out laughing. He turned to Ilsa and took her hand.

'Take him away, for God's sake, and look after him.'

Ilsa led Friedrich up the stairs to a small room at the rear of the hotel. At his rank, he hardly deserved better. Still, the room had a bathroom of its own with a toilet, and the bed, though intended for one person, was certainly large enough for two. Still Friedrich contemplated the option of sleeping together but not having sex. He would explain his reasons to her and she would understand. After all, he'd told her all about Christiane and she could not doubt that he loved his wife deeply.

But Ilsa was no beginner. From the start she'd understood exactly the kind of man Friedrich was. And she understood his loneliness and his needs. Part of the service she gave was to encourage men like him to open up and talk about their loved ones so they no longer felt so lonely. She gave them the companionship that only women can give, the gentleness and understanding. She attended to the mind and then she attended to the body. Friedrich was as vulnerable as a rabbit in a snare. He hadn't managed to utter a word before she'd begun to undress.

She let her dress fall from her shoulders into a heap on the floor and stepped casually out of it. Her eyes never left his. She sat back on the edge of her bed and undid her suspenders. She rolled her stockings off one by one, slowly, languidly. Friedrich could not drag his eyes away. She removed her suspender belt and undid her bra. Her movements were practised and fluid, and more sensuous than anything Friedrich had ever seen. His eyes moved to her breasts, noting their roundness and the youthful tilt of her nipples. Then she stood before him, naked holding his hands. Any last remaining vestige of good intentions vanished. His penis pushed painfully against the cloth of his trousers, demanding release, demanding freedom. He surrendered utterly and completely, and let her remove his uniform piece by piece, teasingly, until his body ached with desire and he could no longer hold back.

At first he wasn't gentle with her as he was with Christiane. He made love desperately, with an urgency born of loneliness, separation and a soldier's fears. He heard himself sobbing but didn't care. He'd found his comfort. Oh yes, he'd found his comfort.

* * *

He was awoken at six and told to dress immediately. The General was leaving. He washed and threw his uniform on. He hesitated at the door. This was no way to leave Ilsa, no way to leave any woman who had been so kind and understanding. There had been times during the night when he'd genuinely believed he loved her — not in the way he loved Christiane — but love nonetheless. He turned back towards her but she gently rebuffed him.

'Go now. Go back to your General. Go back to your war.'

'Perhaps . . .'

'No. Just go.'

The longer he looked at her the more he became aware of his naïveté. She'd done her job and that was that. He turned and raced downstairs to find Rommel pacing furiously back and forth across the foyer. Other officers stood nearby, waiting for transport, their faces drawn.

'Come!'

Friedrich didn't need to be told twice. He followed his commander out to the car. The driver saluted as they climbed aboard but Rommel ignored him. Friedrich waited until the car was well under way before he asked the question burning on his lips.

'Do we have a problem, Herr General?'

'Yes, we have a problem.'

'Have the British broken through to Tobruk?'

'No. We have a much bigger problem.'

'May I ask?'

'The Führer has just invaded Russia. God help us all!'

* * *

Friedrich left Rommel at a staff meeting in Benghazi, and flew back to the front alone on a Junkers crammed with supplies.

Though he sat at the rear of the cockpit, the crew could see that he was preoccupied and left him alone. Friedrich was devastated. All hope for a quick end to the war had vanished along with any possibility of a German victory. The Führer had brought Britain to her knees and failed to push home the advantage. He'd held North Africa in the palm of his hand and let it slip through his fingers. How could they possibly conquer a land as vast as Russia? How could they protect their supply lines? The Australians holed up in Tobruk had already shown how difficult that could be and not even Rommel had been able to shift them. How on earth would they now cope with a front line that stretched from the Mediterranean to the Baltic Sea?

Perhaps the Führer could once more work his magic. Perhaps the master magician was privy to information no one else had. It was a slim hope, but there was nothing else for him to hang on to. With all resources committed to the Eastern Front, he knew they now had no hope of getting the precious fuel and reinforcements they needed. And even less hope of going home to Christiane and the stranger who was his son.

Chapter Twenty

Guido Mila was reunited with his unit in June 1941. While he'd done all he could to delay the day, it was fortunate that he was recalled when he was. Otherwise he risked being sent to Russia as part of the hastily organised *Corpo di spedizione italiano*, Mussolini's gesture of solidarity with Hitler's strike at the heart of Bolshevism. If he had, he would most certainly have perished, if not by Russian ordnance then by the cold — Il Duce sent his troops to Russia wearing the same summer uniforms and cardboard shoes that had served them in the French campaign.

Of course there were tears at the Villa Carosio as Andre the chauffeur drove the Count and Guido down the hillside to the barracks at Menaggio, but Cecilia had to wave her farewells dry-eyed. Though she and Guido had grown close over the previous months, it was not her place to weep lest her emotions be misinterpreted. If Signora Mila had intended that Cecilia only read to her husband on rare occasions, her wishes were soon overruled. Guido demanded her presence. His wife and daughter brought him back to health but Cecilia brought him back to life. The two became inseparable, the gifted storyteller and the battered hero.

Often the garden rang to their laughter and even Signora Mila had to concede that the reading sessions were far more beneficial than her and her daughter's ministrations. Nevertheless, Cecilia's close relationship with her husband made her feel uneasy, yet she'd been given no reason for disquiet. She'd surprised them often enough by bringing them unasked for pitchers of lemonade, or coffee for Guido, and there'd never been any suggestion of intimacy. But there was no doubting their friendship. Perhaps that was all there was to it. Maybe she envied the fact that Cecilia could make Guido laugh as she never could and this made her a touch jealous. She should be grateful to Cecilia. But instead she was resentful, and she didn't understand why.

Cecilia was well aware of what was going through the Signora's mind but was powerless to do anything about it. She knew she should pull back from Signor Mila but couldn't bring herself to do it. She'd caught looks from the Signora and was now woman enough to comprehend their meaning. Still the understanding was wasted as she fell increasingly under Guido's spell. She'd never spoken so openly to a man before nor exchanged ideas so freely. And never before had any man treated her as an adult or an equal, nor shown genuine interest in what she had to say. It was as if he were midwife to her intellect, drawing it out into the light and allowing it to stand on its own merit, to exercise and grow. Guido encouraged her to think for herself, not to accept things at face value, and to be unafraid to express her thoughts.

'If you don't think,' he told her, 'you will never have a point of view of your own. If you never have your own point of view, you will never be independent. If you are not independent you can never be free.'

Cecilia hung on every word. Except for her mother, she'd never been as close to anyone, and she was intoxicated by the experience. But freedom always comes at a price and Cecilia still had to pay her dues. Guido was as committed to the downfall of the fascists as the Count was to their success, and gradually he brought her around to see his point of view. He had to break down the walls of her conditioning, instilled by her schooling, her reading and the pronouncements of the Count. But through Guido she began to see Mussolini in another light. She saw the shallowness of his posturing, the foolishness of the alliance with Germany, and the growing disillusionment of the Italian people. Guido blamed the Duce for the defeat of Italy which he saw as inevitable. Yet she still had to attend to the Count, to share his prejudices and his blind loyalty to the Duce. Of course the two were irreconcilable.

It was then that Cecilia discovered her talent for duplicity. At a time when most people were forced to take sides and commit themselves, she vacillated. Her ability to shut out one world allowed her to roam freely in another. She found she could become two people, each part of the same but independent of the other. One a fascist, the other an anti-fascist. Each half was earnest and sincere in the part it played. She saw no conflict because to her there was none. The Count and Guido each had their own Cecilia and she was true to both. This ability to separate her being meant her real self had to withdraw, to retreat to that hidden place within her. But without it, she would not have survived the war.

Of course, all Cecilia was doing was role-playing. Perhaps it was the reading she had done which enabled her to play her parts so skilfully. She became the consummate actress, wholly immersed in each character she played. She slipped from one to the other with scarcely a thought. She even created a special Cecilia for her mother. That is the greatest sadness. It is tragic to think she could not be herself with the person she most loved and trusted in the world, but her involvement with the Count precluded it. Maddalena would have been devastated if she had discovered the truth. How could a mother live with the thought that she'd delivered her daughter into the hands of a man who molested children? So Cecilia invented a role for herself and allowed her mother to believe that it was her skill at reading — learned at Maddalena's insistence — that had raised her to her present standing.

Guido's departure coincided with the readmittance of Maddalena to the staff of the Villa Carosio for four days a week. Cecilia was elated. For almost three years her only contact had been through her school friend intermediary, Giuseppina Cerasuolo. Doubtless she would have happily continued as conduit if the war hadn't interfered and removed the necessity. The day came when the Count could no longer shield Stefano from being called up to the military, and the Villa lost the only young man on staff and the young house-maid, Anna, lost her lover. She couldn't bear to remain without Stefano, and chose to train as a nurse and care for wounded soldiers. Perhaps she entertained visions of nursing a wounded Stefano back to health, whereupon he'd pledge his undying love and gratitude, finally offering her the wedding ring she craved. Whatever her motives, her departure created a vacancy which, with a reshuffle of staff, gave Maddalena her old job back.

Cecilia was ecstatic. Her mother more than filled the void Guido left behind and, though she missed the stimulation of their conversations, she had little cause to complain. Between the conclusion of school and her mother's return each night to her little home above Ravello, the only times Cecilia left her shadow were when the Count asked her to read to him, on the lawn in the afternoon sun. Then Maddalena would sneak away from her chores to watch them, and her heart would fill with pride.

Cecilia was the one joy in Maddalena's life. She quickly picked up on the fact that her daughter deferred to no one on staff except Signora Mila. But what impressed her most was the fact that Cecilia took her evening meal with the Count, except when he entertained the local fascist hierarchy. Not even Signora Mila did that! As she scrubbed and rubbed, Maddalena's mind filled with the prospect of Cecilia meeting and marrying someone of wealth and substance. Why not? She was beautiful and intelligent, and clearly the Count had adopted her as his ward. Then she would be beyond poverty and a life of despair. Then she would be free.

. . . Other servants would look at Maddalena and wonder why it was that the lowliest of servants, the one whose work was a never-ending cycle of drudgery, was always the most cheerful.

* * *

Following the bombing of Pearl Harbor in December 1941, the first of Guido's predictions came true. For most Italians, the inconceivable happened. They woke up one morning and discovered they were at war with America. How could this be so, they wondered, when so many of their countrymen and women and their families had emigrated to America? How could they go to war against their own kin?

Mussolini's popularity, already on the wane, slumped

dramatically. The ordinary Italian had had enough of fascism and more than enough of Mussolini. It was the Duce who had dragged them into the apocalyptic alliance with Hitler. Virtually overnight anti-fascist publications began to appear, dedicated to the overthrow of fascism.

This development may well have passed Cecilia by if a well-wisher in Milan hadn't forwarded on the illegal pamphlets to the Count. He insisted on her reading them to him. But Cecilia had barely begun before he interrupted her with torrents of abuse aimed at the people behind them.

'*Stronzi!*' he bellowed. 'Ungrateful shits. This is how they repay Il Duce for all he has done for them! Communists! Dirty reds! Il Duce will hunt them down and destroy them and all of Italy will cheer!'

'And we will cheer loudest of all!' Cecilia looked up at the Count full of indignation and outrage.

'That we will! Read on my child, let's see how these traitors hang themselves with their every word.'

Cecilia read on, her voice sharp and shrill and edged with anger. She wasn't acting but reacting in the manner which seemed entirely appropriate to the occasion. But deep inside, Cecilia was fascinated. Guido had predicted that the people would turn against Mussolini and the words he'd used kept recurring in the words she read. She put her thoughts to one side for later consumption as the Count rose to his feet once more and burst into another tirade of abuse. Cecilia waited until he'd run out of breath and stood shaking and gasping for air like a freshly landed fish.

'Count, you mustn't let them upset you like this. Every loyal Italian can see through these lies. Please, let me help you back into your chair.' Cecilia helped him sit and covered his legs with his blanket. The colour drained from his face and his skin resumed its normal deathly pallor. 'These papers are worthless and meaningless. They don't deserve to be read. Let me take them away immediately and burn them.'

'You are a good girl, Cecilia. But burn them here.' He waved his hand in the general direction of his fireplace. 'I will enjoy watching them burn.'

'And have them stink out your study? No! We should not give their authors that satisfaction. Let the cook burn them in her stove. Yes! Let their subversion fuel the stoves of honest, loyal Italians. Let that be our answer!'

'Yes, throw them in the stove!' The Count laughed. 'The evening meal will taste all the sweeter for it. Go! Take them!'

The Count was still chortling to himself as Cecilia left the room. She walked briskly down the hall towards Signora Mila's office. She paused in the doorway.

'Yes, Cecilia? What is it? What was the Count raging about this time?'

'He asked me to read these anti-fascist pamphlets to him,' said Cecilia innocently. 'They are quite scurrilous.' As Cecilia expected, the Signora's eyes narrowed sharply and she looked intently at the papers in her hand. 'I have promised him that the cook will burn them in her stove as fuel to heat the evening meal of loyal Italians.' Cecilia hesitated. The Signora watched her intently. 'Perhaps, Signora, you may wish to pass them on to the cook yourself, to ensure that the Count's instructions are carried out.'

A slow smile of comprehension spread across the Signora's face. 'Yes, very wise, Cecilia. You are a good girl. Here, give me the papers. I will see to it.'

'Yes, Signora. Oh, and Signora . . . ?'

'Yes?'

'When I read them I could hear the voice of someone we both know well.'

'Who?'

Cecilia laughed and withdrew.

*　　*　　*

Cecilia passed the pamphlets on to Signora Mila because she knew she would be interested in reading them. It was a spur of the moment decision. She had no inkling of the effect her ostensibly trivial action would have on the Signora or of the consequences that followed. Had she anticipated the shattering effect it would have upon their lives, she would have taken the pamphlets straight to the kitchen stove herself, and stood over them while they burned.

Cecilia wasn't the least surprised when the Signora called her into her office the following day. Staff shortages had disrupted the normally smooth running of the household, and Cecilia was often called upon to help out. Even the Signora's daughter, Carmela, had been pressed into service. It wasn't until Signora Mila closed the door behind her that Cecilia suspected this meeting would be any different from the others.

'Cecilia,' the Signora began, 'I know I can trust you so I want you to speak frankly. I want to hear from your lips what you and my husband talked about while you were reading to him.'

'We discussed the war, Signora, and your husband's attitude to Mussolini and fascism. But surely you know that?'

'Of course. But I want to know if you share Guido's beliefs?'

Cecilia hesitated. The only beliefs she shared were the beliefs of whoever she was with at the time. 'Do I think Il Duce was wrong to take sides with Hitler? Yes. Do I still believe that he is the saviour of Italy? No. Do I think Italy will win the war? No, we will never beat America. Even if Germany conquers Russia, we will never beat the Americans. But you must understand, Signora, I will give exactly the opposite answers to the Count.'

'Of course. As we all must do. That is, if we wish to remain at the Villa Carosio.'

'What do you want from me, Signora?'

'Your complete trust, Cecilia. Nothing less. I have to know that in the times ahead, I can absolutely rely upon you. Can I?'

'Signora, when I first came here, you tried to warn me about the Count's "tastes". You told me I could always come to you whenever I needed to as one woman to another. In return you asked me to promise that I would never lie to you. You tell me, Signora, have I ever lied to you?'

The Signora took her time answering. She looked hard at the fifteen-year-old girl in front of her and wondered — not for the first time — how she could possibly be so calm in the face of her questioning, and so mature in the way she responded. On the surface at least, it seemed Cecilia would be ideal for their cause, but what went on behind those beautiful, deceptively passive eyes? She shook her head as if to dismiss further speculation and reached across the table to take Cecilia's hands in hers.

'No, Cecilia, you have never lied to me. You are a good girl and I have said that often enough. I can also see that you are brave.' The Signora hesitated once more before taking the plunge. 'Cecilia, remember how we once promised each other that one day we would get even with the Count for what he did to you?'

'Yes, Signora.'

'Do you still feel the same way?'

'Yes, Signora. You know I can never forgive him.'

'Well, Cecilia, the day has come.'

Cecilia gasped and her brow furrowed. It was one thing to entertain some vague notion of one day making the Count pay for what he'd done to her, another to confront the reality. How could she, the daughter of dirt-poor, illiterate peasants, possibly have the means to take revenge on someone as powerful and important as the Count? It defied credulity and, worse, hinted at sacrifice. She'd been through too much to give it all away now. The question burst from her lips. 'But won't we jeopardise our place here at the Villa Carosio?'

'Not necessarily. We can hurt the Count without him even knowing it. We can get our revenge on him over and over and he will never suspect a thing. We can hurt him where it really matters. Does that appeal to you?'

Cecilia smiled. She couldn't imagine what the Signora had in mind. But, yes, provided it didn't cost her her place in the Villa it appealed to her! She waited for the Signora to continue.

'Cecilia, we may receive an unexpected guest tonight. A man who needs our help. Whether or not he comes depends on you because you are vital to our plan. The man is an escaped prisoner of war. A British pilot.'

Cecilia could not restrain herself. Her sharp intake of breath silenced the Signora. She could scarcely believe what she was hearing. It all seemed so impossible, so unreal.

'A British pilot? Here? At the Villa Carosio? Signora have you gone ...' Cecilia caught herself in the nick of time. 'Signora, do you think that is wise?'

The Signora laughed. For the first time ever, she'd ruffled Cecilia's calm. The girl was human after all. But Cecilia was only surprised, monumentally surprised. She looked closely but could find no sign of fear.

'Have I gone crazy? No. Do I think it is wise to bring the airman here? Yes. Who would think to look for him here in this bastion of fascism? Who would dare to hide an escaped prisoner right under the Count's fascist nose? Don't you see, Cecilia? At last we can do something for Italy, something worthwhile. At last we can do something to help end this madness and bring our men home. At last we can get our revenge on that disgusting old goat upstairs. Oh, Cecilia, can't you see?'

Cecilia took her time to digest what the Signora was saying and the fact that she was being asked to become involved. She had to admire the Signora's audacity. It was true, nobody would think to search the Villa Carosio for escaped prisoners of war.

'Cecilia, we need your help.' The Signora had become her normal business-like self. 'The pilot is ill. He was trying to climb across the border to Switzerland when our people found him. He was exhausted and feverish from too many nights sleeping out in the cold. It was a miracle he was picked up by us and not by the militia. He needs a warm bed and someone who can feed and look after him. We are hoping he can stay in your room. He could have Anna's bed.'

'But Signora, what if he is discovered there?'

'He won't be. Carla and Antonella have the room next to yours. They have already helped me out on other occasions.' The Signora noticed Cecilia's eyes widen. 'Yes, they have sheltered deserters overnight. Men like Guido who were sent home to recover from wounds and couldn't face going back to the war. You read those pamphlets, Cecilia, you know they called upon our soldiers to desert. Well many have. Some of them slept in the room next to you and you never knew. Why should you? You don't go into their room and they don't go into yours. Cecilia, now that Anna has left us, no one goes into your room now except you. Unless you have a Stefano you haven't told us about.'

Cecilia blushed at the thought of the nights she'd lain in bed pretending to be asleep, and watched while Anna and Stefano had made giggling love on the bed opposite. But what the Signora had said was true. She hadn't known that Carla and Antonella had sheltered deserters, and no one had any reason to enter her room except herself. All the same, she had reservations. The two women next door might take in deserters for the occasional night, but who knows how long a sick airman might remain?

'The cook is also sympathetic and so is Roberto.' The Signora set about allaying Cecilia's concerns. 'Guido also had a word in their ears while he was here. The only people we have to fear are the old goat himself, Signor Calosci, Andre and Piero the handyman. Perhaps we don't have to worry about Piero because he keeps so much to himself. Nobody has asked him where his sympathies lie, and even if someone did there's no guarantee he'd answer. The others, however, are a different matter. Signor Calosci and Andre have been with the Count for years. They are totally loyal to him and to the fascist cause. Give them half a chance, they'd shoot any deserter on sight. And anyone who helped them. But Cecilia, they have no reason to go anywhere near your room. I doubt they even know where it is. Besides, they have no reason to suspect anything. After all, only a fool would seek refuge in the Villa Carosio.' The Signora's face once more broke into a taut smile. 'Well, Cecilia, what do you say?'

Cecilia saw the wonderful irony of the Villa Carosio sheltering escaped prisoners and deserters. She understood the cleverness of the Signora's appeal to her. Yes, this would be a cunning way of exacting revenge on the Count. But she also saw the danger and could imagine the Count's fury if he ever found out. Nothing could save them then. He would have them shot. She hesitated, but the Signora's assurances had quieted her instincts for self-preservation, and the temptation to humiliate the Count as he had humiliated her was irresistible. One day it would all come out. The war would end or — heaven forbid — they would be caught. Either way, the Count would not escape humiliation nor the contempt he deserved.

'Signora, I have never turned away anyone who needed my help.'

'Good girl!' Signora Mila squeezed Cecilia's hands tightly.

'But Signora, promise me this. Please don't involve me any

more than you have to. I spend more time with the Count than anyone except Signor Calosci, and his suspicions are easily aroused.'

'You have my word. Oh, and Cecilia, when you help serve those preening fascists the Count invites to his dinners, try to keep the smile off your face.'

* * *

As it turned out, sheltering the sick pilot proved more complicated than anyone had envisaged and the Signora's assurances seemed paper-thin. By the time they'd sneaked him into the house, along the corridor and up the narrow stairs to Cecilia's room, he was practically unconscious. They laid him down on Anna's bed and listened to his laboured breathing. It was obvious his lungs were severely congested.

'He will die unless we help him cough up the phlegm,' said the Signora. 'We will have to take turns. Roll him onto his stomach. That's it. Now, watch carefully, I want you to beat on the back of his ribs like this.' She began to pummel the airman's back firmly and rhythmically. The airman's body spasmed and he coughed wetly, dislodging dense mucus onto the floor. 'Cecilia, you'd better fetch a pail, and let us hope for all our sakes that he doesn't make too much noise.'

Cecilia ran off downstairs, ignoring the house rules. She was under no illusion as to the risks she ran. She'd helped the old Count clear phlegm from his chest on hundreds of occasions and he'd made enough noise to wake the dead. What chance did they have of not waking Signor Calosci or Andre?

For the next twenty-four hours they could not leave the young airman alone for a second. When he wasn't coughing or choking on phlegm, he was calling out in his delirium. Someone always had to be there to muffle the sound. Carmela helped Cecilia to look after him before and after school when the absence of the other servants would be most noticeable, and took over when Cecilia was called away by the Count. They bathed his forehead and pummelled his back, and prayed to God that no hostile ears were eavesdropping. Perhaps it was the danger they shared that brought the two girls close together, because for the first time they opened up to one another.

Early on, Cecilia had made overtures of friendship to Carmela but her advances had always been rebuffed. Even when they sat together on their Sunday expeditions to church in Menaggio, the silence between them was rarely broken and then only through necessity. Carmela was never rude to her. They'd co-existed in polite *détente*, separated by status. But it hadn't taken long for Cecilia to realise that the Signora was as much a victim and slave to circumstance as her own mother, and both wanted the same thing — a better life for their daughters. Surely this common goal should have brought them together but the reverse was the case. As the two girls began to confide in each other, the truth emerged.

'I always wanted to be your friend,' Carmela revealed. 'I hoped you'd help me with my reading and maybe we'd do our homework together. But whenever I suggested it, my mother refused point blank. Usually when I want something badly, I can make my mother change her mind. But when it came to you, my mother was adamant. She went out of her way to discourage any friendship between us.'

'Why?'

'Oh, Cecilia, you must know! Gradually, my mother revealed the nature of your relationship with the Count. I was horrified, but at least I could understand why my mother kept us apart.' Carmela lowered her eyes in embarrassment.

'You understand, but I don't,' snapped Cecilia bitterly. But of course she did. This was no shattering revelation to Cecilia, but to hear confirmation put so matter-of-factly was a bitter pill. What she didn't understand was why she must always bear the shame for the sins of others. It didn't make sense. Surely people realised that what the Count did had nothing to do with her. The Count was one person, she another. The Signora of all people should know that. Yet once again she was an outcast, damned by association.

'I'm sorry, Cecilia, really I am.' Carmela could see that she'd hurt Cecilia and was anxious to make amends, to show sympathy and demonstrate that they were on the same side. But if Cecilia was wise for her age, Carmela was anything but, and the words that tumbled from her mouth, however well-intended, were ill-considered. 'Is it . . . is it really awful?'

The airman stirred and opened his eyes. He looked upwards at the two girls and smiled weakly. He attempted to speak but this triggered another bout of coughing. The girls quickly rolled him over so that he lay on his stomach with his head over the bed. Carmela began to pummel his back with the heels of her hands. The airman gagged and brought up more dense gobs of mucus. Perspiration lathered his face and tears ran from his eyes. Meanwhile Cecilia went to the window as she often did to make sure the coast was clear. Her blood froze.

'Wait!' The urgency in her voice was unmistakable. Carmela stopped as if shot. The colour drained from her face and her eyes flared. Even the airman managed to control his reflexive coughing.

'What is it?'

The handyman, Piero, was standing directly beneath the window staring up at it. Cecilia calmly met his eye and waved. He ignored her and kept staring. She began to unbutton her tunic, stopped, waggled a finger at him in admonition, and drew the curtains. She held her breath and peeped through the tiny gap between them. Piero was still staring up at the window but his face was strangely twisted. Cecilia had no reference but she could swear he was smiling.

'What is it? Tell me!'

'It's Piero,' said Cecilia levelly. 'He heard.'

*　*　*

Whether Piero heard or not he never let on. But how could he not hear? He was standing directly below the window. He couldn't have helped but hear the airman coughing. What could they do? No one dared confront him in case there was doubt and they served only to confirm his suspicions. It was like living with a time bomb that could explode at any moment without warning. Unfortunately the young British pilot was still too ill to be moved, and they had no option but to carry on as they were.

So Cecilia continued to care for her patient and, in between times, she read to the Count, sitting naked inside her unfastened dressing gown in front of the open fire in his stuffy, shuttered bedroom. Some people would have found the tension too great to bear, but not Cecilia. When she was with the Count the airman ceased to exist. Instead she slipped into the old game of reading but not absorbing the filth he gave her, and pretending her beautiful young body was no more or less than one of the statues in the garden. When Cecilia had explained to Carmela the strange rituals that passed for intimacy with the Count, Carmela could not comprehend how she could remain so remote and aloof. But Cecilia had become a chameleon, and only one person would ever again catch a glimpse of her true self — the Oberstleutnant.

* * *

'Lucio, what are you doing? You can't break the story there.'

'I can, Neil. I can break it wherever I like. It is my story. I have decided it is time for coffee so it is time for coffee.'

'But what about the young pilot? Did he escape or what? And what about Piero?'

'Lucio, you don't have to answer any of this.' Milos reached across and took his arm. 'You are quite right. It is your story. You determine when and how it is told. Last week we overstepped our rights as an audience in forcing you to continue. We won't do it again.'

'That's okay, Milos. If someone can organise our coffees, I don't mind answering your questions.'

'Gancio's already taken care of it. Now, what happened?'

'For what it's worth Neil, the young airman recovered. When he was strong enough he was helped over the border into Switzerland. What happened afterwards, I've no idea. Maybe he made it back to England and came back to bomb us. Who knows? Over the following months Cecilia helped shelter many deserters and escapees. And Piero, if he'd guessed what was happening, he elected to keep the information to himself. The point is that Cecilia had allowed herself to be directed along a most dangerous path, one that for the duration of the war would put her life in constant danger. Why? Yes, it was an opportunity for her to get revenge on the Count, but I can't believe that was the main reason. I believe she did it because someone asked her to. Because someone needed her help.' Lucio's voice became unsteady and thick with emotion. 'The truth is, she was neither fascist nor anti-fascist, but a child caught up in grown-ups' games wanting only to please and be accepted for who she was, not what other people made her. She risked her life as calmly and as matter-of-factly as she made beds or polished silver. Fifteen years old and she'd already buried her emotions to the point where very little could reach her, let alone touch her. If Piero had reported them to the fascists or *squadristi*, I believe she would have faced the firing squad with the same equanimity.' Lucio paused momentarily, all life drained from his voice. 'I'm told that this reaction is common among victims of sexual abuse and that, my friends, is the real tragedy. She no longer valued herself beyond her usefulness to other people.'

The table fell silent. Neil looked away awkwardly, as did Milos and Gancio. Lucio seemed unaware of the tears that welled up in his eyes and turned the rims red.

'Perhaps so, Lucio. But when you think about it, Cecilia has always avoided confrontation and done everything in her power to accommodate the needs of others. Go back to the beginning, even before her father raped her. Look how she took on all those household chores to accommodate her mother and keep the peace. Perhaps her desire to please was ingrained in her from birth.' Ramon could not see the distress on his friend's face but he could sense it and so, having said his piece, cautiously set about changing the subject. 'Now Lucio, may I inquire, will we be hearing more about Colombina today?

'Yes, Ramon, I will tell you more about Colombina.' Lucio's weariness was now clearly evident. 'But first, I must also take you back to Germany, to Christiane. This story is taking longer to tell than I ever imagined. I apologise.'

'Lucio, there is no need to apologise. You hold us all in the palm of your hand, no?'

'Nevertheless, Milos, I would rather you were in the palm of someone else's. I wonder sometimes how I will get through the next few weeks. Soon my story will run on its own momentum as it accelerates to its terrible climax. In the meantime I must supply you with all the necessary background so that you can make your final judgement.'

If Ramon had been the storyteller, they would have suspected trickery, more of his storytelling theatrics. But Lucio had always worn his heart on his sleeve and his distress was genuine. His audience became concerned, both for him and for where the story was headed. They recalled Ramon's cautions and Lucio's denials, and began to review the story in their minds and speculate on its conclusion.

Maria arrived with the coffee and grappa. Gancio helped her serve it. As he sat back down he put his arm around his fellow countryman's shoulders.

'I'm glad now that you're telling this story for very selfish reasons. It is strange. We had to come to Australia to discover that our pasts are somehow entwined. It is possible you may clear up some things that have always troubled me. It seems they have also troubled you. That's why I don't understand why you didn't leave things as they were. Why are you telling this story?'

'You have your reasons, don't you, Lucio?' All eyes turned to Ramon. 'A few weeks ago, you accused me of testing our friendship, of placing our lunches in jeopardy. Well, I suspect Lucio is about to test our friendship again, indeed, test it to its limits. I am tempted to walk away now. But just as Cecilia could not refuse a request for help, I cannot abandon a friend on mere suspicions. Lucio, you can take that as a warning.'

Lucio did not respond. The friends sipped in silence while they waited for him to begin the second instalment. If Ramon had cause to question the audience's attentiveness before, he had no reason now.

Chapter Twenty-One

By Christmas of 1941, Hitler had every right to curse Mussolini. The rescue of the Italian army in Greece and the subsequent action in Yugoslavia to protect his access to the Balkan oil fields had delayed his onslaught against Russia by five weeks. Those five weeks were to prove critical, as winter set in just as the German army was knocking on the door of Moscow. However, the mood in Germany as the new year began was still optimistic. They'd made massive gains in Russia and everyone expected the advance to recover its momentum with the thaw. Stories of the appalling hardships and suffering by the soldiers at the front had not yet received wide currency. Besides, they were doing so well in other theatres. Rommel was on top in North Africa, and the U-boats were causing havoc in the North Atlantic. The Allied bombing was the one major negative, though it still hadn't achieved the intensity or level of accuracy whereby it seriously disrupted the German war effort or caused significant loss of morale. On the contrary, the bombing had the effect of bringing people together with a singleness of purpose, and hardening their defiance. Bomber Command should have realised that. The same phenomenon had occurred at the height of the blitz on London.

Friedrich was given leave to fly home in late February 1942. After attack and counter-attack, both sides were grateful for the easing of hostilities, to lick their wounds, and garner what reinforcements they could. At last Friedrich could go home to see his son and hold him in his arms. In true soldierly fashion he took his comforts. He forgot about the war and immersed himself in domesticity. Nothing else mattered. His universe became defined by Christiane, Helmuth and the Schiller family. But if he'd hoped for a repeat of the joyful Christmas of '39, he was destined for disappointment. The eldest of Christiane's two sisters, Lisl, had married a young doctor in his final year at Dresden's Medical Academy, and moved in with his family at Wuppertal-Barmen. Ernst had enlisted and been accepted by the Panzer Korps on his eighteenth birthday and been sent to Weimar for training. So it was a subdued household, though nevertheless precisely the tonic that Friedrich needed.

But the nights cast a shadow that neither Christiane nor Friedrich could ignore. No matter how tired they were when they went to bed or how tender their love-making, Friedrich always awoke panic-stricken, believing he was on fire. The first warning would be a strangled scream, then Friedrich would sit bolt upright and furiously beat at his chest and legs. Christiane learned to throw herself against him, trapping his windmilling arms, and smothering him with kisses and soothing words. Then she'd wipe his brow and hold him tightly to her until sleep once more claimed him. But often sleep was no more than the commencement of another cycle, which would end inevitably in another imaginary conflagration. Christiane was stunned and wondered what horrors could instil such fears in a man as strong-willed as her husband.

Yet she also felt a little disappointed in him. The war hadn't ended as quickly as she and her father had thought it would. But it was only a matter of time. How could it possibly continue? Her father was certain that Hitler would soon call a truce and sit down with Churchill, Stalin and Roosevelt to redraw boundaries. The other powers would welcome the opportunity for peace. She couldn't understand why Friedrich didn't share her optimism.

* * *

In the summer of '42, the tide of the war turned conclusively against Germany. The Russian counter-offensive began which would result in the disaster of Stalingrad, from which the German army would never fully recover. In North Africa, despite the fact that his Panzers were heavily outnumbered by British tanks, Rommel once more had the Allies in full retreat. The Desert Fox out-thought and out-manoeuvred the British so comprehensively that, had the Führer even obliged with half of the reinforcements and matériel he requested, they would have seized the canal. But yet again Rommel had been forced to halt, and his advance lost its impetus. Meanwhile, fresh reinforcements poured in to shore up the British defences at El Alamein.

The First Battle of El Alamein in July ended all hopes of a German victory. The men of the Afrika Korps were exhausted and heavily out-numbered. First the British repulsed their attacks, then subjected them to counter-attack. All the while the British forces grew stronger as more men and tanks — including the fearsome American Sherman tank — came to their aid. On October 23, with Rommel absent in Austria convalescing, Montgomery ordered the attack which signalled the beginning of the Second Battle of El Alamein. The Axis troops crumbled before the superior force and began their headlong retreat back across the desert.

Rommel was ordered back to Africa but it was too late. Panzer units became isolated by the speed of the attack and were destroyed. Mines laid by both sides failed to distinguish between friend and foe, and the horrible death envisaged by Friedrich became commonplace, as violent, fiery eruptions ripped through the underbellies of Panzer and Sherman alike.

Still Friedrich survived. His experience and ability to read a battle enabled him to extricate his unit in the nick of time, and support Rommel in his retreat. But they hadn't counted on an increasingly unstable Führer.

The General called his senior officers together and grimly read them the latest despatch from Hitler. 'There can be no other consideration,' he read, 'save that of holding fast, of not retreating one step, of throwing every gun and every man into the battle. You can show your troops no other way than that which leads to victory or death.' If Friedrich had suspected the Führer was out of control, he now had the evidence. Hitler was ordering the annihilation of their entire forces, themselves included. Reluctantly Rommel ordered a halt to the retreat. But two days later, at risk of court-martial, he reversed his decision. Even so the delay was costly. They turned west once more with the remnants of their armoured and motorised units, gathering up what foot-soldiers they could. Hundreds of thousands of men, mainly Italian soldiers, were left behind to surrender.

Friedrich allowed his tank to become festooned with soldiers, as many as could find a place to sit and hold on. Among the soldiers he rescued this way was an Italian tank crew, whose own vehicle had succumbed to the infiltrating sand and lack of spares.

* * *

On November 8, the Allies, under the command of General Dwight Eisenhower, landed on the beaches of Morocco and Algeria and began their advance on Tunisia. Hitler immediately despatched a quarter of a million German and Italian troops to hold Tunis and, along with them, new Panzer IVs and the mighty Tiger tanks. If he'd sent a fraction of this force a few months earlier, in time for the First Battle of El Alamein, Rommel's victory would have been assured. Instead, under the command of Colonel General Jurgen von Arnim, they began a desperate defence of Tunis against the Americans attacking from the west, and Montgomery's forces from the south-east.

When Friedrich heard of the arrival of the Tiger tanks and reinforcements, he was absolutely incredulous. Why not before when they had victory in their grasp? Why now, when they faced certain defeat? It was clear to him then that Hitler the magician had not just lost his touch, but his mind as well. They should be evacuating North Africa for Sicily, not adding to the weight of their defeat. He raced around to see his commander.

'Friedrich! Come in.' A ghost of a smile flitted briefly across Rommel's face. His attempt at good cheer failed dismally. Friedrich was dismayed. Sickness had taken its toll on the General but that alone did not account for his appearance. What Friedrich saw etched into the lines of his face was the bitterness and disappointment of defeat; of a man defeated not by his enemy but by his own High Command. Friedrich could see that Rommel had nothing left to give.

'General.'

'Sit down, Friedrich, I know why you are here. The wheel has turned the full circle. Where once we prospered from the mistakes of our enemies, they now prosper by ours. I have proposed a plan to combine all our resources and drive westward to Tebessa. That way we can cut the Americans' communication and supply lines to their bases in Algeria. If we have learned nothing else in our campaigns here we have learned this. Armies cannot function without supplies. That also is the fundamental principle of blitzkrieg. We need to strike now, yesterday! But von Armin isn't sure and he will let the opportunity pass. You see, my friend, we have learned nothing. We ignore all the tactics and principles that made us successful in the first place. We are now driven more by hope than intelligence, fuelled by memories of invincibility. Instead of striking a mortal blow we will probably be sent northward to Thala where the Americans are expecting us.'

'General, it is not too late for a staged withdrawal to the coast and evacuation. That is the only way we can save our forces.'

'Yes, that has been discussed. But the Führer is adamant that we should hold out here until our final victory.'

'Final victory?' Friedrich made no attempt to conceal his feelings.

'Major, I told you once before that your tongue will get you into trouble. By all means think these things but, oblige me, do not say them out loud. Our final victory is not in question.'

'Of course, Herr General.'

'Do you know that Ziegler destroyed more than one hundred Sherman tanks at Fa'id? Dear God in heaven, Friedrich, think what we could have done with just fifty Tigers. Not even your blasted Matildas could have withstood their 88 millimetre guns.' The General seemed to lapse into a reverie that Friedrich was reluctant to interrupt. Slowly he pulled back from his thoughts and looked up into Friedrich's eyes. 'One thing, Major. I was fortunate in one respect. I could not have asked for better officers and men.'

Friedrich rose from his chair and snapped to attention.

'Herr General, it has been a privilege to serve under you. All of us feel honoured.'

'Thank you, Major. Now let us hope that my brilliance and your willingness will enable us to overcome a vastly superior number of Sherman tanks.' He smiled thinly. 'But Friedrich, I wouldn't count on it.'

The attack on Thala, though initially successful, was finally repulsed by fresh reserves. It was a familiar story. Superior German tactics overwhelmed by superior forces. For General Rommel, the attack on Thala was his penultimate engagement with the enemy in North Africa, following which he relinquished his command. For Friedrich, the Thala offensive was the last action he saw in Africa.

His Panzer took a disabling hit at the beginning of the engagement. As he was helping his crew from the turret, fuel leaking into the hull ignited. The blast knocked him backwards. He regained his balance only to see his gunner's agonised face above the turret and hear his screams of pain. He raced over and grabbed the man beneath his armpits. Flames licked up around his own arms and ate into his flesh as he dragged him clear. The gunner's clothes were alight from his chest to his feet. Friedrich beat desperately at the flames, his arms windmilling frantically. As quickly as he extinguished them they seemed to re-ignite, but gradually his flailing arms won out and he collapsed exhausted. He'd saved his gunner's life but had badly burned his own arms in the process. He stared up at the sky, so distant and blue, and waited for the peace to descend upon him as it had at the Battle of Arras. Instead he felt a sharp, stinging sensation, first in his hands and then his arms. It grew and intensified and doubled and redoubled until he thought his mind would snap. But it didn't. This time there was no merciful unconsciousness.

Friedrich was evacuated by air to Palermo in a Junkers crammed with wounded. He'd foregone the offer of morphine in favour of others more severely wounded than himself, and regretted his decision the instant the plane had begun to taxi. He tried to lift his arms high so that they didn't rub against those next to him. But the jostling and jolting caused them to flail around like straws in the wind, colliding with everything.

He wasn't the only one suffering. Despite the deafening noise of the engines he could still hear men cry out and moan. He was close to adding his voice to theirs when two arms reached from behind him and steadied his. He tilted his head back as far as it would go to see who his benefactor was and to thank him. He saw another patient in the uniform of an Italian tank crew, whose head was encased in bandages from above his eyes to the back of his neck.

'*Come sta, compagno?*'

'*Va bene, grazie a lei.*'

'You don't know me but I know you. You are Major Friedrich Eigenwill and I am Guido Mila. You gave me a lift on your tank all the way back to Benghazi.'

Friedrich looked again at the Italian. Yes, even upside down and partially obscured by bandages, the man was vaguely familiar. 'I am in your debt.'

'And I in yours.' The Italian laughed throatily. 'A lot of good it will do us. Still, maybe we are lucky. Maybe we are now out of this stupid war. Maybe now I can go home to Ravello.'

'Where is Ravello? Tell me about it.' Despite Guido's kind assistance, the pain in his arms was becoming unbearable and he was desperate for distraction. Guido sensed his need and began a long, glowing monologue which embraced the district, the people, the food and the wine, and lasted till touchdown.

As the medics helped him to his feet, Friedrich turned to Guido in gratitude. 'Thank you, *compagno, grazie.*'

'No thanks are necessary. My head feels like it was run over by a Sherman tank not just grazed by a bullet. The distraction served me equally.'

'Perhaps we will meet again.'

'Perhaps.'

The two men parted friends, bonded by trial and hardship, little realising that the next time they met they would be mortal enemies.

* * *

Friedrich stayed in hospital in Palermo for eight weeks, while skin from his buttocks was grafted on to his hands and lower arms. Each night he added his nightmares to the chorus as men's minds struggled to come to terms with the horrors they'd witnessed. Now Friedrich had no choice but to surrender to the flames and each night he met a painful, fiery death, his arms held helplessly away from his body in restraints. He craved the drugs that brought him peace but they were all too few.

With Gottfried's help, as soon as he was fit enough to travel, he scrounged a flight to Rome and then to Berlin. He knew only two certainties. He wanted to get home to Christiane and his son, and he never wanted to set foot in a tank again. When Gottfried met him at the airport, he wasted no time in pleading his cause for a transfer. Friedrich's preoccupation with escaping from the Panzers made him insensitive, and he was slow to pick up on the fact that Gottfried wasn't responding as he would have expected. He paused mid-sentence. The look on his friend's face was enough.

'My God, Gottfried! What has happened? Has something happened to Christiane? Or Helmuth?'

'It's Ernst. He was killed in the retreat to the Dnepr. The news came through last night.'

'Dear God . . .'

'Dear God is right. He was just a boy. Our armies are made up of boys. God forgive us.'

'Do Carl and Clara know?'

'They told me. I would like to come with you to Dresden but it is impossible. Are your travel documents in order?'

'Yes, thank you. And Gottfried . . .?'

'Yes?'

'I'm sorry.'

The old General bowed his head. 'Look after them, Friedrich. You are the soldier. They will need your strength. I will see what I can do about a transfer. It shouldn't be difficult. You have no unit to return to. All the forces we sent to Tunisia and the remnants of your Afrika Korps are lost, thanks to the genius of our Austrian corporal. Your father was right. We cannot defeat every country at once. We never could. Take care of my family. And look after young Jutta especially. She was very close to her brother.'

For a while they sat in silence, each alone with his thoughts, but Friedrich had been deprived of news for too long. In the end he couldn't resist questioning Gottfried. 'How bad are things in the east?'

Gottfried's shoulders heaved and he turned slowly to face Friedrich. 'How bad? As bad as they could possibly be. Stalingrad is just the beginning. When we attacked Russia we estimated that they had around two hundred divisions. Within a couple of months we had identified three hundred and sixty. As fast as we destroyed them others replaced them.' He looked sharply at Friedrich. 'What do you know about the T-34?'

'I've heard it is formidable.'

'Formidable is a good word for it. Again, when we attacked Russia we knew nothing about them. Can you imagine how our commanders felt when they encountered the T-34 for the first time? We believed our tanks were the finest in the world. Now we had to learn differently. They are faster, more manoeuvrable, better armed and better armoured. Our 50 millimetre shells bounced off them. We may as well have fired peas at them. In the beginning the only way we could destroy them in numbers was to somehow get in close and have our Panzergrenadiers place Teller mines on the rear of their turrets and blow them off. What bravery! Our new Panthers and Tigers are putting up a better show, and our 88 millimetre anti-tank guns are highly effective. But Friedrich, we are only staving off the inevitable. They will overrun us unless we can negotiate a ceasefire. No. Call a spade a spade. Unless we negotiate a surrender. Do you want to be the man who suggests to our Führer that the time has come to surrender?'

Friedrich didn't bother answering, the question was obviously rhetorical. He sank back into the seat, allowing the collar of his greatcoat to creep up to his jawline. But it wasn't the cold that had him shivering. Gottfried had the ear of the OKH, the Army High Command, and there was no reason to question his analysis. It wasn't just the hard, clinical facts that depressed Friedrich but the lifeless manner in which they had been relayed. It reminded him of his last conversation with Rommel. They kept their respective silence until they reached the station.

Friedrich stood and watched until Gottfried's car had disappeared into the evening gloom. Ernst, he thought, poor Ernst. But why not Ernst? Why not any of them? Who in Germany was safe now?

Chapter Twenty-Two

War does not impact upon everybody equally. In her home in Prager Strasse, Christiane believed she was safe, at least as safe as anyone in Germany. Dresden had been spared the terror and destruction of Allied bombing because it was at the very limit of the effective range of most bombers. Even with the introduction of the Lancaster and Flying Fortress it was spared because of its lack of military targets. Apart from the Sachsenwerk plant which manufactured parts for radar, the Siemens glass factory and the Zeiss-Ikon optical factory which produced, among other things, bomb sights, the Saxon capital had little to interest the planners of Bomber Command. The Ilse Bergbau Synthetic Oil Refinery in nearby Ruhrland was another story though, and attempts to bomb it occasionally caused Dresden's *Fliegeralarms* to be sounded. But no bombs fell on Dresden.

Other cities in the west had not been so lucky, and already Dresden's population had begun to swell with an influx of bombed out families. Most of the refugees were rehoused near the industrial plants so that their contribution to the German war effort could continue with as little interruption as possible.

Even so, Christiane's decision to remain at Prager Strasse — however reluctantly made — increasingly proved to be the correct one. Particularly in the west, where the housing shortage was more acute, the Housing Ministry was forcing families to open up their homes to others. With two families already sharing Prager Strasse, Christiane had succeeded in buying time.

There were food shortages but, again, nowhere near as

severe as in other parts of Germany. Fresh vegetables and fruit were no longer in abundance for bottling and pickling, even in season. But for the arrival of Helmuth, there would have been no milk. But they made do with no real hardship. Besides, they could always hop on a barge down to Pillnitz and for a few days enjoy life with few restrictions. There was always someone who had eggs and butter for them, or rabbits, or smoked trout, and milk in unlimited quantities. But, best of all, there was usually meat, fresh pork to roast or fry in fillets, and serve the traditional way with hot fat instead of thickened gravy. They scavenged in the fields for mushrooms — the *Pfifferling, Steinpilz, Speisemorchel, Waldergerling* — and edible toadstools, the *Hallimaschen*, which they'd once enjoyed only for their novelty value.

Unfortunately, apart from a few mushrooms, they couldn't bring any of their bounty back to Prager Strasse for risk of being searched and branded black marketeers, an offence which could result in execution. Nevertheless, Christiane and her family fared far better than most. She tried to keep this in mind as she waited for Friedrich on the station platform. Despite the fact that the clock was just ticking over to three am, more refugees had just arrived, distinguishable by their few meagre possessions and dark-ringed, haunted eyes. They moved like sheep, unthinking, blindly following instructions.

Christiane had been as devastated by the news of Ernst's death as her parents. It had been bad enough when Friedrich was wounded but at least they'd felt some relief that he wasn't killed. There was no such relief with Ernst. For all their insulation and good fortune, the war had found them and wounded them as surely as if the projectile that killed their son and brother had also torn through their own flesh.

Nevertheless Christiane tried to put Ernst out of her mind and look on the bright side. She still had a husband and she didn't want him coming home to tears and more suffering. They had to look after the living and she was under no illusion as to the job that lay ahead of them. Friedrich's letters, all written in strange hands, gave no indication of how the injuries had occurred, but she could guess. How many times had she held down his flailing arms? Although he'd given a brief description of his burns and made light of them, eight weeks in hospital told a different story. Still, she'd know soon enough. She stamped her feet and rubbed her gloved hands together, but it seemed nothing could keep out the cold night air. Where was he? She longed to throw her arms about him, to give comfort and receive it in return. She fought back her tears. Poor Ernst! Poor Friedrich! She looked up as an old, tired train slowly drew up to her platform, sighing and wheezing and sadly discharging billowing clouds of steam. She willed her face to smile.

She stood still, scanning the faces emerging from the train, and waited. She waited for what seemed like an eternity as soldiers helped disabled comrades off the train. Nobody rushed and nobody complained. She became concerned as the crowd gradually thinned and there was no sign of her husband. Then she saw him. He stepped down stiffly from his carriage and looked around. She was about to call out, but hesitated. It was as if she was looking at another man. He seemed so remote and distant. So ... lifeless. Again she had to fight back her tears and hold her smile. Then he saw her. He stared at her without moving. Slowly, he cocked his head to one side, a mannerism which always seemed to capture both his gentleness and his strength. He raised his arms, inviting her embrace. She began to walk towards him, slowly at first, then broke into a run. She threw her arms around him and pressed her face hard against his chest. All her sorrow and anxiety rushed to the surface. She waited for his strong arms to envelop her, hold her, caress her and protect her as before. But there was nothing. She was about to pull back when she felt them, the lightest touch on her back, and then not even all the dams of the Ruhr could have held back her tears.

* * *

Christiane could not understand why Friedrich was so insistent that they uproot and move west. She wanted only to help him forget about the war, however temporarily, and for his arms to heal. But he was relentless, and they argued and debated in circles.

'Can't you see?' she reasoned. 'We are so much better off

here. We are too far away for the bombers and so far from the Eastern Front it doesn't matter. Why do you think refugees are coming here instead of us going there? Because it is safer here.'

'Christiane, it won't always be this way. Yes, it is relatively safe now but it won't be when the Russians come. And unless someone can persuade Hitler that it is all over, they will come. And they will not be forgiving. They will destroy us as we set out to destroy them.'

'Friedrich, what kind of talk is this?' Carl cut in, siding with his daughter. 'It is true we have had our reversals. But we will strike back. Hitler is too clever for them and our armies too strong. Ernst did not die for nothing, Friedrich, he did not die for nothing.'

Friedrich always dropped the argument whenever Ernst's name was mentioned. It would have been cruel to continue. But he was determined not to give in. Once in bed, he'd again press Christiane until she turned away in tears. He didn't shout or raise his voice, but he was unrelenting and his constant outpouring gradually wore away at Christiane's resolve.

'There are many places to go in west Germany that have never been bombed,' he'd insist. 'Lisl is as safe as you think you are. Wuppertal-Barmen has never been bombed. But you don't even have to live in a city. We can find a place in the countryside where you can escape the war altogether, where farmers will give you eggs and milk and fresh vegetables like our friends at Little Pillnitz.'

'Mummy and Daddy would never agree. Besides they still have Jutta.'

'Carl and Clara must make up their own minds. So must your sister. Just as we must make up our minds. You are my wife now and my responsibility. We both have to think about little Helmuth. We must do what is best for him.'

Christiane would finally close her ears and bury her face in the pillow. They'd lay awake in the darkness, each agonising over the decision they faced. But gradually Christiane mounted less and less resistance. Friedrich was her husband and ultimately she had to obey his wishes, even it meant tearing herself away from her family. She agreed to take

Helmuth to visit Lisl and see for herself how things were in the west. Lisl was seven months pregnant with her first child and would be glad to have someone from her family on hand.

Having won this concession, Friedrich relaxed and once more became the caring, thoughtful man she married. They decided to take the barge down to Pillnitz to enjoy some unrationed food, and let the warm sun and fresh air of the approaching summer work its healing magic on Friedrich's arms. They intended to test his recovery on a few unwary trout. Two days later, as Christiane prepared some mushrooms for breakfast, they heard on the wireless that Wuppertal-Barmen had been devastated in the worst area bombing of the war to date, and raced back to Dresden.

*   *   *

The twin town of Wuppertal-Barmen at the eastern end of the Ruhr could consider itself unfortunate in a number of respects. The chronic inaccuracy of Allied bombing demanded a change of tactics, clearing the way for area bombing of civilian targets. Because they couldn't hit selected military targets, Bomber Command was directed to strike at the people who worked in them. That way, if they didn't manage to destroy the factories at least they would disrupt their productivity. And, at the same time, they would be executing that part of the Casablanca Directive which required 'the undermining of the morale of the German people'. In the eyes of Bomber Command, houses destroyed and civilians killed equated with working days lost.

Wuppertal-Barmen was not the first German town to be bombed. Berlin had been bombed as early as August 1940 and many others subsequently and regularly. But the twin city was among the first to feel the weight of three new developments. British scientists had at last been able to fashion anti-radar metal foil to the correct dimensions to blind the German early warning systems. As a result, ground defences could no longer predict the bombers' likely target to alert anti-aircraft batteries or accurately direct their night-fighters. The second was a tactic designed to counter creep-back, or the early release of bombs by 'rabbit' crews. The fires from their bombloads would often deceive following crews into also releasing their bombs too early. At Wuppertal-Barmen, the aiming point was set at the most distant end of the target and the seven hundred and nineteen bombers that took part in the raid were instructed to fly down the length of the twin city. This way, any early release of bombs would still result in significant damage. The third development was a variation in bomb loads. In the main the planes carried two types of bombs: thin-walled 1,000- and 4,000-pound blast bombs designed specifically to destroy the roofs of houses and shatter their windows; and small incendiaries in the form of phosphorus canisters to exploit these openings in the houses and set them on fire.

Even so, a successful raid still depended on a measure of luck, and that night fortune smiled on the attackers. As the Pathfinders moved in to drop their 1,000-pound marker bombs and incendiaries, the Wuppertal flak remained silent. The defence controllers did not believe Wuppertal was the designated target and chose not to reveal the city's location. It was a costly mistake. Unhurried and unharassed, the first wave struck with rare accuracy, creating an unmistakable fiery beacon for the following aircraft. As a result there was little appreciable creep-back as the majority of the bombers managed to drop their loads within three miles of the aiming point. It was a triumph for Bomber Command and a disaster for the citizens of Wuppertal-Barmen. An estimated 2,450 people died and more than a hundred thousand were left homeless. The result was a loss to the German war effort of fifty-two days of industrial production.

* * *

All of Carl's attempts to phone Lisl amounted to nothing. They appealed to Gottfried in Berlin but he was no more successful. The family were distraught as days passed and they heard no word, other than the tales of horror which spread out across Germany like ripples on a pond. Friedrich offered to go to Wuppertal himself and look for Lisl, but the last thing the authorities there needed was another anxious citizen suffering from burns. Besides, it was doubtful if he could have got the authority to travel. Just as they were sitting down to dinner on the fourth day after the raid the phone rang. It was Ulla, Lisl's mother-in-law. She and Lisl had just arrived at Dresden Main Station.

Carl, Friedrich and Christiane raced downstairs and out into the street, leaving Clara and Jutta to take care of dinner and make up beds. They turned right up Prager Strasse and began to run towards the station.

'Slow down, slow down,' called Carl. 'This is foolish. We only have to walk back again with their luggage. Let's save our strength. They are here and they are alive, and they're not going anywhere.'

Friedrich and Christiane slowed down and grinned at each other. The short run had discharged the tension and anxiety that had been building up. They'd lost Ernst, but Lisl and her unborn child were saved. That was something to celebrate.

Their joy was soon tempered by reality. They found Lisl and her mother-in-law, Ulla, easily enough, but were shocked by their appearance. Their coats were torn and covered in soot. Their faces spoke of trials that went far beyond mere exhaustion. They were drawn and hollow and their eyes wide and staring, yet they gave the impression of seeing nothing. Friedrich recognised the look immediately. He'd seen it often enough on the battlefield. The only colour in Lisl's face came from a burn on her cheek. She had no eyebrows and her hair looked like it had also caught on fire. How many faces had Friedrich seen like that? He shivered as the old horror re-surfaced. The older woman had Lisl's hand and, though she hadn't fared much better than her daughter-in-law, she was obviously in charge. If Carl had been concerned about carrying their bags, he need not have worried. They had nothing except the filthy clothes they stood in.

Christiane rushed to embrace her sister while Carl graciously attended to Ulla. Even under these most trying circumstances, they greeted each other as formally as they had at Lisl's wedding. Friedrich couldn't help but wonder as he witnessed this bizarre ritual, dapper Carl still in his slippers and chubby, dishevelled Ulla in men's shoes many sizes too large. Ulla was a strong woman, she'd proved that, but

Friedrich knew what she wanted and it wasn't just to shake hands. Though they'd never met, he walked up to her and without saying a word, put his injured arms around her and gently pulled her to him. He could feel her relax with a suddenness that momentarily made him think she was falling. Then she began to sob quietly, insistently, her arms about him and her hands gripping the back of his jacket with all her remaining strength. She'd brought Lisl this far, but could not take another step. They stood there unmoving while the station emptied and Carl went to look for transport.

They bathed both women and called the doctor. Ulla's feet were so badly infected nobody could believe she'd actually stood upon them let alone travelled all the way from Wuppertal. The doctor treated Lisl's burns but he couldn't treat her real injuries which went much deeper. All he could do was provide sedatives and entrust her recovery to the care of her family. At least the baby had come to no harm. They put both women to bed and spoon fed them soup thickened with potato. Ulla and Lisl ate as best they could, but it was clear their tiredness claimed priority. Clara, Christiane and Jutta left them to sleep and retreated downstairs where a grim-faced Carl and Friedrich had opened their last precious bottle of whisky.

Chapter Twenty-Three

The two refugees slept through to late morning. Lisl had a slice of toast thinly spread with jam before slipping back into sleep. The indefatigable Ulla wanted to borrow some clothes so that she could join them for lunch. It was pure bravado on her part for, at last given permission to heal, her feet had swollen monstrously. Nevertheless it said much about her courage and dignity. Clara forbade her to set foot on the floor for a week. Since Ulla couldn't join them, they decided to join her. Friedrich helped Carl move a small table and some chairs into her bedroom.

Lunch was more of the soup she'd had the night before, complemented by thin slices of pumpernickel and even thinner slices of *schlachtwurst*. A humble meal, but for the visitor from the west an apparent feast. Clara dipped into her precious hoard of coffee beans and they sat back to hear Ulla's story. She sat straight-backed and upright against her pillows with her hands clasping and unclasping before her as she began her harrowing tale.

* * *

'There were only four of us in the house that night. As Lisl has probably told you, her husband Nikolaus has been sent to an army hospital in Silesia. Lisl went to bed about ten o'clock and Ludwig and I followed shortly after. We were fortunate because up until two days ago, Ludwig was working night shifts. I remember hearing our maid Käte clanging around downstairs before I drifted off to sleep. She had only been with us for three weeks. She was also pregnant but not showing yet. Her boyfriend was a soldier and she'd allowed herself to be convinced that it was her patriotic duty to have a child by him. He was killed within days of arriving at the front. But that's another story. At around eleven-thirty the air raid warnings sounded and I thought to myself, "What poor souls will be on the receiving end tonight?" Other than that I didn't take much notice. No Wuppertalers did. The *Fliegeralarms* were always going off but no bombs ever fell on Wuppertal. At first we used to climb up to the top windows and watch the bombs fall on Essen and Düsseldorf. We could hear them and the anti-aircraft guns quite clearly and see the flames reach up into the sky. Sometimes it seemed that nobody could possibly survive and we were always surprised in the morning at how low the casualty figures actually were. The raids didn't last long, never more than twenty minutes, then we'd go back to bed and thank God it wasn't us who was bombed.

'This night didn't seem any different. Suddenly there was a deafening crash and non-stop banging and we realised the Wuppertal anti-aircraft guns had opened fire. That was the first indication we had that we might be in trouble and it was chilling. Of course, this wasn't the first occasion our guns had fired on passing aircraft, but somehow this time it felt different. I think we knew we were in for it. I raced in to Lisl's room while Ludwig ran downstairs to wake Käte. Between bursts of ack-ack we could hear the droning of the bombers' engines right over our heads.

' "Come! Come quickly!" I yelled. Lisl jumped to her feet, deathly white.

' "My baby," she said. "What about my baby?"

'I grabbed her arm to drag her to the door. "Your baby will be all right so long as you are all right," I told her. "So long as you do as you are told. Now come quickly." Already we could hear bombs exploding nearby. I pushed Lisl ahead of me and we raced down the stairs. When we reached the hallway I stopped her to get her coat off the hallstand and pass her some shoes. She took them and kept going down to the cellar. I grabbed my coat off the hook but I couldn't find my shoes. Then the lights went out. I turned on my torch to keep looking. Where had I left my shoes? Next moment I was flying through the air. A bomb had landed in the street outside and blown in the front of the house. I landed halfway down the stairs to the cellar. My chest felt like it was crushed and I couldn't breathe. I couldn't call out for help and, even if I could, nobody would have heard me. The noise was incredible, endless and louder than anything you can possibly imagine. I'd lost my torch and it was pitch dark. The stairs shook and pieces of glass and bricks began to shower down. Suddenly I felt arms under my shoulders lifting me and dragging me down the rest of the steps into the cellar. Someone shone a torch at us and I could see it was Ludwig who had risked his life for me. If I'd died then in his arms I would have been happy. Lisl and Käte came over to see how I was while Ludwig closed the cellar door. There was another enormous explosion and our house began falling down above us. Just as I was getting my breath back, the cellar began to fill with acrid, stinging smoke. Then my husband was shaking me.

'"Ulla, Ulla are you all right? Can you move? We have to leave here."

'I was still too stunned to be frightened and my head was still filled with silliness. I thought Ludwig was magnificent, so in control. I don't think I ever loved him more. I remember smiling up at him and he got so exasperated.

'"Ulla, we have to get out of here. Now get to your feet! Now!"

'"Come on, mother, please!"

'Lisl added her pleas to my husband's and finally my mind began to work properly. I was amazed to stand and find I hadn't broken anything. I put my coat on over my nightie and we crawled through a hole in the wall into our neighbour's cellar. In the west all homes have to have tunnels through to the cellar next door. Now we knew why. If we'd been stuck in our cellar we would have suffocated in minutes. Even so, the tunnels were rarely as big as they should have been and we had to crawl through on our hand and knees. Poor Lisl with her swollen tummy really had to struggle.

'There was no one in the cellar next door and it too was full of smoke so we kept going. We went through cellar after cellar. Our lungs were bursting and our throats stung. Bombs were still falling all around us. We broke through to another cellar and — unbelievably — we could see the sky. At first we didn't notice the other people climbing over the smoking rubble, trying to get out. We followed them. I tripped over something in the dark and fell. They were a man's legs. The poor man was crushed under the rubble and certainly dead. I probably knew him. But I did a terrible thing. I took his shoes. I took shoes off a dead man. God forgive me! I'd reached the stage where the pain in my bare feet was intolerable. They were badly scraped and bleeding. It's funny how little things at times like that can seem so important. So I took my neighbour's shoes and followed my husband and Lisl. Käte was standing on top of the rubble helping to pull us up.

'"The street's on fire!" she kept saying. "The street's on fire."

'And it was. Houses all around us were ablaze and toppling into the street. Trees were alight. And even on the road the tar had melted and ignited in places. Because I had tripped we were last out and we couldn't see where everyone had gone. We didn't know what to do. We were surrounded by falling bombs and fire and there seemed no escape.

'"Follow me!" Ludwig yelled and took off across the road. There was our fire warden with his torch, bless him, calling us over towards the house opposite. People criticise we Germans because we are too structured and orderly. But German discipline saved our lives that night. The fire warden was just one example. He led us into this house. The whole front had been blown off but it was of very solid construction and most of the rooms and the staircase were still standing. I wish I had the name of the builder because he will be very popular after the war. When I looked up the staircase I could see trails of fire tumbling over the steps. How could this be so? It was the same with the walls that were still standing. It looked like they were splashed with fire. Nothing escaped the splashes. I have never seen anything like it but that is why everything had caught fire so quickly. The warden ushered us down the steps into the cellar and closed the door behind him. There were at least fifty people sheltering there. The cellar was large with strong vaulted ceilings, unlike ours.

'Above the noise from outside I could hear people crying out for help. There were people with broken limbs and gaping wounds and others who were badly burned. There were children there too and they broke your heart. The poor little things were shaking and cowering with fear, clutching on to whoever was near and could comfort them. A little boy about five or six attached himself to Käte. He had no idea where his parents were. But still we weren't out of trouble. A bomb must have hit the building above us because there was a deafening roar and the cellar shook. Dust and mortar squirted out of the bricks above our head and the ceiling began to sag ominously.

'"Prepare to evacuate!" called the warden. But where would we evacuate to? Every house in our street and in every street around us was on fire. Where could we go? But as the cellar once more filled with smoke, it was obvious we couldn't remain where we were. We hadn't escaped from our cellar just to suffocate in someone else's. Amazingly there was no panic. Perhaps everybody was as shocked as we were. The warden opened the hole through to the cellar next door and made sure everybody filed through in an orderly fashion.

'"Keep going until we reach the corner house," instructed the warden. "Then we will make our way to the public shelter. We will be safe there."

'The public shelter was at least a block away but the warden made it seem like a comfortable stroll. We crawled through cellar after cellar, Lisl first, then Käte and the boy, then me, then Ludwig. It was horrifying. People were crying out in fear and from the pain of their injuries. I never saw such suffering. And still the bombs kept falling. We knew that few raids lasted longer than twenty minutes but this seemed like an eternity. Suddenly the people in front of us stopped. Word was passed back that the way ahead was blocked. We'd all have to try and make our way up into the open as best we could. Ludwig still had his torch and he flashed it around the cellar we were in trying to find the doorway. But there was too much smoke.

'"Hold on," he shouted and started to feel his way along the wall. He disappeared into the smoke and all we could see was a weak glow from his torch. The glow brightened so we guessed he must have found the door. He had, but it was blocked.

'"Everybody back one house!" he called. We were running out of time. There were now no more than eight to ten people besides ourselves in the cellar. We all turned and squeezed back the way we came. The heat and smoke were becoming unbearable. We were sure then that we would all die. We linked hands and followed the orange glow from Ludwig's torch. Once more the cellar door was blocked. Two men joined Ludwig and they pushed on the door with all their strength. It gave a little. They pushed and pushed and forced a small opening but it wasn't big enough for an adult.

'"Where's the boy?" shouted Ludwig.

'Käte took the boy up to Ludwig who bent over him and shouted in his ear.

'"Little man, we need your help. We want you to crawl through this hole and see if you can move whatever is blocking the door. Will you do this for us?"

'The boy nodded. He was so brave. He was shaking with fear. He started to cry as they helped him up through the hole but he still went. Ludwig passed him his torch and we were left in darkness. There we were, ten adults trusting our lives and our only torch to a boy of five. One of the men cried out suddenly. The boy had dropped a brick through the hole. Then another and another. We stood back as brick after brick tumbled out of the darkness. Then the torch appeared in the hole and we could see the boy trying to climb back down. Ludwig grabbed hold of him.

'"Push," the boy shouted. "Push the door!"

'So the men pushed and the cellar door opened another ten or twelve centimetres.

'"We will have to squeeze through," my husband shouted.

'Lisl began to panic. How could she get her swollen tummy through that tiny gap? But we had no choice. Our eyes were watering and the smoke and dust made it very difficult to breathe. Ludwig sent the boy and Käte up first. Then the other people. Then me. He told me to wait on the other side to help Lisl through in case she got stuck. I climbed through the doorway and looked up. Boards from the upper floors were dangling ablaze above my head. Burning pieces fell on

my head and arms. I wanted to run but I had to help Lisl. I
tried to grab her hands but then some burning piece of debris
would land on me and I'd have to brush it off. Lisl twisted
and turned and slowly began to wriggle her way through.
She'd taken off her coat to reduce her bulk and I could see
her stomach scraping hard against the rubble. She was crying.
I grabbed her hands and pulled. She looked up at me helplessly and something fell through the air and landed on her
face. Maybe it was burning carpet, I don't know. Her hair
began to smoulder and she screamed. There was nothing
she could do. She was trapped and I had hold of her two
hands. I pulled as hard as I could. Lisl screamed. I pulled and
pulled but she wouldn't budge. But suddenly she was free. I
smothered her burning hair with the front of my coat.

'Once more we made our way up onto the street. The
flames were worse but there were fewer bombs. We looked
around but we couldn't find Käte or the boy. We started to
run as best we could towards the shelter when a house wall
collapsed and fell right across the road in front of us. Surely
now we would perish. But no. Ludwig found a path through
the shell of a burned out house. It must have been a corridor
which had run from front to back. We ran down it with our
arms over our heads in case anything fell on us. We came
into a clearing which had been the garden. Walls had collapsed and we could see a possible escape route. We dashed
from garden to garden until we finally reached the corner.
But the heat and smoke had taken its toll. We were on the
verge of collapse. All I wanted to do was lie down. We
staggered out onto the road. If we'd died and gone to hell it
could not have been worse. We no longer had the strength
to weep, and what tears were left dried in the searing heat
before they left our eyes. We were finished. It felt like the air
was being sucked from our lungs. Ludwig took my hand. He
knew it was all over. We put our arms around Lisl. It was her
we felt sorry for, her and her unborn baby.

'Then came our miracle. Out of the smoke a truck appeared.
Men in strange coats and gas masks leapt off the back and
lifted us up onto the tray. They were from the *Sicherheits und
Hilfsdienst*, the rescue and repair service. They were so fast,
so brave and so disciplined. There were at least ten or fifteen

other people like us crowded onto the back. We turned down a street, one we must have known well but was now unrecognisable. We clung on desperately as the truck kept swerving around debris without slowing. Then I saw two figures — one large, one small — silhouetted by the flames. It was Käte and the boy. I grabbed one of the rescuers and pointed to them. He banged on the side of the truck to stop it. Käte and the boy were crossing through a burning building. They were running towards us. As the flames were reaching up around their knees Käte swept the boy up into her arms. One of the rescue men leapt off the truck before it had stopped and ran into the flames. He grabbed the boy from Käte and to our amazement stood there momentarily hugging him. As he turned and began to race back, a wall collapsed and fell on Käte. I saw her fall into the flames on the ground and the bricks pile up on top of her. The rescuer stopped and hesitated. What should he do? Save the boy or imperil us all by trying to save Käte? Houses were collapsing all around us and bombs were still falling nearby. The truck could easily be trapped. He put the boy on his back and began clawing at the bricks and stonework on top of Käte. Another rescuer ran into the flames and began to drag the man and the boy away. They left her there. Poor Käte! She never stood a chance.

'The rescuers leapt back on the truck and we raced off down the street. I couldn't stop thinking about poor Käte. If it hadn't been for the boy she would probably still be alive. But she never could have left him to fend for himself, what woman could? I hoped she had been killed instantly when the bricks hit her. It would be terrible to be trapped and burned to death. But there was another miracle. Quite extraordinary and touching. People talk about them but I never expected to witness one. The rescuer with the boy ripped off his mask and kissed him. The boy stopped crying immediately.

'"Daddy!" he screamed. He had been rescued by his own father! No wonder the man had run into the flames. No wonder he'd tried so desperately to save Käte, to repay his debt to her. He hugged the boy to him and tears flowed down his cheeks. Tears I thought were gone forever also flowed from my eyes, mixing with the soot and grime. Tears for Käte. Tears of relief. Tears for the boy and his father. Tears for Germany which had been destroyed. Suddenly we drove out of the fire. One moment we were in hell, the next in Wuppertal-Elberfeld. It was unbelievable. The path of the bombers was as precise as if they'd drawn a line. In Wuppertal-Elberfeld nothing had changed. It was all so unreal, so normal. Of course there were people running around everywhere, but the only signs of damage were broken windows. The most unusual thing we noticed was the sudden wind and the cold. Gales of cold air were rushing in to replace the oxygen burned in the fires and we went from nearly being roasted alive to freezing. But nothing made sense that night.

'The truck took us to a school which had been converted into a casualty station and centre for processing victims. We sat huddled together until a doctor could see us. He gave us cotton wool and some liquid to dab on our burns, and a tiny bowl of antiseptic for our cuts. It was hard to know where to begin. They told us the bombers had dropped little bombs filled with phosphorus which split open on impact and splashed fire everywhere. That was what I'd seen and why nothing could escape the flames. They told us the phosphorus keeps eating away at flesh until neutralised. Clearly that was the case with some of the less fortunate people around us who were in agony.

'I tried to get my shoes off but my feet were badly swollen. The shoes were many sizes too big but now I filled every centimetre. Ludwig who had been so brave and strong was almost in tears when he finally managed to take my shoes off and saw my feet. They were cut and raw. You saw them last night but they were much worse then. He bathed them in antiseptic as gently as he could, but every touch of the cotton wool was like hot needles. A woman from the *Frauenschaften* came and took our names. We told her about poor Käte. She asked if we had any relatives who lived in Elberfeld. I said we did and gave my sister's address. Then she ordered us to leave.

' "If anyone asks for you, that is where we will send them. Go now."

' "What do you mean?" I asked. "How can you expect us to go anywhere? Look at us! Look at my feet!"

'"I am sorry," she said, and I believe she was. "There are more people coming and we need the room. There are people much worse off than you. I am sorry."

'It was true. There were many people who were badly burned or unconscious and the room was rapidly filling up. Dear God! Once more I had to put on those shoes. We walked out into the night. The bombers had gone but the night was still filled with the roar of fires and the crash of buildings. Everyone who had a siren was using it. My sister lives about three kilometres away from the school but it may as well have been thirty. We had to ignore the pain and the icy gale that swirled about us, ripping off roof tiles and chimney pots as it rushed to fuel the flames. That would have been the final injustice. To be killed by a flying chimney pot! After one kilometre I knew I could go no further. We should have just banged on the nearest door and thrown ourselves on the mercy of whoever lived behind it. How could they turn us away? Of course they wouldn't. But despite our pain, we still couldn't bring ourselves to do it. We heard a truck labouring up the hill and Ludwig stepped out onto the road in front of it. The truck was going to collect more sand to put on the fires and the driver gladly gave us a lift. He dropped us right at my sister's front door. His kindness was typical of what happened over the next few days.

'My sister wept to see us. She ushered us in to her drawing room and made us coffee, real coffee. God only knows where she got the beans from. Everyone except us seems to have a secret hoard of coffee beans. Her husband had gone to help fight the flames and she had been sitting up alone, worried out of her wits about us. Her daughter was putting her three children to sleep in the bedroom at the top of the stairs. My sister gave Ludwig and I her bed, and made up another on the sofa for Lisl and stayed with her. Lisl was in shock, she still is. My sister washed her and tended her burns and put her to bed and sat with her, holding her hand for the rest of the night.

'When her husband came home he was so exhausted he lay down on the landing half way up the stairs and fell asleep without washing or changing his clothes. There were bodies everywhere. It was clear to us that her little house was crowded even before we arrived, so in the morning we made up our minds to move on. All Lisl talked about was going home. She sat on the sofa rocking backwards and forwards and the only words she said were "... home ... home ..." Ludwig decided I should bring her to you. He wanted to stay and see what he could save from our house. He said he would find somewhere to live and send us a telegram when he had. He also said he'd send you a telegram to warn you we were coming. My sister made us some breakfast and lent us some of her clothes, but they were threadbare and she didn't have any coats to spare. She wanted to give me some shoes, but my feet were so swollen the only shoes I could get into were my dead man's shoes. I felt guilty every time I put them on. But I would have perished in the fires without them.

'When we reached Elberfeld station, we were given our tickets free and told where to go for food. Sometimes it takes a disaster like we had experienced to bring out the best in people and officialdom, and that was certainly the case. Having never been bombed before we had no idea that this had been by far the worst air raid of the war, and the whole country was galvanised to help its victims. We were given some bread and a little sausage and some kind of paste. God knows what it was made of. I told Lisl to eat only a little because we had no idea how long the train trip would take.

'As it was, it took three days and we had to change trains four times. They were all very crowded but each time somebody gave us their seats. One look at our faces and our filthy clothes and they knew we were from Wuppertal. People brought us drinks and shared what little food they had with us. One woman even lent us a blanket. People were so kind but even so the journey was interminable. Every time I got to my feet was agony. I could put off going to the toilet but not Lisl because of her pregnancy. And every time I had to go with her so she wouldn't get lost. Poor Lisl! All she could say was, "My baby, my baby ... what has happened to my baby?" By the time we reached Dresden I was at the end of my tether. I have never been so relieved to see anyone in my life. I can't tell you how glad I was to see you. The moment you put your arms around me, I knew my ordeal was over.'

*   *   *

Ulla finished speaking and sank back in her bed. She picked up her coffee but it had long gone cold. Clara took it from her and disappeared back to the kitchen to warm it up again for her. But mostly, she went because she didn't want Ulla to see her tears. What could anyone say to this brave woman who had been through so much and could still inject touches of humour into her narrative?

'Thank you for bringing our daughter back to us.' Carl went over to Ulla, knelt down and put his arms around her. He'd spoken from the heart and for everyone.

Ulla began to weep silently. Christiane fought back her tears then made her decision.

'Ulla, you must stay here in Dresden with us and Lisl. We will all stay here. We are safe in Dresden.' She turned defiantly to Friedrich. 'We are staying here. I am staying here.'

Friedrich turned away without a word and went down to Carl's study. He needed time to think. How could he persuade Christiane to take their son to the west now? Yet if they stayed they would have to face the Russians. Germany was sliding inexorably towards the brink of the abyss, trapped between two unspeakable horrors. He deferred a decision. Perhaps Dresden was the safest place for the time being. Perhaps the Russian war machine would falter. Perhaps the Führer would bow to the inevitable and sue for peace. Perhaps, perhaps, perhaps! Friedrich knew in his heart that they had to move west, to a small village somewhere that had no attraction for bombers. But it would be a harsh decision given the events of the previous days, and in the end he made no decision. He would not get the same opportunity again.

*　　*　　*

Lucio finished speaking but nobody spoke. The same sense of impending doom that had consumed Friedrich now enveloped them. Friedrich had backed down when he should have stood firm. It was now clear to them all where the story was headed for they all knew the terrible consequences of his indecisiveness. They thought about Christiane and Helmuth, Lisl and her unborn child, Carl, Clara and the courageous

Ulla. They thought about those lives, each with its hopes and aspirations for the future. And they thought of the impending carnage. It just didn't seem fair.

'Jesus,' said Neil finally, 'somebody tell a joke.'

'We don't need a joke, Neil, we have you.'

'C'mon, Ramon, you know what I mean. We need one of Lucio's bedtime stories otherwise we all might as well just go home and open a vein.'

'I think Lucio has done enough talking, no?' Milos looked around the table seeking consensus.

'Yes, he has done enough talking. Milos' comment is obviously aimed at me. I want to hear more about Colombina and Lucio had promised to enlighten us.' Ramon paused. 'But I don't need to see his face to know that he is tired. No one can tell such stories without becoming affected by them. He has his tiredness and Ulla's. He has his despair and Friedrich's. And he bears the sorrow of the story yet untold. I release him from any promises. Besides, Milos has indicated that he will intercede to prevent a repetition of last week.'

'Thank you, Ramon.' Lucio exhaled and slumped back in his chair. 'I was prepared to continue. I just needed to catch my breath. You are quite right, you know, a storyteller does live his story and I feel the combined weariness of all the characters. I will never tell a story like this again. It is too exhausting. I promise I will begin next week with Colombina. In truth, I should end with her tonight to give you something to think about over the coming week. But, dear God, today has been harrowing enough.'

'You've given us plenty to think about. It's really strange to hear about the war from the German side. All my life I've been taught that the Germans were the baddies and the only good kraut was a dead one. I thought they were all Nazis.'

'No Neil,' said Milos, 'most Germans were just very ordinary people with very limited choice. The German people were the first victims when the Nazis came to power. The ordinary citizens had two options. They could speak out against the atrocities, the treatment of the Jews and the loss of civil rights. But to do so was to invite a visit from the Brownshirts or the Gestapo, and not just them but their whole family would be made to suffer. Bear in mind also, that they would be making a stand against the one man who could put food back on their tables and fuel in their fires; the one man who could unite Germany; the one man who could give them back their sense of pride. Even so, a large number of German people were appalled by what the Nazis were doing. But here again, you have an example of Hitler's evil genius. He could always find justification even for his most vile actions. He revived the belief in the primacy of the German race. It was ingrained in most Germans that they were special people whose birthright was at risk because of the influx of foreigners. He pounded his message home until belief was accepted as fact. That gave dissenters an easy way to salve their consciences. Now if they weren't prepared to stand up and take their chances with the Gestapo, they were no longer cowards but patriots, allowing the Nazis to reclaim what was rightfully theirs. Of course, the Nazis' methods were distasteful, but few could argue against the justice of their cause. Besides, most people believed Hitler would stop once they had their *Grosswirtschaftsraum*. Once the war had escalated and started to go against them, most people were happy to distance themselves from the Nazis. But by then it was all too late. The man who'd promised to set them free was now their gaoler, and the instruments used for repressing the Jews and the Slavs were now poised above their heads. There were informers everywhere and no one could be trusted. Imagine how they felt. There they were, ordinary people doomed at the hands of the Russians, the Allies and in fear of their own leaders.'

'Well said, Milos.' Ramon turned to Neil. 'You must remember, Neil, history is always written by the victors. If Hitler had won, Stalin, Roosevelt and Churchill would have been the villains and you here in Australia would have been none the wiser.'

'We'd be Japanese, that's what we'd be, wise or otherwise.'

'There were bad things on both sides,' said Gancio gloomily. 'That's why it's all best forgotten. There is no right or wrong in war, just winners and losers. And there are always more losers.'

'That's it! I am going to open a vein.'

'No! Neil you can save your razor for your chin.' Everyone turned to Ramon. 'Gancio should go and get us a bottle of his best grappa instead. I will pay for it. Then we can all phone for a taxi to take us home.'

'Or a bloody hearse,' said Neil grimly.

FIFTH THURSDAY

'We've got to find some way to lighten up,' said Neil. 'Last week I'd had my best day in years and you still managed to spoil it. I used to look forward to these lunches. Remember when we used to enjoy ourselves? I'd always go straight from here to my girlfriend's and round out the day in the nicest possible way. I tell you, she got to look forward to our Thursdays as much as I did. Now — shit! — they're about as much fun as making love on a sandy beach with an on-shore breeze.'

'Half your luck!'

Neil paused and looked at Milos. 'Half my luck? Milos, you are an ignorant man. I have made love in phone boxes, movie theatres, small cars and even on a motorbike. I've made love on a concrete patio till my bum was rubbed raw. I've made love on my desk with a secretary who should have been a jockey, and spent the next ten minutes pulling glider clips and staples out of my back. I have made love by moonlight and by cellulite. But mate, there is nothing worse, no pain on earth to compare with having sand blown up onto the sticky bits when you're heading for the happy ending. No don't laugh. Don't any of you bastards laugh. You're all reffos and you know nothing. You wouldn't know a rabbit was up you until he had a nibble at your carrot.'

Gancio saw his friends laughing and came scurrying over to the table to see what was happening.

'It's okay, Gancio, you've missed nothing.' Lucio smiled. 'We've swapped roles. Neil has turned into me. He was just recounting some of his more intimate experiences.'

'Maybe you'd be better off doing the same,' cut in Neil.

'C'mon, mate, give us one of your tales for old times' sake. Give us all a laugh for a change.'

Lucio thought for a moment. A little digression would do no harm. Neil was right. They could all do with a laugh. 'Okay,' he said. 'I have a story to tell which is worse, much worse, and much more painful.' His four friends sat up expectantly. This was the Lucio of old, the one they'd come to love. 'As you are all aware, there are times when my member could be accused of irresponsibility. When I was a young man in Varese, I fell in love with a beautiful woman. She could have been anything. A famous model, a movie star, who knows. She had the sort of body that makes men groan in their sleep, and the face of pure love. I tried hard not to learn her name so that I wouldn't give myself away by calling it out aloud when I was with another woman. But it was no good. I thought about her the whole time. Finally I lost my appetite for food and for sex. It is true. How could any other woman interest me when I had discovered the one woman I wanted more than life itself? I knew then the full agony and despair of lovesickness. I knew then why lovelorn men shoot themselves and throw themselves off bridges. Life no longer has purpose.

'I decided I had to meet this woman, to talk to her, hopefully to seduce her and maybe one day ask her to be my wife. But there were difficulties. I was only nineteen and she was twenty-one. And she still lived with her parents. Her parents were very devout and went to church every day and twice on Sundays. My love, this woman, went with them on Saturdays to confession and Mass on Sunday morning and evening. What could my angel possibly have had to confess? She had no life. Her parents watched over her like eagles over their chick. She could never leave the nest without them.

'As I watched I saw other men try to get close to her. Her parents would glare at them and that seemed to frighten them off, because either there'd be a different man trying his luck the following Sunday or nobody.

'I bided my time and one Sunday morning I sat next to her. I never looked at her or spoke to her. I did the same in the evening but this time I smiled at her. She smiled back and her parents scowled. I can't tell you how wonderful it felt just to be next to her, just to be near her, to breathe the same air. She was so pure and virginal, and so very desirable.

'As we were leaving, I discovered I was alongside her. She smiled so I spoke to her. Oh joy! She had the voice of an angel. She could sing like an angel and now that angel voice was talking to me. She told me her name. It was Pia. Pious Pia, I thought. Then she leaned close to me and said, "I know what you want." I was stunned. Could she read my mind? I thought of all the thoughts that had gone through my head as we'd knelt together in prayer. I began to blush. And do you know what? As we walked down the aisle to the exit her hand brushed my fly. Now I was really blushing. I hoped God wasn't watching. She took my hand and led me over to her parents.

'"Papa, Mama," she said, "I would like you to meet Lucio. I have invited him to have coffee with us."

'She had? When? It didn't matter. Her parents just shrugged their acceptance although their annoyance was unmistakable. We went back to her home and we sat in their lounge room sipping weak coffee. It was more milk than coffee, exactly the way I loathe it. The room was small and the house was small. It was crowded with furniture and religious icons. Every wall had a crucifix or a Madonna or a baleful looking Christ. We talked about my job and my mother. Her parents said nothing. They just watched and wilted. We talked about the flowers in church. I was so polite my jaw ached. Then her parents stood up and announced that they were going to bed and that it was time we did too. I stood to leave but Pia grabbed my hand and pulled me back down onto the sofa.

'"I haven't finished my coffee," she said. "Neither has Lucio. Surely it would be rude to ask him to leave before his cup is empty. What would he think of our hospitality?"

'It was clear to me that neither of her parents could give a damn what I thought of their hospitality, but equally they were almost asleep on their feet.

'"You go on to bed," Pia told her parents sweetly. "Lucio can finish his coffee and go. We will only be ten minutes."

'Well her parents looked at her doubtfully, but they were tired and there's not a lot that can happen in ten minutes, particularly when the preliminaries haven't even begun. Pious

Pia had done nothing to arouse their suspicions or, more to the point, anything to arouse me. It was hard to believe that this was the same girl who professed to know what I was thinking and whose hand had brushed my fly. At that stage my disinterest was palpable. So they left to go to bed. I sat there on the sofa wondering what was going on. Pia sat in the chair opposite and talked a lot of rubbish about the service. I thought now was probably a good time to leave. She was beautiful but there is a limit to what a man can stand, even for love. Every now and again she'd stop talking and listen. I opened my mouth to speak but she put her finger to her lips for silence. I heard her mother go to the toilet, then her father. I heard them brush their teeth. I heard one of them fart. There are noises everybody makes that are best not shared. I'll be charitable and say it was the father. I heard him go to bed and then her mother suddenly opened the door.

'"Not finished yet?" she asked pointedly.

'"Mother, we were just discussing the sermon." Pia looked up at her mother all starry-eyed and innocent. It was the truth. She was discussing the sermon when her mother came in.

'"Good night, then," says her mother. "Don't be long. Finish your coffee."

'She closed the door and we heard her walk into the room alongside and climb into bed. What now? What was the point? If we could hear them, surely they could hear us. What did Pia hope to achieve? Well, I wasn't left to wonder. I have seen strippers have more trouble getting out of their clothes than Pia had getting out of hers. I have never seen anyone undress so fast. Her clothes flowed off her and she was standing in front of me absolutely naked, eye-balling me with her nipples. She'd made no attempt to dim the lights so I missed nothing. Even now I can tell you, I have never seen anyone or anything as beautiful in my life. I remember every detail. Her skin was flawless and almost as pale as the English. Her breasts were erect — that is the only word to describe them. I have never seen nipples point so high. Like anti-aircraft guns. Next thing she was undoing my trousers. She lay back on the sofa and invited me in. I wanted to shout, to scream, to whoop for joy, but what could I do? I climbed out of my trousers and onto her nest. I needed no encouragement. My thing was like a space probe, a Saturn rocket and only centimetres from the moon. And, my God . . . what bliss! She moved slowly beneath me as if she knew every squeak in the sofa and how to avoid them. Oh God, I was scared to breathe. I didn't want her parents to come in and interrupt this ecstasy. And it *was* ecstasy. Round and round she went and up and down. Slowly. Expertly. But how can anyone be ecstatic in silence? She was coming to a climax and so was I. Her eyes were shut and her face screwed up. Round and round she went. I crossed my eyes, I crossed my toes, I crossed my heart! Nothing in my life would ever be better than this. I knew then with absolute certainty that when we came we would wake the dead. We would wake all of Varese. Our cries would reach out to the galaxies to all the stars in creation. Just as nothing can stop the sun from rising nor the tides, nothing could stop us from howling the house down. But Pia had thought of a way. Without warning she sank her teeth into my shoulder. Not like a love bite but like a wild animal. Like a vampire. Any other time I would have gone soft with the pain. But I couldn't stop. Not now. Not now! Round and round she went, faster and faster, hanging on by her teeth. I don't know to this day which was the greater sensation, the orgasm or the pain in my shoulder. All I know is we came to a gasping, shuddering, wonderful climax, with after-shocks rolling on and on like waves onto a beach, and neither of us had made a sound. Not a peep! She because she had a mouthful of my shoulder. Me because I was gritting my teeth so hard to block out the pain. Next thing I knew she was up and getting dressed. She threw my pants at me to put on. It wasn't easy. My shoulder ached and already the blood was sticking to my shirt. She sat down opposite me and watched me as she calmly finished her coffee.

'"That's it," she said. "Coffee's finished. Will I see you in church next Sunday?"

'Well of course I said yes but in truth I wasn't sure. I wasn't sure my shoulder could go another round and, besides, she'd ruined my best shirt. I didn't know what to make of her. I was utterly confused. I'd hoped to seduce her but had no idea how to go about it. Instead she'd seduced me and knew exactly how to go about it. I went to the café where my friends hang out. We'd been talking a while when I took off my jacket. My shoulder was stiff and sore and I wanted to rub it. They saw the blood and one of them pointed and shouted, "Hey! Look! Lucio's been to church!" Then I understood why no man sat with her twice. They all had scars on their shoulder. They'd all felt the bite of my love, my unassailable virgin. The bitch had sunk her teeth into half the men in Varese.'

The friends collapsed in laughter. Other diners turned around, curious as to the disturbance. Gancio returned to the kitchen to fetch the next course, colliding with chairs and diners as he went. This was more like it. This is what the Thursdays used to be all about. But just as an entree is often no guide to the main course, their levity was no indicator of the tale to come. Lucio had set the parameters of his story and there was no changing course now.

Chapter Twenty-Four

Colombina was devastated. She stood stunned, motionless on the narrow pathway as the calamaris she'd intended for lunch leaked water through their paper wrapping. The grass between the pavers that had felt the weight of her feet, slowly unwound and tentatively reached back up for the sky. What did the woman next door mean when she said, 'He's gone.' Did that mean he was dead, or simply not there? Please God! Please don't let him be dead! She looked over to the window to see if the woman had reappeared but her curtains were drawn. Colombina didn't know which way to turn. Little by little the Oberstleutnant had taken over her life. He was all that mattered to her. His death, and the manner of it, had become the focal point of her existence. He had to be made to confront his past and face his guilt. He had to pay for the death of her mother. She felt a massive emptiness inside.

Colombina returned to her car and sat slumped over the steering wheel. Disappointment and bewilderment fought for ascendancy. And there was another emotion, also insistent and intrusive — a deadening sense of loss. She discovered she was crying but her confused mind couldn't pinpoint the cause. All her life she'd managed to keep her emotions under tight control. Now that they'd escaped the restraints, they ran riot and Colombina lacked the experience to rein them in and deal with them in an orderly fashion. If she had, perhaps she would have discovered a few truths and faced up to the new knowledge. Instead, she sat in her car and let the waves of distress wash blindly over her until she calmed down. Then she began to consider her next steps coldly and logically.

She would ring the hospitals until she found him or, at

least, someone who knew what had happened to him. She started her car and drove home. She sealed the calamaris in a plastic container and put them in the fridge. She put away her pasta and olives, and sat the artichokes in a fruit bowl. She washed her face and hands and changed her dress, and wondered why fish shops bothered to put their goods in plastic bags when they neglected to seal up the necks. Her soiled dress would have to be dry-cleaned. She made herself a coffee and sat down at the phone.

Colombina had recovered her strength. If the Oberstleutnant was dead then he was dead, and that was the end of it. There was nothing she could do about it except forget him, and forget that she'd ever had a chance, however briefly, of avenging her mother. In a way she felt as though she'd been relieved of a burden. By the time she'd got through to the reception desk at the Mona Vale Hospital, she'd convinced herself that the old man and her burden were gone from her forever.

'Hello, I am Mrs Galli. I am making inquiries about a Mr Heinrich Bose. I believe he was brought in on Wednesday some time.'

'Could you repeat the name?'

Colombina smiled and did as requested. Hospitals everywhere were seemingly untouched by the life and death dramas enacted within their walls. The people who serviced her car showed more emotion.

'B3.'

'I beg your pardon?'

'He's in B3. That's the ward.'

He was alive! Colombina supressed her excitement. Or was it relief? 'Could you tell me his condition, please?'

'I'm sorry. I'm not allowed to pass on that information. Would you like to speak to the sister?'

'Please.' Colombina hung on while she was put on hold and the phone played a jingle for margarine. The commercial ended and they crossed to the news just as the ward sister answered.

'Sister . . .'

'Hello. I'm Mrs Galli. I'm ringing about a friend of mine who is in your ward. Mr Bose.'

'Are you a relative?'

'Mr Bose doesn't have any relatives in Australia.' Colombina could see the trap coming and decided to bend the truth a little. 'I help take care of him and bring him meals. I am his closest friend.'

'You're not Cecilia by any chance?'

Colombina felt her blood run cold. She was stunned speechless.

'No,' the voice on the phone continued. 'I don't suppose you could be. He called her name out all the time in his sleep after the operation and now we tease him about her. He says she's someone he knew in Italy or somewhere. Hello . . . ?'

'I'm sorry. You mentioned an operation. I was out of town when he was taken ill. What was the problem?'

'Kidney stones.'

Kidney stones. Colombina didn't know whether to laugh or cry. Of all the possibilities that had gone through her head! She was prepared for a stroke, a heart attack, a fall. Nothing had prepared her for kidney stones!

'May I visit him?'

'Certainly. Visiting time is from two until four, then from six until seven-thirty.'

'Thank you, I'll come this evening.'

'I'll let him know when he wakes up. He's still under mild sedation and has a lot of pain passing water.' She paused and added knowledgeably, 'Fragments.'

Colombina hung up. She wondered momentarily if it was her cooking that had caused the kidney stones. Then her mind moved on to the greater issue. She found it hard to believe he'd be calling out the name of a lover he hadn't seen for nearly fifty years.

*   *   *

'Hello, Heinrich.' Colombina had brought a bunch of flowers she'd picked from her garden, four kiwi fruit which she knew he adored, and a half bottle of red wine. She also brought her Walkman, some opera tapes and a small transformer so that he wouldn't always be replacing batteries. She knew how much the Walkman would be used.

'Colombina!' The old man opened his eyes and the delight in them was overwhelming and genuine. 'Colombina. I was so worried. I didn't think you would be able to find me.' His speech and his movements were slow but the sedatives hadn't suppressed his emotions.

Colombina was touched. At that moment she was the old man's closest friend and nothing more. She watched as tears washed over the old man's eyes and made them shiny. She placed his flowers on the bed tray, his fruit and wine on top of his cabinet, and bent over and kissed his cheek.

'You shouldn't have worried, Heinrich. You should have known I would find you. I would never stop searching until I did.' Colombina chose her words deliberately and watched closely to see what effect they would have. But he appeared to take them at face value, as a declaration of affection.

'What is this?'

'Opera, Heinrich. I know you can't live without it and I thought I'd save the hospital the trouble of having to dispose of your body.'

The old man smiled, delighted with both the gift and the irreverence. Colombina took his hand and squeezed. A long time ago it was his smile that had cut through her defences. Her response was entirely reflexive, familiar and learned. But there was danger in its familiarity, unequivocal confirmation of her true identity, and she was quick to cover up. She used the gesture to hand over the Walkman. Heinrich gave no flicker of recognition, no hint of an acknowledgement other than gratitude at her thoughtfulness.

'So who have you brought me?' He reached across to his cabinet for his glasses. He examined each cassette minutely as if their contents took a while to register. 'Ah . . . *Lohengrin*, a very old friend. And Elisabeth Schwarzkopf.' He peered up at Colombina over his glasses. 'When I die, Colombina, I would like them to attend my funeral. I can imagine no finer farewell. Would you do that for me?'

'First you have to die.'

He peered at her intently and Colombina had the distinct impression that something beyond the obvious had at last penetrated his drug-induced haze. She held her breath. Was this the moment of truth, when they both stopped playing games? Instead he slowly smiled.

'Colombina, you are a tonic. An absolute tonic!' He began to chuckle.

Colombina joined him. She'd learn no more that day and dared not throw any more hints. If he knew she was Cecilia then he'd kept the knowledge securely to himself. Even with his brain undermined by sedatives he hadn't flinched. She'd tried three times to unsettle him — twice deliberately and once accidentally — yet there'd been not the slightest indication. Surely there would have been. Surely his sedation would have worked in her favour. Did he know who she was? Did he know she suspected he knew? Surely in his weakened state with his mental processes inhibited, there would have been some indication. But maybe not. Maybe the sedatives worked against her and masked any reaction on his part, giving him the opportunity to examine her words later. If so, she'd blundered. She had revealed her doubts and he had revealed nothing.

Colombina visited him every day for the next fortnight, always in the evening because she'd learned that John and Edna often called by in the afternoons following their Meals-on-Wheels duties. She never tested him again — she had no need to. She was now convinced that he knew who she was. He would not have cried out her name unless she was on his mind. He was playing her game and she believed she understood his motives. At first she'd thought he'd gone along with the charade preferring to have the company of an enemy he liked rather than no company at all. Certainly he was confident enough to pit his wits against hers. But if he was doing it simply for amusement he was taking an entirely unwarranted risk. Then it dawned on her. It was so blindingly obvious she was astonished by her stupidity. After all this time, he still loved her. The thought came unbidden and brought with it half a century of pain. Suddenly it all made sense. And another possibility occurred to her. Maybe she hadn't found him. Maybe he had found her.

The more Colombina thought about it, the more certain she became. They were both refugees but only one a fugitive. Only one needed forgiveness. And only forgiveness and the

rekindling of love could justify his empty, meaningless existence through all the lonely years. Yes, Colombina thought, if
I forgive him and open my heart to him once more, his
penance will have been worthwhile. It will all have been
worthwhile. That is why he persists. He loves me and I am
his only hope for absolution. He wants me to absolve him.
But there could be no absolution, only retribution. Her fingers
unconsciously searched out the hasp on her locket and flicked
it open. They picked at the photograph of Mario and removed
it so that Maddalena's faded image gazed up at her, a silent
but insistent plea for justice.

She drove the old man home from the hospital, promising
to look in on him every day to make sure he was all right,
knowing full well that she would never have a better chance
to kill him. His legs would still be weak. It would be understandable if he fell. Forget the poison. She could confront
him. Force him to face up to his guilt. And his fate. Then she
would drag him through to the bathroom. If his head didn't
hit the toilet or the edge of the bath the first time he fell, it
certainly would the second.

But dear God! To think how easily it could all have been
so different! To think he still loved her after all those years.
All those wasted years! And to think she still loved him. Yes!
Of course she did. She could admit it now that the end was
imminent. Of course she still loved him. That was the terrible
thing. They were still in love and now she had to lose him
again.

Chapter Twenty-Five

By June 1943, the Duce was sick, dispirited and ineffectual. Hitler, once his friend and ally, now made no secret of his contempt for him and everything Italian. Mussolini's country had turned against him and there were dark whispers of revolt from within his own ranks. His army was in tatters and, worse, those soldiers who were prepared to fight were defecting to the resistance. But he still had some friends and none were more strident than the Count d'Alatri.

The Count's arch-enemy, the communists, had risen once more and struck at the country's heart. Massive strikes had swept Milan and Turin. This show of strength had galvanised the Count into action. As Mussolini faltered the Count grew stronger. He wrote to the Duce every day, forcefully suggesting punitive action against the strikers and their families, and offering to finance a bounty on the head of every killed or captured communist leader. He also railed against what he saw as cavalier treatment of Italy by the Germans, and insisted that the Duce demand more aircraft and weaponry. When local fascist leaders came to dinner he berated them for their ineffectual attempts to deal with the partisans and escaped prisoners.

Increasingly Cecilia found herself less of a companion and more of a secretary. The Count had acquired a typewriter which she now used to type his letters as he dictated them. She developed the knack of capturing the sense and flavour of his rantings and composed her own sentences. It not only added to the comprehension but enabled her to keep up. The Count constantly sent letters to the Duce, and began to network his old friends in the fascist hierarchy. Even when she was at school, Cecilia had never worked so hard. She longed for the afternoons when the Count would retire for his siesta and she'd have the chance to talk to Guido Mila.

There'd been no hero's welcome this time for the wounded soldier. The Count failed to understand how Guido could allow the Italian army to be weakened twice by his absence. He accused him of malingering and, in fact, he wasn't far from the truth. The bullet which had creased Guido's head had travelled a long way to find him and no longer had the energy to penetrate his skull. By rights it should have, and the doctors who attended him were curious as to why it hadn't. They attributed his survival somewhat facetiously to the thickness of bone and the absence of brain. But Guido was no fool. He made the most of his misfortune and milked it. He had the perfect injury for a soldier who wanted to take no further part in a war that was already lost. Head wounds were a passport out of uniform because no doctor could ever be certain of the extent of the injury. So Guido complained of severe headaches he never had, dizziness he never felt, and blinding flashes of light he never saw. He was well versed on the symptoms, as most of his fellow soldiers were. Head wounds were precious and not to be wasted.

At first he allowed Cecilia to bathe his forehead and minister to him, relishing her care and concern. One day he told her the truth and she nearly hit him. Then she laughed. It was another blow against the Count. He was now sheltering a malingerer. Nevertheless she maintained the charade and continued to nurse him and pander to him to avoid suspicions. Besides, the daily ritual gave them the chance to be together and talk.

She never asked herself what was at the root of her attraction to him, possibly because she didn't want to know the answers. But she lapped up his company and hung on his every word. When he told her how proud he was of her for helping deserters and escaped prisoners, she glowed.

'You risk your pretty little neck,' he said. 'You risk your life for men like me, poor men who can never repay your kindness.' He put his hand up to her cheek as a father would to a favoured daughter. 'After the war when Italy names its brave, you will be there at the top of the list.'

He made all the risks she'd taken and would continue to take seem worthwhile. There was nothing she wouldn't do for him, no risk she wouldn't be willing to take. He was her hero and she adored him. If only her own father had been like Guido. So every day she swung between the fascist and the anti-fascist, the fanatic and the reluctant soldier, the deviant and the hero. She balanced the opposing forces and was unswervingly loyal to both. Cecilia was happy and would have been content if things had remained as they were. But the time was fast approaching when loyalties would have to be declared and consequences acknowledged. Change was inevitable and, as it happened, the Count was the catalyst.

One evening over dinner he announced that he had to see Mussolini in person. 'My child, we will write to the Duce tomorrow. You will accompany me to Rome. There are matters I need to discuss with him which I can only do in person. He is surrounded by traitors. It is not something I can put in letters. Who knows who has access to his mail?'

'Will I meet the Duce?' Cecilia looked up at the Count, her eyes shining brightly. She knew exactly how to react.

'If the opportunity arises, of course you will. In fact, I will see to it that you do. He is a great man, Cecilia, but never too great to shake the hand of his supporters, whoever they may be. Andre can drive us to Milan. We can catch a train from there.'

'Thank you,' said Cecilia. She reached across and squeezed the Count's hand.

'You are a good girl, Cecilia. With people like you I know our cause is not yet lost.'

He kept Cecilia busy all the morning of the next day, writing letters and making travel arrangements. For a while it seemed that he would work through lunch and forgo his afternoon sleep. But eventually tiredness crept up and claimed him. As soon as she was free, she dashed away to find Signor Mila and tell him the news. She found him sitting alone in the shade of a plane tree, gazing out over the lake.

'How is your headache?' she asked.

'For once I do have a headache — two headaches in fact — because I'm getting another headache just trying to think of a cure for the first.'

Cecilia laughed. 'Have you heard about my little journey?'

'Yes, I have heard,' he said. 'It is a pity I don't have a hand grenade to give you, to slip down the front of Il Duce's trousers. That would cure my headache and spare us all a lot problems and hardship.'

Cecilia laughed along with him. She loved him when he was in this mood. But he turned serious and took her hand.

'Cecilia, when you come back from Rome you will be on your own.'

'What do you mean?' Everything suddenly went deathly quiet. If the birds still sang she never heard them. For a moment the earth ceased spinning and time froze. Her mind focused exclusively on his next words, seeking enlightenment.

'It is almost certain that the British and the Americans will land somewhere in Italy. When that happens the fascists will grab every man they can get their hands on to go and fight them.'

'But you can't . . .'

'No, I can't. And I won't. Nevertheless, it is time for a full recovery. Things can't stay as they are. Signor Calosci is already suspicious. He fought in the first war and you can't fool old soldiers. Cecilia, I'm going up into the hills to find others like me. We will become partisans. We will fight the fascists and the Germans when they come. Germany is our enemy now, not Britain or America.'

'But what will happen to the Signora and Carmela?'

'You know what will happen. The Count will throw them out. He won't have the family of a traitor living under the same roof. I will take advantage of the Count's absence to slip away. It will also give the Signora time to make other arrangements. I assume Signor Calosci is also accompanying you?'

'Yes.'

'Then we will have time. The Signora and Carmela will have a home until the Count returns. There's nobody with enough authority to throw them out. Perhaps the Count will let them stay on a while. Who knows? He is a selfish man and does not like to go without his comforts. Maybe he will keep them until he finds someone to replace them.'

'Maybe.' Cecilia could not keep the doubt out of her voice.

Her mind was reeling and not up to playing along with patently false hopes. She suddenly realised how much she'd come to depend on the Signora. Her presence was a strength she could always draw upon. And even Carmela. They'd become close friends. What would she do now? The thought burst like a bubble from her mouth.

'What will you do? Cecilia you will continue to do what you've always done. You will take care of the Count. You will be faithful to him and Mussolini. It will be hard, Cecilia, but you can do it. We both know you can. You will stay here at the Villa. The time may come when we will need you.'

Cecilia knew she would cope, she always did. But there was the other part of her loss which had nothing to do with being isolated. Guido was going away. She might never see him again or talk to him. She knew from the men she'd helped that life on the run was desperately hard. The only things they could be certain of were starvation and deprivation. She glanced up at the hills, welcoming now in the warmth of summer but desolate in winter. He could starve, he could freeze to death or he could get shot and die. Surely he couldn't escape with just being wounded a third time. She thought of that kind and decent man dying alone in the mountains with no one to care for him or comfort him. Maybe what she felt was only puppy love or the love of a daughter for a father. Whatever it was, it was still love and Cecilia felt heartbroken. How could she explain that to Guido? She felt like crying but wouldn't allow the tears to form, not even when Guido leaned across and kissed her cheek.

'Be careful,' she whispered and walked slowly back to the house.

* * *

The trains had adopted the practice of running at night to avoid possible attack by marauding Allied aircraft, even though they were still safely beyond fighter range. For once, the Italian bureaucracy had anticipated the need. To Cecilia's surprise, the Count slept through the entire journey and even snored. He seemed to relish being active and having a sense of purpose once more. Overnight, the years had fallen away and he'd become a much younger man. When they arrived in Rome, he had to be dissuaded from going straight to the Palazzo Venezia and joining Mussolini for a surprise breakfast. Instead they went to the Count's apartment which had been rapidly vacated by his nephew and family, who normally enjoyed the privilege of staying there. Cecilia had written the letter warning them of the Count's arrival.

All she wanted was a hot bath and a bed, and time to get used to the fact that Guido was now probably gone from the Villa Carosio, and that the Signora and Carmela would soon be as well. But the Count had found untapped sources of energy and was eager to bring forward his meeting with the Duce.

'Wait till you see him, Cecilia, he is magnificent. You can feel the power radiating from him. He is an inspiration. You will have to wait of course, until we have completed our business. After all, that is why we are here. But Cecilia, I promise you, it is an experience you will never forget.'

For once Cecilia's enthusiasm failed to live up to the required levels.

'Cecilia, I am talking about meeting the Duce.' His voice grew hard. 'What are you saying? Is the Duce no longer important to you?'

Cecilia forced a tired smile. 'Count, if the Lord struck me dead the moment after I met him, I would die happy for I know that nothing else that might happen in my life would ever compare.'

'That's more like it!'

'But Count, I am not used to sleeping on trains. I did not sleep all night. Signor Calosci can confirm this.'

'In that case go and sleep. I will call you at lunch time. By then I will have some letters for you and hopefully a typewriter. Go!'

Cecilia found her way to the servants' quarters and lay down. She knew well that it wasn't tiredness that had caused her façade to slip but distraction. Guido had upset her equilibrium. She could not allow it to happen again. The Count was neither tolerant nor fair and was liable to do anything in one of his rages. What would she do then? She put Guido in a corner of her brain where he could hide and sealed him off.

She thought about meeting the Duce and made herself feel excited. She remembered everything she'd read about him, to her father and to the Count. She thought of the march on Rome, and the triumphant procession through Rome with Hitler. She cheated her mind until her weariness overcame her and she fell into sleep. But she couldn't cheat her dreams.

*   *   *

The Count strode into the Palazzo Venezia as though he'd borrowed the legs of a much younger man. He was imperious and his reception justified his attitude. He was warmly greeted by the Duce's personal staff, veterans of the march on Rome, and led away immediately to his private chambers. Cecilia was taken to one side and offered a chair away from the traffic and virtually out of sight. Yet she was happy to be tucked away. She found the Palazzo overwhelming and intimidating. She didn't belong there. She'd always thought that the Villa Carosio was grand but it paled into insignificance by comparison. So she watched and waited and did her best to appear invisible.

She heard a door bang and a woman's voice ring out. Cecilia stirred and looked around. Down the stairway came a young woman talking animatedly to the man who was with her. She was beautiful and elegant and looked to Cecilia as if she'd stepped out from the pages of a magazine.

'*Buona sera*, Signorina Petacci!' someone called. The Signorina waved.

'Who's she?' wondered Cecilia.

Time and again Cecilia heard footsteps and doors open and close and looked up expecting to see the Count. But each time she was disappointed. She glanced repeatedly at the clock which seemed as bored as she was, and only moved on reluctantly out of habit. Three hours! For three hours she'd sat silent and invisible, blessing her foresight in going to the toilet before they left the apartment.

'Signorina Ortelli?'

Cecilia started. Where had he come from? She rose from her chair as if it had suddenly become scaldingly hot. The man smiled. He was as old as Signor Calosci and dressed the same way. Doubtless he had similar duties.

'Yes.'

'The Duce will see you.'

She followed the old man as if in a trance. She had no need to fake excitement. Her hands trembled and she could feel her mouth drying up. She sucked her cheeks in as she did when she was reading and worked her tongue around them, searching for moisture. He led her away up the stairs.

'One moment, please.'

They waited outside a room while her escort knocked discreetly. How had they got there? Which way had they come? Cecilia had never felt so nervous before. There was a sign on the door which read 'Zodiac Room'. It meant nothing to her. Her escort turned the handle and opened the door. He stood aside for her, then followed her in.

'Ah, Cecilia. Come here, girl.'

There were two men in the room, both seated and partly silhouetted by the table light behind them, but there was no mistaking who was whom.

'The Duce has asked to meet the person whose hand-writing he so admires. He wants us to dispense with the typewriter. It is a poor substitute for your hand. Duce, allow me to present Cecilia Ortelli.'

Cecilia curtsied and offered her hand. What was it the Count had said? He was never too great to shake the hand of his supporters. So she held out her hand for him to shake. As he turned she could see his face clearly. She was stunned. He was old and what . . . ? She'd expected to see the proud head with the forward-jutting chin. She'd expected to see a man of destiny, precise of gesture and clear of purpose. But instead of a legend she found a mere mortal, bowed down and beaten and very, very ordinary. Where was the power the Count spoke of? Where was the aura? Where was the magnificence? Where was the Duce of all the books and papers she'd read? Was this the man she'd trembled to meet? She wanted to laugh. The Duce rose slowly from his chair and took her hand. He raised it to his lips and kissed it. The gesture was supposed to be grand and gallant but struck her as incongruous and faintly ridiculous.

'Signorina, it is a pleasure to meet you at last.'

'And I am honoured to meet you. It is the proudest moment of my life.'

'The Count has told me all about you. I could not allow this opportunity to pass without meeting you. I would invite you to join us for coffee but alas I have other demands on my time. Count d'Alatri has invited me to the Villa Carosio. I look forward to meeting you again under less pressing circumstances.' He drew himself up to his full height, bent stiffly forward and gazed into her eyes as he once more kissed her hand. Perhaps he imagined he still had the seductive charm of his youth when women competed to lie alongside him, but the sixteen-year-old Cecilia could find no trace of it. He turned to the Count. 'Again I thank you for your advice and counsel. I will of course value it. In these times it is reassuring to know I have friends such as yourself whom I can always count upon. Goodbye, my friend.' Mussolini escorted them half way to the door where his servant took over.

'What did I tell you?' said the Count exultantly, once they were on the other side of the door. 'Isn't he magnificent?'

* * *

Andre met them at the station in Milan and the Count's rage grew with each passing kilometre. Cecilia had hoped they'd stop in Como for coffee where, on the pretext of visiting the toilet, she could sneak away to a telephone and warn the Signora. But the Count was in no mood to dally. He raged at Andre's report of Guido's treachery and vowed to have the Signora and Carmela shot in retaliation. Their betrayal was an affront to his name and reputation — he, a confidante of Il Duce! The insult! The shame! The humiliation!

Cecilia had never seen the Count so angry, not even during his most strident, anti-communist ravings. She had little choice but to sit quietly by, listen and occasionally echo his sentiments. After all, what point was there in defending the indefensible and incurring his wrath as well? Yet she was concerned for the Signora and Carmela. The Count's threat to have them both shot worried her, and with some justification. They wouldn't be the first people shot for harbouring partisans. She'd heard the rumours, and the anti-fascist pamphlets seemed to confirm them. So much for Guido's optimism. If the Count kept the Signora and Carmela on at the Villa Carosio it would only be to imprison them until the militia arrived. Cecilia felt she had to do something, but what could she do without embroiling herself?

Signor Calosci and Andre sat mutely up front, concentrating steadfastly on the road ahead. Both old soldiers, they knew well when to keep their heads down. But in Signor Calosci, Cecilia saw a possible, if unwilling, ally. As they negotiated the narrow winding road alongside the lake, Cecilia decided to make her move.

'How could Signor Mila be so treacherous?' she asked, indignation colouring her every word. 'How could he insult the Count who has been so kind to him? Signor Calosci, you were once a soldier, you tell me. How can a soldier who has brought us honour, turn and shame the Villa Carosio like this? And even his own family! The Signora must be mortified — she who has always been so loyal! You tell me!'

Signor Calosci squirmed in his seat. He could see what Cecilia was trying to do and wanted no part. But the silence begged a response.

'Men change, *piccolina*.'

'But to betray his own family as well!'

Signor Calosci sank further into his seat. He looked to Andre for support, but the chauffeur stared intently at the road as if expecting it to rise up like a snake and bite them, grateful that Cecilia hadn't picked on him.

'What are you saying, Cecilia?' interrupted the Count. There was a quiet menace in his voice that Cecilia had learned to fear. 'Are you suggesting that the traitor Guido did not discuss his plans with his wife? Of course he did! Those two have always been as thick as thieves. I have never trusted them!'

'If Signor Mila told the Signora of his intention, I'm sure she would have talked him out of it. At least, she would have tried. She is a loyal Italian. She is loyal to Mussolini and she has always been loyal to you, Count. Ask Signor Calosci! Signor, has the Signora ever been disloyal to the Count?'

Signor Calosci sighed and bowed to the inevitable. 'No,

she has never been disloyal, not to my knowledge. Nor has she ever been dishonest. But Cecilia, who knows what people think in their hearts? Even if she was always loyal, we must consider what happens when that loyalty is divided. Should she be loyal to the Count or to her husband? I say she should be loyal to the Count whose generosity she enjoys. The church, however, may insist that a wife remains loyal to her husband. If so, then she must accept the consequences of that course of action.'

'And if she has remained loyal to the Count, what then are the consequences?'

Signor Calosci was lost for words. He'd been out-manoeuvred and knew it. She'd turned his own argument against him. The old soldier's instincts told him it was time to run for cover, but what cover was there? He could feel the Count's eyes on him and he shrank under their intensity. What if the Signora had remained loyal to the Count? He considered that possibility for the first time and the injustice that may be her only reward. The tide had turned and the old soldier climbed out of the trench one more time.

'Then Cecilia, it is a matter for the Count's discretion. The Count is never disloyal to those who are loyal to him. But how do we know whether she has remained loyal to the Count or not?'

'Perhaps you could ask Andre.'

They were travelling on one of the few good stretches of road, along the waterfront at Tremezzo, yet the car swayed suddenly as if forced to avoid a pothole.

'Well, Andre?' The Count's voice had lost none of its venom.

'Her husband ran off into the mountains the night after you left. She told me in the morning and I drove down to Menaggio and informed the militia. He stole some bread, sausage and flour. The Signora has remained and run the household as efficiently as always. She has also replaced everything that traitorous bastard stole at her own expense. She could have run away but she hasn't. But where could she go that the Count could not find her? I can't answer your question.'

'But you have!' Cecilia turned to the Count triumphantly. 'See? As soon as she realised her husband had run off to join the partisans she told Andre so he could tell the militia. She is loyal to us. She is loyal to you! I knew it!'

'We'll see!' The Count still scowled but his voice showed definite signs of a thaw. He liked the idea of the Signora reporting the defection of her husband. He liked the thought that her loyalty to him was greater than even the bond of marriage. Yes, perhaps he'd been a little too hasty. Perhaps she was a true fascist. Only fascism and the justice of their cause could command such loyalty. Perhaps he had misjudged her.

* * *

As their car swept into the driveway, the Signora appeared on the front steps as she normally did. At least their system of lookouts still worked efficiently. The moment they came to a halt, Signor Calosci jumped out to open the rear door.

'Welcome home, Count.' The Signora smiled stiffly. Cecilia was impressed that she'd managed to smile at all.

'Welcome home indeed! To what? Infamy and betrayal! I want to see you now! In my study!'

Before they'd even begun unpacking the car, they could hear the Count berating the Signora. Everyone except Signor Calosci made themselves scarce, but there were few places in the villa where the Count's shouts did not penetrate. But tiredness finally caught up with him and his voice weakened until he could no longer be heard beyond the walls of his study. Cecilia went in search of Carmela to comfort her. She was with her when her mother finally emerged from the study, teary-eyed and shaken. The Signora turned to Signor Calosci hovering in the hallway.

'He's letting us stay on. I can't believe it. Thank God!'

'Save your prayers woman and thank Cecilia. The Count was going to have you shot. The girl talked him around. She is smarter than the rest of us put together. And braver. However, if I were you I would not chance fate a second time. Do not make any attempt to contact your husband. Do you understand?'

Oh yes. The Signora understood. She also understood the extraordinary risk Cecilia had taken. Signor Calosci was right.

Cecilia was brave. But neither of them suspected how brave she was or could even guess at the risks she'd soon be asked to take.

*　　*　　*

The Count's visit to Mussolini proved futile. Three weeks later his Party turned against him and the Fascist Grand Council voted to dismiss him. The following day, King Vittorio Emanuele III ordered Mussolini's arrest. He was imprisoned first on the Island of Ponza, then on a remote island off the coast of Sardinia. But fears of possible rescue and reinstatement by the Germans led to him being moved once more. This time to a hotel high on the Gran Sasso d'Italia, considered unassailable.

The Count was devastated. He couldn't imagine how the Duce had even allowed the vote to take place. He had warned him himself! He turned his fury against the conspirators but what could he do? Marshal Badoglio had now taken over as the head of government and he was sure to surrender to the Allies. Italy was finished. Fascism was finished. Both sacrificed by the men Mussolini had most trusted. On September 8, Marshal Badoglio confirmed his worst fears and Italy capitulated.

The Count alternated between rage and despair, and only Cecilia and Signor Calosci were spared the sting of his tongue. For two months his staff hung on grimly, to be summarily dismissed for some slight which usually existed solely in the Count's mind, only to be rehired when passions had cooled. Then came the radio broadcast, the miracle he never dared dream of.

'Blackshirts,' it began. 'Men and women of Italy. After a long silence you hear my voice once again, which I am sure you recognise . . .'

Incredibly, Mussolini had been rescued from his prison in the Abruzzi. In one of the most audacious missions of the war, German glider-borne troops had crash-landed on the slopes and whisked the Duce away to Munich. The Count's excited shouts brought people running from all over the Villa and they listened with decidedly mixed feelings as Mussolini announced the dissolution of the monarchy and the establishment of a new Fascist Republican Government. Italy was not only back in the war but engaged in another which was much more insidious — civil war.

The Count wept for joy.

Chapter Twenty-Six

Despite all the representations Gottfried made on his behalf, Friedrich was destined for the Eastern Front and command of another Panzer unit. The army was desperate for officers with his experience, courage and tactical knowledge, attributes Rommel had unwittingly confirmed in his reports back to the OKH, army headquarters. He was promoted to Oberstleutnant and placed on standby. His old fears were rekindled. The Russians had already developed a method of knocking out German Panther tanks by climbing aboard and firing flame-throwers through the engine vents. The crews were under no illusion as to what would happen to them once the tank was disabled. During the daytime Friedrich could dismiss his fears, but they crept up on him at night and attacked him in his sleep.

But once again Friedrich gained an unexpected reprieve. The Allies stormed ashore on the beaches of Sicily. Expecting a second landing on the toe or shin of Italy, Hitler rushed to protect his exposed underbelly and diverted all available men and matériel south. Friedrich was available. Although he wasn't relieved from command of tanks, at least he was spared the Eastern Front.

He was sent to help shore up Kesselring's defences along the Gustav Line formed by the Garigliano and Sangro rivers, north of Naples. Earlier in the war, the German army had proved itself irresistible in attack. Now, on the defensive, it was proving impregnable. Through the autumn and winter it held out against the Fifth Army and the Eighth Army, halting its advance northwards along both coasts.

At first, Friedrich had impressed his men with his courage

and bravery under fire. Even in the thick of battle he was to be seen standing upright, more out of the turret than in, issuing orders and calling in the range. The young Panzer-grenadiers accompanying the tanks took heart in his bravery and were inspired. But the older heads among the tank crews knew better. They didn't question his courage except in one respect. They knew the real problem. Clearly, their commander would rather be killed than set foot once more inside a tank.

Inevitably, Kesselring heard about his conduct and sent for him. He could hardly accuse an officer who had repeatedly distinguished himself under fire of being a coward. Equally, his Panzers were too few and too precious to be risked in the hands of a suspect officer. He had no choice but to relieve Friedrich of his command and recommend a transfer out of the Panzer Corps. Friendly sources within the OKH passed the transfer request on to Gottfried who was finally able to use his influence.

Friedrich was appointed garrison commandant in the small northern Italian town of Menaggio. The previous commandant had had the misfortune to be shot by terrorist snipers from the *Gruppi di Azione Patriottica* while pausing to admire the *Duomo* in Milan.

When Friedrich read his transfer papers, he could hardly credit his good fortune. He would be near Milan, a city he'd come to love as a boy. His only regret was that his parents had been recalled to Germany because of the GAP terrorists. He couldn't remember if he'd ever been to Menaggio but he seemed to know a lot about it. Then he remembered the Italian soldier who'd held his arms steady on the pain-filled flight from Tunisia. He smiled at the recollection. Perhaps they'd meet again after all.

* * *

Friedrich took over command of the Menaggio garrison in March 1944. Although he was well away from the front he was hardly out of the action. Following Mussolini's arrest, the Germans had moved swiftly to secure the Italian armed forces and all boys approaching conscription age. They'd given them a simple choice; fight on alongside the Wehrmacht; join volunteer labour forces in Germany; or be sent to a concentration camp. Only diehard fascists chose to fight on. Most resigned themselves to the deprivations and misery of the concentration camps rather than assist the Nazis. Others elected to fight back instead. These once-reluctant soldiers of fascism now had something to fight for that they could believe in. What they lacked in order and discipline they made up for in passion. They fought for themselves, their families and an Italy free of Mussolini. Though hopelessly outnumbered by the Germans, they showed a degree of courage and commitment that had not before been in evidence. But as fast as the occupying German forces had moved, they hadn't moved fast enough. Many soldiers and village boys had anticipated the round-up and those who could had fled to the forests and hills to join the partisans. Where once they'd been little more than an irritation, the partisans rapidly became a significant force to contend with. The will to fight that had been absent through the earlier years now manifested itself in patriotism, and a fierce determination to rid their country of their old allies.

Friedrich had hoped his job would be little more than policing the local population. Instead he found he had a full-time job keeping supply routes open to Switzerland and supplies flowing, safe from partisan harassment. None of his previous experience equipped him for the type of hit-and-run tactics the guerrillas employed, nor had he ever before had to contend with a population that was largely hostile. He needed to understand how the partisans organised themselves, their command structure, their numbers, and where they acquired their armaments. The local militia and the Gestapo were able to help him, with information extracted during interrogations of prisoners. But in addition to hard facts he needed local knowledge. What did the partisans do for food and shelter? Where did they hide in winter? Where and when were they vulnerable? How did they communicate? Clearly their activities were governed by three factors: climate, terrain and opportunity. Friedrich wanted to know how they interacted so that he could anticipate their moves and get ahead of the game. He realised that if he failed to take the initiative the partisans would rule the hills and he'd spend the rest of the war chasing their shadows. He began making inquiries among local dignitaries. Inevitably, they led him to the Villa Carosio.

* * *

Lucio paused for a coffee and much needed rest. Gancio heard the familiar hiss from his espresso machine and glanced up. Maria was learning.

'Bravo,' said Milos quietly. 'I was wondering how you would bring Cecilia and Friedrich together. Well done.'

'Yes, well told.' Gancio spoke softly but grimly. 'But Lucio didn't bring them together. He's not God. All he is doing is telling what happened. If I thought for one second that he was responsible, I would poison his food and watch him choke.'

'Jesus, Gancio, I thought you were the pacifist. I thought you were the one who wanted us all to forget the past. Forgive and forget. Now you're talking about murdering poor Lucio.'

'He was speaking figuratively, Neil, just as you are speaking facetiously.' Ramon paused reflectively. He sensed everyone at the table was waiting for him to go on. 'But you talk about murder as if it were something that couldn't possibly touch you. Murder is what this story is all about, Neil, and murder isn't selective. Very few people who are murdered expect to be, and very few who commit murders ever expect to become murderers. Given the right circumstances, most people are capable of murder, even you. Either directly or as an accessory. What do you think, Lucio?'

'Isn't Colombina proof of that? If someone as nice as Colombina can be pushed to commit murder, anyone can.'

'Anyone?'

'Yes, Ramon, anyone.'

'Even me?'

'For God's sake, Ramon, what is your game?' Milos made no attempt to hide the exasperation in his voice. 'Lucio said anyone, and anyone includes you, unless you've put yourself above the rest of us mortals. Given the last story you told and the fact that you are Argentinian you can hardly claim exemption. I must say that you are beginning to irritate me. You said earlier that you were prepared to let Lucio get on with his story without further cross-examination. Now either include us in your game or keep your word.'

'I apologise, though why I should apologise to fools is beyond me. Nevertheless, I apologise.'

'Then let Lucio continue his story. I think now we all accept that his story is true, no? And it is also obvious to those sensitive enough that the telling is both difficult and painful. We owe it to Lucio to help, not hinder him.'

The men sipped their coffee in silence.

'I'm still not convinced that those two wogs haven't cooked up the whole bloody thing,' said Neil at length, but he was ignored.

Chapter Twenty-Seven

Cecilia had become accustomed to meeting German officers. Since the daring rescue and reinstatement of Mussolini, the Count actively courted them. He forgot that he'd blamed them for the collapse of the Italian army, and had accused them of failing to provide promised weaponry and support. Instead he greeted them as saviours. He discovered in the Germans the discipline and sense of purpose he'd hoped to find but never did in the fascist armies. They were like supermen and he couldn't imagine how they could possibly be defeated. They were his last hope of a bulwark against communism.

The Count entertained the German officers and the senior fascists with lavish meals. He had lambs and calves specially slaughtered, trout netted, and wild fowl shot. He opened his cellars generously. Even if his guests sometimes found his company tedious, the food more than compensated.

Cecilia was never invited to join the company. Instead she liaised between the cook and Signor Calosci, helping prepare each course and serve it. Sometimes she'd catch the officers eyeing her as they speculated on her relationship with the Count, and her possible availability. But she didn't get to know any of them, no matter how often they came. When the previous commandant of the garrison was assassinated in Milan, all it had meant to her was a hastily cancelled dinner and a spare chair the following week. Cecilia was happy with the arrangement. They were her enemies even though she could never acknowledge it. Then everything changed.

Cecilia waited until Signor Calosci had introduced the new commandant to the Count, who had in turn once more expressed his admiration of the German military and his gratitude for Il Duce's rescue. She stepped forward with her tray filled with glasses of wine, expecting the Oberstleutnant to help himself without acknowledging her any more than he would any other servant.

'Aha . . . you must be Cecilia.'

Cecilia nearly dropped the tray in surprise. She looked up into his face and for the first time felt the warmth of his smile. His eyes weren't cold and distant like all the others but twinkled with amusement. Yes. He was playing with her, not cruelly or cynically, but in a way that was both friendly and charming. Encouraged, she smiled back. 'Yes, I am Cecilia.'

'I met your father the other night. He is very proud of you.'

Her father was proud of her? How could he both disown her and be proud of her? She looked up sharply at the Oberstleutnant to see if he was taunting her but he seemed genuine enough.

'Will you be joining us for dinner?'

Cecilia was embarrassed. If the Count had wanted her to join them at the table, he would have made his wishes clear. She laughed. 'No. My job is to help serve dinner not eat it. What would I do among so many important men?'

'But I insist. Count d'Alatri, could you oblige me by inviting this charming young lady to join us for dinner? I'm sure you can find someone else to do her job. After months of talking only to other soldiers, this is an opportunity I cannot let slip by.'

'Of course.' The Count was only too happy to oblige his latest guest. 'Cecilia, run along and change into something more suitable. Tell the Signora to find someone to take your place.'

Cecilia went straight to the kitchen where she found the Signora, Antonella and Carla with sleeves rolled up, helping Signora Fiorella prepare the dinner. She relayed her instructions.

'Dear God! We are short-handed enough. Carla, find Carmela. Tell her to come and help here in the kitchen. I think she's in the cellar fetching wine for Signor Calosci. Antonella, you take Cecilia's place. Go change into something more appropriate. Signora Fiorella, can you look after things on your own for a few moments? I need to have a word with Cecilia in private.'

The cook threw up her hands. 'Yes! All go away! How am I supposed to cook dinner anyway, without proper help? It's already spoiled. Just go. How can I possibly spoil what is already spoiled?'

'We will only be a moment. Cecilia, I want to talk to you while you change.'

They left Signora Fiorella fuming in the kitchen and climbed the narrow stairway to Cecilia's room. Neither exchanged a word until they'd closed the door behind them. Signora Mila sat down on Anna's old bed and ran tired hands down her face.

'Dear God, Cecilia, when will things get back to normal?' She waited until Cecilia had pulled her uniform up over her head, then leaned forward secretively. 'Do you realise what an opportunity this is? Guido would give his right arm to have friendly ears at that table! You know the sort of things they discuss in there. You could find out when convoys are coming. You can find out which ones are heavily protected and which ones aren't. You can find out when and where the next *rastrellamento* will be. Imagine that, Cecilia! If we can find some way to tell Guido when and where the Germans and the Blackshirts are planning their next sweep, they can set up an ambush or make sure they're on some other mountain. For once the partisans will have the advantage. Think of it, Cecilia!'

Cecilia did. Helping hide deserters was one thing, but the Signora was asking her to become a spy and inform on the Germans. She hesitated. It sounded dangerous, but what really were the risks? After all, she'd only be repeating what they'd said. Besides the Signora was right. The information would be invaluable to Guido and could save many partisan lives, even his. She thought of how pleased he'd be with her and her mind was made up. Cecilia waited until the Signora had helped her on with her dress before answering.

'I will do what you ask.'

'Good girl, Cecilia. Guido will be so proud of you. I am proud of you!' She hugged Cecilia and kissed her. Then her voice became serious. 'You realise what you will have to do?

You will only be invited back to the table if the new commandant wants you there. You have to make him want you. Do you understand?'

'Yes, Signora. I understand. And Signora ... I have conditions.'

'Conditions?'

'Yes. It is too much to expect me to betray my father or Alfredo and Elio. I want an undertaking from Signor Mila that he will do everything in his power to see that they are not harmed if they are caught up in an ambush. Similarly, if they are captured.'

'That is reasonable.'

'Also they should take care not to shoot the new commandant. If he is killed, I will lose my place at the dinner table.'

'That makes sense.' The Signora smiled. Yes, if Cecilia's information proved fruitful, they'd make sure the commandant survived any engagements. That made sense. But as for her father and brothers well ... they were soldiers. They'd just have to take their chances along with everyone else.

'Signora, what if the commandant doesn't want me? After all ...'

'After all nothing! You are beautiful. Of course he will want you. You don't need a pretty dress or make-up. Just touch him with your eyes. That will do it. The new commandant will fall at your feet. Look! You are blushing!'

The Signora's accusation made her face blush even brighter.

* * *

By the time Cecilia returned downstairs, the guests had already taken their places at the dinner table. Cecilia gasped when she saw the one available chair. They'd placed her between the Count and the new commandant. Of course they would.

'Ah, Cecilia ... you've rejoined us.'

The new commandant stood as Signor Calosci held her chair for her. He was the only one who did. She smiled and did her best to conceal her nervousness.

'Would the Signorina care for some wine?'

It was Signor Calosci treating her like she was one of the

guests. If the Count had turned communist she couldn't have been more surprised. She was aware that everyone at the table was watching her. She looked up at Signor Calosci and he smiled. Barely perceptibly, but a smile nonetheless. Could it be? Was that old dried stick actually proud of her? Dear God! 'Thank you, Signor Calosci.' She looked at the bottle he held. 'That is my favourite Pinot Grigio.'

The Count laughed delightedly. 'You see how well I treat my staff? This is her favourite Pinot Grigio!'

'It is a pleasure to share the table with a connoisseur.' The Oberstleutnant raised his glass to her. 'I have never tasted a finer Pinot Grigio myself.'

Cecilia raised her glass to her lips and sipped. There was no doubt in her mind. She'd often had a glass of wine with the Count at mealtimes. It was certainly the finest she'd ever tasted. She forgot all about spying and concentrated on the more urgent matter of fitting in, winning over the Oberstleutnant, and controlling her racing heart. She gained respite once the food arrived. Signora Fiorella had done them proud and it was far too good to be ignored. The guests gave it their full attention and commented only upon its excellence. But between courses, the Oberstleutnant gave Cecilia a lesson on how to extract information.

He began by telling an anecdote, then attaching a question to the tail of it as if it were a logical progression. Often he posed his questions in a way that suggested naïveté on his part. The Count and the other guests fell over each other in their race to provide the answers. Cecilia sat alongside, mesmerised. In no time at all he'd established the estimated size and nature of the partisan bands roaming around the hills between Como and Switzerland. His questions revealed things that Cecilia never knew. The communist Garibaldi and socialist Matteotti bands tended to operate further south around Milan and were more or less controlled by their political parties. The same applied to the Actionist groups, which were second only in size to the Garibaldi brigades. The Christian Democrat Green Flame bands operated to the north and east of the lake. In between were groups like Guido's, that owed allegiance to no political party and whose sole commitment was to free Italy from fascism and the hated Germans.

The Oberstleutnant probed unobtrusively but insistently, switching his questions from guest to guest until there was competition for his attention. He probed for weaknesses. How did they get their arms? Who kept them supplied with ammunition? Where did they get their explosives from? What type of explosives did they prefer, and what weapons? Where did they get their food supplies from? He mixed his questions with anecdotes from Spain and North Africa. He was witty, charming and deadly.

Cecilia listened and waited for an opportunity to make a contribution. She knew that if she remained silent her first dinner would also be her last. But what could she contribute without appearing uninformed or foolish? It occurred to her that she wasn't expected to contribute but just laugh at the witticisms and look beautiful. Perhaps later there'd be an opportunity for talk. But that wasn't the custom. The Count's guests usually made a hasty exit as soon as the meal was finished, before the Count had the chance to launch into one of his anti-communist harangues. Her one chance lay in the hope that the new commandant was too courteous to allow her to be ignored through the entire meal. She turned in her chair so that she intruded further into his line of vision when he addressed the Count. If he was a gentleman, he would have to acknowledge her sooner or later. He did.

'Gentlemen, I feel I have monopolised conversation enough. This young woman joined us at my request and we have ignored her.' He turned to her. 'Please accept my apologies. Put soldiers together and we inevitably discuss the war.'

'Put any two people in Italy together right now, Herr Oberstleutnant, and you will find they inevitably discuss the war as well.' Cecilia smiled but she could see that the commandant was taken aback. The table fell silent and she could sense the Count's disapproval. 'I have discussed the war with the Count since the beginning of hostilities and I am as interested in the subject as anyone else. You asked some interesting questions, Herr Commandant, but you have missed perhaps the most important issue.'

'And what might that be?'

'I don't believe you are any closer to understanding your enemy than you were when you arrived. You know their numbers and disposition, their armaments and affiliations, but what have you learned about the men themselves? Who are they, these partisans? How determined are they? What is the picture you carry in your mind of the typical partisan? How true is it? You see, Herr Oberstleutnant, you can find the answer to all these questions right here at the table. If you only ask.'

'Cecilia, that is enough! You are dismissed.'

'Wait! Count d'Alatri, I feel I provoked Cecilia's response and it was entirely justified.' He put his head back and began to laugh. It came easily and naturally and soon it infected everyone. 'Everything she said is true. I came here hoping to learn more about the nature of the partisan and all I have succeeded in doing is confirming what I already know. I have been in the company of soldiers too much and women not enough. Cecilia, please forgive my arrogance. Now tell me the answers to the questions I should have asked.' The commandant had enormous charm and used it. Cecilia could feel herself begin to wilt. But this was her one chance, and she couldn't let it slip by.

'In this winter just passed, many partisans in the hills died of cold and hunger. The others barely survived. Those who survived have grown hard. They lead a desperate existence, hiding by day and moving by night. They are being hunted down relentlessly by your troops and by our Blackshirts. So they are always on the move. And with every day and every hardship their hatred and resentment grows. They are fighting for their homes, for their wives and families, and for Italy. The one reason for their existence is to destroy fascism and drive out the German army. Of course, some fight for one political flag or another, but mostly they fight for their families. They are our mortal enemies and they are very determined. Many of them are trained soldiers hardened in battle. Others are mere boys who ran away to avoid conscription or being sent away to Germany. But don't underestimate them either. It is impossible to survive in those hills without becoming a man very quickly. They also have a strong leader.'

'Cecilia that is enough. You sound like one of them. Where did you learn all this nonsense?'

'Count, these men are your enemies. Therefore they are my enemies. I hear this from the staff. Whenever somebody goes to the village or down to Menaggio, they come back with more stories about the partisans. If the Oberstleutnant wants to understand them, he needs to know this.'

'Please, Count d'Alatri. Allow Cecilia to continue. Tell me about the leader.'

'Cecilia . . .'

She heard the Count's warning and the undercurrent of menace but chose to ignore it. She had the Oberstleutnant's wholehearted attention and there lay her strength. 'The leader of the local partisan group was a tank machine-gunner. He fought in Abyssinia and in Libya. He is very smart and cunning, and he despises fascism. He is passionate in his beliefs and will not compromise them. When he joined the partisans he left his wife and child behind because they did not share his beliefs. He loves both of them dearly, yet he was prepared to abandon them because they were still loyal to Mussolini. He is a hard man and a strong man, the sort you'd much rather have by your side than as your enemy.'

'You obviously know this man?'

'Yes, Herr Oberstleutnant, I do. After Mussolini and the Count, he was the man I most admired in the whole world.'

'You know him that well?'

Cecilia could hear the Count squirming in his seat.

'Yes. Before he betrayed us he was our friend. He worked here at the Villa Carosio. His wife is the Count's housekeeper, Signora Mila.'

'It's true.' The Count jumped in to justify his position. 'It is not news to anyone else at this table. He is a traitor but the Signora and her daughter are proof of the strength and greatness of fascism. They put the Duce ahead of their husband and father. I respect that and I am not in the habit of allowing loyalty to pass unrewarded.'

'Very laudable and honourable of you, Count d'Alatri. You are to be commended.' The commandant was both well mannered and skilled in conversation. His words expressed all the right sentiments and were exactly what the Count wished to hear. But Cecilia could see that other matters preoccupied him.

'This man, Mila. He fought in tanks, you say? In the western desert?'

'Yes.'

'Tell me, do you know if he suffered a head wound around February last year?'

Cecilia's jaw fell open. She couldn't keep the surprise out of her voice. 'Yes. I helped to nurse him back to health.'

'Then he must be Guido Mila. I know him.'

Cecilia's wide eyes and open mouth gave him all the confirmation he needed. He laughed once more. 'Ha! I wondered if I would ever meet him again. I should compliment you. Your description of him was very accurate. Cecilia, you are a mine of information. I have learned more from you than I have from all the conversations I have had since I arrived. Guido Mila, eh? There will be no complaints now about the image I carry in my head of the partisan. He is precisely defined. Cecilia, we must meet and talk again.' He stood abruptly. But for the last exchange of courtesies, dinner had concluded.

Chapter Twenty-Eight

From the day her husband chose to join the partisans, the Signora seemed to become more committed to her religion. It was understandable, the war had reawakened the faith in many Italians. While she still attended the church in Menaggio every Sunday with the Count and the rest of the staff, two and three times a week she'd climb the hill to Ravello and pray to the Holy Mother, beseeching her to watch over her husband. Those who witnessed her piety felt nothing but compassion for her. The truth was, Guido had been lucky to survive as long as he had and, unless the war came to a speedy conclusion, his luck would inevitably run out. Under-armed, under-fed and always weary, the partisans suffered fearful losses. Every time she visited the little church in Ravello she would also confess her sins. Nobody thought to question why the Signora should feel the need to confess two or three times a week.

In the gloom of the confessional, she told Father Michele of her sins, and whatever information she'd been able to gather about supply convoys and troop movements. In return he gave her light penance — her sins were few — and news of Guido. He gave her messages to pass on to the families of other partisans who accepted them without questioning her source. On this day, however, the Signora told Father Michele about the dinners at the Villa Carosio and the good fortune that had placed Cecilia at the table. She told him how Cecilia had succeeded in winning the new commandant's confidence and friendship, and the hopes she had for the quality and quantity of information she could provide. The Signora could no more keep the pride out of her voice than her confessor could his astonishment. They parted with the usual blessing.

That night at seven o'clock, he rang the church bell. Seven slow, ponderous beats to mark the hour ... a pause ... then another ... and another. At any other time, the parishioners might have wondered about the eccentric time-keeping of the priest, but lately they'd become accustomed to the bell's erratic behaviour. They'd learned to count each peal up until the pause and ignore any others, should there be any. But higher up in the hills other ears listened, and any variation was passed on to others who passed it on to others until it reached the high summer pastures. One extra peal meant a rendezvous, two demanded Guido's presence.

Father Michele woke at five and went straight to his back door. He looked down at the step where generations of priests had worn a hollow in the stone. In the middle, like a sparrow's egg in an eagle's nest was a single, smooth pebble. Some brave soul had breached curfew to let him know that the meeting was on. He sighed grimly and prepared himself for the rigours ahead. He glanced over to the east where the first fingers of dawn reached for clouds that weren't to be found. A light breeze touched him but he ignored its chill. It would get warm soon and then, if the breeze failed to pick up, uncomfortably hot, particularly for anyone foolish enough to climb the mountains.

Father Michele would have made a good soldier but for his vocation. In his mid-thirties and the peak of health, he was a prime candidate for conscription. But he believed in the commandments and didn't believe that the politics of men overruled the laws of God. For years he kept himself apart from the war and ministered equally to anyone in need, regardless of the uniform they wore. Eventually the excesses of the fascists and the Germans, and the suffering they wrought upon his flock made him take sides. He now saw the war in the context of the eternal battle between the forces of good and evil, and believed the church should no longer stand by. When Guido had slipped down from the hills one night and asked him to become a conduit between the partisans and their supporters in the village, he'd agreed without hesitation. But the nature of some of the information he carried troubled him deeply. He knew that it would often result in the deaths of young men and that he bore part of the responsibility for those deaths. But what could he do? He bore the fifth commandment like a cross.

His vocation gave him a singular advantage over other men. On the pretext of serving his outlying parishioners he could roam the hillsides at will. Occasionally he would encounter a Blackshirt patrol. They'd ask to look inside the haversack he carried and always found no more or less than they expected. Of course, they suspected he had contact with the partisans, but he also had a legitimate reason for being there. Once or twice they'd followed him, and he'd spent a fruitless day dropping in on the surprised old men and boys tending the sheep and goats, and the herds of small, grey-coloured cattle.

Father Michele set out at first light, his haversack weighed down with his Bible, a pouch with the Eucharist, his stole, two one-litre bottles of water, half a kilo of cheese and a loaf of bread. He would have liked to take more bread to the partisans or some white flour because he knew how starved they were for carbohydrates. But if he encountered a patrol, nothing could more clearly signal his intentions. He made rapid progress in the cool mountain air, anxious to put as much distance behind him as he could before the sun became too hot. For once he was oblivious to God's annual miracle, the reawakening of nature. He ignored the new shoots and the budding leaves and the birds' morning song. Instead he was consumed by the conflict raging inside his head. That morning his cross was especially heavy. He climbed up the lower pastures and into the pine forest which ran like a belt across the hillside on slopes too steep for cultivation. While it was cooler in among the trees the going was hard, and he was glad when he was through them and out onto the rock-strewn summer pastures.

'Good morning, Father.'

The voice took him completely by surprise and he whirled around. His mind raced as it considered possibilities. Who could it be? How could he have allowed himself to be so distracted? He'd made a beeline for the rendezvous without checking to see if he was being followed and without making any attempt to disguise his route. He recognised the big man the moment he moved out from behind the rock that sheltered him.

'Piero. You startled me.'

'If you were a rabbit and I a fox you would now be my breakfast.'

Father Michele accepted the rebuke, shamefaced at his lack of caution.

'And you, Piero? Who was it this time?'

'Jews.'

'You've booked your place in heaven, Piero.'

'So long as they're not expecting me soon.' The two men laughed. Father Michele pulled a bottle out of his haversack and offered it to the big man. He took a few grateful swallows and handed the bottle back.

'*Grazie*.'

'Piero . . .'

'I know what you're going to say and I will give you the answer I always give. When the war is finished I will come and confess. It may take a whole day, so be warned. But I will not confess and seek absolution now for deeds I will only repeat later. I am not yet sorry for the things I do.'

The priest reached out his hand and placed it on the older man's shoulder. 'You're a good man. May God care and look after you, at least until I hear your confession.'

Piero laughed. 'Today I am indestructible. I also have the God of the Jews looking after me. Goodbye, Father, and God take care of you, too. Whichever God takes care of rabbits.'

Father Michele watched Piero make his way wearily down the mountain hugging the shadows, and wondered how many kilometres his aging legs had covered that night. The encounter had been salutary. He put his problems aside and concentrated on the task ahead. It was high time the rabbit assumed the cloak of a fox. He climbed steadily, criss-crossing gullys along paths worn by sheep and shepherd. The trees thinned out and what few remained offered little relief from the sun. He reached the rendezvous point, where coarse mountain grass and lichen fought each other for a toehold, and sat down. His legs ached from effort and he struggled to suck in lungfuls of air. He knew the partisans were there already, somewhere, watching to see if he was followed.

His heavy soutane was stained with his sweat. He took out his bottle of water, swallowed deeply to make up for the fluids he'd lost, and lay back exhausted. How did the men cope who roamed these hills day after day? His tiredness and the hot sun made him drowsy. He offered little resistance and quickly succumbed.

'Is this what you call God's work, Father?'

'Guido . . .' Had he been asleep? How long?

'You wish to speak to me.'

Father Michele looked up. Guido was standing over him. His eyes were tired and wary, and sunk deep into their sockets. Suffering was etched into every line of his face. How long had it been since they'd last met? Five months? His clothes hung limply, as if borrowed from a larger man. The priest was shocked by how much weight he'd lost.

'It's been a hard winter, Father.' Guido smiled grimly. 'I can see what you're thinking. How are my family?' He sat down beside the priest.

'They are well and send you their love. And a message.'

'Yes.'

'The girl Cecilia, you know her?'

'Yes, I know her.'

'Do you trust her?'

'I trust her.'

'Then let me tell you why I needed to see you.' Father Michele told him all about the dinners at the Villa Carosio and how Cecilia had come to be invited to attend them. The partisan's eyes widened in astonishment and delight. 'She is in a position to cultivate the new commandant,' he continued. 'If she is as clever as your wife seems to think she is, there will be nothing the Germans or Blackshirts can do that we won't know about.'

'It is a godsend.'

'Perhaps, but I think you should be aware of . . . of . . . of complications.'

'What sort of complications?'

'The girl is putting herself at tremendous risk. It is up to us to afford her as much protection as we can. It is vital that as few people as possible know about her role. Already three people know. You, your wife and me. That is enough. No one else must know.'

'Agreed. But what is the complication?'

Father Michele hesitated, searching for the right words. 'When you found me here, you asked me if this was God's work? The answer is yes, it is. And I am a man of God. You asked me to be your go-between and I have never shirked my responsibilities. But I must draw the line between carrying messages and sending young boys and men to their deaths. We both know what you will do with the information Cecilia provides. You will ambush patrols and strike hard at supply columns you know are poorly defended. You will kill more Germans and Blackshirts because of Cecilia's information. I will not be her conduit. I will not be instrumental in killing.'

'What about the partisan lives her information will save? All you will be doing, Father, is altering the balance. More of my men will be saved, more of the enemy will be killed. Good men will still be killed either way, whether you bring the information or not. Isn't it better that they be the enemy?' Guido's voice was hard, bordering on contempt.

'I hear what you say. God knows I've thought about nothing else since your wife came to see me. But my mind is made up. I will not be instrumental in more killing.'

'Do you think any of us are here by choice, Father? Do you think any of us want to live up here? Do you think we enjoy shooting people? Do you think we enjoy dropping burning bottles of fuel onto trucks? Do you think any of us enjoy this killing? This is war, Father, and war deprives people of choice.' Guido's voice rose in anger until he was shouting. 'We didn't ask for war! We were given war! What makes you so special? Why do you have choice and we don't? Because the only way the killing is going to stop is if they kill all of us, or if we kill enough of them so that they leave!' He glared at the priest, but he could see he was wasting his words. He turned and spat into the dust. 'Is that all you have to say or do you have a proposal?'

'The girl will have to talk to you herself. You will have to arrange to meet her further down the mountain.'

'You know what you are asking.'

'Yes. It will be very dangerous for both of you.'

'But we have no choice.'

'No. I'm sorry.'

'So am I, Father. I will find a meeting place and send word. Goodbye, Father.'

'God be with you, Guido. Oh, here is something for you. No more than usual.' He handed him the bread and cheese, and the empty water bottles. 'I wish you hadn't told me what you use these for.'

'And I wish the Germans dropped a bomb on your parents' house,' Guido said bitterly. 'Then you'd have no trouble bringing me Cecilia's messages. Then you'd have no trouble bringing us bottles. Dear God! Don't you think the girl's taking enough risks?'

'I know you don't mean that, Guido, and anyway, you're wrong. Please, my friend, I hear your disappointment and wish with all my heart that there was some other way. Please don't let us part as enemies.'

Guido put aside his anger and reached for the priest's hand. 'Let me know if you change your mind. If I say any prayers tonight, that's what I will pray for. Now go. Give my family my love.'

Father Michele turned and began the long journey back down the mountain. His haversack was lighter but that didn't compensate for the weight on his heart.

* * *

Cecilia had no idea her fate was being decided high up in the mountains. Nor did the men who made the decisions realise the tragic chain of events they were setting in motion. Cecilia was happy to have survived the dinner, to have made a contribution and to have extracted a commitment from the Oberstleutnant to meet again. Beyond that she had no plan. She had no clear idea of what sort of man he was or what his interest in her was. Perhaps he did value her as a source of information, though she suspected it had more to do with the fact that she was seventeen years old and attractive. What if that was the case? What if that was the price of his friend-ship and the information she sought? When it came to the crunch, she wasn't sure how she'd react. But that was a problem for later, if there was a later. The next move was up to him.

Chapter Twenty-Nine

Friedrich Eigenwill sat in his office in the Menaggio barracks and contemplated the situation he found himself in. Mussolini's Salo Republic was a joke. The Duce's government had responsibility but no power. The Nazis ran practically everything and even censored his government's letters. Six hundred thousand Italians had been hauled away to Germany as cheap industrial labour, along with the machinery from entire factories. Those men and boys who had escaped the round-up had become partisans and there was little he could do to stop others joining them. Mussolini had dissolved the *Carabinieri* and replaced them with a Republican National Guard comprised of *Carabinieri* and old fascist militia. As a police force they were hopelessly ineffective and defection to the partisans became a daily fact of life. The Ministry of Police ran its own security force, the *squadristi*, who were a law unto themselves. To complicate matters, he had to contend with private police forces run by the local senior fascists. Then there was the Gestapo and the SS, whose job had grown from hunting down Jews and anti-fascists, to ensuring the full commitment of the Wehrmacht. It was a mess.

All Friedrich had to help him round up partisans and keep the road to Switzerland open were his own troops, a combination of untested boys and First World War veterans numbering about fifty, and roughly seventy fascist soldiers, raggle-taggle remnants of Marshal Graziani's forces. What the Italians lacked in skills and equipment, they made up for in local knowledge. What his men lacked in local knowledge they made up for in weaponry and discipline, so the two forces were reasonably complementary. He had five machine-guns, six mortars, three covered trucks, two field cars, two motorcycles, one motorcycle combination and two Lancia Aprilia staff cars. This is all he had to patrol forty kilometres of road and all the hills north of Menaggio and west of Lake Como. He had one other weapon which he was loath to use — fear.

The previous commandant had posted warnings in every village informing the population that anyone possessing weapons or harbouring partisans would be shot; that soldiers would use their rifles against any gathering of more than two people; and that any village whose inhabitants insulted German soldiers would be burned to the ground. Coupled with these warnings was the threat of reprisals, the cold-blooded shooting of civilians in revenge for partisan activities. Friedrich prayed that that was one measure he would never have to take. Yet his first duty was to protect his men and that begged the question: What measures could he take to avoid the necessity for reprisals? He had no stomach for shooting innocent women, old men and children.

All over northern Italy partisan forces were growing bolder as they grew stronger. Sooner or later activity would pick up in his area. At the moment they were no more than a nuisance with their strike and fade tactics, hitting and running before the mortars and machine-guns could target in on them. It was only a matter of time before the partisans engaged them in serious battle. More and more regularly the Americans dropped supplies to the partisans by parachute, and the last drops had included light cannon. The partisans had left the cannon behind on the ground because they were too heavy to transport. But one day soon they'd have the means and he was powerless to prevent it.

He summoned his staff and the commanding officer of the Blackshirts and outlined his strategy. He intended that they would use the same tactics as the guerrilla forces they opposed. They would harry them constantly, and delay the day when the partisans could truthfully claim control of the hills. When that happened, all was lost. He wanted to step up the patrols and frequency of the combined forces' sweep through the hills. But above all he wanted information. He wanted the Blackshirts and the local fascist militias to establish informants throughout the hills. He instructed them to offer exemptions from conscription, release of imprisoned relatives, money, threats and any other form of coercion they deemed necessary. The hills were too many and his forces too few to waste time chasing shadows. He terminated the meeting without allowing questions or anyone to introduce any suggestion that his requests may prove too difficult to fulfil. Then he turned his attention to personal matters.

As he'd predicted, the Russian advance was proving inexorable. As dedicated and tenacious as the German armies were, the result was a foregone conclusion. Unless the Allies could speed up their advance through Italy and open a second front in France, the Russians would sweep through Germany. Before that happened he wanted to get Christiane and Helmuth as far west as he could. But getting them to move from Dresden was proving harder than stopping the Russians. He couldn't order them or send direct instructions because of the censors and the threat of execution that hung over the heads of any defeatists. All he could do was allude to places in the west they'd never been and relatives they didn't have, in the hope that Christiane would take the hint. He spoke of returning to those places after the war knowing full well she'd understand his meaning. But she remained in Dresden, stubbornly defiant. She played his game and never failed to mention her sister Lisl, Ulla or the unfortunate Käte, an obvious allusion to Wuppertal-Barmen and the devastating bombing of German cities. It seemed to him that Christiane still hadn't grasped the seriousness of the situation they were in, and still clung to the foolish notion of Hitler's infallibility. He knew that in her heart she still believed that somehow everything would work out all right because her father said it would. His despair and frustration grew. What chance did she have of seeing the light? The only information anyone in Germany got was the lies fed to them by Goebbels via the Nazi-controlled radio and newspapers. They were forbidden to listen to foreign broadcasts on pain of death. How could Christiane be made to face reality? Only the bombing and the desperate shortages of food, fuel and clothing gave any real indication of their plight. He wrote guarded letters to Gottfried in the hope that he could talk some sense into her but nothing had come of it. Daily his anxiety grew until he was forced to seek distraction.

Friedrich was a loving husband and his love for Christiane was beyond question. But he was also a serving soldier a long way from home, and there'd been many days when he'd been fortunate just to survive to see the next. General Rommel's advice had become his justification and he took his comforts where he could. The girls in the brothels provided solace of a kind but it was never satisfactory. They took care of the body's needs but usually left the mind to fend for itself. He longed for the company of a woman with whom he could talk and relax, share intimacies and ultimately seduce. What he wanted was love and affection, not abstract and distant, but here and now that he could feel and touch. He was a soldier in need of gentle reminders that he was also a functioning human being. He needed Cecilia.

He rang the Villa Carosio and invited himself to lunch on the pretext of discussing the morning's strategy meeting with the Count. He specifically requested that Cecilia join them for lunch. He resolved to determine the extent of the Count's hold upon her and her receptivity to his advances. He was thirty years old yet he still felt the same thrill he had as a teenager, the thrill of the chase. That surprised him. But he would have been even more surprised if he'd known whose ears would ultimately share their lunchtime conversation.

Chapter Thirty

Colombina had every chance to become the Oberstleutnant's killer, but instead she became his nurse. Time and time again she steeled herself to confront him but couldn't go through with it. It wasn't just her weakness but also his weakness that was his salvation. She simply couldn't bring herself to commit the final act when the old man was so helpless and dependent upon her. Arguably, he was lucky to have survived the operation. For many elderly, the trauma and the effects of the anaesthetic often prove too much. The old man soldiered on, although he was nothing like his former self.

Colombina stayed with him through most of the day and sometimes overnight, sleeping as best she could on his old sofa. He kept apologising to her and telling her how much he appreciated her help. But while his body was weakened, his spirits were high and he engaged her endlessly with his wit and humour. She was both mother and daughter to him and he both child and father to her. She cancelled Meals-on-Wheels and cooked for him instead. She bathed him and did his laundry and helped him to the toilet. And each time she guided him on his unsteady legs to the bathroom, she held his life in her hands. Sooner or later she'd have to face him and let him know what she intended to do and why. But she kept putting it off and putting it off, and every day her attachment to the charming old rogue grew. As he won more and more of her heart, the excuses for her inaction became easier to find.

She justified her indecision in many ways, both rational and fanciful. The fact was, though, there was no urgency. The old man's recovery was painfully slow. She decided she

wanted to know about his life in Australia, to fill in the gaps
in her knowledge. It seemed foolish to send him into the next
world without discovering all he'd done in this. Afterwards,
she'd always wonder, and never have the opportunity of
finding out. So she asked him.

He seemed taken aback by the question, and took his time
before he answered.

'What part would you like to know?' he asked cautiously.

'How do I know? All you ever talk about is opera, food and
football. And politics a bit.' She laughed. 'Come on! You've
spent a lifetime here, something interesting must have happened. Start at the beginning, when you first set foot on
Australian soil.'

'All right,' he replied slowly. 'On one condition. When I
am finished, you must tell me the story of your life in Australia from the time you arrived.'

'I was born here. I told you.' She looked hard at the old
man. He'd definitely flinched. She laughed to cover his error.
'I can tell you about my mother and father and the night
when the moon was full and they made love beneath the
stars and their fruit trees. Don't you think that is a romantic
way to begin life? I'm surprised they didn't name me after a
variety of plum or peach.'

The old man laughed with her. 'My parents never talked
about such things. They were just like the English — they
pretended they didn't have sex.'

Colombina wasn't certain but an edge seemed to have crept
into his voice, a tension, a guardedness. She felt a coldness in
her belly. Perhaps their little game was drawing to a close.
Perhaps today would see it reach its conclusion. Would she
be up to it when the time came?

'When I arrived in Australia, returned soldiers had the first
pick of what jobs were going. Who could blame the employers?
But it wasn't exactly ideal circumstances for a non-combatant
Swiss with a German accent. I ended up on the Snowy Mountains project surrounded by other Europeans like myself. I
had trained as a lawyer back home in Sankt Gallen so they
made me an explosives expert. The hours were long and the
work was hard, but it was never boring. There is something
about gelignite that demands the whole and undivided atten-

tion of the people who handle it. One day, one of my fellow experts didn't concentrate hard enough. His charge exploded just as I was fitting detonators to fuses. When the blast hit me I was measuring off fuses. If I'd been holding the detonators I would have lost both hands. As it was, my clothes ignited and I had to beat out the flames with my arms. All I lost was skin, my colleague lost his life.

'I would have stayed on but by then things were becoming unpleasant. There were Italians, Balts, Jugoslavs, Poles, Hungarians and Germans. Unfortunately, some of them brought the war with them to their new country and someone was always accusing the Germans of being war criminals. I myself was accused without evidence. It became an unpleasant place to stay. So I took to the road and did whatever work came along. For a while the burns on my arms restricted me and I was fired from some jobs. Can you imagine labouring for a bricklayer with burns up to your armpits? I thought I could hold my arms away from my body and I could, but not all day.

'I got a job in a bakery in Melbourne making pastry. For two weeks I worked in the fridge carrying fifty-six pound blocks of butter and margarine from one place to another. They always gave Europeans the jobs in the refrigerator because they thought we didn't feel the cold. Maybe they didn't read about all the soldiers who froze to death on the Eastern Front. After two weeks they took me out of the fridge and put me on a machine which broke the butter and margarine into twelve pieces about five pounds each. I did that for ten weeks, then they put me on a brake which rolled out the pastry. For a year I rolled and folded, rolled and folded until I nearly went insane. I ran out of daydreams very early on and the only way I could keep my sanity was to compete against myself. So every day I tried to roll more pastry than the day before. There was a little counter on the machine so I always knew how well I'd done. Of course the bosses were delighted. Unfortunately the union wasn't. They told me if I didn't slow down they'd go on strike. They threatened to break my hands. Why? All because I worked too hard and showed up the laziness of others.

'I left and got a job in a plastics factory making light-fittings.

The same thing happened there. I found I was no good at repetitious jobs. That is, I was too good. I had to compete with myself or die of boredom. I worked as a storeman in a brewery, a lathe operator, and a bus driver for a private bus line which took kids to school. I liked that job but the company went broke.

'I heard there was a shortage of electricians so I went to a company and asked them to take me on as an apprentice at apprentice wages. The boss was a good man. He said the law wouldn't let him do that but he'd teach me anyway. For eight hours a day I learned my trade, then I put in another four hours in the warehouse packing heavy electrical equipment without pay. Once I qualified, I shook hands with the boss and left. With my new trade I found I could go anywhere and get a job. So I did. I crossed this country so many times I lost count.'

'Did you ever marry?'

'No. Sometimes I lived with a woman as man and wife. It's fashionable now but let me tell you, it wasn't very fashionable then. In the end, they'd leave me or I'd leave them. They always wanted more than I was prepared to give. They always wanted to pry. Pry. Pry. Pry! In the end I became a confirmed bachelor, confirmed and selfish in my ways. A bottle of Scotch, football and opera. They became my passions. And once a year I went back down to the Snowy to catch trout. Not much of a story. Not much of a life.'

Colombina didn't know how to respond. Everything except the incident with the explosives seemed to fit. Perhaps it had taken place and his friend was killed, but she knew damn well that wasn't how he'd burned his arms. He'd lived the life of a fugitive, not knowing when to stop running. What had driven him on? Who did he think was pursuing him after all those years? Perhaps he'd simply spent his life running away from his guilt. She looked back at him and found him watching her closely. She smiled. 'You should have stayed in Switzerland. Instead of making holes through mountains, you could have made holes in cheese. It's a lot easier, tastes better too. I'll go make a cup of tea.'

She put the kettle on and noticed the worn flex. She'd become so familiar with it, it had ceased to represent a hazard.

But why would an electrician put up with it? If anyone knew about the dangers, he would. It occurred to her then that the whole of his story might be fiction, a carefully prepared, deliberately boring history to be wheeled out on request. Had he been hiding for so long that he'd forgotten how to trust? She felt cheated and hurt. She was his friend, nurse, cook and companion. Her every waking moment revolved around him and his needs. The fact that she was also his would-be murderer was inconsequential. He didn't know that. For most of her life she'd lived in two worlds and expected to be taken at face value in each of them. It rankled with her that the man who called himself Heinrich Bose did not repay her kindness and trust.

'Here's your tea. By the way I don't believe a word of your story. I can't imagine you as an electrician or a pastry cook.' She said it flippantly, almost in jest, as if to convince herself that she didn't care whether he told her the truth or not. For a moment he said nothing. He just looked at her steadily then cut the ground away from beneath her.

'And I don't believe you were born in Australia or that your name is Colombina. It isn't, is it, Cecilia?'

She was lost for words, stunned speechless. There it was. He knew. He'd probably known all along. He looked at her with a mixture of hurt and accusation. She didn't know where to turn or what to think.

* * *

Lucio stopped speaking and glanced over to Gancio, who caught his signal that the day had concluded.

'Maria!' Just as the name passed his lips to hurtle towards the kitchen, they heard the telltale hiss of the old espresso machine.

'*Subito!*'

'Maria's improving,' observed Neil drily.

'So is our storyteller,' cut in Milos.

'Yes, well done, Lucio. You've given us a lot to think about over the coming week. I must admit I'm intrigued to know how long the Oberstleutnant has known Colombina's true identity and what he thinks her motives for lying may be. It must be terrible to be caught telling lies by someone who regards you as a trusting friend. What do you say, Lucio?'

'What can I say, Ramon?' Lucio said evenly. 'When somebody tells lies they must be prepared to face the consequences if they're found out.'

'Are you prepared, Lucio?'

'Have I told lies?'

'Ramon,' cut in Milos. 'You are like a cracked record and they are best thrown away.'

'Thank you for your simile. I was merely offering Lucio ground to manoeuvre, room to correct any misunderstandings he may have inadvertently given.'

'He has refused your kind offer, no? So drop it.'

Ramon shrugged. Lucio's ending to the day's storytelling had surprised him. The old man was obviously on his guard. That wouldn't make things any easier for Colombina. Perhaps he'd been too hasty in leaping to conclusions. Maybe it was he who hadn't been listening as well as he should. Either that or Lucio was a far cleverer storyteller than he gave him credit for.

SIXTH THURSDAY

'Before Lucio takes us back to Lombardia, I am going to take you there.' Gancio spread his arms wide. 'Today everything on the menu is from Lombardia. Everyone who eats here today is eating in Lombardia. If anyone wants *spaghetti bolognaise* they'll have to eat somewhere else.'

'Do we assume from this that today's story will centre around Como?'

'Yes, Ramon,' Lucio said evenly. 'You know it does. You can see further ahead of a story than even the storyteller.'

'What about Colombina and Heinrich, or is he now Friedrich?'

'We'll get to them.'

'Soon?'

'When I'm ready. Now let Gancio tell us all about the treats he has in store for us.' Lucio smiled inwardly, a smile of satisfaction. Ramon was coming along nicely.

'We begin with *bresaola*, cured dried beef served wafer thin with olive oil and pepper. It was a perfect food for the partisans because it didn't spoil. Unfortunately, they only had it when they had money to buy a cow, and time to slaughter it and to cure it. Then *polenta taragna*, buckwheat *polenta* served with butter and cheese. *Polenta* was a staple food for the partisans but they couldn't get enough corn to make that either so they used to stretch it with pine tree sawdust, sometimes flour if they could get it, and barley husks. Mostly they ate it cold because they didn't want to attract the attention of the Germans by lighting fires. They didn't have butter either. So they ate it cold and rock hard with a parmesan

319

cheese. Sometimes they'd try to soften it up with milk. It tasted like shit but it filled stomachs.'

'Jesus, Gancio, what are you doing to us?'

'Relax, Neil, you are not a partisan and my *polenta* is famous. Besides, I have made a special meat dish for you, *rostin negaa*, veal chops braised in white wine.'

'That's more like it.'

'The rest of you will have something special — *foiolo*, tripe cooked with butter and onions and served with grated cheese. It is delicious. During the war the people in the villages often didn't have the money to buy meat and so they had to make do with tripe. But in Lombardia, we are very good with tripe. You'll see.'

'I'll stick to my chops.'

'As we knew you would. God only knows how bored your taste buds must be. Afterwards, a little *formaggio*. Gorgonzola of course, and *stracchino* which is made from the milk of tired cows. *Strecco* is a local word for tired. The cows get tired on the long walk down from the alpine pastures. It's a nice, smooth, full-flavoured cheese. To finish, *torta paradiso*, sponge cake. I wanted to make you *busecchina* which is boiled chestnuts and cream. The partisans sometimes boiled chestnuts on their little primus cookers, or when it was safe to light fires but they had to eat them without the cream.'

'*Bravo*, Gancio.' Lucio sat back and applauded the menu. 'It is entirely appropriate to the story I will be telling today.'

'Yeah, nice bit of cooking, Gancio,' cut in Neil. 'But why do I get the feeling you two are cooking up something more than lunch?'

'More to the point,' said Ramon quietly, 'how come you know so much about what the partisans ate?'

Chapter Thirty-One

Cecilia and Guido became lovers. Some claimed it was inevitable, that she had designs on him from the first day they met, and they'd point to the way that she'd never missed an opportunity to sit and talk to him. It's true that Cecilia was fond of him and had grown to love him, but it was more the childish crush a girl might feel for her teacher than adult passion. More accurately it could be argued that their affair was a by-product of the war, begun as an act of kindness to a lonely, desperate man, or as a means of bringing comfort to one another in the face of shared dangers. But the end result was the same. They became lovers and once more Cecilia was destined to bear the blame.

She was horrified when the Signora passed on Father Michele's message but did her best to conceal her fear. The idea of breaking curfew and sneaking out of the house alone in the dead of night to climb to a secret rendezvous in the hills terrified her. But how could she refuse the Signora? If Father Michele wouldn't act as courier, she had no choice. She knew how important her information was to Guido. The Signora named three meeting places where the lower pastures met the forest, none much more than five kilometres above her old home. Each place had a codename which would change each time she met with Guido, so only the two of them would ever know exactly where the next rendezvous would take place. Cecilia knew she could find her way to these meeting points in the dark provided she didn't come across any patrols or escapees or deserters. That's what worried her most. What chance would a young woman alone have then?

The first night she crept out of the sleeping house she would never have known if she was being followed or not. The pounding of her heart made her deaf to the inadvertent snapping of twigs or any other sound that didn't belong naturally to the night. She skirted around Ravello and the farm houses she knew had dogs and avoided open spaces. Her breathing was strained, not so much from exertion as from fear. She paused every two hundred metres as she'd been told, to listen for pursuers, but all she heard was her own breathing. She kept clear of the shepherds' overnight huts and the outlying stables, which often provided welcome shelter for fugitives and were a target for patrols. She climbed and climbed until genuine tiredness softened the edges of her fears and her brain could begin to function almost normally. As she drew closer and closer to the rendezvous point she paused again to listen. When she heard nothing, she continued. But the closer she got to the shallow cave the more desperate she became for Guido's protection. She ignored all her warnings and scrabbled forward as fast as she could. She reached the mouth of the cave. 'Guido!' she called. But there was no response. She peered into the gloom trying to penetrate its depths. 'Guido?' she asked again softly. Again there was no reply. She began to panic. Surely not. Surely her efforts hadn't been for nothing. He had to be there! 'Guido?' she asked once more. Tears began to well up in her eyes. She couldn't believe it had all been in vain and she still had the return journey ahead of her. She began to sob.

'What is the point of having passwords if you don't use them?'

'Guido!' She spun around and threw herself sobbing into his arms. She clung on to him fiercely, pressing herself tightly against him until he responded in kind. He bent down and kissed her, the top of her head, her cheeks then her lips. She responded hungrily until he gently eased her away.

'Oh Guido, I was so frightened. You weren't here . . .'

'I was here waiting for the password. I listened to you climb up here.'

They'd picked their rendezvous well, tucked away in a hollow sheltered by trees. Even so, some pale moonlight managed to filter through and Cecilia could clearly make out the face in front of her. Her heart went out to him.

'Romeo.'

'And I reply?'

'Margherita.'

He laughed. 'Well, Margherita, what news do you have for your Romeo?'

Cecilia told him everything the commandant had told them over lunch and, as she did, she saw his face grow hard.

'Dear God,' he said finally. 'I thought we were over the worst. I thought now at least we would have some respite. Still, now that we know what they plan we can take counter measures. If we strike first maybe we'll force them to change their plans.'

Cecilia studied his face with eyes grown accustomed to the dark and could scarcely believe how much Guido had aged. She saw that the news had hit him badly. Once more he would have to dig deep to find the strength to fight on.

'Dates, places. Do you think you could find out?'

'Of course I will try.'

'You're a brave girl, Cecilia.' He squeezed her to him and in that gesture Cecilia felt his loneliness and his despair. She hugged him back, reached up and kissed him. It was a signal, a beginning, and both knew where it would lead them but neither did a thing to prevent it. They sank gently to the ground where lichen and moss made a soft bed for them. What began as a tender kiss gave way to the full flood of passion and for the first time Cecilia experienced the urgent caresses and pleasure of a lover of her choice. They took each other hungrily and noisily, with an urgency born of desperate times, almost in blind panic. But it wasn't enough. They'd barely rested before Cecilia began again. She rolled on top of him and unbuttoned her blouse, making him a present of her breasts. She took him inside her impatiently, urgently seeking the fulfilment she needed and cried out when she found it. For Cecilia the experience of her first climax with a man was overwhelming and her emotions ran riot. She loved Guido more then than she ever believed it was possible to love anyone. She wept and held on to him and never wanted to let him go. Neither considered the consequences nor questioned its permanence.

Who could blame Guido for succumbing? He'd been denied the love and warmth of his wife and daughter and the comforts of any woman. He lived each day on the run like a wild animal, hunted and hounded, depending for his life on his guile and his willingness to endure. Cecilia gave him something every bit as precious as the food they managed to buy and scrounge, and the arms and medical supplies dropped by the Americans. She gave him love, a balm for his soul, sustenance for his will, and a reminder of why he persevered. Along with her information she brought comfort and who could say which had the greater value?

Cecilia returned down the mountain and, rather than being fearful of her next foray, waited eagerly for the signal. That evening had established a pattern which she knew would be continued. She loved him and boldly believed he loved her equally. In a strange way, perhaps to allay her feelings of guilt, she saw herself as an extension of the Signora and Carmela, delivering in person the love they were unable to share. She never considered what would happen when the Signora and Guido were eventually reunited. At any event she felt neither shame nor regrets, nor gave Signora Mila any cause for suspicion. Guido simply became another part of her life, the part that took place on the mountainside, remote from anything else and irrelevant to her relationship with the Signora and Carmela. But nobody can so compartmentalise their life that they become entirely disassociated episodes. Cecilia played many different roles but they were interrelated and impacted upon each other in ways not easy to predict.

* * *

Ironically, Cecilia's relationship with Guido depended upon a continuing involvement with the Oberstleutnant. If she was not immediately aware of his ultimate intentions, the Count summoned her to his study and made them abundantly clear.

'The commandant is joining us for lunch once more,' he chortled. 'He pretends it's me he wants to see but it's you, Cecilia. Ha! The man's fallen for you. Head over heels. You can see it, he's smitten. Well, what are we going to do about it? I don't want to spend my few remaining years as a gooseberry in the middle. I'm going to let him know that I give him my permission to court you. It's up to you, Cecilia, now to do your duty. And I want to know everything that happens. Everything!'

'No. I'm sorry, Count, but that is impossible.'

'What do you mean? I forbid you to refuse him!'

'Count, I have no intention of refusing him. But I have every intention of refusing you.' She laughed and put her arm around the Count's thin shoulders. 'What happens between two people is their affair. It is private. For example, I have never told anyone about what used to pass between the two of us. Would you prefer I did?'

'No, of course not.'

'You see? If the Oberstleutnant and I become lovers — and I'm not as certain as you that that is what he is after — then you can rest assured that your secrets are as safe with me ... as are his.' She smiled.

'Ha! Signor Calosci warned me that you are a clever little vixen and you are. Now you blackmail me. Who taught you to be so devious? Ha! It must have been me. Ah ... what does it matter? I'm too old now anyway. After you've done your duty at least entertain me with an edited version.'

'Perhaps, but Count, remember that rewards should not be given without effort. And the greater the effort the greater the appreciation of the reward. Would you deny the commandant full appreciation of his reward? Surely it is my duty to heighten his appreciation to the fullest?'

The Count laughed. 'Then God help him! '

*   *   *

Cecilia began to see the Oberstleutnant. Mostly twice a week but sometimes three when the Count entertained. They ate in the local restaurants and occasionally in the barracks. One day Friedrich commandeered the mayor's motor launch and took her out onto the lake for a cruise. He was stunned to learn that she'd never been out on the lake before. She loved it. They visited Bellagio and Ravenna which she'd looked upon all her life and yet knew little about. He bought a guide book and they became tourists. They discovered the Villa Giulia, the retreat of Leopold the First, King of the Belgians, and the Villa Serbelloni. They crossed back to Tremezzo and strolled through the gardens of the Villa Carlotta. But what gave the Oberstleutnant the greatest pleasure was the discovery of the Villa Margherita where Verdi had composed *La Traviata* almost a hundred years earlier. From then on they took the little boat out whenever they could, often on the warm summer evenings.

For Cecilia it was a duty, but it a became a very pleasant duty. If her heart didn't already belong to another, it could easily have fallen into his hands. He was precisely the sort of person her mother hoped she'd meet and marry. He was handsome, witty, clever and oh so charming. He made her feel special and important. Where once she'd have thought herself lucky to wait upon his table, he now held her chair for her and entertained her with his stories.

He told her about Christiane and Helmuth and it was plain to see how much he adored them both. She liked him all the more for that. He was kind and patient. She was grateful for his patience and the fact that he hadn't forced his affections upon her, but her gratitude blinded her to the dangers. She knew the value of prolonging the chase. She'd even flaunted its merits to the Count. But she failed totally to see that its appeal also worked in reverse. As the weeks passed and grew into months, she became increasingly attached to him.

Of course, in a small town their relationship could hardly go unnoticed. People who used to exchange greetings with her at church or in the street now ignored her and worse, hissed softly as she passed. But she dismissed this and bore the insults with dignity. After the war, she would be revealed not as a collaborator but as a brave heroine. Guido never ceased to remind her of the fact. She had every right to hold her head high.

Once a fortnight and sometimes twice, she'd slip out at night and into the hills, bearing her precious information. She became skilled in hugging the shadows and avoiding humps or ridges which could silhouette her against the night sky. But more than anything she learned to listen. She became familiar with the night noises, associating each with a particular animal or trick of the wind. She learned to listen for the night birds and to take alarm at their absence. Silence, she learned, often warned of the presence of others, and she'd hide and wait until she'd heard them pass. Whether friend or foe, she had no intention of letting them find her. Her confidence grew and so did her caution.

Increasingly it was duty not her love for Guido which drew her back, for she could no longer be certain of meeting him. The risks were just too high. At any time it was dangerous for partisans to come down from the heights where they were safe. But with the increased activity of the German soldiers and fascists as they tried to carry out their commandant's instructions, the risk of being shot or caught had trebled. More and more often, Guido sent his trusted lieutenant in his place. The first time, Cecilia had been heartbroken and found it hard to hide her disappointment. The man who simply identified himself as *il ascia*, the axe, had laughed at her then grabbed her, suggesting she gave him what she normally gave Guido. He tried to force her down onto the ground but she kicked out and slapped him. He called her a bitch and a whore and asked when she'd become choosy. Everyone knew she was also fucking the Oberstleutnant.

Cecilia was humiliated and blamed Guido for allowing it to happen the next time she saw him. To her surprise and mortification he just shrugged. 'These are desperate times,' was all he'd said. 'And he is a desperate man. It is a long time since he has had a woman. But I will speak to him.'

That was not the reaction Cecilia had hoped for. That was not the reaction of a lover whose best friend had betrayed his trust. She'd expected him to rage and threaten to kill him. She'd expected sympathy and comfort. Instead she had the distinct impression that Guido would not have minded greatly if she had extended her comfort to his lieutenant. When Guido lay his coat on the ground for them to lie on, there was no sweet preamble, no prior exchange of endearments. What had once seemed special had become a habit and expected. Nevertheless she'd lain with him but it was a coupling from which she drew little satisfaction.

Cecilia still loved him and was prepared to accept that

what had passed between them that night was an anomaly that would be forgotten the next time they met. But the next time was long coming, and three times in a row she'd had to put up with the lewd suggestiveness and leers of the man who called himself 'the axe'. When she finally met up with him again he was more like the Guido of old, gentle and thoughtful and not distracted. When they made love she'd expected it to be a replay of the first time and was more than a little surprised when it wasn't. She couldn't help comparing him with the other man in her life and Guido did not stand up well to the comparison.

She'd been shown another kind of love that made her feel happy and want to radiate her happiness to all around her. There was nothing furtive or secretive about it. She loved the little attentions and the courtesies and the implications they brought that she was somebody worthwhile. She loved its openness and honesty and sex was not yet a part of it. She loved the way the Oberstleutnant paid attention to her mind, rather than just her obvious beauty. He'd introduced her to opera. When she'd told the Count how they'd sat and listened to Wagner he'd put his head back and laughed. 'Imagine,' he'd cackled, 'a German introducing an Italian to opera! What has the world come to?' He also awakened in her an appreciation of beautiful things, and constantly surprised her by pausing to admire a flower, a tree, a building or even something as mundane as an old doorway. This was not what she expected from a feared soldier of the Reich. He gave her gifts, often trivial but always thoughtful. He also inadvertently gave her information but she never allowed herself to consider for a second that she was betraying him. She forbade herself to think that way when she was with him. He was no longer the enemy but a charming and engaging companion. The information she gathered was incidental and belonged in another compartment of her life. Besides, she wasn't betraying him but serving the just cause of the partisans. What was wrong with that?

She never asked him any questions that had any direct bearing on any activity he might be planning, so he never had any reason to suspect her when partisan activity intensified. He saw it instead as a reflection of the increases in

partisan attacks taking place all over occupied northern Italy.
He came to respect his adversaries for their uncanny selection
of which convoys to hit, and for their sixth sense in melting
away whenever a *rastrellamento* was planned. He'd tried
assembling troops and then disbanding them so they'd never
know whether a sweep was going to take place or not. He
thought this tactic would keep them safely on the retreat up
into the mountains and so allow his convoys to pass unmo-
lested. Sometimes, when the information they'd gathered
from informants seemed particularly reliable, he'd assemble
his troops at short notice for a lightning thrust into the hills.
Yet rarely did they catch the partisans by surprise and often,
when it seemed that they had, they'd be lured into an ambush
by a stronger force. Then by the time he'd brought his mortars to bear they'd be gone. Casualties were always reasonably light, though Friedrich regretted the loss of even one of
his men so close to the end of the war.

He had his successes. Sometimes his forays into the hills
slipped through the web of informers, and he'd kill a few
partisans and take many more captive. By the time the fascists
or the Gestapo had finished with them, many of the partisans
wished they'd been killed on the mountainside. He accepted
that the partisans had informers but never for a second
suspected that Cecilia was one of them. Instead, he continued
to court her as if they were young lovers, relishing the chase
and her company, not at all anxious to move in for the kill a
moment before it was due.

Throughout that summer and autumn, Cecilia kept up her
double life, loving the Oberstleutnant by day in the way
that they both found easy and comfortable, and loving Guido
by night on the increasingly few occasions he risked the
journey down the mountain. But as the Allies advanced
northwards and the German defences along the Po Valley
began to crack, the strain started to tell. The partisans grew
bolder and their attacks more ferocious and prolonged. But
still they slipped away before the mortars and machine-guns
could pin them down. Friedrich called for more troops to
help contain them but the High Command could ill afford
to spare more troops from the front. Instead he found himself
under pressure to order reprisals. But what village should he

hit? The partisans kept away from all the villages and spread their activity widely to protect the people who lived in them. For their part, the villagers gave no obvious support to the partisans, complained endlessly about the grain and livestock that they'd stolen, and gave the Germans no cause to take action.

After a series of attacks on supply convoys, Friedrich's pleas for assistance were heard. When the SS truck pulled into the barracks compound, and he went to greet the officer who led them, he instantly regretted ever having made the requests.

'You!'

'Yes indeed, Herr Oberstleutnant. Tell me, does Christiane's uncle still pimp for you?'

Chapter Thirty-Two

As winter closed in the partisans moved down from the heights, caught between the savagery of nature and the gathering storm below. Yet they could claim to have more control of the hills than ever as more and more soldiers deserted the fascists to swell their ranks. But the presence of the SS in force in Menaggio kept them on a nervous alert. They could no longer rely on messages coming through from Cecilia and their other sources, as few were prepared to brave the fog, the snow and the bitter cold. There was also the risk of leaving behind an incriminating trail in the snow. Nevertheless, Guido was desperate to know when and where the SS would make their move. He fed messages via couriers to Father Michele and on to the Signora with the same urgent plea. Cecilia must find out when the *rastrellamento* was planned and get the information to them.

The tension and urgency began to make its mark on Cecilia. She cut off the Signora every time she tried to remind her of the urgency, and had to endure her reproachful looks every time she returned from a meeting with the Oberstleutnant without the information. Cecilia had not actively sought specific information before and was reluctant to start now. Besides, the arrival of the SS had brought a change in Friedrich she found unsettling. He was still as thoughtful and courteous as ever, but she could see he had other matters on his mind. He apologised for his preoccupation and insisted the situation was only temporary.

Cecilia was soon to understand the nature of the Oberstleutnant's distraction, in a way that brought home to her the reality of the risks she ran as a matter of course every day of her life. She heard Signora Fiorelli scream and rushed to the kitchen to see what the problem was. She imagined the cook had burned herself dropping a pan of boiling water or soup, or at least a mishap of that kind. Instead she ran into the barrel of a sub machine-gun and was pushed abruptly to the floor. She screamed, adding her voice to the chorus that grew around her. She looked up into the hard eyes of an SS soldier and the weapon pointed at her head. In panic she looked for Signora Mila. Wherever she looked there were SS soldiers and cowering staff. She saw Carla and Antonella, Roberto and Andre the chauffeur up against the end wall, hands raised. The soldier standing over her kicked her foot to get her attention. He pointed to the others.

'Schnell!'

Cecilia jumped to her feet and ran over to them. Her mind was racing. Where was the Signora? What did they know? Surely they weren't going to be taken out and shot. Where was the Count? And Friedrich? Surely Friedrich could help? Then the realisation hit her that if the SS were there because of her activities, there'd be no help coming from either Friedrich or the Count. Her heart pounded and she wanted to be sick. The walls she'd so painstakingly constructed between the different parts of her life began to crumble and seem foolishly artificial. She heard a scuffle in the corridor and looked up in time to see two soldiers dragging the Signora and Carmela into the kitchen. The Signora was irate and cursing the soldiers with every breath.

An SS officer appeared at the doorway, briefly silhouetted by the daylight outside. Cecilia looked up into the eyes of the coldest, hardest man she had ever seen. He seemed to tower over everyone else and his sheer presence was overwhelming. Even the Signora ceased her raging.

'Who is in charge here?' he asked and an officer translated his question into Italian. Signora Mila shrugged off the hands holding her and stepped forward defiantly.

'I am. I am the housekeeper. Who are you and what is the meaning of this?'

Sturmbannführer Dietrich Schmidt looked calmly at the indignant woman in front of him while he listened to the translation. He looked straight into her eyes as she glared back at him, his thin lips twisted into what might once have passed for a smile. He waited and waited until he'd waited her out and she lowered her eyes. Still he looked at her, unwavering and unblinking. To Cecilia's horror the Signora seemed to crumple up in front of her. Just when she thought she'd fall, the Sturmbannführer spoke once more.

'Where is the man Piero?'

Piero? Were they after Piero? Were they safe after all? Or was he an informer? Surely not, or he would have informed on them before. Cecilia felt her hopes rise and saw some stiffening return to the Signora's back.

'Piero is our handyman. He could be anywhere in the garden or sheds or in the cellars. Or in his room above the workshop.'

'I ask you one last time. Where is the man Piero?'

The SS officer had not moved nor raised his voice, yet Cecilia felt an icy hand wrap around her heart. She'd never heard anything so laced with menace before in her life. The man was a killer, who'd obviously killed many times and would kill again without hesitation or remorse. The Signora hesitated, eyes wide with fear, her mouth dry, perfectly aware of the threat she faced. She obviously didn't know where Piero was. She glanced over to the staff helplessly, pleadingly.

'Signora . . .' It was Roberto. 'Excuse me, Signora, but I believe Piero is in his room. I heard him in there. He will still be there unless the noise of the soldiers has frightened him off.'

'Scharführer!'

The SS sergeant leapt to obey his superior. He grabbed hold of Roberto and pushed him through the doorway into the yard. Four soldiers followed.

'Why do you want him? He is an old man.'

The Sturmbannführer ignored her question and looked right through her. He waited patiently for his men to return with Piero and wasn't made to wait long. The sergeant stepped back into the kitchen pushing Roberto in front of him.

'Herr Sturmbannführer, the man Piero is under arrest.'

Dietrich looked calmly at the cowering staff and turned to leave.

'One moment if you don't mind!' The Count stood in the

doorway from the corridor, his face crimson with rage, Signor Calosci at his side. 'What is going on here? Who the hell do you think you are? I will have you skinned alive for this.'

'I think not. Our interrogators tell us a man called Piero is responsible for ferrying Jews over the mountains to Switzerland. There is a man here called Piero who meets the description we have. We are taking him in for questioning.'

'You will do no such thing! That man is a loyal servant. I trust him completely. What gives you the right to burst into my home like this? Release him immediately or I will insist your superiors have you shot!'

'My superiors will probably give me a medal. Now, if you don't mind . . .' Dietrich turned on his heel and walked out into the yard. His troops hesitated for a moment to see that nobody took any action to prevent him, then followed. The Count watched them go, too stunned to move.

'Oh dear God . . .' Carla sank to the floor sobbing. Cecilia exchanged a brief glance with the Signora, acknowledging the relief they both felt, then walked past her to the Count.

'Count, you were magnificent. We must get in touch with the Oberstleutnant immediately. He will make sure Piero is released. We can't let them get away with this. We must also tell the Duce. He will be furious. He will make them pay for insulting you like this.'

The Count let Cecilia take his arm and lead him away, grateful to be given his next course of action. All his bluster had gone and he'd turned as white as a sheet. He shook from head to toe. 'You are right, Cecilia. We can't let them get away with this. Mussolini must be informed. This is an outrage! An outrage!'

* * *

Oberstleutnant Friedrich Eigenwill was waiting for Dietrich when he returned to the barracks.

'Sturmbannführer! One moment of your time please!'

The SS officer walked casually across to where Friedrich was standing. 'You wish to see me, Herr Commandant?' He contrived to make 'Herr Commandant' sound like an insult and said it just loud enough to draw a snigger from the men closest to him.

'In my office.' Friedrich whirled around and marched into his office. He pushed the door open and left it that way for Dietrich. 'Close the door.' He waited until Dietrich had complied then turned on him. 'What the hell do you think you're doing? I've just had the Count on the phone to me. I'm expecting a call from Marshal Graziani at any moment. How dare you insult the Count like this! How dare you go behind my back. Why didn't you inform me of your suspicions and I would have had the man arrested myself? In fact the Count would have brought him to us if I'd asked him. What the hell game are you playing?'

'Let me ask you something, Herr Oberstleutnant. How many Jews have you arrested since you have been commandant here? I'll refresh your memory. Precisely eleven. Yet we know this area under your command is a major escape route for Jews. We know it is a major escape route for deserters. Again, you have caught precious few of them. May I remind you that you requested help to do your job as you are so obviously incapable of doing it yourself. Do you think I wanted to come to this fart-arsed little hole? No! This is not a game. This is war. My place is at the front line not holding the hands of gutless army officers . . .'

'Sturmbannführer!' Friedrich reacted in outrage but Dietrich had touched a nerve and made accusations he would find hard to defend. He knew what horrors lay ahead for any Jews that were captured and he had no stomach for hunting them down. He was a soldier and his war was against other soldiers, not defenceless women and children. Hunting Jews was one part of his duty he had not pursued with all vigour, justifying his inaction by convincing himself his limited resources were better applied against the partisans. Others would not be so easily convinced.

'Hear me out, Oberstleutnant. I am not accustomed to repeating myself. It is my intention to clean up the shit in your nest as fast as possible and get back to the front. I will use whatever methods I deem necessary and you will not interfere. When I leave you can play soldiers as much as you like. While I am here, we play by my rules. If not I will have you shot. Don't interrupt! I will have you shot. Not up against a wall but on the field of battle. Things can become very confused there as you know. In the meantime I will thank you not to make demands of me in front of my troops otherwise I will be forced to ignore them. Do I make myself clear, Herr Oberstleutnant?'

'Have you finished? Good. Understand this. I am the senior officer here and I will give orders. If I choose to give you orders in front of your troops I will do so and you will obey them. Or I will have you arrested and shot. And it will be up against a wall, Herr Sturmbannführer, and I will make sure the spectacle is well publicised. Do I make myself clear?'

'It appears Herr Oberstleutnant that you have difficulty hearing. Any attempt to arrest me will be met by gunfire from my men. Who would you back, yours or mine?' Dietrich began to laugh. 'You're as full of shit as your pimp, the Generalleutnant.'

Friedrich gritted his teeth. If it came to a showdown he had no illusions over who would win. His force was no match for Dietrich's elite SS troops. 'Sturmbannführer, you are required to apologise to the Count and release his man immediately.'

'No, I don't think so. If you want the Count to receive an apology, you apologise. I imagine you're good at that. As for his man, I've already handed him over to the Gestapo. They are anxious to talk to him. If he cannot add to their knowledge in any way, he will be released. Anything else?'

Friedrich gripped the edge of his table in rage, his knuckles white. 'I could have you arrested now.'

'No. We have discussed that. That would be most unwise. One other thing. I am drawing up plans for an attack on the partisans. I have an idea how to lure them down to attack us. You and your men will be the lure.'

'I already have a plan.'

'Ah ... not a very good one I'm afraid. Please organise a meeting tomorrow morning and bring your Blackshirt commanders.' Dietrich looked at his watch. 'If you hurry you will have time to see the Count before dark, to offer your apologies and screw his mistress. I won't keep you.' Dietrich's lips twisted in a travesty of a smile as he turned and left the room.

Chapter Thirty-Three

Cecilia learned about Dietrich's plan over the dinner table at the Villa Carosio. The Count laid no blame at Friedrich's feet for the humiliation he'd received, indeed he was grateful to Friedrich for finally rescuing Piero from the Gestapo. The old man had been frightfully beaten but was still in one piece. He'd told them nothing and had steadfastly maintained he was a servant of the Count and had nothing to tell. So the Count had no hesitation in extending an invitation to Friedrich.

Dietrich's plan was bold and the fascists made no secret of their admiration for Friedrich and the part he was willing to play. They praised his bravery while secretly laughing at his stupidity for accepting the part. Cecilia sat and ate and talked and listened and mentally took notes. She felt no elation at finally learning what Guido so desperately needed to know. Rather, she felt concern for Friedrich over the risks he was taking. She was horrified. He'd be a sitting duck in any ambush, a free target for a machine-gunner or for petrol bombs. She felt like bursting into tears. It wasn't just the actress in her responding, her concern was genuine. Perhaps she should have paused for a moment to consider what that meant.

As soon as the dinner concluded, she sought out the Signora and told her to arrange a rendezvous. Signora Mila did not disguise her delight with Cecilia. She grabbed her and hugged her and let her tears of gratitude fall openly. Cecilia thought of the nightmare climb ahead of her, of the patrols that would be stepped up as a precaution, and the ever present threat of storms. She began shivering and the warmth of the Signora's gratitude could not stop the icy shudders rippling through her body. She went to bed fearful for herself, for Guido and for the Oberstleutnant.

But fate had another card to play, one which would begin to tear apart the walls that separated the different parts of her life. It was inevitable, of course. Sooner or later the contents of each compartment had to spill over, one into the other. For Cecilia, the time was fast approaching.

She awoke the following morning with a light headache and put it down to a restless night during which all her fears manifested themselves in nightmarish dreams, until she was too scared to close her eyes. Only exhaustion had brought what little sleep she'd had. By evening, when Father Michele's bell pealed confusingly across the hillside, her headache had intensified and her limbs grown heavy. The soreness in her throat and her watery eyes were symptoms easily recognised, and her sickness too obvious to be ignored. Cecilia, brave heroine of the partisans and all Italy, had caught a cold.

* * *

While the soldiers prepared their trap in Menaggio, Cecilia lay in bed and briefed the Signora. There was no choice. Father Michele still refused to carry information that would lead directly to the deaths of others, and they didn't dare involve anyone else in their secret. Cecilia painstakingly explained the location of the rendezvous and the best route to get there, cautioning her to take the safer, more round-about path which avoided open meadows, even though it would add more than an hour to her journey. She gave the Signora the passwords and insisted that she wear the coat and hat she herself normally wore. 'Guido will be expecting me,' she explained. 'If you don't look like me he might suspect a trap and withdraw.' On the evening of the rendez-vous, she told the Signora the details of Dietrich's plan.

It was simplicity itself. The idea was to draw the partisans out so that they revealed their main force, which would then be encircled. The Oberstleutnant was to drive to Porlezza on the eastern tip of Lake Lugano the day before to collect captured partisans, deserters and Jews, many of whom had escaped the Germans and Blackshirts only to be turned back by Swiss border guards. The following morning he would return accompanied by two covered trucks filled with soldiers, and the prisoners in a covered truck between them. His Lancia would head the convoy. Another armed convoy would precede them by ten minutes, with an armoured car clearing the road ahead of it. Instead of a normal armament shipment, the enclosed trucks would carry more soldiers. Meanwhile, the SS would make a very public withdrawal from Menaggio, making it plain to anyone who cared to listen that the winter conditions were unsuitable for a *rastrellamento* and they were returning to the front. Instead, they would drive south to Argegno and double back overnight on secondary roads around the southern shore of Lake Lugarno. They'd hole up on a deserted stretch of road near Porlezza and wait until they received the signal that the Oberstleutnant had left. Then they would pursue them, again allowing a ten-minute gap between. The Blackshirts meanwhile would be trucked into positions on by-roads north and south of the highway, ready to come to the assistance of the commandant.

Dietrich believed that sympathisers would inform the partisans of the two convoys and that the second would prove irresistible. After all, how often did they get the chance to kill the area commandant and free their own captured men? The force accompanying the prisoners was strong enough to require attack by the main body of partisans, but not so strong that it would be a deterrent. He expected the partisans to follow their usual practice of strike and fade, hitting the convoy and retreating up into the hills. But this time they would be trapped. The instant the ambush occurred, Friedrich would radio the codeword and troops from both the preceding and following convoys would immediately disembark, and set off on converging courses up the hillsides. The partisans would then be surrounded on both flanks, and from below by the survivors of Friedrich's force and the Blackshirts coming to their assistance. The final nail in the coffin would be provided by a spotter plane which, weather permitting, would plot the partisans' retreat.

The Signora listened grimly to how the SS planned to kill her husband. If she'd had any reservations about making the hazardous trip, she had none now. She knew that Guido could not resist the chance to free his men. Everyone knew what happened once the Gestapo and the fascist interrogators got hold of them. Of course Guido would try to save them. She looked at the sick girl in the bed in front of her and took her hands in hers.

'I thank God for sending you to us, Cecilia. Think how many lives this information will save, Guido's among them. Next time I see your mother I'm going to give her a big hug.'

Cecilia laughed just thinking of her mother's surprise. But the day was not yet won nor the information delivered. She knew the risks the Signora faced. God help them all if she was caught. 'Go carefully, Signora. Remember, time is your ally, speed is your enemy. Never hesitate to stop and listen. In this weather you won't have the birds to warn you.' She squeezed the Signora's hands. As she left her bedroom, Cecilia lay back in bed and wondered if Guido would also lay down his coat for his wife. That was one aspect she hadn't considered, not even for a second.

* * *

The Signora waited nervously for the staff to finish up in the kitchen and go to bed. On these bleak winter nights there was nothing for them to stay up for. She heard footsteps on the stairs up to the servants' rooms, some hushed 'good nights', then silence. She slipped into Cecilia's coat and hat and slid quietly out the back door. The cold hit her as solidly as if she'd plunged into an icy stream. She glanced up at the sky and saw the hard twinkle of winter stars. It would be bitterly cold but at least it wouldn't snow. She hesitated to give her eyes a chance to become accustomed to the darkness before moving on. But the darkness was near total. She hadn't expected it to be so dark. She felt the first twinge of panic. Would she be able to find her way?

She opened the side gate, grateful for remembering to tell Roberto to oil its hinges. She crept down the narrow laneway to the meadow which marked the beginning of her climb. She'd hardly made it halfway along before she tripped and fell headlong onto the ground. She cried out in surprise. Dear

God! Had anyone heard her? She'd hardly begun and she'd fallen already. It was just so dark, so hopelessly dark. She considered the magnitude of the task ahead and knew it was beyond her. How could she help but fail? How could she find a secret place she'd never been before when she couldn't even see her own hand in front of her face? Bitter tears flooded her eyes. She had to go on, however hopeless, for Guido's sake. She couldn't fail him. She gathered her breath and her wits and prepared to pick herself up.

'Signora!' The whisper came soft and urgent and scared her out of her wits. She lay there, not daring to breathe.

'Signora, it is Piero.'

She felt his hands under her arms helping her to her feet. She was surprised at the old man's strength.

'Piero, what are you doing here?' She only whispered but the force of it in the still night air made it sound almost like a shout.

'Signora, keep your voice down. Better still, keep your mouth shut. I will do the talking. Do you think I don't know what's going on? I have been following Cecilia off and on since spring to make sure no harm came to her. I don't know who she meets because I stop once she gets near to her meeting places. It would be too dangerous for me to go on. I assume whomever she meets has lookouts, too. I don't know who she meets but I can guess and I think I know why she goes. She is a remarkable young girl. I have learned to associate her trips with a particular ringing of Father Michele's bell. Now that Cecilia has a cold, I assumed you would go in her place. When I heard you'd told Roberto to oil the gate I was sure. So I've waited for you. Signora. On a night like this, you would never make it on your own. Now tell me, where are you going? I will take you.'

The Signora hesitated. It could be a trap. After all, Piero had just been released by the Gestapo — an event rare in itself — so perhaps there'd been a trade-off. Information for his freedom. She tried to look into his face to search for the truth there, but the darkness would not permit it. If he knew about Cecilia, perhaps he was setting her up so they could also catch Guido. She considered her options and realised she had no choice. She could never find Guido without Piero's help, she was now certain of that, and if she didn't find him to give him the message he was doomed anyway. 'Okay,' she said, and told him. But as she told him, she realised how much she was asking of Piero. The man was still covered in bruises from his beatings and barely out of bed. 'Piero,' she said when she'd finished, 'Are you sure you are up to this? You've done enough.'

'Ha! What is a little pain compared to the pleasure of revenge? Guido will give them a beating in return. That will be my revenge.' He spat on the ground. 'Come along. Stay close behind me.'

They set off at a pace that staggered the Signora. It was all she could do to keep up with the dark shape in front of her. Piero moved as assuredly up the hills as most people did down their hallways. He seemed to know every bush, rock and overhanging branch and, more importantly, how to avoid them. They climbed until her breath rasped and she could no longer climb silently. Piero paused then briefly, to listen and give her time to recover. But the halt gave the seeping cold a chance to envelop them and they had to move on before it cramped their muscles. The Signora could feel herself begin to perspire and knew the dangers as her sweat dampened her underclothes. Wet clothes and cold were a potentially fatal combination. They climbed and climbed until she'd lost track completely of where they were and she could think of nothing else but her blind pursuit of the shapeless form in front of her. Then he stopped and pulled her to him. He held her so tightly and crushed her face so hard against his coat she couldn't breathe. What on earth was he doing? She wanted to scream. Was he trying to kill her? Then she heard a voice, muted and curt. She didn't understand the words but she recognised the language. German. She pressed herself harder against Piero, trying to melt into him, wanting to become invisible, wishing to be anywhere else but where she was. Piero stood as motionless as stone, waiting until his ears told him it was safe to proceed.

He gently eased himself apart from the Signora and continued the climb, more cautious now. A German patrol was unusual. Whatever information the Signora was carrying, the Germans were doing their utmost to ensure it didn't reach the partisans. They crept on upwards, pausing every hundred metres until they were close to the meeting point. He pulled the Signora to him once more and whispered in her ear.

'You go on now. Go straight on up the hill. You see that big rock silhouetted against the sky?'

The Signora strained her eyes and could just make out the outline. 'Yes, I see it.'

'Head for that rock, Signora. That is what Cecilia does. Somewhere between here and that rock someone will find you. Let's hope it is the person you want. Go now. I will wait for you here.'

The Signora looked up at the rock, wobbly on her feet now that she no longer had Piero to follow. She climbed a step at a time, unwilling to take her eyes off the rock up ahead in case she lost sight of it. She tripped, but caught herself as she hit the ground. She found herself among rocks and began to climb over and around them, desperately keeping an eye out for her marker. She climbed with as much urgency and strength as she could muster but the rock never seemed any closer. She nearly screamed out loud when hands grabbed her from behind.

'Well . . . well . . . if it isn't Guido's brave little whore.'

She fainted.

* * *

When she came to, she could see the shape of a man kneeling over her, then felt his hand slapping her face.

'Stop! Stop it!' she cried hoarsely. 'Who are you?'

'Who am I? Who the hell are you?'

She remembered the passwords. 'Margherita.'

'Ah . . . Margherita. *Bene!* I am your Romeo. Guido couldn't make it. It is too risky. There are too many patrols. Now is not a good time to lose our leader so he sent me instead. Tell me what you know — quickly before we both freeze to death!'

'No! First, you tell me something. Why did you call me Guido's whore?' The Signora was confused and disappointed. She was looking forward to seeing her husband again, however briefly. Tiredness, fear and her fainting spell had taken its toll. How did he know that she was bringing the message this time, and why when she was his wife did he call her Guido's whore? It didn't make sense. 'Tell me. Why do you insult me? Why do you call me Guido's whore?'

'What does it matter to you? I thought you were his darling Cecilia. Everybody knows that slut is fucking Guido.' The partisan laughed. He waited for a response and became curious when he didn't get one. He misunderstood her silence. 'What's the matter? Don't tell me he's fucking you as well?'

'Yes, he is as a matter of fact.' Her voice seemed to come from far away, not sad nor accusing but filled with pain. 'I am Guido's wife.'

Chapter Thirty-Four

'I thought you were dead.' He sat propped up in his armchair, a tired old man supported by pillows and cushions. Colombina looked down at her hands, unable for a moment to meet his eyes which had become shiny with tears.

'I thought you were dead,' he said again, his tone still accusatory. 'But then one day without warning you walked back into my life. It was pure chance, an act of God! A blessing! I didn't recognise you immediately but I recognised something familiar about you. At first I was cautious, wondering who you could be. But then you appeared on my doorstep one Sunday with *Rouladen* and *Blumenkohlsuppe*. That was not the kindness of a stranger who had met me only once. No! You had gone to too much effort. That was the act of a friend or of someone who wanted to be my friend, someone who wanted to get close to me for whatever reason. Naturally I was suspicious, but it was easy to hide my suspicions behind my excitement at the prospect of real food. German food! It was only when you asked if I'd like a coffee that it began to dawn on me that it was you and that somehow, miraculously, you had come back to life and into mine. I said, "I drink tea" and you replied, "Of course". Oh, you covered up well but it was the way you said it that triggered my memory. It reminded me of a beautiful girl in Menaggio who had been my lover and then my sole reason for living. But how could that be? You were dead. But deep inside me I knew it was you. A tiny spark of hope re-ignited the pilot light within me, and its heat began to course through my body. It was like coming alive again after a century of hibernation. It was like being reborn. As we talked I became more and more certain. You had the same mannerisms and the same confidence. I escorted you to the door so that I could look at you more closely in daylight. Dear God, you had changed Cecilia, we have all changed, but you were still beautiful and I recognised you. I wanted to shout "Cecilia! It's me, Friedrich!" and grab you and hold you. But then I realised you already knew who I was but were pretending otherwise. So I covered up. I was stunned. I couldn't understand why — why you would want to taunt me that way? And I still don't.' He paused to look at Colombina, his hurt still undiminished.

'Each time you came back I expected you to admit to your true identity but you didn't. As time went by I realised you had no intention of doing so. I was mystified. Obviously you were not going to report me to the authorities or you would have done it. So I decided to play your game and a game of my own, a game you should have been familiar with. I set out to seduce you again, to win you over as I had back in Menaggio. With patience, thoughtfulness and sincerity. In truth, that is all I have left. I could sense that I was succeeding. Then, when you came to visit me in hospital I was sure I had. Have I, Cecilia? Have I succeeded in making you love me again?'

'Don't call me Cecilia. My name is Colombina now.'

He accepted the rebuff and its implications in silence. Once he never gave away a hint of what he was thinking, but now his hurt was plain to see. His eyes grew shiny once more. Finally he managed to put aside his disappointment and found the strength to face up to her.

'But if you don't love me, why have you come back to me? Why befriend me? Why care for me? Why have you done so much for me?'

'To get my revenge, Friedrich.'

'Revenge . . . !' He stared at her open-mouthed, the fugitive cornered when he least expected it, gasping like a stranded goldfish.

'Revenge Friedrich, for killing my mother!'

'Your mother? I don't understand.' He looked up at her bewildered.

Colombina grabbed the locket around her neck and jerked

it so that the clasp broke. She opened it and took out her late husband's photo. Maddalena's face stared up at them. Her hands shook as she held the faded image right up to Friedrich's face. He fumbled for his reading glasses, put them on slowly and deliberately and studied the picture in front of him.

'I swear, Cecilia, I have never seen her before in my life.'

'Think again! Think back to the square in Ravello. Think back to those eight women you murdered.'

'Nooo . . . !' His cry of anguish was genuine and heartfelt. What had he done? His world crashed in on him, crushing his dreams, burying his hopes. The picture was small and old and faded brown. But, yes, she was the woman who had argued with him and cursed him before the firing squad had shot her. She was the brave one. Dear God! What had he done?

'When she was told I was dead she was torn apart by grief. She always maintained I was the only good thing in her life. She went to the church to try and find some reason behind it all. To try and find some comfort. Instead she found you and you killed her!'

'Oh dear God! Oh Cecilia! Honestly I didn't know. I swear I didn't know! How can you ever forgive me? How can I ever forgive myself? What have I done? Oh dear God, what have I done?' He cupped his face in his hands and began to weep. His shoulders shook and Colombina could hear him struggle for breath as he sobbed.

The anger had gone from Colombina as quickly as it had flared. The secret she'd carried gnawing away at her insides was now out in the open. She felt empty. She looked at her mother's picture and at the distraught figure slumped over in the chair. She knew what she had to do. She closed her locket and put it in her pocket. She sat down on the arm of his chair and put her hand on his shoulder. 'Why, Friedrich? What made you do such a terrible thing?'

He looked up and turned his tear-streaked face to her in astonishment. 'How can you ask me that? I did it because of you! Because of you! Because of what they did to you.' His voice shook and he looked beseechingly into her eyes. She turned away, forced at last to face a truth she'd always known — a truth too painful to admit, a pill too bitter to swallow. She lowered her head. It was her turn to weep. Yes, she had been instrumental in the death of her mother just as she had with her brother Alfredo.

'My tea is cold,' she said finally. 'I'll go put the kettle on again.'

* * *

'That, I take it, is our cue for coffee, no?'

Lucio nodded. He picked up his napkin and wiped his forehead.

'Well done, Lucio, your story grows more complex and tantalising by the minute.' Ramon reached over and patted his shoulder. 'And thank you for telling us about Colombina so early in the piece. I thought you were going to keep us waiting until the end of the day like you usually do.'

'There is more to come, Ramon.'

'More?' Ramon's surprise was genuine. 'A double ration?'

'Yes. My story has begun to accelerate towards its climax. Soon it will be someone else's turn to put up with your cross-examinations and insinuations.'

'It all adds to my enjoyment of the story, Lucio. Isn't that what we come here for?'

Chapter Thirty-Five

'We were betrayed!' Dietrich stood leaning over Friedrich's table, his face flushed with rage. 'They knew every detail of our plan. I want everyone who was at the briefing rounded up and questioned by the Gestapo. Now!'

'No, Herr Sturmbannführer! You have had your chance. You wanted your way and you got it. You have given the partisans in this region their biggest victory so far. We will now be made to pay for your blunder all winter! If you want to know who to blame, look no further than yourself. You come up here and presume to tell us how to do our job. Now perhaps you have a better understanding of the problems we face. Of course there are informers and of course they will slip your net. This is their country, this is their home. They know every bush, tree and pathway. Your plan had a major weakness — it took too long to organise. When you are surrounded by a hostile population, time is not something you have. But you wouldn't listen. Besides, your tactics were blatant. The SS does not advertise its movements but you did. Do you think for a second that anyone actually believed you were withdrawing? The whole affair has been a disaster and it is a disaster of your making. You can explain to High Command how you sacrificed twenty-seven of my men and a third of the Blackshirts, and lost every single one of our prisoners. Explain the genius of your plan to them. I assure you, it is all in my report, and I mean all!'

'We were betrayed. How did they know to dynamite the bridge at San Pietro just as we approached it? How did they know to move down the mountain after the attack instead of up as they usually do? And tell me this, why are you still alive?'

'No, you tell me, Herr Sturmbannführer. It was your plan. You tell me.'

'One of those fascist bastards betrayed us!'

'Unlikely. Their losses were the highest.'

'Who else could know?' His eyes narrowed as a thought occurred. 'You discussed it didn't you, over dinner, up at the Count's Villa. Yes! I bet you did. You discussed my plan with no more thought for security than if you were discussing the weather. Admit it!'

'I admit it. Do you think that raving fascist up there would betray us? He is a personal friend of Mussolini.'

'What about the servants? What about the girl?'

'The servants were not present. The doors were closed. The girl is as loyal to Mussolini as the Count. Do you think for a second she could have survived there if she wasn't? The same is true of all his staff. Besides, the girl has been sick and confined to bed since the dinner took place.'

'I want her interrogated. I will do it myself.'

'For God's sake you are clutching at straws. The girl's father is the local fascist cadre. He is a slow-witted fool but a committed fascist. Everyone at the Villa Carosio is a commit-ted fascist. The manservant and chauffeur took part in Mus-solini's march on Rome.' Friedrich had listened enough. It was time he dismissed the Sturmbannführer and sent him back to the front with his tail between his legs.

'What about the housekeeper, the partisan leader's wife? I want her interrogated. I want them all interrogated by the Gestapo!'

'No, Herr Sturmbannführer. What you want no longer matters. You are dismissed. As of this instant, you are ordered to rejoin your company as soon as possible. Here is confir-mation from General Wolff. I have been in contact with him.' He handed Dietrich a radio despatch. Dietrich read it and crumpled the message up in his fist.

'You bastard! I will get even with you for this!'

'Don't let me delay you, Herr Sturmbannführer.' Friedrich stood and glowered at the SS officer. For the second time in his life he thought Dietrich was going to strike him. Instead, he whirled on his feet and stomped out of the room.

Friedrich watched him go then sank back into his chair. He ran his hands through his hair. He had a lot of thinking to do. Dietrich was right on a number of issues and there were many questions that begged an answer. Of course, they'd been betrayed. The partisans not only knew every detail of the plan but had even had time to devise a brilliant counter. But that didn't explain why he was still alive. Did they simply prefer the devil they knew to the devil they didn't? Why not? The ambush certainly called for reprisals which the partisans could reasonably assume he wouldn't take. But could they be as confident with his replacement? And what if Dietrich had been left in charge? Friedrich shuddered. Dietrich would have ordered reprisals and they would not have been token. Did that explain his reprieve or was somebody protecting him? If so, who? And why? He went over the failed trap in his mind, seeking inspiration.

The whole thing had been a disaster. The first two convoys had left right on schedule without incident. But the SS had barely travelled a few kilometres before the San Pietro bridge was blown up, effectively isolating the SS on the wrong side of the river and the mountains. When they'd gone to inspect the damage, they'd come under mortar fire. Three men had been killed before they'd managed to withdraw. Friedrich's convoy had continued unawares until the partisans opened fire on them with captured *Panzerfausts*. The shells had ripped through the two trucks carrying troops, completely disabling them. They'd known exactly which trucks to hit. Then his men had come under a hail of grenades taped to petrol bombs. His driver had had no choice but to accelerate away, expecting a *Panzerfaust* to line up on them at any moment. But it hadn't, and Friedrich was at a loss to know why. They could have blocked the road and petrol bombed him or fired on the Lancia with their light automatics. One short burst would have been enough to do the job. It was almost as if the partisans wanted to separate him from the battle.

He'd ordered his driver to stop once they'd rounded a corner and could take to the covering trees. While he'd tried to double back, his men had taken a merciless beating. They'd had no chance to use their mortars or unload their machine-guns. All but a few of the soldiers in the first truck were wiped out and those in the second were forced down into the trees by mortar fire. Those guarding the prisoners had jumped for cover the moment the partisans had struck, only to surrender immediately to the desperate men pointing their short-barrelled *parabellos* at their hearts. Then, as quickly as they'd struck, the partisans melted away back up the hill with their prisoners.

But they didn't continue on up the hill. If he'd needed more evidence of betrayal he needed to look no further. The partisans had doubled back and withdrawn down the hill. It was a tactic they'd never employed before. Meanwhile, the troops from the lead convoy raced uphill in precisely the opposite direction in a bid to intercept them. Whoever had briefed the spotter plane had also failed to consider this possibility, and it had circled in futile loops over the heights.

Worse was to follow. As the Blackshirts raced up the mountain to his rescue, one of the units ran straight into an ambush. The partisans had been absolutely ruthless on their countrymen whom they considered traitors. They'd slaughtered them, and in the process ignored all attempts by the soldiers to surrender. Friedrich found this hard to reconcile with the treatment his own men had received. Those who had surrendered had been tied up but unharmed less than a hundred metres away. The partisans had eventually escaped up the Sanagra Valley unopposed.

Who had betrayed them? Who could he trust in future? Perhaps one of the Blackshirt brigades had been infiltrated. Perhaps one of the Blackshirt officers was too trusting. The more he thought about that the more it seemed the most likely scenario. After all, only one of the fascist units had been hit. The informant would have made sure his unit was spared. What could he do but caution his Blackshirt leaders to secrecy once more, and make sure he told them no more than was absolutely necessary for them to do their part in any future action. He did not even momentarily consider the leak came from the Villa Carosio. Who in their right mind would?

Chapter Thirty-Six

Cecilia looked up as Antonella opened her door and came in with a box of Swiss chocolates, gift-wrapped with a note from Friedrich. But not even this could cheer her up. It was not just the cold that kept her in her bed but the heaviness in her heart. Once again she'd failed to foresee the natural consequences of her actions. In her mind, her motives were always pure and she was always surprised when others interpreted them differently. The Signora had been unforgiving and flatly refused to hear any explanation or even discuss the subject. Surely the Signora could see that what went on up in the mountains had nothing whatsoever to do with her own relationship with Guido, that she'd had no intention of ever coming between them. In Cecilia's mind they were separate worlds. What she'd done up there she'd done for Guido, in response to his needs and deprivation. That was how she justified in her mind what had taken place. She ignored the fact that she'd loved him and had entertained the belief that he'd loved her equally in return. To her, the affair was nothing more than an act of kindness. Why couldn't the Signora see it? Besides, she'd already decided to terminate it.

She'd tried to explain to Carmela in the hope that she would intercede on her behalf with her mother. The two had grown very close. But Carmela had just slapped her face and contributed another stream of invective over her betrayal of their trust. After that, she deliberately and pointedly ignored her, at times refusing even to face in her direction.

Cecilia felt sorry for herself, wondering why it was that once again she had to bear the blame alone. Perhaps she could get Guido to explain what had happened. She clung to the hope briefly then dismissed it. She'd done so much and risked so much to help others and now once more she was an outcast. It wasn't fair. She wondered how she'd ever manage when she was back on her feet, and obliged to face the Signora and Carmela every day. Dear God! And she'd suffered more than either of them.

Her mother Maddalena had been allowed up to her room to bring her the bad news. Her eldest brother, Alfredo, had been killed in the partisan ambush. She'd had to comfort her mother and at the same time face up to the fact that she'd contributed to his death. It didn't matter that he was a Black-shirt and her enemy, or that he'd treated her so cruelly after she'd been thrown out of her home. He was still the brother she'd grown up with and loved. She now had to live with the fact that she'd also betrayed him.

Maddalena had been surprised at the depth of her daughter's grief and put it down to the sibling affection which runs so deep in Italian families. It gave her comfort and made her feel proud of her daughter.

'You're a good girl, Cecilia,' she'd said over and over. 'You're a good girl.' Her daughter had just clung to her in silent grief as she'd stroked her hair.

Cecilia now had no one she could turn to and call her friend. Except one. She looked at the box of chocolates and wondered when they'd meet again.

Chapter Thirty-Seven

Christmas approached cheerlessly in uneasy truce, while the Germans licked their wounds and the partisans occupied the lower slopes, taking what respite they could from the cold, the snow and incessant fogs. Convoys passed through infrequently, depending on the state of the main supply route through Como. At the Villa Carosio, there was no truce. Time did nothing to soften the edges of the Signora's anger nor take the sting from her bitterness. She only spoke to Cecilia to convey instructions and her coolness couldn't help but infect the staff. They squabbled and niggled at each other, not sure why things had changed, only that they had, and that Cecilia was somehow to blame. They resented her for that and Cecilia found herself more and more isolated.

Her mother was her only comfort but even in her company Cecilia sensed her silent reproach. She yearned to talk to her and tell her what had really happened, but how could she? She had no one to talk to so she convinced herself of her innocence and absolved herself of any wrongdoing. She was, after all, a heroine. She risked her life for Guido, the partisans and for Italy. One day her story would be told and everyone would see how wrong they'd been. In the meantime she resolved to hold her head high and be stoic in the face of the silent accusations and resentment. If people wouldn't speak to her, she'd speak to them. And if they didn't answer, she'd carry on as if they did. She would rise above it all. The staff interpreted her conduct as pride and arrogance when perhaps a little humility was more appropriate, and their resentment hardened. In truth it was little more than childish petulance.

The Count could offer no comfort. The cold weather had

found the weakness in his chest and he rarely left his bedroom. When Cecilia kept him company, all he did was complain. He no longer found distraction in his books and the newspapers only depressed him. He dictated long, rambling, disjointed messages to Mussolini which Cecilia never bothered to send, converting them instead to Christmas greetings or similar messages of cheer. But mostly the old man slept or sat huddled up in front of the fire, staring at the flames as if imagining what might have been. Perhaps he saw again Mussolini's triumphant torchlight procession with Hitler past the burning Colosseum, or the hopes of his youth. Whatever he found in the flames brought him solace and released Cecilia from his presence, giving her the opportunity to see the Oberstleutnant.

He often sent the Lancia to collect her and bring her back to the barracks, where he taught her to cook the solid, warming Saxon and east German food. The day before Christmas he sent the car for her and they made *Dresdner Stollen*, Saxon Christmas fruit bread, without which Friedrich insisted it was impossible to celebrate Christmas. He had the glacé cherries, raisins, currants and almonds brought in from Switzerland on one of the convoys, and scoured Como for the remaining ingredients. They made it together in the little kitchen attached to his quarters, taking turns to knead the dough until it was smooth and elastic and all the flour incorporated. They opened a bottle of wine and turned the occasion into an event.

For Cecilia, the time she spent with Friedrich was like a tonic, relief from the siege. She could relax and laugh and chat, knowing that her goodwill would be welcomed and repaid many times over. There were no recriminations here with her enemy as there were with her friends, just genuine warmth and affection. They teased each other, laughed at their mistakes and shared their triumphs as their culinary endeavours turned out exactly as they should. But they weren't siblings, nor cousins, but two healthy young people with normal desires and weaknesses. Their time together was an anomaly, an oasis of calm in the eye of the storm that raged around them. It was time out from the fears and concerns and the reality of their lives. Who could blame them for seizing it with both hands?

They became lovers as the *Dresdner Stollen* cooled on the wire rack above the stove, flushed with success, wine and the rum left over from cooking. It began with a kiss and a joyful embrace which lingered a little longer than expected. Friedrich gave her the chance to withdraw, but instead she put her mouth over his and traced his lips with her tongue. He pulled her gently to him so he could feel her breasts pressing against his chest and returned her kisses. They stood there together in the kitchen, locked in their embrace, oblivious of their surrounds, rocking gently, lost in each other.

He bent over, slipped his arm behind her legs and picked her up. She held on, her arms locked around his neck and buried her head on his chest. He didn't carry her to his bedroom but lay her down instead in front of the fire in the room that served as both dining room and lounge. It was spartan but at least it was carpeted. By the flickering light of the fire he removed her clothing, not in haste but slowly as if savouring every moment. Cecilia could feel her breasts swell and her nipples harden. Then he undressed and lay beside her.

Cecilia wanted him inside her then, to pick her up and sweep her away in a frenzy of passion. She was ready and told him so. But he ignored her and silenced her by putting his lips over hers so lightly that they barely touched. He ran his hands over her body, cupping her breasts, tracing her navel, caressing the swirl of her hips, so gently she was never entirely certain where they were. She wanted him but still he played with her. She reached down and found his penis, alert and ready. What was he waiting for? But still he just stroked her and kissed her and her body flooded with the most delicious sensations. But it wasn't enough! It wasn't enough. He moved on top of her and slid his body lightly along hers. She could feel her wetness and her tension grow. Then he entered her and her back arched in welcome. But there was no frenzied rush to fulfilment as there had been with Guido. Instead a slow, slow, ever so slow quickening then easing of intensity. He brought her on and on teasingly, skilfully, crescendo to decrescendo, until she could stand no more. She cried out. Her orgasm racked her body in endless waves from her head to her toes. But, dear God, he wasn't finished and not yet finished with her. He took her with him until he could hold back no longer and released the flood gates.

They lay together not moving while the after-shocks subsided, holding onto each other and the moment. Cecilia was in love. She realised she had been in love with Friedrich for some time and it was only her duty to Guido that had prevented her from showing it. But now there were no such restraints. Typically she didn't consider the fact that he was married. There was plenty of time for that later. All she knew was that she loved him and he loved her. Yes! He loved her! It occurred to her that their time together had been a long, elaborate courtship and that he'd been in love with her all along. The way he'd made love to her was ample evidence. Yes, he loved her. They were lovers and in love, and would remain lovers forever. Forever. Cecilia accepted the lie because it was what she wanted to believe with all her heart. There'd be time to come to terms with that later. But not now. She rolled over on top of him and slid her legs on either side of his. She propped herself on her arms and knees and slowly revolved her lower body over his. She felt wanton and shameless and sinful and more confident than she'd ever felt in her life. She arched her back and closed her eyes.

Chapter Thirty-Eight

For Friedrich, the *Dresdner Stollen* had a bitter taste. Instead of elation he felt guilt and remorse. He thought of all the women he'd lain with over the course of the war, and knew Cecilia could not be dismissed as lightly. He also knew where the blame lay. He set out to court her and seduce her for his own amusement, but in doing so he had grown extraordinarily close to her. He couldn't accept that what he felt for Cecilia was love because he loved Christiane, but anyone witness to their affair would have found it hard to draw that distinction. He knew he should sever contact with Cecilia. He knew in his heart that that was what he should do before either of them got in any deeper, but couldn't bring himself to do it. Besides, he rationalised, it would be too cruel to Cecilia, to lead her on for almost a year and then drop her the instant they made love. It was not as if she was a girl who gave herself readily. Their courtship was testimony to that. No, he'd set out to make her love him and want him, and he'd succeeded. Now he must manage the consequences until the war moved on and took him with it.

He'd left his quarters to join his men once Cecilia was on her way back to the Villa Carosio for dinner and the giving of gifts. He'd saved a little of the *Dresdner Stollen* for Cecilia and given the rest to his men. Even so it was a subdued Christmas, as his men contemplated their prospects and the plight of their families in the face of the inevitable defeat. Not the wine Friedrich allowed them nor the Christmas bread could cheer them up. That required nothing short of surrender and there was precious little hope of that.

In his guilt, Friedrich's thoughts turned to Christiane and

her refusal to move west. Nothing, it seemed could make her change her mind. She spoke of Dresden as being a free city, a refugee city, a fact that was respected by the Allies and pointed to the fact that Dresden hadn't been bombed to validate the belief. He couldn't convince her that bombing wasn't as much of a threat as the Russians, who were massing on the Vistula in preparation for a spring offensive. When they came they would show no mercy. Rumours of Russian tanks driving straight over refugee columns in the East Prussian district of Gumbinnen had even reached him in Italy. Surely working with the *Frauenschaften* she must have come in contact with refugees and heard the stories. Why didn't she heed them? He could see the hand of Carl Schiller in her intransigence.

The writing had been on the wall for more than two years but Carl still steadfastly refused to read it. He refused to believe that Hitler would allow Germany to be overrun and clung to the fond hope that somehow a solution would be worked out. But any hope of surrender had died when the bomb plot to kill Hitler had failed. Friedrich could imagine Carl, having filled her head with nonsense about the invulnerability of Germany and the infallibility of Hitler, now trying to convince Christiane and himself that, even if the unthinkable happened, Dresden would somehow still be spared. Friedrich wanted to fly home and shake some sense into him. But years of Goebbels' propaganda and news deprivation had denied the citizenry any basis upon which to make a judgement. They believed what they wanted to believe, and those with doubts wisely kept them to themselves.

Understanding the problem, however, didn't automatically produce a solution and Friedrich fired off yet another letter, carefully worded to hide its intent from the censors. He talked about having a second child named after a non-existent uncle who lived in the Black Forest, and even expressed the hope that the child be born there. He could hardly have been more blatant, but had no reason to hope that this plea would be any more successful than those that had preceded it. Damn Carl! Why didn't he let Christiane move out from under his wing while she had the chance?

As winter tightened its grip, Kesselring held firmly to his defensive positions along the Po Valley and the Allies closed down their offensive to wait for spring. The partisans in the hills above Menaggio gave up all thoughts of harassment as they concentrated on the more urgent problem of finding food and safe shelter.

Friedrich and Cecilia took full advantage of the lull and were never far from each other's company. Cecilia was young and in love and didn't care if the whole world knew. The old men muttered obscenities behind her back and the women snubbed her. Even the Signora and Carmela were openly contemptuous of her, though they knew of her secret agenda. But Cecilia didn't care. She learned about German food and German composers and how to make tea the way he liked it. Friedrich would have had to go a long way to find a more attentive student. She adored him and everything about him. She didn't care that he was the enemy or what people might think. When the war ended, they'd discover the truth. Guido would make sure of that.

But the war hadn't ended for them, it had just gone into hibernation. When the awakening came there was no gradual quickening of activity, but a sudden thunderclap both un-expected and devastating. Cecilia was with Friedrich on the morning of February 14 when the news came through. She'd spent the whole night with him swaddled in blankets in front of the fire, and was preparing his breakfast when she heard the discreet knock on the door. She took little notice of it. She heard Friedrich turn the handle and open the door as she poured boiling water from the kettle into the teapot. She heard him say good morning to the communications clerk as she stirred the brew the mandatory three times. She put two cups and saucers on the tray, a little jug of milk and a bowl of sugar. She picked up the tray, carried it into the main room and placed it on the table. She'd expected Friedrich to already be seated at the table. She looked up, curious to see where he was. She was surprised to find he was still standing by the door.

'Friedrich?' she said tentatively.

He didn't move or even seem to hear her. He just stared at the message in his hands.

'Friedrich, what is it?' She sensed something was terribly wrong. 'Friedrich!' She ran over to him. Bumped him as she reached him. But he didn't seem to notice. He didn't seem to hear her or see her. He seemed oblivious of everything. He just stared at the message, the message that changed both their lives forever.

Chapter Thirty-Nine

Adversity brought out the best in Christiane. The combination of years of near starvation rations and the day and night bombardment by the RAF and the USAF had left the German population weak and demoralised. They longed for peace and the return to some kind of normal life. It was increasingly apparent that the war was lost, yet most people didn't expect Germany to be overrun. The army would defend their borders and, if the situation became utterly hopeless, negotiate a peace as they had at the conclusion of the First World War. East Prussia aside, it was inconceivable that a single enemy soldier would set foot inside German territory. So they clung on, freezing inside clothing made from wood pulp which retained little warmth, and subsisting on what little food was available.

In Dresden, food, fuel for fires and electricity were in critically short supply. The flood of refugees had swollen its peacetime population of just over six hundred thousand to around one and a quarter million. Horses and dairy cattle were killed for their meat and black marketeers were executed on the spot. Relief supplies were shipped in from all over Saxony, but even so people barely survived.

The Schillers got by on their diminishing store of preserves which they used to supplement their rations. Where once they'd laughed at Christiane's zeal for bottling everything she could get her hands on, they now had reason to be grateful. Their illicit supply of dairy food and eggs dried up once they'd surrendered Little Pillnitz to the Housing Department to provide temporary shelter for refugees. Christiane willingly gave up those precious little extras along with their country home. The Fatherland was in trouble and it needed her help. What's more she needed to help, to be useful, in the belief that firm resolve and self-sacrifice on her part would somehow help save Germany. She was by no means alone in her belief. It was a national characteristic to ignore the larger issue in the conviction that if everybody obeyed their orders and did their duty to the fullest, somehow everything would resolve itself for the good. That was the light they searched for at the end of a long, bleak tunnel.

Christiane believed she was safe in her free City of Dresden, and that it was her duty to help others less privileged. Helmuth was four and a half years old, not yet of an age for school, but able to be left in the care of her father and her sister Lisl, who was still exempted from work to care for her daughter. So Christiane threw herself into her work with the *Frauenschaften*. Her experience at the Semper Picture Gallery had made her a good administrator so she was assigned to help organise and process refugees from Silesia as they passed through Dresden on their way west. Her enthusiasm and energy was an example to others and gave heart to the weary, desperate refugees. Just as she drew strength from Carl's confidence and conviction, the refugees drew strength from her. She told them where to go and what to do and relieved them of the necessity of making decisions for themselves. They followed her instructions blindly, willingly and to the letter, and the processing of refugees under her control ran more smoothly and efficiently than anywhere else.

Christiane knew she was doing a good job and put in longer and longer hours. She worked by night when the trains ran to avoid being strafed by American fighter planes and light bombers. Sometimes she stayed on to help feed the hungry, exhausted women and children held over on the station platforms. Inevitably, those who excel in providing such much needed service sooner or later come to regard their contribution — and themselves — as indispensable. Friedrich's urgings for her to move to the west with Helmuth hadn't fallen on barren ground, at least not entirely. It wasn't just his letters that caused the change of heart but the stories of Russian atrocities the fleeing Silesians, East Prussians and Pomeranians brought with them. But just as she'd resolved to join them in their flight, the number of refugee trains had doubled. She saw the potential for chaos and unselfishly threw herself into the fray, telling herself she was only deferring the move. She thought the upsurge in traffic was only temporary and that it would soon ease. Then she'd comply with Friedrich's requests. In the meantime she couldn't leave, not while she was so desperately needed. Anyway, she'd have to wait until things eased before she could hope to get permission to travel.

On the night of February 13 she was called in on duty. Among the refugees she had to organise and despatch were two trains from Königsbruck filled with children — *Deutsches Jungvolk*. She left Helmuth playing with his grandfather. She walked carefully through the black-out to Central Station counting the steps between each intersection, never more than an arm's length from the old stone and timber houses which were her only guide. They were good old houses, butted tightly together as if to share their warmth, even though some now leaned away from the original angle of their construction. They'd housed and sheltered Dresdeners for centuries. That night, there was hardly a home that didn't also shelter its quota of refugees. Occasionally a vehicle passed cautiously by with hooded lights.

As she walked through the Altmarkt, Christiane snuggled deeper into her coat to escape the icy wind, wishing she'd been sent to Dresden Main Station instead which was less than a kilometre from her home. But Central Station had become the centre for refugees and she had no choice but to grope her way across street and square for three painstaking kilometres. Every Dresdener believed the winters were getting progressively colder but in fact the only thing that had changed was their sensitivity to it. It wasn't just the lack of fuel which caused this but the changes in their diet. They were a people accustomed to eating lots of fat and would relish a pork dish served with pure pork fat instead of gravy. Traditionally this is what had insulated them from the cold. Now, with no fats to be had, the cold cut through to their bones.

It was little warmer inside the station. Not even the mass of humanity crowded there could heat it. The ceiling was too high, the walls too wide and the main hall too cavernous. There was little chance of the glass ceilings retaining heat anyway. She went straight down to the vaulted basements which were the refugees' temporary homes and reported for duty. In the weak, flickering light around her, exhausted Red Cross workers and labour force girls battled to feed the starving and tend to the aged and sick. Yet few complained. They'd been driven from their homes and lost everything except the clothes they wore. Some had lost children or partners, parents or friends. Yet they waited patiently and stoically, unshakable in their conviction that somehow the Reich would provide for them.

The two trains filled with the *Deutsches Jungvolk* had been sent out onto a siding while space was cleared for them inside. Christiane was sent to join them. As she passed through the crowded throng, she spoke to everyone who caught her eye.

'*Grüss Gott!*' she'd say optimistically. 'Soon you will be on your way west. There are nice homes and places for you to stay where the terror fliers never go. You are the lucky ones.' Some of the refugees reached out to touch her as she passed and thanked her. Christiane had never felt so proud in her life. She loved being so useful and helpful and wanted. It was like a drug to her. Every reaching hand and uttered thanks inspired her to greater effort.

She could hear the children before the trains loomed out of the darkness ahead of her. They were singing. She could hear the strident voice of her *Frauenschaften* colleague leading them. It was a silly childish song but it brought a smile to her face. She tried to imagine how Helmuth would cope with the boredom and inactivity of being cooped up in a railway carriage for days on end. She opened the door of the first carriage and climbed aboard. She pulled aside the black-out curtains and slipped into the compartment. One solitary lantern provided the only light, illuminating a sea of young, upturned faces. The children noted her arrival with their eyes and instantly decided she didn't warrant an interruption to their song. Christiane smiled. It was a tonic to see these ten year olds and enjoy their good spirits. There was nothing passive about them. The war, hunger and their nightmarish trip had failed utterly to strip them of their right to behave like children and enjoy themselves. What was the flight west except an adventure?

She glanced over to the woman she was about to relieve, who sang heartily but with tiredness etched into her face. She rolled her eyes at Christiane, finished the song and handed over. She waved to the children as she left but they'd already forgotten her. She was just another face in a sequence that had begun hundreds of miles away to the east. Christiane judged that her charges had had enough of singing for a while and wanted to sleep or amuse themselves. She let them. There was little for her to do. Their names had all been checked and numbers counted to make sure nobody was missing. They'd all been given a bowl of soup and a piece of coarse bread. She noticed that they'd all kept half of the bread they'd been given in case of emergency. Obviously they'd been caught out before and learned the hard way. She wandered from carriage to carriage then crossed over to the second train, but it was clear everything was under control.

As she was crossing back she heard the sound of an aircraft high overhead. She felt no sense of alarm but looked up anyway. As she watched, the clouds above her began to glow red, faintly at first and then progressively brighter. She was mystified. Suddenly she realised she could pick out things around her, the station building, the railway lines and the houses backing onto the track. She could see each of the carriages clearly. An aircraft roared low overhead without lights and she ducked instinctively. The awful truth began to dawn on her. But why were there no searchlights? Why no air raid alarm? Why no anti-aircraft fire?

Unfortunately for Dresden, the myth of its status as a free city had even penetrated High Command. They'd taken away the batteries of searchlights and sent them to cities more in need. They'd taken away the 88-millimetre anti-aircraft guns and sent them to the Russian front to combat tanks. To soothe the nervous citizens, they'd replaced them with wooden and papier-mâché replicas. That night, as one of the deadliest bomber formations of the war closed in, Dresden was undefended.

The rumble of the approaching RAF formations grew louder

and louder. Surely it couldn't be an air raid. Dresden was a refugee city, the whole world knew that. She wondered if her father had heard the aircraft and taken Helmuth down to the cellar. Helmuth! She thought of her little child and wanted desperately to run to him, to be with him, to shelter and protect him. But she had her duty and she couldn't abandon all these other children in her care. 'Dear God, dear God! Look after Helmuth. Please! Please!' These were her thoughts. She was unaware that she was saying them out aloud. She turned and ran from carriage to carriage and ordered them to extinguish the lights. She thought she was doing the right thing but immediately she could see black out curtains being pulled back and young faces appearing at the windows. The flares were clearly visible now and falling about a kilometre to the east.

She looked at her watch. It had just turned ten o'clock. She saw men racing through the strange orange light towards the engines. They were going to move the trains! Thank God! She climbed aboard the nearest carriage as they began to clank and creak. Slowly the wheels began to turn and carry their precious cargo back into the protection of the station.

The children had turned deathly quiet. In the orange glow she could see anxious eyes watching her.

'There is no cause for alarm,' she said. 'It seems the RAF are going to bomb the marshalling yards at Dresden-Friedrich-stadt. We're going back into the station until it's over. Come on! Let's sing a song and show them we're not scared.' A couple of girls began to sing *Bund Deutscher Mädchen* — the Hitler Maids — and gradually the other children joined in. She wondered how they were coping in the other carriages. Maybe they'd hear their singing and join in. The night grew dark again as they entered the station.

The roar of the bombers swelled louder and louder until it drowned out the singing. Dear God! thought Christiane. They must be right above us. She heard another sound and recognised it instantly from Ulla's description and the film footage she'd seen at the cinema of their own bombers.

'Lie down!' she ordered. 'Everybody lie down on the floor!'

The children did exactly as they were told, pulling whatever cover they had over them. They heard the first bombs land but they were some distance away. Christiane's spirits rose. Maybe they wouldn't be bombed. Maybe they really were going to bomb the marshalling yards. Then another thought struck her. Maybe the bombs were landing in Prager Strasse. The explosions came closer and suddenly it appeared as if the whole station had exploded. The windows of the carriage blew in as she threw herself to the floor. The carriage rocked and threatened to leap off the rails. Everywhere she could hear children screaming in fear. Two floors above them the roof of the station collapsed in sheets of flame, clearing the way for a hail of incendiary bombs. They fell among refugees racing for shelter, they fell down the elevator shafts and made rivers of fire down the stairways, igniting piles of baggage and anything and anyone in its path.

The carriages rocked violently and endlessly as massive 8,000-pound and 4,000-pound blast bombs caved in walls and roofs, but they lacked the ability to penetrate the thick concrete through to the lower reaches of the station. But smoke and poisonous fumes did. Christiane felt the fumes sting her eyes and burn her throat and smoke began to catch in her lungs. She began to cough and gasp for breath. She buried her head in her coat and took a deep suck of clearer air to steady her breathing.

'Cover your faces! Cover your faces!' She looked up to see frightened eyes running with tears staring back at her. 'Cover your faces! You and you! Cover your faces!' She realised they couldn't hear a word above the noise of the bombs and so mimed what she wanted them to do. The effort took its toll. She gasped and coughed, each mouthful of air stinging and burning her lungs. Her eyes streamed and her temples felt like they were going to burst. But just as she was about to collapse from lack of oxygen she felt a gust of cold air on her face. The fires raging on the levels overhead had begun to suck air in through the tunnels and up the stairways. The wind roared past them taking away the smoke and fumes. Christiane sucked in the cold, clear air in great lungfuls.

'Stay calm!' she ordered but she knew it was as much for her sake as the children's.

Suddenly the carriage jolted and began to move. Christiane began to panic. What were they doing? Why were they taking them out into the open to be killed? Light and smoke filled the carriages but still they continued up the grade into the open. Christiane climbed onto a seat and peered out through the shattered window. Houses blazed on both sides of the track and none were spared. But she made a discovery that overwhelmed her with relief. The bombing had stopped. They'd survived. Barely fifteen minutes had passed since the first bombs had fallen and the raid was over.

The train took them back to the siding and stopped. Christiane stood and began to move among the children.

'Everybody sit up,' she ordered. 'The air raid is over and we are all safe. You can resume your seats. Is anyone hurt? If anyone is hurt please raise your hands.' She had no trouble seeing. The flames from the burning buildings had turned night into day. Children were coughing and crying and holding onto one another fiercely, but it was clear that none had raised their hand. She moved on into the next carriage and the next. It was the same story in each. The children had been badly frightened but in the main had suffered only minor cuts from the flying glass. A few children, however, had deep cuts to the hands and faces that needed attending to. Christiane decided to go back into the station and see if she could coax some bandages and disinfectant from the Red Cross. Perhaps she could even get to a phone and call home.

She climbed down from the train and hurried back along the track. A gust of wind hit and nearly lifted her into the air. She staggered, trying to regain her footing and fell. Incredibly, she felt herself being dragged along the ground into the tunnel. She grabbed hold of the rail and hung on for dear life. The station was ablaze. What about all the people inside, she wondered? They couldn't all have been killed or she and the children would have been killed too. She waited for the wind to subside then dashed into the tunnel. She ran blindly, hoping there wasn't a train moving towards her. She knew she wouldn't have a hope of hearing it before it knocked her down. The roaring of the fires and the wind, mingled with the crash of falling masonry, obliterated everything. She saw a light up ahead and ran towards it. She climbed up onto the platform and stood uncomprehending.

Sicherheits und Hilfsdienst crews — the rescue and repair

service — moved among the refugees, rolling them over, checking them, then moving on. Every now and then they'd call for a stretcher. Were they the only ones hurt? Or were they the only survivors? She looked at the grim faces of the rescue workers and knew the answer. Hundreds — no thousands! — of refugees had suffocated or been asphyxiated by carbon monoxide fumes as they lay huddled together. The same people she'd walked among spreading her cheer, telling them they were the lucky ones. They were all dead.

As she reached the stairs, the corpses took on a different look altogether. Here were the victims of the blast bombs and incendiaries. Some were limbless or headless, others so badly charred they were barely recognisable as human corpses. Christiane was stunned by the magnitude of the horror that confronted her. It exemplified how unprepared Dresden was for a bombing attack. The refugees had been sheltered in the vaulted basements but the authorities hadn't thought to protect them with blast-proof doors.

She looked to where the Red Cross post had been but it had been obliterated along with everyone close by. As she climbed the stairs the horror increased. The floors were covered in dead and wounded. Some people cried out in pain but, for the most part, those who had survived just sat looking blank as their minds struggled to cope with the terror and horror they'd witnessed. The fire roared on the level above them and she dared go no further. She realised that there was no help for her there. They had greater problems than a few children with deep cuts. She turned and made her way back down to the platform.

The wind had intensified. It was unlike any she'd ever known before. As she watched, it picked up bodies and threw them onto the railway lines. She felt it lick around her and try to drag her back up the stairs. She crouched down and held onto the rails. But as quickly as it had swept in it eased and she was caught in a backdraught. As it lifted her, she swung onto the platform and raced back to the tunnel. Someone called out to her but she ignored him and kept running. She jumped down onto the rails and ran. She could see the glow of the fires up ahead and ran for it. Please God! Don't let the wind come now! As she burst into the open, she saw

the telltale swirl of smoke and dust rush towards her and
threw herself onto the ground. The wind rushed over her,
hurling burning debris and roof tiles like missiles. As she
hugged the rail line, she made a startling discovery. The rail
was warm. She could feel it on her cheek. She hung on and
hung on, waiting for the gust to subside, then made a dash
for the nearest carriage.

She burst through the door gasping for breath.

'Ah . . . there you are! Did you get any bandages?'

Christiane looked up into the eyes of an SS-Sturmbann-
führer. She noticed he only had one arm. He caught her
glance and shrugged.

'I left it behind in Russia. Perhaps one of the Ivans has kept
it for a souvenir.'

'Who are you?'

'Sturmbannführer Georg Hoffmann. And you are the woman
from the *Frauenschaften* who is supposed to be in charge of
these children. I have been entertaining them in your absence.'

Christiane wasn't deaf to the officer's implied criticism and
couldn't ignore it. 'Thank you for standing in for me. I would
have thought, however, that your services might be better
employed helping the injured and dying inside the station.'

'What use is a one-armed man?'

Christiane bit her lip. 'I'm sorry.'

'Don't be. I thought about helping in there but what could
I do? I could hardly carry a stretcher. Besides, someone has
to look after the living.' He looked around at the wide-eyed
children inside the carriage watching their exchange. 'Our
future.'

'Then please continue. Don't let anyone outside and keep
them away from the windows. Better still keep them all on
the floor. That wind could carry a child off into the flames.'

'As you wish.'

Christiane picked her way down through the children and
crossed into the next carriage. She found a labour force girl
calmly bandaging a little girl's head with strips of material
she'd torn from the lining of her coat. She couldn't have been
much older than fifteen herself.

'Do you need any help?'

'No, Frau Eigenwill.'

'How did you get here?'

'I was ordered here, Frau Eigenwill, along with some other girls and some old men from a labour force. I think they are Poles.'

'Is there someone in each carriage?'

'Yes, meine Frau, I think so.'

'Thank you.' Christiane turned and gradually worked her way along the length of the train, stopping to help where needed. She gave each supervisor the same instructions she'd given the SS officer and turned back. Time and time again she heard the clanking and felt the thump that suggested the trains were going to be moved off somewhere else. But it was only the buffeting of the wind. She was exhausted by the time she'd made her way back to the Sturmbannführer. She collapsed onto the first seat where the carriage wall offered some protection from the wind. She looked at her watch. It was twelve thirty, barely two hours since the raid had finished.

The SS officer was telling a story and made it just rude enough to delight his listeners and make them forget the flames and collapsing buildings on either side of them. He saw Christiane, frowned, and began to wind up his story. She suddenly felt overwhelmingly ill. She leaned out of the carriage and vomited. She continued to retch long after her stomach had emptied itself of its contents. Her head pounded and sweat poured from every pore in her body. She tried to undo the buttons of her coat but her hands lacked both strength and dexterity. Her arms fell helplessly to her side and she began to weep silently. She felt more than saw the officer sit beside her. He put his hand to her forehead.

'Here,' he said. 'Drink this.' He handed her a small hip flask. She looked up in gratitude. The heat and her exertions had caused her to dehydrate and she craved a drink. She unscrewed the top and took a sip. She was expecting water and instead swallowed a mouthful of brandy. The fiery liquid sapped her breath and made her gag. She doubled over, tears streaming for her eyes.

'I'm sorry, Gnädige Frau, I thought you realised. I wish I had some water for you but there is no water left on this train. I'm sorry. This is the best I can do.'

Christiane handed back the flask and nodded her thanks.

He took a sip, placed the bottle between his knees and screwed the top tight. 'You must be strong, Frau. Relief services will be coming here from all over Saxony and even further. No matter what else, you can always rely on German organisation. That is our strength.' He put his arm around her shoulders and squeezed gently. 'Come now, Gnädige Frau. You have been so brave. You must be brave for a little while longer. For the children.'

She dried her eyes. The carriage suddenly shook violently and everything loose in the carriage was sent flying. A couple of children screamed in fright. Instinctively she grabbed on to the man alongside her, and held on until the wind once more abated.

'What's happening?' she asked. 'Why is the wind like this?'

'Firestorm.'

'No . . . no!' Christiane tried to get to her feet but the officer held on to her firmly. Christiane had heard about firestorms and knew how severe the bombing had to be to begin one. She'd heard the stories from the refugees who had earlier come from the west. Surely it couldn't happen in Dresden? That's what happened in the industrial towns and the ports. Why would the Allies firebomb a city like Dresden that had so few factories? The officer had to be wrong! But another gust rocked the carriage and she couldn't deny the evidence of her own eyes. She tried to peer through the fires raging all around her home in Prager Strasse. It was no use. Dresden was ablaze.

'Helmuth!' She tried once more to stand, her fears restoring her strength, but the officer still held firm. 'Let me go! I must go to my son!'

'Calm down, Gnädige Frau. You are no use to him dead. You wouldn't last a minute out there. The raid finished two hours ago. Either your son is safe in a cellar somewhere or he is dead already. I'm sorry, there is nothing you can do about it except pray that he is safe in a cellar. In the meantime, your duty is here, with these children.' He spoke firmly but not unsympathetically. Christiane collapsed back on the seat and fought back her tears. She knew that what he'd said was true. Either Helmuth was alive in a cellar somewhere or he was already dead. She thought of the dead children she'd seen in the station huddled up to their parents. She thought of Helmuth dying alone without her and of life without him.

'Oh Helmuth ...' she sobbed, and the words came in a groan filled with pain and despair, straight from the heart. Why shouldn't a mother cry? She buried her head against the Sturmbannführer's chest to drown out her sobbing and hide her tears. He let her stay that way for some time, patting her back as a father would a distraught child. But they had their duty to perform and children to care for. Duty took priority. He shook her gently.

'Gnädige Frau, it is time to tend to the children. You are needed here.'

'Yes.' Her answer was mechanical. She had her duty. She was needed. She stood and began to thread her way through the children. She glanced outside the window at the inferno that raged around them. But once more the world around her changed colour and seemed artificial. She risked putting her head out of the window and saw flares hanging in the sky directly above them.

'God in heaven!' she heard the Sturmbannführer say. 'They're coming back!'

Chapter Forty

'Friedrich! What's wrong? What's happened?'

He handed Cecilia the message.

'Friedrich, it's in German!'

He looked at her, barely comprehending.

'Come!' ordered Cecilia. 'Come and sit down.' She took his hand and guided him to the little table. He sat down. He wanted time — time to digest the full import of the message, but Cecilia was insistent. 'Read the message to me! What does it say?'

He took the radio message back from her and began to read. 'Dresden bombed. Two raids approx. 2210 and 0120. Dresden centre and Altstadt destroyed. Firestorm in progress. Heavy casualties reported. Have tried to contact Carl Christiane. Unsuccessful. Phones electricity ARP control destroyed. Communication not yet possible. Any news will advise. Take heart. Gottfried.' He could see the horror in her eyes and it cut through the numbness that had encased him.

'Oh dear Mother of God! Your wife . . . your son . . .!'

He slumped back in his chair, his mind trying to add flesh to the terse message, trying to imagine where Christiane and Helmuth might have been when the raid began and what might have happened to them. Clearly the house on Prager Strasse would not have survived, but had they? He thought back to Ulla's story of the bombing of Wuppertal-Barmen and tried to imagine what it would have been like in Dresden. In his mind he saw Christiane running through flames clutching their precious little Helmuth to her chest like the maid Käte had. Dear God! Don't let them burn to death! Not burn! His control began to wilt as the old horror took hold of him. He began to shake.

Cecilia slapped his face. When that didn't work she hit him again with all her force. 'Friedrich! Friedrich! Stop it!'

Slowly his tremors eased and he turned to look at her.

'Friedrich, you don't know for sure what has happened. Your wife and your son could be safe somewhere in a bomb shelter. You don't know what has happened to them. You don't know for sure!'

He looked at her and saw the glimmer of hope. It was enough to help him gather his wits together. 'Yes, the house in Prager Strasse has a strong cellar. Perhaps they are safe.' But he knew there'd be little hope for people trapped in the centre of a firestorm. Maybe the firestorm didn't start until the second raid. Maybe they escaped from the cellar after the first. 'I must send a message to Gottfried.'

'No, Friedrich. As soon as your friend hears anything he will tell you. I imagine he is doing everything in his power. Now, I'm going to pour you a cup of tea and you will drink it before you do anything else.' She poured the tea in silence and they drank it in silence, each grateful for the chance to examine their thoughts. Cecilia was upset for Friedrich — who wouldn't be? Yet it hurt her to see the depth of his feelings for his wife and son. Would he react the same way if it was her who'd been bombed? She knew the answer almost as soon as she phrased the question. She'd ignored the fact that he had a family and commitments elsewhere, even though he'd made no secret of his affection for them and often spoke about them. She'd simply pushed that to one side as an issue irrelevant to her role as informant and made no adjustment as the circumstances had changed. She realised bitterly that she'd deliberately misled herself; that she'd invented her own convenient little fantasy, another little compartment, without regard to reality. Yet hadn't he done the same? He seemed to love her, even told her he loved her, and they were lovers, as closely entwined as lovers could be. The bitter truth was that once more she had to share the affections of the man she loved, and accept that the division was unequal and that another had greater claim. She glanced up at Friedrich. He'd barely sipped his tea and a skin was forming on the top. There were no tears from this man, no hysteria and not even anger. He sat straight-backed and stared unblinking at the table top. Only the ashen pallor of his skin gave any indication of the pain he felt inside. Cecilia's heart went out to him.

* * *

Friedrich alerted the radio operator to bring him all signals the instant they arrived and remained in his room with Cecilia. The operator didn't need to be told. He liked Friedrich, as did all the men under his command, and knew his family lived in Dresden. At one thirty another signal came through from Gottfried. The operator read it and smashed his fist into the wall in rage. Fierce pain shot up his arm to his elbow but it was pain he was glad to bear for his commandant. He took the message up the stairs immediately as instructed.

Friedrich read the message aloud in stunned disbelief. '1210 Dresden bombed by heavy force of American bombers strength estimated 1000 plus. Communication intermittent. No casualty lists yet available. Will keep you informed. Gottfried.' He turned to Cecilia. 'Why?' Once more his control was shaken. He collapsed back on his chair at the table and reread the cable. 'Why Dresden? It doesn't make sense. There is nothing in Dresden worth bombing. Why bomb it three times? Why bomb it at all? It is a refugee city. Where is the point in taking the war to people trying to escape it? How does that help the British and Americans? How does that help anybody?'

Of course Cecilia had no answers. She sat down next to Friedrich and took his hand in hers. What could they do but sit and wait?

* * *

For the next two days, Friedrich stayed in the barracks. He organised patrols as usual but charged his Hauptmann with the responsibility of carrying them out. He instructed the junior officer to withdraw and inform him instantly if they made any substantial contact with the partisans. He was loath to venture out himself in case a message arrived. In every other way it was business as usual. He gave his men no reason to believe their welfare was being compromised by his personal trials. He knew the communications clerk would share the news with the men because he'd given no instructions forbidding him to do so. While none would presume to address him directly on the issue, they showed their support in many subtle ways: by holding a salute a fraction longer; by standing straighter and performing their allotted tasks with more zeal and military exactness; and by the quiet they maintained around his rooms. He was a tower of strength but every tower needs solid foundations. Cecilia was his. He didn't weep on her shoulder or cling to her desperately in the lonely hours of night. Nor did he open his heart to her and pour out his sorrow. But Cecilia was well aware of his unspoken need and stayed with him as much as she could.

He tried unsuccessfully to make contact with Dresden by phone and radio. As the days passed, his despair grew. If Carl, Christiane or Lisl had survived they would have sent a message through to Gottfried somehow. What petty bureaucrat would refuse to transmit a message to a Generalleutnant? He now knew for sure that Prager Strasse had been razed to the ground, but he clung to a slim shred of hope that the cellar would have held up under the bombardment, and that the rescue and repair service would dig down and find the occupants alive. He'd heard of such miracles happening after the firestorm bombings of Hamburg, Darmstadt and Heilbron.

On the morning of the fourth day after the bombing his phone rang, startling him out of his reverie. He recognised the voice immediately despite the crackle and distortion on the line. 'Gottfried!'

'Friedrich! Listen carefully, our time is limited. I have been to Dresden. I still have no definite news. The *Vermissten-Suchstell* — the Missing Persons Inquiry Office — is only beginning to compile lists but, my dear friend, it doesn't look good. For either of us.'

Friedrich's heart sank. Gottfried was softening him up, preparing him for the worst. He knew what he was going to say. Had suspected it all along. But that didn't make it any less painful.

'All of central Dresden has been flattened from the Dresden-

Friedrichstadt Sportsplatz and Central Station to Dresden
Main Station and the Great Gardens back to the Elbe. They
are digging for survivors but there are too many cellars and
too few labour gangs. So far they have not been very successful. Those who survived the blast from the bombing had the
air sucked out of their lungs by the firestorm or were overcome by poisonous gases. They say the temperatures reached
eight hundred degrees centigrade. If Carl, Lisl and Helmuth
remained in the cellar after the first attack then there is little
hope.' Gottfried paused to allow that information to sink in.
Friedrich wanted to respond but no adequate words came to
mind. Gottfried continued, his voice matter-of-fact and soldierly. 'I was referred to a woman from the *Frauenschaften*
who knows Christiane. She says Christiane relieved her at
Central Station.'

Once more the voice on the other end of the phone hesitated. Friedrich closed his eyes as the cold fingers of dread
took hold of him, squeezing out the last of his feelings and
desensitising him. He braced himself for the next blow.

'Friedrich, Central Station was the aiming point for the
second attack.' Again Gottfried paused as if he found the next
words difficult. 'Christiane was assigned to look after two
trains filled with *Deutsches Jungvolk*. Both trains had been
moved out onto a siding after the first attack. The second
attack caught everyone by surprise. There was no time to
bring the trains back under cover. Both were completely
destroyed. We don't know yet if any of the occupants had
time to find shelter elsewhere, but none of the *Jungvolk* have
been reported to the *Vermissten-Suchstell*. Nobody left aboard
either train survived.'

'Gottfried, is there no hope?'

'Perhaps it is too soon to give up hope entirely. There are
always the miracles, those who survive against all the odds.'

'Dear God!'

'I'm sorry, Friedrich.'

'Gottfried? Will you go back for me? If they have been
killed, at least see that they are properly identified and buried.'

'I will do my best. Goodbye, my friend. It seems that
Dresden has been made to pay for all our sins. Perhaps we

will all be made to pay. I will get back to you the instant I hear any more.'

The line went dead. Friedrich stared at the phone, letting the realisation wash over him that he no longer had a wife and child to love and be loved by. That his beloved Christiane and precious Helmuth were gone forever. Along with Carl and Clara, Lisl and her little baby Trude. They were all gone as if they'd never existed, wiped off the face of the earth. And why? All because of the little Austrian corporal and his insane ambitions. The nightmare they'd unleashed was coming home to haunt them. He sat at the little table almost catatonic, unseeing, unfeeling, unhearing.

He still hadn't moved hours later when Cecilia arrived. She immediately guessed what had happened. She was unsure what to do, to comfort him or leave him alone to grieve. She walked up behind him and put both hands tenderly on his shoulders.

'They're gone,' he said flatly. 'All gone.' He turned and looked up at her and she was struck by his appearance. His skin was grey and his eyes dull. It was as if his life had also been drained from him and only the husk remained. He was beyond pain and despair. 'They're all gone,' he repeated. 'There is only the two of us left. Just the two of us.'

Chapter Forty-One

'God abandoned Dresden on the night of February 13, 1945, that much is certain. But for you I would have killed myself or allowed the partisans to do it for me.' There was no life in the old man's voice. He occasionally looked up at Colombina in the armchair opposite him as he told his story, but mostly he stared at the worn patch in the carpet around his feet. Every now and then he paused to sip his tea.

'I have read every book there is to read about the bombing of Dresden and I believe Gottfried's first instincts were right. Dresden was destroyed as punishment for the atrocities committed by the Reich. It is impossible not to see the hand of God involved in it. Almost the whole of continental Europe was shrouded in cloud that night, yet the British weather forecasters were able to predict one brief window in the cover. That window was estimated to last for between four and four and a half hours. It occurred between ten in the evening and two the following morning, right above Dresden. Can you believe that? The very night the raid was planned, the heavens parted to make it possible. Even the timing is significant. Ten o'clock was the earliest possible time the British bombers could reach Dresden without risk of being attacked by our fighters in the last moments of daylight. Two o'clock is also significant. It allowed the RAF to complete the second raid before the clouds closed in once more. Half an hour earlier and the second attack would have been called off.

'A lot of people blame Bomber Harris for the attack but that is too simplistic and too convenient. Churchill himself was an advocate of area bombing and was even quoted as saying ". . . it was better to bomb what we could hit than to carry on bombing what we couldn't." The theory was that if the RAF wasn't accurate enough to hit the factories, they could disrupt production by striking at the people who worked in them. It was also Churchill's decision to bomb Dresden or, at the very least, his War Cabinet's. One thing is certain, he approved both of it and the manner in which it was carried out. The most convincing explanation I can find for why the attack took place at all rests with Churchill. He, more than any of the other Allied leaders, recognised the threat Russia might pose in the post-war years. He wanted to give them a demonstration of Allied power should they be tempted to overstep the mark. Dresden was perfectly placed a mere eighty kilometres or so from the Russian front to provide the example. The instructions given to Bomber Harris are clear evidence of this.

'Bomber Harris's responsibility was to carry out his instructions. In his defence he was only carrying out orders to the best of his ability. But that is not a defence that works particularly well in trials for war crimes. Many of my ex-comrades were testimony to that. The records prove that his plans for the attack were focused squarely on Dresden Centre, radiating out from the Dresden-Friedrichstadt Sportzplatz in the shape of a slice of pie to include all of the old city. The target sector markings totally ignored military targets to the north, and the Dresden-Friedrichstadt marshalling yards to the east which were full of trains carrying supplies to the front.

'Because of the nearness of the Russian Front he chose the elite Number Five Pathfinder Force to lead the attack. They used radio waves and radar to pinpoint the exact location. As they closed in to drop their markers, they realised to their astonishment that the city was undefended. They were able to drop their primary markers within one hundred metres of the aiming point. It was the most accurately marked raid in the whole of the Second World War. The Master Bomber took advantage of the lack of defences to call the bomber force in below the level of what little cloud there was. Naturally, the lower altitude and lack of ack-ack ensured their accuracy.

'They had no night fighters to contend with. Because of the diversionary attacks on Bohlen, Nuremburg and Magdeburg, and the jamming of German radar, Fighter Control had no idea where the main force of bombers was headed. They didn't consider Dresden. When it finally dawned on them that Dresden was in fact the target, they scrambled fighters from Dresden-Klotzsche, but they didn't receive their orders until nine fifty-five. The marking had already begun. By the time they'd climbed to attack altitude, the first attack was over.

'Only two hundred and forty-five Lancasters took part in the first attack but their accuracy and the high concentration of incendiaries made a firestorm inevitable. Dresden was ill-equipped to handle any air raid let alone one of such severity. By law — the *Luftschutzgesetz* which had been in force since August 1943 — all homes had to provide fire syringes, grappling hooks, ropes, ladders, first-aid chests, beaters, fire buckets, water tubs, sand-boxes, shovels, paper sandbags, spades, sledge-hammers and axes. Few people in Dresden bothered to comply though it is unlikely these precautions would have had much of a bearing on the final result even if they had. But people did prepare their cellars and excavate tunnels and holes between buildings to enable evacuation. The authorities even built water towers at strategic places. While the intentions were laudable they brought tragic results.

'The damage done to Dresden by the first raid should have been enough. It is hard to believe that any civilised people would not be satisfied with the havoc they had caused. But Bomber Command and Bomber Harris had been instructed to leave a message that the Russians would find unmistakable. The first raid wiped out the Air Raid Protection Command Centre so there was no co-ordination of emergency services. It also wiped out the power supply and telephones. As news of the catastrophe spread, emergency services began to pour in from all over Saxony. But Bomber Command had anticipated this and timed their second attack accordingly. Just as help arrived in the stricken capital, the second raid began without warning, trapping and annihilating the would-be rescuers. This time there were more than five hundred and forty bombers.' The old man paused as his voice gave out. He covered his face in his hands. His whole body shook.

'Friedrich, there is no need to go on.' Colombina was too emotionally drained to go to him and comfort him. She wasn't sure she wanted to anyway. She wanted to bring him back to the square in Ravello before her own strength deserted her, but she was powerless to intervene. She was held captive by the horror of his words.

'You talk about murder, Cecilia. That was murder.' He looked up at her briefly then reached for his cup. The tea was cold but did its job in enabling him to continue. 'The temperature at the heart of the firestorm reached 1,000 degrees. The winds reached 200 kilometres per hour. The smoke rose over five kilometres into the air. Pilots in the second attack reported that they could see the glow of Dresden's fires from 350 kilometres away. As far as I have been able to ascertain, this was when Christiane was killed. Cecilia, can you possibly comprehend what it must have been like? Rock takes millions of years to metamorphose but in Dresden it took a single night. People in cellars were reduced to piles of ashes as if they'd sought refuge in a crematorium's furnace. Roads melted. Pots and pans and even bicycles melted down to pools of metal. And those poor people who sought refuge in the water towers were either overcome by the heat and drowned, or boiled to death.

'Once again the fighters were caught off guard. Most were refuelling after their abortive attempt to engage the first wave of bombers. In all, only twenty-seven night-fighters took to the air to fend off the most devastating air-raid in history. Ten minutes after the second attack finished the cloud closed in with fifteen square kilometres of the city destroyed forever. A total of 1,400 bombers had been used in the night's operation. I hope the Russians were suitably impressed. But Dresden's trials were still far from over.

'At twelve fifteen on the following afternoon, just fourteen hours after the first attack had begun, 1,350 Flying Fortresses and Liberators attacked the Dresden-Friedrichstadt marshalling yards. Because of their high altitude and the cloud cover the bombing was largely ineffective and the bombs hit everything but their target. But worse was to come. The bombers rendezvoused over the target with P51 Mustangs. Their primary job was to protect the bombers from day fighters which they succeeded in doing, and secondly, to strafe targets of opportunity. Targets of opportunity! Would somebody please explain to me exactly what that means! They dropped to roof level and machine-gunned the columns of refugees streaming from the stricken city. They dropped down over the Elbe and machine-gunned the people sheltering from the fires on the river banks and bridges. In the reports and books I have read, many people claim it was only then that the city gave up. It seemed that the horror would seek them out no matter what they did. Dear God! To have survived the bombing and then be caught like sitting ducks by fighters and machine-gunned.'

'Yes, Friedrich, it was unforgivable. But you make it sound as though the bombing of Dresden was the only atrocity of the war. What about what Nazism did across the length and breadth of Europe? What about the death camps?'

Friedrich ran his hand tiredly across his scalp, his fingers tracing the line of the old scar from France. 'Cecilia, I can't defend Hitler or the German people for the terrible things that happened. I can only tell you what happened in Dresden. I can't explain the war or how things were allowed to occur. You know yourself that the war was far too complex for any single point of view, whether German, Russian, British or Jewish. We all see the war in our own way with a different perspective, according to how we were affected. I don't think anyone will deny that the bombing of Dresden was an atrocity, but I think you will be surprised at how few know the full extent of it. Are you aware that in the entire war, German bombers killed fewer than 52,000 people in the whole of the British Isles? Allied bombing killed more than 635,000 Germans, around 135,000 in Dresden alone. Yes, we committed more than our share of atrocities and for that many of my former comrades were damned as war criminals. But if they were guilty, isn't Churchill equally guilty, and Bomber Harris? Does all the guilt have to be concentrated on the side of the losers?' Friedrich looked up to see his point strike home.

Colombina slumped back in her chair and stared at him. It was now clear to her what he'd been doing all along. The old man may have aged but his brain was still as sharp as ever.

'Were you ever accused, Friedrich?'

'Of a war crime? No, they didn't catch me to accuse me. If they had, I probably would have been, as you well know.'

'Then you would have been accused falsely.'

A ray of hope flickered across his face. 'Do you mean that, Cecilia?'

'Yes.' She waited to see his look of relief, then struck. 'What you did wasn't a war crime, was it Friedrich? It was a crime of passion, revenge for what had been done to you. For Dresden and for me. What you did, Friedrich, wasn't a reprisal but revenge. It was murder. Cold-blooded, premeditated murder.'

'No! Don't say that!'

'Yes, Friedrich. Yes!'

He stared at Colombina. All his years on the run had come to nothing. He'd been caught just as salvation and perhaps even forgiveness had beckoned. 'What are you going to do?'

'I don't know. I don't know!' How could she know? Nothing was clear cut any more. After all, she'd just learned she was the cause of the shooting. How could she blame him and not herself?

* * *

The four friends stared at Lucio willing him to continue, but it was clear that he'd finished for the day.

'Jesus Christ, Lucio, and all the saints on little motorbikes, you can't stop there!' Neil turned to the others in exasperation.

'Oh yes he can!' Milos broke into a broad smile. 'Ramon was right. We've all underestimated Lucio. I tell you now, if I have to crawl on broken glass and old razor blades to get here next Thursday, I'll do it. We would all do it, no?'

'No.'

They all turned to Ramon. His voice was hard and showed none of the delight that Milos had found in Lucio's storytelling. 'The truth is, we may all be better off if none of us comes next Thursday.'

'Explain yourself, Ramon.'

'You show delight in Lucio's storytelling, Milos, but I still don't believe you are listening to him. Lucio says his story is true and Gancio confirms it. So let me ask him once more.'

Ramon turned his body so that his sightless eyes faced Lucio. 'Has the story you are telling already been resolved? Has it reached its conclusion? The truth please, Lucio.'

Lucio hid his face from Ramon even though he knew his friend could not see him. But the others could and he didn't want them to meet his eyes either. He kept his head hung in an attitude of shame. His voice barely rose above a whisper yet no one had the slightest difficulty in hearing his admission. 'The story is not yet resolved.'

'I knew it!' Ramon thumped the table in anger. 'You lied to me Lucio, you lied to me! Mother of God, you have some explaining to do.'

'Shit! If the story's not yet resolved that means we could all be party to . . .' Neil's voice faded away as he realised the sickening implications.

Milos sat stunned, a look of horror on his face. Only Gancio's doleful expression remained unchanged. 'I warned you. I warned you at the start. I didn't expect Lucio to pull a trick like this, but we should never have let him tell this story.'

'Who are you, Lucio? Where do you fit in?'

'Haven't you guessed, Milos?' Gancio looked around the table. 'Haven't you all guessed? Colombina did not have a son but she did have a beautiful daughter, the sort that would undoubtedly appeal to our little fat friend. Lucio is Colombina's son-in-law. Right?'

Lucio nodded.

'Holy shit!' Neil closed his eyes. 'Holy shit!'

'So now Colombina is planning to kill the man who ordered the execution of her mother.' Ramon tried to keep his voice even and matter-of-fact, but the way he measured his words served only to underscore his anger. 'The trouble is, she is no longer as sure as she was and has asked Lucio for his advice. That would have taken place six or seven weeks ago when Lucio usurped Milos' right to tell a story, so we can draw some comfort from that. Colombina is obviously in no hurry to consign herself to hell and us possibly to prison as accessories. Lucio warned us at the start that he would need us to resolve the ending, a warning some of us chose not to heed. The point is, do we assist Lucio in his job as judge and jury and implicate ourselves in a murder, if that is what Colombina elects to do? Or do we blow the whistle on her and ring the police? Now! Right now! In that event, Colombina would get off with a warning but we would probably lose Lucio's friendship forever. I for one am not convinced that would be a bad thing. After all, what sort of friend implicates his companions in murder?'

'I didn't implicate you in a murder,' said Lucio quietly. 'Nor did Colombina tell me this story so that I could become sole judge and jury.'

'What are you saying?'

'What I am saying, Milos, is that it was Colombina not me who implicated you. It was Colombina who chose to make you — all of you! — judge and jury. She knows all about you and our storytelling. She learned about you through me and throuːh me is asking you for your help. That is the truth! She respects your independence and trusts you to be fair. She swears she will abide by your decision. She wanted to come and tell you her story herself and beg your assistance but I wouldn't let her. I thought it would be too hard on her and she has suffered enough. So I volunteered to tell her story for her. And now as your friend, I'm asking for your help. I'm sorry I had to lie to you, Ramon, but I had no choice. I'm mortally ashamed of what I did, you should know that, but I couldn't let Colombina down. She is counting on us. Please help us! Help her!' It was a cry from the heart and his plea had not fallen on deaf ears. But that didn't make his audience any happier.

'Dear God, Lucio, and you had the audacity to accuse me of testing our friendship.' Ramon put his head in his hands, pushing his dark glasses up so that he could massage the bridge of his nose. 'I need a drink.'

'I will get the coffee.'

'No, Gancio, you stay right where you are. Maria can bring our coffee. I can hear her making it. Just make sure she brings some good grappa. You're going nowhere until we've worked out what we should do.' Ramon removed his glasses altogether, an act so rare and unthinking, it brought the table to immediate attention. 'I assume we accept Lucio's request for assistance whatever the consequences may be. Alternatively,

Milos, I must ask you to make a phone call to the police. Well? We hold Friedrich Eigenwill's life in our hands. Do we help Colombina, or call the police?'

'I think for the moment at least we should accept Lucio's request. His story is not yet finished. I want to know what happened to Cecilia. Remember the Oberstleutnant said that he shot the women for Cecilia. I want to know about that. I want to know what happened to Cecilia that enables him to say that. I want all the evidence before I make up my mind. From what Lucio has told us, I don't believe Colombina will act precipitately. We must have at least another week. I don't believe we need to make a final decision today.'

'Milos, how do you think the police would regard somebody who is in the position to prevent a murder yet waits a week before doing anything about it? No! We must decide today! Now!'

'Then I will support Lucio for the sake of our friendship. Besides, I don't think we can presume that we will sentence Friedrich to death or even that we can reach unanimity. I don't think there can be any presumption of guilt until we've reviewed all the facts. We may well advise Colombina against taking any action against Friedrich. Tell me, where is the crime there? Neil, what do you think?'

Neil often gave the impression that he would have liked nothing more than to be a barrister and was in his element. 'I said earlier that I like to see war criminals hounded to their graves. I don't believe that time excuses anything. By the same token, I don't believe that millions of tax payers' dollars should be spent on bringing them to trial and gaining a verdict. We have the opportunity here to administer justice. If the circumstances demand an acquittal, then we will acquit. If they don't, then we can let Colombina get on with what she has to do.'

'Neil, sometimes I get the feeling you are living in the wrong century and wrong country. The American west could have done with you. But I gather you are in favour of assisting Lucio. Gancio, what do you think?'

'We help Lucio. This is just another sorry chapter in a war that is best forgotten. I don't think we should bring in the police. I agree with Neil that there is no point in going to the police and bringing this business to trial. It would just drag on and probably fail to reach a resolution because of insufficient evidence. I think Friedrich would be lucky to survive the process. To commit him to trial would be the same as condemning him to death. That would not be fair either. No, it is better that we deal with this matter, honestly and honourably. I disagree with Neil on one point. I believe time does excuse. We live in different times. It is impossible for us to make judgements relevant to the time these events took place. I think we should forgive and forget. However, I am prepared to listen to all arguments. Besides I know what happened to Cecilia. Ramon, what do you think?'

'I think I am out-voted. I don't believe we have any right to be anybody's judge and jury. However, Lucio is our friend — despite the fact that he lied to us — and he has asked for our help. I think his request is outrageous. Nevertheless it is also genuine. I may never forgive him for asking or myself for accepting. God help us!'

'Then we are all agreed?'

'Yes, Milos, we are all agreed. Isn't that just what I said?'

Maria served the coffees and grappa and retreated to the kitchen. She listened at the door to try and hear what had gone wrong and why everybody was upset. But the silence that had greeted her arrival at the table remained unbroken. After a while she gave up and went to stack dishes.

SEVENTH THURSDAY

Gancio watched the four men arrive as he attended the tables of other diners. Their usual jaunty steps and smiles were absent, replaced by grim looks that mirrored the television images he'd seen of jurors filing back into court, head down, burdened by the weight of their decision. He cursed as more diners arrived. He wanted to be with his friends but his other obligations demanded his attention. He made up his mind to serve his friends slowly so that they wouldn't start the story without him. They'd grumble, but what the hell? As Ramon had remarked, they were all in it now.

The table was unusually subdued and the tension palpable. All four men would have gladly skipped lunch to get on with the story. They waited impatiently with no appetite for small talk either, sitting like poker players unwilling to say anything that might give the others an indication of the cards they held. They carefully avoided the subject they'd come to discuss until Neil could no longer stand the inertia and prolonged silences.

'Well, I haven't changed my mind,' he announced.

'That's a pity,' Ramon snapped. 'Any mind would have been better than the one you've got.'

'Thanks.'

Milos smiled. 'Whatever your decision, Neil, I think you should keep it to yourself until Gancio has joined us and Lucio has finished his story.'

'That's fine by me. We can always discuss the wallpaper. Anyone have any idea why Italians have such a passion for shitty wallpaper? And look at those bloody lights. Who in their right mind would choose lights like that?' He stared at the wall morosely until another thought occurred to him. 'Hey, Lucio, speaking of our absent restaurateur mate, what do you make of his assertion that he already knows your story?'

Lucio looked up, grateful for the opportunity to speak and ease away some of the tension he felt. Nevertheless, he was determined to tread carefully. He'd come too far to lose control now. 'Does this mean that you no longer think that Gancio and I have cooked up this story between us?'

'I gave that away a long time ago, Lucio. Now answer my question.'

Lucio looked thoughtful for a few moments. 'To be truthful, I really don't know where he fits in. Don't think I haven't given it a lot of thought. He really rattled me that first day. My guess is that he knows the story from the point of view of one of the other participants. He said as much. There were plenty of them if you think about it. At one stage there were more than three hundred partisans in Guido's brigade. Then you can add in everybody who lived in Ravello and Menaggio — in fact, any of the towns around that part of Lake Como. The story of Cecilia and what happened to her couldn't help but spread. Even after the war people were split over whether she was a heroine or a Nazi sympathiser. Doubtless they argued the pros and cons of her case in cafés, some to justify what had happened, others to see justice done. There are many people who know her story, or at least parts of it. That is why Colombina wanted to leave Italy and why she replied to Mario Galli's letter in the Lecco newspapers. Of course, you could argue there was nothing to keep her in Italy. Her mother was dead and so was her father, executed alongside the mayor of Menaggio by the communists after the shooting of Mussolini. But the truth is, her name could never be cleared completely. There would always be nagging doubts and suspicions about her. Always innuendoes. She had to get away where nobody knew her, recognised her name or told her story. You ask me, how does Gancio know Cecilia's story? I think you'd better ask him.' ·

'What did happen to Cecilia?'

'For heaven's sake, Neil! Does nothing penetrate that cotton-wool mind of yours? We have talked about this and agreed that it is unfair to have these discussions in Gancio's absence. Do you think we might do him the courtesy of waiting for him?'

'Jesus, back off!'

'Ramon's right. And Ramon . . . back off. Don't ride Neil so hard. We're all aware of what today means and we're all concerned. But turning on each other isn't going to solve anything. Neil is no different to any of us. He can't sit still and his mind is bouncing off everywhere. This is not normal Neil behaviour, no?' Milos looked away from Ramon to Neil and Lucio. 'Old habits die hard, my friends, but we must all get used to the fact that we are now five.'

'And we are also hungry. Well I am anyway.' Neil scanned the restaurant. 'Where the hell is that wog bastard anyway?'

Lucio was apprehensive about telling the remainder of his story. With only one exception he knew how the vote would go and would vote accordingly himself. All the same he knew he had to confirm Milos and Gancio in their opinion without shaking Neil. The exception was Ramon. Only Ramon was undecided which was exactly how he hoped it would be. Ramon would wait to hear the others out before finally making up his mind and casting his vote. Then he would understand the true measure of friendship. Ramon would be made to decide.

Chapter Forty-Two

By the beginning of March, the German army in Italy was in a critical position and its collapse was imminent. It still held its defensive positions along the Po Valley as the Allies prepared for their spring offensive, but its forces were continually being depleted by the demands of the Russian Front. Division after division was pulled out and sent to shore up the Reich's eastern defences as the Russians surged towards Berlin. The remnants of Mussolini's army were used to fill the gaps but their reliability was, to say the least, questionable. Seemingly overnight, the numbers of partisans doubled as Italian soldiers defected to their ranks.

For days following Gottfried's phone call, Friedrich retreated into the responsibilities of command. He was riven by grief and guilt. It wasn't just his loss that haunted him but the memory of what he'd been doing the night his wife and child were killed. His self-recriminations were bitter and damning. Yet he didn't attempt to blame Cecilia or turn from her. She may have been the source of his guilt but she was also his only source of comfort. He needed her by him and it was unthinkable that he should lose her too. She was the life-raft he clung to in his despair. She stood by him and it was her strength, her seemingly bottomless reservoir of strength, that he drew upon. No, he didn't blame her. She was all he had left, apart from his duty.

The war did not wait for Friedrich to recover from his grieving. As the cold weather eased, the partisans once more made their presence known. He was forced to concede that he'd lost control of the hills, and that it was only a matter of time before the partisans took them on in set battles as they had further south. But he still had to keep the road open to Switzerland and keep Kesselring's desperately needed supplies flowing, as ambushes and air raids claimed more and more convoys. The Lugarno–Menaggio road was hardly a major arterial road, but as the USAF and the partisans attacked the more direct supply routes to Como, an increasing number of arms shipments were diverted their way. He'd escort them down as far as Menaggio then transfer them by ferry to Bellagio or Ravenna so that they could bypass Como.

Friedrich knew he had to go on the offensive to contain the partisans but lacked the force to do the job. Reluctantly he sent a request to headquarters for reinforcements. He never thought for a second that they'd send Dietrich Schmidt once more. After all, his first foray had ended in disgrace. Perhaps they sent him because he had previous experience in the area; or because he'd let it be known that he had a score to settle; or because High Command felt an elite corps was necessary to secure the road and their supplies. Perhaps it was just one of those curious decisions that armies the world over feel obliged to make that defy any rational explanation. Whatever their reasons, it was a decision destined to cast a shadow over the remainder of Friedrich's life.

The cable from High Command was curt in the way all orders are and told him only to expect Obersturmbannführer Schmidt and a company of one hundred and fifty soldiers and vehicles. It gave no detail of what armaments they were bringing, only that they were due one week from the date of the message. Dietrich groaned inwardly. *Obersturmbannführer* Schmidt! They now shared the same rank! Friedrich had no doubts that once more Dietrich would take charge of the operation and there'd be little he could do about it.

That day he received a second cable. It was from Como, advising him that a large shipment of arms was being diverted through Menaggio three days hence owing to partisan activity around Como. The cable stressed the vital nature of the cargo and the need to secure the road. Friedrich shook his head in wonder. Why did it take a week for reinforcements to arrive, and why couldn't they delay the shipment if it was so vital? But he already knew the answer. Two different commands, two different imperatives. Nobody would have informed Dietrich about the arms shipment and the organisers of the convoy wouldn't know about the pending reinforcements.

That night as Cecilia cooked and shared his dinner, he told her all about the reinforcements, the convoy, and how he'd had to compete with Dietrich for Christiane's affections. He told her all about the fateful dinner. These days he told her everything, as if sharing his knowledge helped him understand it better. He was rather surprised when Cecilia announced that she had to return home to the Villa. He hid his disappointment, sent a message for his driver and kissed her goodnight.

* * *

Poor Cecilia. Once again she was torn between opposing forces. But what could she do? She was desperately in love with Friedrich and wanted nothing to do with anything that could put him at risk or add to his troubles. By the same token, the partisans depended upon her for information. How could she not pass on what Friedrich had told her? They'd want to attack the convoy and then fade away to the north before the SS troops arrived. They couldn't rely upon Cecilia to help them outsmart the SS twice. Besides, the SS would want revenge and there'd be no limit to their savagery. The partisans had to be given the chance to fade away before they arrived.

Cecilia went looking for the Signora the instant she arrived back at the Villa and found her in her office.

'Signora . . .?'

The Signora pointedly ignored her until she finished the column of numbers she was adding. Her attitude changed the moment she saw Cecilia's face.

'Come in, come in child. Sit down.' She lifted a bundle of folders off the only other chair and placed them on her desk.

'Signora . . .'

The Signora could see that Cecilia was clearly distressed. Her attitude softened. Time, the great healer, had begun its work. 'It's all right Cecilia. Tell me, you have been talking to the Oberstleutnant and you have learned something you want to tell us, yes?'

Cecilia nodded.

'Ahhh . . . Cecilia.' To Cecilia's surprise, the Signora reached over and took both her hands. 'Perhaps we were too hasty in our judgement of you. I have spoken to Guido. But I suspect Guido is the least of your problems. First you must tell me what you know. If you have information you know we must pass it on to our men in the hills. We are their lifeline. Without us, without the courage of people like you, the Germans would have captured or killed them long ago. So tell me what you know and then we'll talk about your other problem.'

The Signora was calm and reason itself. Cecilia had never expected to hear a kind word from her ever again and her tone and attitude implied forgiveness. Her uncertainty and doubt evaporated in a wave of gratitude. She wanted to reach out and throw her arms around the Signora and hug her. Instead she told her everything she knew.

The Signora listened attentively to every word, asking questions to clarify detail, gently but skilfully drawing out every scrap of information.

'You are a good girl, Cecilia. Now I must keep my side of the bargain. You have fallen in love with the Oberstleutnant — no, don't say anything. That is clear not just to me but to everyone in Ravello and Menaggio. We have, of course, also heard of his tragedy. That has saddened us all. He is our enemy but he is also a decent man. But that has clear implications for you. He is no longer a married man.' She paused as if that phrase triggered feelings she was trying to suppress, then continued. 'Tell me, do you have any plans?'

'If we are separated before the war is over, he will send for me. I know he will. I will probably have to move to Germany as it is unlikely that it would be possible for him to return here. Signora, I don't want to inform on him any more! Surely I've done enough!'

'Yes, Cecilia,' the Signora said softly. 'You've done enough. I will never ask you to inform again.'

'Thank you, Signora!' Cecilia couldn't restrain herself. She stood up and threw her arms around the Signora's shoulders and hugged her. The burden was lifted. She was free.

'One more thing, Cecilia,' the Signora said, once she was

able to disentangle herself and speak. 'It may be better if you spent less time at the barracks and more time here at the Villa. There are two reasons. The old man needs you. I believe he is heading for pneumonia. It would be foolish to risk losing the protection of the Villa Carosio now. The other reason concerns your welfare. Try to understand that you have become one of the most hated people around here. You are vilified wherever you go. People see you at best as a sympathiser, at worst as a traitor. Once this war is done, there will be no mercy for traitors or sympathisers, and few people know of your other role. There will be a period of time between the departure of the Germans and the discovery of your true role as informer and patriot which will be very dangerous for you. Even when people are told that you spied for the partisans, don't blame them if they don't rush to embrace you in their gratitude. Their memories of you parading with the Oberstleutnant and the hatred they felt towards you may take time to fade. Many will believe you played both sides and to be honest with you Cecilia, there have been times when that is how it has even appeared to me. No, don't look at me like that. I have never doubted your courage or your honesty. The fact that you came to me tonight only confirms my opinion of you. But I'm telling you the truth. I'm telling you how people see things. The strength of your affection towards the Oberstleutnant has been your greatest asset. That is what has protected you. But it won't protect you after the war. Cecilia, you must talk to the Oberstleutnant and make him understand. It is for your own good. People will find it easier to forgive if you leave him now. You should cease going down to Menaggio. You should remain as much as possible behind the walls of the Villa. If you must go out, go only to Ravello. Go and talk to Father Michele. It can only do you good if you are seen with him and appear to enjoy his protection. Everybody knows he sends messages to the partisans. Everybody knows his bells have a secret meaning. If you are seen with him they may take this as an act of contrition at the very least, and it will also help them accept that you have been working for the partisans all along.'

'But Signora, you are asking . . .'

'I know I'm asking a lot. I know he needs you. I know you

need him. But you have to make this one last sacrifice. This time for your sake. Trust me, Cecilia, you know what I'm saying is right.'

Cecilia nodded. She thought of Friedrich bearing his grief alone and her heart ached for him. The Signora was right. The Signora was always right. But she couldn't give up seeing Friedrich yet, not yet, not while he needed her.

'Talk to your mother, Cecilia. You'll see she agrees. Do you think she's not concerned? Do you think she's not hurt by what people are saying about you?'

All doubt vanished. It was the Signora's trump card and she'd finessed it to perfection. Maddalena was Cecilia's greatest vulnerability. The arrow struck home. Cecilia would do anything to avoid causing her mother distress.

'Either Piero or I will take the message to Guido. I want you to alert Father Michele. Tell him how important it is and that we can't afford for him to wait until the evening before he rings his bell. At the same time take the opportunity to have a talk with him. Have a coffee in the square, or whatever it is they're serving in place of coffee. Let people see you together. And Cecilia, you must smile and say good morning to everyone you meet. Ignore anyone who is rude to you. Spend time with Father Michele. He won't mind. He owes you that and he knows it. Now run along.'

'Signora . . .'

'I'm sorry, Cecilia.' The Signora realised she had been too curt in her dismissal. She could never entirely forgive Cecilia but it was better that she appeared to. Besides, the girl was the main reason that Guido and most of his followers were still alive. She reached over and kissed Cecilia on both cheeks like she used to. 'Goodnight, Cecilia.'

'Goodnight, Signora.' Cecilia left the tiny office light-headed. She didn't know what made her happier; the relief of not having to inform on Friedrich, or the fact that the Signora had forgiven her and that they were friends once more.

*   *   *

Cecilia did exactly as instructed. But if she'd expected any immediate thaw in the way people regarded her, she was doomed to disappointment. Nobody returned her greetings or even acknowledged her existence. She was stunned. How long had this been going on? When she was with Friedrich they'd obviously concealed their discourtesy, either that or she was too blinded by love to see. The final insult came when Father Michele took her across to the café for ersatz coffee. Their waitress, Giuseppina Cerasuolo, banged her cup down so hard on the table half of its contents spilled over into the saucer. Cecilia was stunned. Giuseppina had always been her friend. When she'd needed to get a message to her mother, Giuseppina had been the go-between. Father Michele reacted angrily and insisted that Giuseppina bring another cup for Cecilia. But she was unrepentant. When it arrived, it was barely warm and undrinkable. There was to be no forgiveness for Cecilia that day.

When she returned to the Villa Carosio she rang Friedrich. She'd intended to ask him to visit her for a change, pleading the Count's illness as the reason. But the moment she heard his voice she changed her mind. It was flat and dead, as it had been when Gottfried's first message had arrived. He sent the car for her.

* * *

'What's wrong?' she demanded as soon as they were alone. He looked at her with a sad, bitter, ironic smile.

'Gottfried said once that it seemed as though Dresden had been chosen to bear the guilt for all our sins, for starting this disastrous war. Only now is the horrendous price becoming fully apparent. He has been unable to find any bodies. Oh there are plenty of bodies, but none that he can claim. The Heide-friedhof cemetery is full. They used bulldozers to push the bodies into deep trenches. Even that wasn't good enough. There were too many bodies. So the SS have begun to burn the bodies in stacks over train rails in the Altstadt. Hundreds of bodies at a time. Gottfried said he saw seven pyres burning at once and still they kept bringing in more bodies by the cartload. It was supposed to be kept secret but how can anyone keep something like that secret? Gottfried was crying as he told me. There are too many bodies to bury. Imagine that. Too many to bury. Some of the bodies are already burned so badly the funeral pyres are only finishing the job. All of the people in the trains were burned beyond recognition. Even their jewellery and rings had melted. When they dug out the cellar beneath the house, it was empty. Perhaps they'd tried to escape and were killed as they ran. It doesn't matter. There will be no graves and no headstones. They are all gone as surely as if they'd never existed. I ask you, what did they do to deserve this? What have I done to deserve this?'

Cecilia listened in horror. He didn't get angry or raise his voice. He laid the facts bare and relayed them in a lifeless monotone. She couldn't begin to guess how deeply his pain ran. She put her arms around his neck and her head on his shoulder.

'What did they do to deserve this?' he asked again.

They stood together holding each other while the minutes ticked away, until he abruptly turned from her. He changed. He became business-like and began to give instructions.

'I think it would be wise for you to stay away from the barracks until the SS have been and gone. I will try to visit you at the Villa Carosio whenever possible but that may not be very often. Try to understand, Cecilia, that I am not asking this of you by choice. You must be patient as I must be patient. This war cannot go on forever. When it is over, perhaps then we will find a place as far away from Germany and Europe and world wars as it is possible to go. Perhaps then we will find some peace. Will you be patient for me, Cecilia? Will you do that?'

She threw her arms around him once more and the floodgates opened. She cried like she had the first time she'd sat on the strange bed with Anna and watched the tiny figure of her mother retreat up the hill to Ravello. She cried for the hurt he'd suffered, for her fears, and for the love she felt for the tall German. But she also cried from relief. For the first time he'd actually said in as many words that his plans for the future also included her. She'd never doubted it, but it was wonderful to have her conviction confirmed. If that wasn't a marriage proposal, what was? He waited until she'd dried her eyes and escorted her to the Lancia.

* * *

Once Cecilia had gone, he applied himself to organising an escort for the convoy. He needed the distraction and his country needed him. He shut Gottfried's last call from his mind. He decided to lead the convoy himself in an armoured troop carrier armed with a heavy machine-gun. He'd arrange for another machine-gun to be mounted on the tray facing rearwards. If they tried to isolate him from the convoy this time, he would be ready. He put his latest acquisition, a heavy armoured car with a turret mounted 30 millimetre gun, at the rear. He spread the trucks carrying his troops evenly through the convoy. He'd instruct his mortar squads to set up within each and to fire through the canvas the moment any attack occurred. These first salvoes would be fired blind and therefore aimlessly, but he hoped they'd cause enough confusion and consternation in his enemy to give his troops time to disembark and take up positions. The plan was for the troop carriers to drive off the road or at least to one side and for the troop to engage the partisans while the convoy made a run for it. He thought that if the troop carriers kept as far to the left as possible and the convoy to the right, the road might stay open even if his troop carriers were disabled by *Panzerfaust*. He decided to commit all his troops and hold the Blackshirts in reserve.

He sat back and considered his plan. If they dynamited the road, they'd have no option but to stand and fight, but this was not a tactic the partisans had employed in his area. The heavy armoured car and its 30 millimetre gun would deter them from engaging in any stand-up fight. If they attacked at all, it would be a return to their old tactics of hit and run. Perhaps when they saw the strength of the escort, they wouldn't hit at all. Unless . . . unless they felt they had a force to match. Friedrich thought of the cannons left rusting in the high pastures after air drops. Had the time come when they had both the means to move and deploy them? If only he had a force strong enough to sweep the hills ahead of the convoy, he thought grimly. That was the only way he could ever be sure that the convoy would go through without incident.

* * *

That night, in the hills high above Ravello, Guido met with his lieutenants and discussed their plans. As Cecilia had suspected, the partisans saw the convoy as the last chance to strike a telling blow before the SS arrived. And, by then, they hoped to be long gone. They made their plans carefully. They focused their attention on the heavy armoured car. The 30 millimetre gun had to be incapacitated as soon as possible. The question was, would it lead the convoy or follow it? If it led, they could isolate it by dynamiting a cliff face or dropping a tree behind it. Then they'd try to fix a mine to the rear of the turret. If it trailed, they'd drop a tree ahead of it. Either way they'd need two dedicated squads, one at either end of the ambush. If the Oberstleutnant decided to lead the convoy there was nothing Guido could do to shield him. He'd have to take his chances along with everyone else. Besides, Piero had made it perfectly clear that Cecilia would not be bringing him any more information from the Oberstleutnant so there was no longer a need to risk the lives of his men in making sure he wasn't harmed.

Guido listened to his lieutenants discuss tactics and watched their excitement grow. Those krauts who criticise Italian soldiers should see us now, he thought. Under-armed, under-fed and under-estimated. Well, he'd give them something to talk about in Berlin. He decided to lead the attack himself.

Chapter Forty-Three

Friedrich picked up the convoy at Albogasio, right on the border with Switzerland. For once he had no eye for the beauty of Lake Lugarno in the still morning air nor for the trout rising in their quest for tasty insects. He was surprised on two counts. First that each truck was sealed and guarded so that no one — not even he — could determine their contents. And, secondly, that there were only eight trucks. He couldn't imagine what they were carrying that could be so precious, but precious it obviously was. Maybe Hitler the magician had one last card up his sleeve, a new and devastating weapon. But would it change the course of the war? No, it was far too late for that, but it could change the course of the peace. Whatever was in those trucks, Friedrich resolved to protect with all his might and even, if necessary, with his life.

They drove along the northern side of the lake, past Porlezza and the bridge which had earlier halted Dietrich's SS troops, and into partisan territory. He wished he had a spotter aircraft to warn him of any ambush, but they had other priorities. All he had was his eyes and a soldier's instincts for trouble. They scanned the hillsides and searched into shadows, but found nothing. The convoy ground on and began the steep descent towards Lake Como. He allowed a little optimism. Perhaps his convoy was too well protected to tempt the partisans. Perhaps he'd over-estimated their strength.

The first he knew of the attack was a blast from the rear as the partisans attempted to immobilise and isolate the heavy armoured car. Then a shell from a Panzerfaust, fired in haste by an over-excited crew, ricocheted off his carrier's armour plate. Almost instantly his forward machine-gunner returned fire. He turned his attention to the convoy and his mouth fell open in surprise. The canvas covers on the convoy trucks as well as those on his troop-carrying trucks shredded before his eyes. Mortar and machine-gun ripped them apart from within. Then there were soldiers everywhere, his and Dietrich's SS. Now he knew what the convoy was carrying and why it was so heavily guarded. This time Dietrich had used himself and his troops as bait. He watched in admiration as Dietrich's troops bled around the ends of the convoy and charged up the slopes to outflank the partisans and prevent their escape. Once they had them pinned down, their mortars would range in and massacre them.

With no convoy to protect, Friedrich jumped off the tray of his troop carrier and ordered his troops to engage the enemy head on, to pin them down while Dietrich completed his encirclement. At first they met little resistance and soon learned why. The partisans had begun their withdrawal the instant the SS had revealed themselves. Many had escaped before the encirclement was completed and were being fiercely pursued by the SS. But the partisans were expert in hit and fade and carried lighter arms and less equipment than the SS. The pursuits would end in countless hastily arranged ambushes and rear guard actions until the SS called off the chase, and the surviving partisans made good their escape. But their numbers would be severely depleted.

Those who had reacted too slowly realised their fate and began their fight to the death. Friedrich engaged them with light arms until he'd brought his machine-guns and mortars up into position. The partisans were in a hopeless position, but if any attempted to surrender they failed to make their intentions clear.

When Friedrich realised that their fire was no longer being returned he ordered his men to cease. He called out to the surviving partisans in Italian, telling them to throw down their arms and show themselves. Fewer than ten were able to comply and, of these, three were wounded. Friedrich was shocked by their ages. Some were old men, others mere boys. He advanced slowly, his gun at the ready. His men came with him, checking the dead and wounded. He heard a gun shot and looked up. SS troops were moving back down the hill towards him, shooting the wounded as they came. His prisoners raised their hands even higher and moved nervously towards him for protection.

'What's this?' he heard Dietrich ask. 'Prisoners? We don't take prisoners.' Without warning he opened fire on the prisoners with his machine pistol and his men did likewise. It was all over in an instant. The partisans crumpled into bloody heaps one on top of the other. Friedrich was speechless.

'Cease fire!' he yelled. 'My God, what have you done? Those men had surrendered. They were my prisoners!'

'Correction, they were my prisoners,' said Dietrich coldly. 'My prisoners, taken as a result of my ambush.' He smiled. 'You were obviously mistaken. We don't take prisoners. There is no point. Being a partisan or aiding them or withholding information about them is an offence punishable by death. I would have thought you'd be aware of that.'

'They were soldiers who had surrendered,' said Friedrich through gritted teeth.

'Soldiers? The only soldiers I see are soldiers of the Reich. The rest are partisans. Partisans are not soldiers but terrorists. Now, let's see how many of these terrorists wish they hadn't got out of bed this morning.' He looked for his sergeant-major. 'Hauptscharführer! Start counting.'

*   *   *

It was almost noon when old Mentore Parente put down his tools and eased himself out from under the old Fiat he was repairing. He'd heard the rumble of trucks and crawled out to see them pass by. He stood there watching silently as truck after truck filled with German soldiers drove past. He was curious as to why the soldiers were singing at the top of their voices and why their canvas covers were pulled down. That was unusual these days. They'd be sitting ducks for snipers. To his surprise an armoured troop carrier pulled out of the convoy and ground its way into the square. He recognised the Oberstleutnant first, then noticed the SS officer. They appeared to be arguing.

'Why are we stopping here?' Friedrich was clearly irritated.

'We are stopping here, Friedrich, because I am thirsty and I'd like a cup of coffee. I think you should join me. It is time we recognised that we are both fighting on the same side.'

Friedrich gritted his teeth. Now that they were of equal rank, Dietrich had taken the liberty of calling him by his Christian name. 'You won't get coffee here.'

'Then, Friedrich, we will drink whatever it is they do have here.' He turned to his corporal. 'Rottenführer! See that our coffee is not interrupted!'

'Herr Obersturmbannführer!' The corporal ordered all the soldiers except the machine-gun crews off the truck and positioned them around the square. Dietrich strode casually over towards the café, and sat down at the table closest to the counter. Friedrich joined him. Dietrich looked for the waitress and found her standing nervously behind the bar. He smiled with satisfaction. Yes, she was the one who'd served him on his previous visit and chatted to his men. Everything was falling nicely into place. He called out to her in German.

'Two coffees, you understand. Not the slop you usually serve. I want real coffee. Or I'll add your worthless body to the heap up the hill.'

'*Un momento, Signorina,*' Friedrich interrupted before she had a chance to move. 'She doesn't speak German, certainly not enough to understand what you said.' Friedrich turned to the girl and ordered in Italian. 'Two coffees. And you'd better find some real coffee beans. My colleague here has his heart set on real coffee. Do you understand?'

Giuseppina Cerasuolo nodded, too terrified to speak. She understood all right. She'd even understood most of the German. It was one of the conditions of her employ. She had to understand German so that she could speak to the German soldiers who stopped by. It made the café popular and helped pay her wages. So she studied the language and practised daily on her customers. She was surprised the Oberstleutnant wasn't aware of it. The SS officer certainly was. She'd waited on his table the last time he'd come to Ravello. But of course, on the few occasions she'd served the Oberstleutnant he'd come with Cecilia and they had always spoken Italian. It was a point of pride with him. She raced off to find the owner and to beg for some cherished coffee beans. The owner's wife, who had heard the exchange, was waiting for her out the back. She gave Giuseppina half a cup full of beans and ushered her back out into the bar.

'You see, Friedrich, what can be accomplished when you are firm with these people? I wonder how many cups of slops you've had here for want of a little show of strength.'

'None actually,' said Friedrich, ignoring the insult. 'I normally drink tea. Today I will drink coffee to oblige you.'

To his credit Dietrich laughed. Why wouldn't he? Just when he thought he held all the aces he'd been handed another. Friedrich wasn't aware the girl spoke German. An unexpected bonus. He could afford to be a little generous.

'So, Friedrich, what did you think of my little strategy?'

Friedrich waited until Giuseppina had finished grinding the coffee beans before answering. 'I can't deny that it was effective.'

'Effective? No, Friedrich, it was more than effective. We left one hundred and thirteen corpses on that hill. And that doesn't include the ones my men killed higher up. You can add at least another thirty to the total. When was the last time you killed one hundred and forty-three partisans?' Dietrich began laughing. 'And all you can say is you think my strategy was . . . what was the word you used? . . . effective!' He laughed again.

Behind the counter, Giuseppina listened in horror. What were they talking about? One hundred and forty-three partisans killed! She could hardly comprehend the number or the scale of the tragedy. Now she understood what the SS officer had meant when he said he'd add her body to the heap on the hill. She mumbled a quick prayer for those killed and crossed herself.

'My men contributed their share.' Friedrich was determined not to allow Dietrich to claim all the glory. They'd fought bravely with great discipline and deserved recognition for that. 'They engaged the partisans head on to give you time to outflank them. You may have also noticed that my strategy in respect to setting up machine-guns and mortars within each truck was identical to yours.'

'Yes, that is fair.'

Dietrich's unexpected generosity stunned Friedrich and put

him off balance. It was so out of character. What was he playing at?

'Our strategies were not quite identical, Friedrich, although the principle was the same. You set up mortars, we didn't. I had the top of my trucks covered with three layers of canvas and pulled tight to deflect their blasted petrol bombs. However, I wasn't convinced our mortars could penetrate them. Nevertheless, you are to be congratulated. And so is your Italian whore.'

'What do you mean? Are you talking about the Count's companion?'

Giuseppina froze, her ears tingling, fixed on the conversation.

'Companion ... yes ... not the word I would use to describe her but it will do. Remind me, what is this companion's name?'

'Cecilia.'

'Yes, Cecilia.' Dietrich smiled. 'Well, Cecilia is also to be congratulated for the part she played.'

'What do you mean?'

'We have Cecilia to thank for setting up our ambush. You told her and she told the partisans who she knew would be unable to resist a nice, fat convoy before the wicked SS troops arrived. Yes, Cecilia is to be congratulated.'

'Dietrich that is preposterous!' Friedrich glanced up at Giuseppina but she seemed preoccupied with making their coffee. What was Dietrich playing at? Whatever his game was, he decided to end it. He didn't realise that the game was already over and won. 'Besides, this is no place to be discussing such things.'

'Then we'll change the subject.' Dietrich smiled innocently. He'd achieved what he wanted. 'How's Christiane?'

'Christiane is dead.'

Dietrich briefly lost his composure. His jaw dropped open. 'Dead?'

Giuseppina lost the rest of the conversation in the spluttering of the espresso machine. But she'd heard enough. The partisans had been betrayed and she knew who had betrayed them. Dear God! One hundred and forty-three dead! More than one-third of the partisans dead! Her hands shook with anger. She put both coffees on a tray and carried them to the table. The men ignored her and seemed oblivious of the fact that her shaking hand had spilled coffee into their saucers. She retreated to the furthest end of the bar to wait until they left or ordered another coffee. She'd heard enough. Her head spun. She didn't want to hear any more.

She watched as the men finished their coffee. Friedrich left a few *lire* behind to cover the cost. She waited until all the soldiers had boarded the truck and it had begun to move out of the square. Then she called the owner's wife and burst into tears.

'What's the matter, girl?' demanded the owner's wife anxiously. 'What did they say?'

Giuseppina only cried harder.

'What's wrong with Giuseppina? What's happened?'

Giuseppina looked up through her tears to see who the newcomer was as more curious women crowded into the little bar. It was the girl from the Villa, Carmela.

Chapter Forty-Four

Cecilia turned away from the troop carrier as it ground its way down the hill, using its lower gears to check its momentum. It wasn't just to avoid getting dust in her eyes but to make it easier to ignore the inevitable whistles and shouted obscenities from the soldiers. She waited for the dust to settle before continuing up the hill. She heard a robin call to its mate and stopped to watch them flitting and darting from branch to branch. She couldn't remember when she'd ever felt so happy or so much at peace. When the Signora had released her from her obligations to the partisans she'd lifted a massive burden off her shoulders. That was one pretence she no longer had to sustain, a lie she no longer had to live. Furthermore the Count was dying. He grew weaker by the day and was rarely lucid for more than a couple of hours a day. She no longer had to play the role of ardent fascist. She still pretended to take his dictation but these days his rantings were less coherent than ever. Instead, she dreamed of the exotic places she'd run away to with Friedrich. Brazil, Argentina, America. Most of all, she wanted to go to America, if only America would have them. But first the war had to end and before that, she had to ensure that it ended satisfactorily for her. She wondered whether Father Michele would already be at the church hearing confessions or still in the rectory. She thought she'd try the church first. If he wasn't around she could kneel and say a few prayers while she waited for him. It did no harm to be seen to be pious. Besides, she now had a lot to thank the Holy Mother for.

As she strolled down the lane alongside the church, she heard the sound of women wailing and keening coming from

413

the square. She frowned. What could the problem be? Slowly it dawned on her that the convoy had been due that morning and an icy shiver ran down her spine. Had something gone wrong? She quickened her step. The keening grew louder. She saw the women gathered by the cafe and spotted Carmela. She hurried towards her.

'Carmela, what's wrong?' she cried. 'What's happened?'

'You! You have the nerve to come here and ask us that. You bitch! You betrayed us! You murderer!'

Cecilia stopped in her tracks, stunned. Bitch? Murderer? What did she mean? Other women took up the cry.

'Murderer! Murderer!' The women started to move towards her, but one had a better idea. She pulled a half-brick from the decaying wall of the *panificio* and hurled it at Cecilia. It hit her on the side of the face and she stumbled. Another brick followed, and another. Cecilia reeled back under the blows. She saw old Mentore Parente screaming at the women to stop and tried to run to him, her mind struggling to comprehend what was happening. Why were they doing this to her?

'Murderer! Murderer!' The women chanted, spurred on by one another, their accusation gaining conviction with repetition.

'Stop it!' Cecilia screamed, but a rock caught her full in the face and she fell. Blood streamed from her nose and mouth as she curled up into a ball to protect herself from the missiles. Bricks and stones pounded into her body, her arms and her legs. One penetrated the protective shield of her arms and thudded into her head. Mercifully, she lost consciousness.

'Murderer! Murderer!'

The hail of rocks and bricks continued and they began to pile up around her body.

'Stop it! Stop it. In the name of God stop it!' Father Michele and Piero charged through the crazed women knocking them flying. Father Michele fought his way to Cecilia's inert body and stopped. He looked up at the now sullen women. 'Oh dear God! What have you done? What have you done?' He stood guard over Cecilia, defying them as Piero bent down and picked her up.

'You stupid women!' Piero glared at them, his eyes awash

with tears. 'You stupid, ignorant women! You've killed her!' He turned in a circle so that he could hurl his accusation at all the women, so none could escape his condemnation. He saw Carmela, still with a rock in her hand. 'You!' he hissed. 'You of all people should know better. Cecilia is the bravest woman in all of Italy and you have killed her! Out of my way! Out of my way.' Piero wept openly as he carried the lifeless girl away, propping her head in the crook of his elbow so that all could look with shame at her face. The women moved back to clear a path for him but the café owner's wife stood firm.

'You're not going to desecrate our church by taking that traitorous bitch in there!' she spat.

Piero lashed out with his boot and knocked the woman flying. 'I wouldn't dishonour her by taking her into your church! It is you who have dishonoured it! You have turned it into a house of murderers!'

'No, Piero!' the priest rushed up alongside him. 'Please carry her into the vestry so I can administer last rites.'

'No, Father. You tend your flock. They need you more than Cecilia does. You try to forgive them because I'm damned if I will. Go! Cecilia has no need for you or any of us any more. Go!'

Piero walked away down the lane with his torn and broken burden, then looked over his shoulder to make sure he hadn't been followed. When he saw the lane was clear, he broke into a run. He knew something no one else did. Cecilia had groaned when he'd picked her up.

*   *   *

Piero left the road and ran into the meadow. He ran into the thicket along the trail the shepherds used. He could feel Cecilia's blood seeping thick and warm onto his arms, urging him on. He ran uphill until his own blood pounded in his head and his old, tired legs threatened to give out. But he had no choice. He reached the old farmhouse and kicked on the door. The woman who opened the door took one look and dragged him inside. She ran to the stables to fetch the fugitive Piero had hidden there the night before. He was another Jew on the run from the Nazis, but not just another Jew. He was also a doctor.

Piero lay Cecilia down delicately on the bed and fell to his knees, not entirely from exhaustion. Piero, the man who had turned away from God and the church for the duration, wept as he began to pray for her life.

* * *

In the Church of San Pietro, Father Michele listened to the women's confessions. Those waiting their turn knelt in silent prayer or sat numbed in disbelief at the magnitude of their sin. As he heard confession after confession, it began to dawn on Father Michele that the information Cecilia had been given was deliberately misleading. It occurred to him that the Oberstleutnant had also been misled. But that didn't forgive the women for what they'd done. They'd jumped to conclusions and seized upon the opportunity to unleash their pent up resentment and jealousy and also their hate. Absolution would not come easy for any of them. But he had other worries. If the story was true about the massacre, he knew that many of the women he now berated would need his comfort and prayers. A car had already gone to investigate.

* * *

In the Villa Carosio, Signora Mila listened in horror as Carmela tearfully told her story. Her first thoughts were for Guido. Had he survived? Had he escaped? Was he wounded? He'd survived this long, surely he couldn't die now! That would be too unfair. Then her thoughts turned to Cecilia. It was inconceivable that she would betray them, not after all the risks she'd taken in the past. But then she thought of how she'd treated Cecilia over the previous months and her growing attachment to the Oberstleutnant, and was no longer sure. But stoning her to death on suspicion! Dear God, and Carmela had been part of it! The Signora forbade Carmela to return to the church and ordered her to her room. She put her head in her hands and squeezed her eyes tightly shut. Sweet Mother of Jesus, where had everything gone wrong?

She little realised that her action might have just saved her daughter's life.

* * *

In the inadequate, little farmhouse above Ravello, Maddalena slumped in her chair. Old Mentore Parente sat opposite her unable to meet her eyes. It didn't matter. She saw nothing and her mind took in nothing, concerning itself only with what was happening within. Her darling Cecilia, gone, stoned to death by women she thought were her friends. The loss stripped her life of all meaning and the emptiness inside her knew no walls. Her life was over as surely as her daughter's. She no longer had the strength even to cry.

'Maddalena . . .' Mentore said softly. 'Maddalena . . .'

His words penetrated her fog-bound mind and she looked up.

'Maddalena, let me take you to Father Michele. Please. Please Maddalena. I am no help to you and I won't leave you alone. Let me take you to Father Michele. Perhaps he can explain.'

Someone could explain? Father Michele could explain? Suddenly she wanted to know why. Why? But what answer could there be for the unanswerable? What could Father Michele say that could make sense of what had happened? She could listen, she could hear him out. Maybe he might help her understand.

'Help me up, Mentore,' she said. 'I will hear what the priest has to say, though I'd be surprised if God himself could find an explanation.'

Old Mentore hastened to take her arm and helped her up the crooked pathway to his Fiat.

* * *

Ravello was not an isolated village quarantined from the rest of the world. Word of the massacre and the stoning of Cecilia filtered down the mountain from shepherd to shepherd, bystander to bystander, house to house. It was couched in terms of stunned disbelief which could only add to its credibility.

Dietrich waited patiently. News of the massacre of the partisans swept like wildfire through the streets of Menaggio, fuelled by bragging soldiers and the gloating of the Blackshirts. Women congregated in the churches and in the square desperate for news of their menfolk, anxious to learn who still lived and who had died. Dietrich primed his men to come to him the instant they heard of any new developments. He was pleasantly surprised at how little time it took.

The news about Christiane's death had rocked him back on his heels but had done nothing to make him change his mind. He would savour this day for a long time to come. He'd get revenge, not only on the partisans, but on Friedrich for the humiliation of his last dinner at Prager Strasse. Nothing would stop him from taking his revenge in full. He marched up to Friedrich's quarters, barely able to keep a smile from his face. He knocked briefly and pushed the door open.

Friedrich was sitting at his desk writing out his report. He spun around at the rude interruption. 'Obersturmbannführer! What is the meaning of this? How dare you?'

'I have come to report another casualty,' he said casually. He leaned arrogantly against the table and put his boot up on a chair. 'You want your report to be thorough, don't you?'

'Just make your report and go!'

'If that's what you wish. It seems our conversation in the café was overheard. The girl Cecilia has been killed. It seems that half of the women in Ravello had fathers or brothers in the partisans.'

'Cecilia . . . killed?' Friedrich was stunned. His mind refused to accept the information. But Dietrich was relentless.

'Yes. Killed. The women stoned her to death in the square. Very biblical, don't you think? Really, Friedrich, you are careless with your women.' He grinned as he watched the blood drain from Friedrich's face. He spat on the floor and sauntered to the door. 'I told you at Prager Strasse that I would get even with you.' He took one more look at Friedrich, saw his face crumple in agony, and left.

Friedrich didn't move, not for some time. His capacity for pain and grief had been exceeded. Slowly his brain began to function once more and he reached for the phone. He rang the Villa Carosio and asked for Signora Mila. He needed confirmation. The moment he heard her voice he got it. She told him about the stoning, omitting any detail that would allow a glimpse of Cecilia's other life and any mention of the part Carmela had played. She said she was sorry, but Friedrich's heart had hardened beyond the reach of any expressions of sympathy. He hung up, buttoned his tunic as he walked to the door, and shouted for his Hauptmann. He had fought his war according to the rules, allowing whatever shreds of decency and fair play his war would permit. But there was no decency in this war, no honour and no forgiveness. He buckled on his holster containing the favoured but superseded Luger semi-automatic pistol and went downstairs. The men were already waiting for him in the truck.

Chapter Forty-Five

Old Mentore Parente gathered up the bricks and stones into a pile as he waited for Maddalena to come down the steps from the church. He looked accusingly at the shame-faced women as they entered and left. A few had gathered at the foot of the steps, perhaps to wait for Maddalena and express ... what? Their condolences? Perhaps to apologise? They would be the lucky ones with no losses to mourn, no dead hero to keen over.

His ears picked up the sound of the truck labouring up the hill from Menaggio. Vehicles were his interest and his distraction. He always stood at the front of his garage to see what passed by. But this time he heard the sound and ignored it.

The *breva* had sprung up but there was no warmth in the wind. It created little whirlwinds in the dust and ruffled the black hems of the women's skirts, and carried the voices of grief from house to house. Old Mentore was so involved with his thoughts he didn't look up again until he saw the Oberstleutnant's Lancia Aprilia pull into the square with the truck close behind it. He looked up at the church steps just as Maddalena appeared. He wanted to call out to her, to tell her to go back inside, without even knowing precisely why. But it was all too late. He watched in horror as the men spilled off the back of the truck and began to grab every woman in sight. He saw the Oberstleutnant, looked him in the eye and knew there was no hope.

'Out of the way, old man,' he hissed, 'unless you want to be shot as well.'

Old Mentore staggered back out of the way, his eyes shut, unwilling and unable to witness any more tragedy. What else could go wrong on this most terrible day? He heard Maddalena curse and Giuseppina cry. Then he heard the explosion of rifles which made martyrs of eight women and a war criminal of the Oberstleutnant.

* * *

The silence hung heavily over the table as Lucio finished speaking, each man aware that the time had come. Lucio looked at each of his friends in turn, wondering who would be first to break the ice. No one was prepared to meet his eye.

'Perhaps we should have coffee first,' said Ramon finally. 'It will give us time to reflect. I heard Maria pour five cups so I assume they are for us. I would not refuse a glass of grappa either. Goddamn, Lucio, I may never forgive you for this!'

'Ramon, that is enough!' Milos turned to the blind man. 'No one forced you to come here today. You came of your own free will because Lucio asked for your help. You knew the temperature of the water before you came. Don't complain now because it is too hot. Frankly, I am disappointed in your attitude. I expected more from you.'

'I am sorry, Milos, but I am not accustomed to aiding and abetting murderers.'

'Colombina is not yet a murderer and may never be.'

'Yes, but it is us who will determine that.'

'Yes, it is us who will determine that. All of us, me included.' Lucio interrupted to cut short the argument. 'Let me begin by thanking you all for hearing me out and for coming today. By coming you have indicated your preparedness to help my mother-in-law and to help decide the fate of Friedrich Eigenwill. That is the act of true friends. I know I have imposed upon all of you, but now that you are aware of the circumstances I'm sure you understand that I had little choice.' He leaned back to allow Maria to serve the coffees. 'Perhaps I should venture the first opinion.' He took a sip of his coffee. 'I assume from your silence that you all agree.'

The friends all shifted forward in their chairs like conspirators, their whole being focused on Lucio's words. He didn't keep them wondering where he stood for very long. The trial of Friedrich Eigenwill had begun.

'Let me say right from the start, that had Colombina sought my opinion alone, the Oberstleutnant would now be dead.' He paused and looked around the table. The first vote had been registered and, even though the men knew the nature of the deadly game they were playing, Lucio's verdict had taken them aback. 'Of course, there are mitigating circumstances. Friedrich suffered horribly. He lost his wife and his child in the most appalling circumstances. Then he was led to believe that he had also lost Cecilia, killed in the cruellest and crudest possible way. I was tempted to accept a plea for temporary insanity, that he acted while the balance of his mind was disturbed. But on reflection I chose to reject that. Friedrich is a true Teuton. Everything he does is considered. Under the stress of battle he was always in control of himself. He has a very logical, ordered mind. I have not the slightest doubt that Friedrich knew exactly what he was doing when he ordered those women shot. It was hardly a spur of the moment reaction. Rather, it was a premeditated act of revenge. Of revenge!

'This leads me to another point. I don't regard his actions as a war crime. On this I am of the same mind as Colombina. It was not a reprisal for the actions of the partisans but the act of a vengeful lover. Therefore it is not a war crime but murder. You can say he was under duress, but what about his victims? Most of them had gone to the church to pray for husbands and sons and brothers killed in the morning's ambush. They too, were suffering. But they didn't take up weapons and order the deaths of eight innocent Germans. To me, the Oberstleutnant's personal losses do not mitigate the barbarity of his crime. He is guilty of the premeditated murder of eight innocent women. My vote says that he should be made to pay, and pay in full.'

'My vote says he has already paid for his crime many times over.' Gancio looked around at the others. 'Does anybody object if I go next? No? Okay. I have said from the very beginning that it does no good to rake over the past. I think it is outrageous and disgraceful that we should even presume to sit in judgement on this man for things that happened half a world away in another time. To say that the shooting was murder and not a war crime is patently ridiculous. Of course it was a war crime! If there was no war the situation would not have arisen. There would be no partisans, no informers, no sympathisers, no ambush. And Friedrich would not have had an army of soldiers at his disposal to kill anybody. It was a crime of war in the time of war. This sort of thing went on every day in occupied countries and virtually all of the instigators have gone unpunished. Unpunished by courts, that is. I believe that Friedrich has served out nearly fifty years of punishment. When he ended the lives of those women he virtually ended his own.

'All his life since, he has been on the run, waiting for a Colombina or a Guido to find him and inform the authorities. I know the sort of life he has had to lead and I believe that Friedrich has been punished enough. He will have regretted his action every day of his life. He has suffered the consequences as have other people. People like my aunt.' He paused and looked around the table. Diners around them chatted and laughed and rattled their cutlery on plates but at their table you could have heard a pin drop.

'I wondered when you'd get to that.' Neil smiled wryly but got no response.

'Guido was a hero at a time when Italy was full of them, and my aunt was a villain at a time when Italy couldn't find enough. Nothing was clear cut after the war. A lot of people waited until the end was inevitable before racing off to join the partisans. They stole the glory from the true heroes, and zealously condemned anyone who had even a whiff of taint about them. My aunt's father, Guido Mila, never got the recognition he deserved.'

'No!'

'Yes, Lucio. There were times in your story when I wanted to scream out and correct you, but it was your story not mine. My father's brother married Carmela. You have also told my aunt's story. Think about that! After the war, she was blamed for the stoning of Cecilia. Why not? Giuseppina Cerasuolo was dead and nobody could remember — or didn't want to remember — who had cast the first stone. Even Guido had difficulty forgiving her but ultimately stood by her. Perhaps because of his own shame at having taken Cecilia for a lover. Perhaps he felt in some way responsible. Whatever, it was because of Carmela that the Signora and Guido never got the recognition they deserved.

'Those who believed Cecilia was a saint spat at my aunt whenever she walked past them. Those who were ambivalent about Cecilia's role wouldn't forgive her either. And those who believed Cecilia had betrayed the partisans for the sake of her German boyfriend were too ashamed of what had happened to forgive her. They all blamed Carmela for the shooting that followed. They saw that as a natural consequence. Strangely enough, nobody blamed the Oberstleutnant. In their communal guilt they found one of their own to blame. They found Carmela. It wasn't fair, but nothing in war is fair. She became an outcast and because her parents sheltered her, they became outcasts too.

'They left the Villa Carosio, but not before the Signora took her promised revenge on the Count. As he lay dying, she told him all about how they had sheltered deserters and prisoners of war. But mostly she told him how his darling Cecilia had betrayed him. He was going to die anyway but that was what killed him.

'They moved across the lake to Ravenna and finally to Bellagio. My uncle had fought alongside my father as a partisan under Guido, and also had Cecilia to thank for his survival. Some say he married Carmela as a kindness to Guido, to repay him for some incident or another or as a vote of confidence in his daughter. But I know better. I have visited their house enough to know the truth. He married my aunt because he adored her. He was the best thing that happened to her. He brought love, kindness and hope at a time when she had no reason to expect any. Sometimes he came home at night from the café with his nose spread across his face because somebody had said something derogatory about her. But he never wavered. He protected her honour and he still does. Gradually things settled down and they were able to live a normal life. But even to this day they are not free from covert looks and dark mutterings. I tell them to leave Italy and its bitterness behind and come to Australia but they won't hear a word of it. Till the day my aunt dies, she will carry the scars of the events that took place in the square at Ravello. And so too, my friends, will Friedrich

Eigenwill. He has served his sentence. Nearly fifty years of it. It is time to forgive. And forget. Let him have a little peace before he dies.'

'Bugger him!' Neil looked dismissively at Gancio. 'The bloke's a cold-blooded murderer. Does anybody doubt that he ordered the soldiers to shoot those women? No? Has anybody produced evidence to suggest that he didn't? No! It doesn't matter that he committed his crime nearly fifty years ago, he should not be allowed to get away with it. He should thank his lucky stars that he's got away with it for as long as he has. The way I see it, we can report him to the war crimes tribunal or whatever, but by the time they gather enough evidence to bring him to trial he'll be pushing up daisies. Christ, he's got to be over eighty now.

'No, I believe the old bastard should be made to face his guilt and be made to face his executioner. I believe it is time Colombina cooked him another kraut meal and laced it with cyanide. He'll die horribly, knowing why. That is justice.'

'That is barbaric!' Milos turned to Ramon. 'My friend, do you mind if I go next? I can't let Neil get away with his nonsense.'

'If I let you go next, mine will be the casting vote.'

'But if you go next, Ramon, I may not even have a vote. If you don the black cap then the trial is over and Friedrich is condemned. At least hear my argument.'

'Dear God . . .!'

'Do I take that as acceptance?'

'Yes! Get on with it!'

Lucio heaved a sigh of relief and immediately hoped nobody had noticed. Things were working out perfectly. He fought back his excitement.

'No one doubts that Friedrich ordered the deaths of those unfortunate women, but it happened against a background of greater atrocities. The lives of ordinary men and women were devalued. I don't want to raise the whole issue of the deaths of millions of Jews in concentration camps. That is a monstrous issue in itself. Rather I'll confine my comments to the subjects that have been discussed.

'Early on in his story, Lucio made the point that all war is an atrocity. The bombing of Guernica, the shooting of the

Jewish girl by Dietrich and so on. The dropping of stick grenades and Molotov cocktails by partisans on trucks crowded with troops is an atrocity. Running over refugee columns in tanks is an atrocity. The bombing of innocent women and children in cities is an atrocity. All war is an atrocity and one of the biggest atrocities of all was the bombing of Dresden. Lucio has spared us little detail about that particular event so it serves no point to go back over it. But let me ask you this, who paid for the crime of Dresden? Does anybody doubt that it was a crime?' Milos looked around the table but nobody chose to contradict him. 'Perhaps Gancio is right. Perhaps it is outrageous for us to sit here in judgement at all. What is the basis of judgement? What constitutes a war crime? It seems to be that criminality in war is determined by the victor. If Hitler had somehow won the war, doubtless Bomber Harris would have been hanged instead of having a statue erected in his honour. If Hitler had won we would not be here now sitting in judgement of Friedrich Eigenwill. He would have returned home a hero. A sad and embittered one, maybe, but nonetheless a hero.

'In light of some of the atrocities that took place during the war, the shooting of the women in Ravello is a piddly affair. Bear in mind, also, that Friedrich would have been perfectly within his rights to have ordered not one shooting in Ravello but several. He had ample cause for ordering reprisals. Lucio made the point that many of the women who were shot were mourning husbands and sons killed in the ambush. Those women were supporting and giving comfort to the partisans. Under the laws of the army of occupation, that was an offence punishable by death. There were posters everywhere informing the populace of this. Arguably, Friedrich was simply enforcing the law as he understood it, even though the event that triggered the reprisal was of a personal rather than military nature.

'I don't believe that Friedrich is a bad man. On the contrary, I would regard him as a very decent, kind, thoughtful and fundamentally moral human being. His reluctance to hunt down Jews is further evidence of that. He is simply a man who cracked momentarily under extreme pressure and made a wrong decision. I believe he has suffered the consequences of that decision ever since.

'I will make one final point. That is to do with Colombina's motivation. She is not seeking retribution for the death of her school friend Giuseppina Cerasuolo or any of the the the other six women. No! She is seeking revenge for the killing of her mother. Did Friedrich Eigenwill deliberately set out to kill Maddalena Ortelli? No! He didn't even know she was in the line up. Had he known, would he have shot her? Of course not! He shot her by accident. Yes, by accident. It was one of those unfortunate accidents that occur every day in a war. There was no premeditation. It was terrible, tragic but not unforgivable. That is my point. What Friedrich did under the circumstances that he did it, is not unforgivable. For my part, I forgive him.'

The four friends turned to look at the blind man who held the casting vote. He alone now held the fate of Friedrich Eigenwill in his hands.

'Well, Ramon, we are tied two-two.' Lucio began to turn the screws. 'How do you vote? You have heard all the arguments and must have an opinion of your own. The final decision rests with you.'

'God above!' he hissed. 'Do you realise what you are asking me to do?'

'We are asking no more of you than we've asked of ourselves.'

'Not so! Everything rests with me. His life is in my hands! The four of you have negated each other. You have left it to me to decide for you. The blood will be on my hands!'

'Does that mean you side with Neil and myself? Does that mean Friedrich must be made to face up to his crime and pay for it?'

'No, it bloody well does not!' Ramon's shout startled the diners nearby who had already begun to cast nervous glances in their direction.

'May I suggest we all keep our voices down?' Milos addressed the whole table, reluctant to single out Ramon as the culprit. Ramon was under enough pressure as it was. 'We don't want to make the whole of the restaurant privy to our discussions, no?'

'Sweet Jesus, I don't want to do this.'

'Ramon, you have no choice. Remember, whichever way you vote you will only be adding your vote to two that have already gone before. It is a shared responsibility, not yours alone.'

'Bullshit, Lucio. It is my decision and you know damn well it is.'

'Cut the shit, Ramon,' Neil snapped. 'Cut this dying swan routine. Just give us your vote and we can all go home and kick the dog or whatever. Show some guts.'

'Yes, Ramon, it is time you cast your vote.' Ramon turned towards Gancio, surprised by the harsh note in his voice. He'd expected support from Gancio at least and was dismayed to discover none would be forthcoming. He cupped his head in his hands, and ran his fingers over his face. His hands shook and his friends could not fail to notice.

'I'd hoped I'd finished with all this sort of business when I left Argentina. But it seems otherwise. Let me say this, I'm not sure the concepts of guilt or innocence as we might understand them apply. It is like Milos said, who determines guilt in a war? Guilt seems to me a very arbitrary thing. It depends, for one thing, on which side the offender is on. Two people may commit identical acts but only one is deemed a crime. The comparison with Dresden is entirely appropriate. That was undoubtedly a crime against humanity. There was premeditation. There were no mitigating circumstances, at least none that amount to much. It seems to me that guilt is a personal thing. If my mother had been shot in the square at Ravello instead of Colombina's, then Friedrich Eigenwill would always be guilty in my eyes and I would demand retribution. Time would forgive nothing. Equally, if my family had been killed in Dresden, I would demand retribution. But my mother was not shot in the square at Ravello, nor were my family killed in Dresden. I feel no personal loss. I can dismiss both events as atrocities of war among many atrocities. I feel perhaps that recriminations and retribution should end with the armistice. But Milos, you raised the issue of the Holocaust. How could retribution for that end with the armistice? The perpetrators of that should be hounded to their graves. So when does an atrocity justify retribution and when doesn't it? Is it a simple matter of body count? The deaths of six million Jews matter but not the deaths of eight innocent women in Ravello? The issue of criminality in war is too big for us to decide. It is too simplistic to say that all crimes should be punished because all crimes will not be punished, because the definition of war crimes is not constant. But that really is not the issue. We have not been asked to decide on the overall issue of war crimes. We have been asked to help one person determine whether or not she is justified in seeking revenge on the man who killed her mother. If it had been my mother who was killed, I would demand retribution. I would demand that Friedrich Eigenwill be made to face up to his crime and the certainty of his death. So how can I possibly advise Colombina otherwise?'

'No, Ramon! Don't say it!' Milos reached over and grabbed his friend's arm.

Ramon snatched his hand away. 'Dear God Milos, do you think I am enjoying this? Don't you think I wish there were some other way?' He paused and dropped his chin on his chest. Seconds ticked away and became minutes, but still he did not raise his head. When he began to speak again, his voice was devoid of all life. Every syllable seemed reluctant to leave his mouth. 'I don't believe individuals are justified in taking the law into their hands. However inadequate our system is in dealing with things like this, it is our system and we should abide by it. Is Colombina justified in seeking revenge? Yes, she is. But should she? The answer is no. If she goes ahead with her plans she will not only break the law but become a murderer too. And she doesn't deserve that. So my vote is split. Colombina is justified in taking her revenge but only within the framework of the law. I cannot sanction the death of Friedrich Eigenwill by her hand.'

'That's a cop-out Ramon, and you know it!' Neil was almost out of his chair in anger. 'You think you should let Colombina kill him but you haven't got the guts to say so. You haven't, have you?'

Ramon remained silent in obvious distress but Neil was relentless. 'You found him guilty. You say that Colombina is justified in exacting her revenge. That is all you have been asked to do. You have not been asked to decide whether or not we are right to sit in judgement or whether or not Colombina is right to be the agent of retribution. We discussed that earlier. We have a system of law and decided not to use it. We decided not to use it for three reasons: expense; the fact that the stress of a trial would probably kill the old man anyway; and, finally, his age virtually eliminates any possibility of him being brought to trial. He will die of old age first. No, we have gathered here to decide whether Colombina is justified in seeking retribution for the murder of her mother. How she exacts her revenge is her affair, and we only have Lucio's word for that. All Colombina has asked us to do is examine the facts and weigh up any mitigating circumstances in his favour. We have done that, each of us in our own way. Lucio says she is justified, I say she is justified, and so do you. You can pussyfoot as much as you like but that is the essence of your decision. So our judgement is made. Ramon's vote has determined the result. Does anyone disagree?'

'No. That is the majority decision, though I wish it were otherwise.' Milos shook his head sadly. 'In passing on our judgement, Lucio, I think you should also communicate a recommendation for clemency.'

'Bullshit!'

'No, it's not bullshit, Neil. Ramon recommends clemency and so do I and so does Gancio. You can have your verdict but we have a majority decision in favour of clemency.'

'Why bother reaching a decision? We're no bloody help to Colombina. What are we going to tell her? Yes but no? For Christ's sake!'

'Well, Lucio, will you do that?'

'No, Milos. Any plea for clemency is outside our terms of reference. Ramon's decision has ended the discussion. As much as he has equivocated, the truth is he has found that Colombina has just cause to take her revenge. That is right, isn't it, Ramon?'

'Yes, Lucio! That is right! What do you want me to say? I will never forgive you for this! You have orchestrated things so that the blood is on my hands. You have, haven't you? Don't insult me by denying it!'

'No, Ramon, I won't insult you. It's true. I knew how the

others would vote as did you. Your only doubt was me. Once I cast my vote you knew you would have to decide the fate of Friedrich Eigenwill. So how does it feel?'

'For Christ's sake, Lucio!' Milos knocked his chair flying as he rose to restrain Ramon. 'How dare you say such a thing! There are five of us. The decision was not Ramon's alone.'

'Oh, yes it was. That was exactly how Ramon likes it. To be in the position of power, to be the one who decides. He plays with our friendship and our affection. It's all a game to him, a game with him in control. So how does it feel to be in control of this game, Ramon?'

Ramon slumped back in his chair, retreating behind the protection of his dark glasses. Milos picked his chair up off the floor and sat back down.

'That's what all this is about, isn't it, Lucio? You're getting your revenge on Ramon for what he did to us in his last story.'

'Not entirely. The main story is true, Gancio can vouch for that. But revenge is not Colombina's sole prerogative. I embellished the story a touch to get revenge of my own.'

'And you have, no? What you have done to Ramon is no more forgivable than what he does to us.' Milos paused, his agile mind leaping ahead. 'Are you suggesting now that our judgement of Friedrich Eigenwill was simply an embellishment?'

'Let me just say it was surplus to requirements. The issue has already been resolved. It reached its conclusion early this week.' Lucio's voice betrayed no emotion. He looked around the table at the stunned faces. Nobody was game to ask the question. Finally Ramon found the courage to break the silence.

'And how was the issue resolved? Given the way you voted I assume you have made us all party to murder?'

'No, Ramon. You have been party to nothing more than an interrupted romance stretching back nearly fifty years.'

'What? For Christ's sake, Lucio, explain yourself!'

Ramon couldn't see Lucio's smile but heard it in his voice. 'They have done what they were prevented from doing all those years ago. They are giving each other the peace and forgiveness they seek. They have laid old memories to rest. They were married on Tuesday.'

'You bastard!'

'Yes, Neil, I am a bastard. I have beaten you all at your own game and humbled Ramon. That is no small achievement for a man you thought could only tell jokes.' He began to laugh. 'Colombina will of course be interested in your opinion, but don't be surprised if we drop a little in her estimation.'

'You are a bastard, Lucio.'

'Thank you, Gancio.'

'Stop being so smug. You have used this story, a tragic story and also the story of my aunt, for what? To score points. I don't give a shit if Ramon never forgives you, I will never forgive you!'

'Ahhh . . . Gancio, what you say is true and I do apologise. But when I began my story I didn't know that you had personal involvement in it. I will apologise more sincerely to you later. But not in my moment of glory. Tell, me Ramon, it was a good story, no?'

'Yes, it was a good story.' Ramon answered for all of them. 'It was a bloody good story and bloody well told. Allow me to congratulate you. You were brilliant.'

'My God, you're all bastards!'

'Yes, Gancio,' said Ramon evenly. 'We are all bastards. The story is the thing, the only really important thing. That and your food.'

Milos and Lucio began to laugh. The others joined in.